"It's all steampunk a[n]d ... [t]he adventures of Elizabeth Barnabas. The [...] [alon]g the way keep the plot tight and fun, and the conclusion sets us up nicely for book two."
The Washington Post

"If I had a bowler hat, I'd take it off to the author of this beautifully crafted steampunk novel."
Chris D'Lacey, author of The Last Dragon Chronicles

"Let's just say I haven't been this impressed by a book in a while... Unseemly Science is a beautifully written steampunk, alternate history novel. Elizabeth, the main protagonist, is a feminist heroine I can get behind – smart, intelligent, and void of the typical fantasy heroine. It's a slow burn mystery but so intelligently written and with a well developed world, I barely put it down... If I were to recommend you pick up anything this week, *The Bullet Catcher's Daughter* and *Unseemly Science* are it."
Adventures in Sci Fi Publishing

"Duncan is an accomplished crime writer, and this detective story with fantastical elements shows his chops to great effect, and the steampunk elements don't overtake the story; instead, they add just enough to make it more interesting. The ending leaves so many wonderful possibilities for more adventures with Elizabeth."
My Bookish Ways

"Steeped in illusion and grounded in an alternative history of the Luddite Rebellion, Duncan's strong supernatural mystery serves ably as both a standalone adventure and the start to a series..."
Publishers Weekly

ROD DUNCAN

The Custodian of Marvels

BEING VOLUME THREE OF
THE FALL OF THE GAS-LIT EMPIRE

ANGRY ROBOT

ANGRY ROBOT
An imprint of Watkins Media Ltd

Lace Market House,
54-56 High Pavement,
Nottingham,
NG1 1HW
UK

www.angryrobotbooks.com
twitter.com/angryrobotbooks
Key items

An Angry Robot paperback original 2016

Cover by Will Staehle.
Set in Meridien by Epub Services.

Distributed in the United States by Random House, Inc., New York.

ISBN 978 0 85766 502 7
Ebook ISBN 978 0 85766 503 4

Printed in the United States of America

9 8 7 6 5 4 3 2 1

CHAPTER 1
September 2009

Take off the disguise and another is revealed beneath. Regard well the many people you must be. There is no innermost layer.

THE BULLET-CATCHER'S HANDBOOK [1]

The question of how to approach Professor Ferdinand presented a singular problem, in that the costume that would get me past his gatekeepers was not the same as the one I judged necessary to engage his curiosity.

On my first attempt I progressed only as far as the entrance hall. The soles of my shoes, being soft rope, made no sound on the flagstones. But before I was halfway across that empty chamber, a side door creaked open and a porter wearing a black bowler hat scurried out.

"Hey! You there!"

I put a hand to my chest, as if expressing the shock of one not used to being hailed in coarse language.

"You can't come in here," he said.

"I'm looking for the Department of Ethnographic Studies."

---

[1] *As recorded in the Harry Timpson manuscript.*

His brow creased. He looked me up and down, taking in the blue calico skirt, the cloth bag hanging from my shoulder and the brass charms on a plaited cord at my waist. His confusion turned quickly to resolve.

"Out!"

"But–"

"I'll get rough if that's the way you want to play it. Don't think I won't." He emphasised the point by jabbing a finger towards me, then back in the direction from which I'd come.

My second attempt to access the inner cloisters was via a narrow passageway running past the college's massive kitchens. Empty crates were stacked waiting for collection outside. I picked one, which bore the legend *Mallaig Kippers*, and carried it before me as if hurrying on a delivery.

This simple device took me between the service buildings, into a lawned quadrangle, past a group of students, who cast me not a glance, and into the shade of a covered walkway overhung by wisteria. It was here that I found my way barred by a janitor, who held a mop across his body like a musket.

"What you got there?" he asked.

"It's for Professor Ferdinand," I said.

Until then I'd had to guess where the professor's rooms might be located. But, on hearing my words, the janitor turned his gaze from the fish crate to the upper storey of an ivy clad building.

"Best I take it," he said.

"I'm to give it to him and him alone."

It was then the janitor noticed the charms hanging from my waistband. I saw the gates closing behind his eyes.

"We don't have gypsy girls in here," he said. "And Professor Ferdinand isn't that kind of man. None of them are. So you can go. Right now!"

"Then you must make the delivery," I said, thrusting the fish-smelling box into his hands.

He fumbled, dropping both mop and crate. I half turned, preparing to run, but his hand shot out and grabbed me by the strap of my bag. I snatched it away, pulling him off balance, whereupon he tripped on the mop handle and went sprawling forwards. There was a sharp double crack, as the crate shattered under him, followed by a groan of pain.

Knowing this would be my last chance, I jumped the poor janitor and lifted my skirts to sprint off towards the ivy clad building. I was in through the door before he'd got back to his feet and had made it up two flights of stairs before hearing his footfalls labouring after me.

At the top of the building, I found a wide, wood panelled corridor. The scent of beeswax was thick in the air. I set off at a run, my feet sliding under me on the smooth floorboards. Each door had a polished name plaque – *Dr Ross*, *Dr Martin*, *Dr Bannister*. Then, at the turn of the passage, I found the one I'd been looking for: *Professor Ferdinand*.

I rapped on the door as loud as I dared. I could hear the janitor's footsteps getting closer, uneven as if he was limping up the stairs. I gave the door one more knock, then opened it and slipped inside.

It was a room of objects. Carvings, ceramics, metalwork. Every shelf and windowsill had been used. A rounded man with salt and pepper hair looked up from a book that lay open on the desk. Spears and other tribal artefacts were displayed on the wall behind him. He reached for his spectacles.

"Professor Ferdinand?"

"Yes. But–"

Whatever he was about to say was cut short. The door burst open and the janitor lurched in. I jumped back as he made to grab my arm, circling away from him, first to the window and then around towards the professor's desk. He advanced, still limping, until I was backed into the corner. My hand found the base of a wooden statue on the windowsill. I gripped it, ready to swing my arm.

"Stop!"

We both froze.

"What is the meaning of this?" the professor cried.

"She's run away," said the janitor. And then: "We don't have her sort here."

The professor glared at me. I released my hold on the statue.

"What have you to say for yourself?"

"They wouldn't let me see you."

"It's a respectable college," growled the janitor.

"And I'm a respectable woman!"

"You're a chancer!"

"I'm nothing of the sort!"

The professor slapped his hand onto the desk, bringing the argument to a stop.

"You are no doubt, as you say, a respectable woman," he said. "Nevertheless, you cannot simply barge in here without appointment. We have systems. We have procedures."

The janitor began to relax. He took half a step back towards the door. "I'll send for the constables?"

I turned to face the professor. The charms on my waistband swung as I moved, catching his gaze. He stared.

"Sir? Am I to throw her out?"

Professor Ferdinand was still frowning, but now it

seemed more in concentration than displeasure. "Perhaps," he said. "Perhaps. But tell me, my dear, why is it you came to see me?"

I gestured to the shelves that lined his room and the artefacts that crowded them. Some might have come from Africa. But there were also objects from the world of the travelling magic show. A trick birdcage. A set of Chinese rings.

"You're an anthropologist," I said. "That's why I needed to see you. I need to ask about this."

So saying, I reached into my bag and withdrew the wreck of a leatherbound volume. There was no need to make a show of it. The book had a presence that drew the eye. Such a journey it must have taken to reach this room. I knew of but a fraction.

"*The Bullet-Catcher's Handbook*," I said.

The professor dwelt for a moment on the gnarled cover, burned at one corner. Then he looked to the janitor.

"It seems the constables won't be necessary," he said. "But perhaps you could see to it that someone brings this young lady a cup of tea."

Professor Ferdinand took his time with the book. I sipped my tea as he examined the binding through a magnifying lens. Then he began to read, his own cup untouched on the desk. The pages crackled softly as he turned them.

My gaze wandered across to the wall, where a row of daybills hung, framed as if they were paintings. When I was a child, we had pasted such advertisements on tree trunks, walls and fences in the towns we visited. If anyone had said they might one day be hung as art, we would have laughed them to scorn.

My cup was empty. The professor's must have been long

cold. The sun moved behind a cloud and the room grew darker. At last he sat back and closed his eyes, his hands interlocked over his stomach. I was beginning to think that he might have forgotten me when he spoke.

"How is it," he said, "that you come to be in possession of such an artefact?"

"It was given to me."

"A singular gift."

"You doubt it?"

He opened his eyes. "Books of this kind are bequeathed, master to apprentice. To sell it would bring disgrace and exclusion. I've never heard of one being given. And to a woman."

"It was a woman gave it to me. She had notice of her death. Before it came, that is. She was the last of her line."

"Ah. That might explain it," he said, nodding as if he had read in my words the bitterness of the memory. "But it's a curious tale – such a book being passed from female to female. You claim to belong to that same world?"

"Claim?"

"You're dressed as a gypsy. That caught my interest – as you must have known it would. Tell me, are you of the Romani people?"

"Truthfully, sir, no."

"So – one subterfuge you admit. Why not another? Why shouldn't I think you stole the book? Why believe you come from a travelling magic show, let alone the world of the bullet-catchers? You bring an object to me – *this* object – and speak of its owner's death. I believe I'm entitled to challenge you."

I got up and reached for the Chinese rings on the shelf.

"Don't touch," he said.

But before he could finish, I'd taken the five steel hoops

and was turning them in my hand. Hidden from his view, my thumbnail dragged over the smooth metal, searching for the invisible break that I knew must be there.

"They are very old," he said. "Very valuable. I would prefer it if you…"

I held one of them apart then clashed it twice back against the others. He winced at each impact. Then, with the third clash, they were linked, as if metal had magically passed through metal.

"My father taught me," I said, placing them back on the shelf and returning to my seat.

The professor took a moment to compose himself.

"I probably deserved that," he said at last. "But this is a peculiar meeting. You mustn't blame me for harbouring suspicions. How did you know to approach me?"

"I read your book, *The Culture and Language of the Travelling Magic Show*."

He polished his spectacles on a handkerchief. "It was a very small circulation. I'm surprised you found a copy."

"It was in the library."

"A library that would admit a woman?"

"I can be persistent," I said.

"So it seems!"

He picked up *The Bullet-Catcher's Handbook*, as if to refresh his memory. "What do you know of it?"

"It's a book of sayings," I said. "When my father met other bullet-catchers on the road, he'd quote lines to them and they'd quote back. It meant nothing. It was like country people talking of the weather."

"Fascinating," said the professor. "But are you certain it meant nothing? Or was there a code you hadn't been told?"

"I… I couldn't say. I was only fourteen when I left."

"Then may I respectfully suggest there was more to it." He patted the cover. "This is not a book of the ordinary sort. Each copy is different. There are famous sayings among the entries that are universal. But others are less common. It's clear that sayings were added as it passed down the generations. In that sense, each copy needs to be seen in the context of a pedigree. The exchange of quotations – precisely chosen – as a formal greeting would remind them of their positions on a kind of family tree. Similar practices are seen in other guilds."

"Are you saying there are things in my book that aren't in other copies?"

"There are sayings here that I've never seen written. But tell me – was it in this condition when you received it?"

"Not exactly. The cover was gnarled. The paper was yellowed–"

"Vellum," he cut in. "It is not paper, but calfskin, scraped with a blade until fine and smooth enough to take quill and ink."

"Vellum then. It had that colour when I first received it. But the damage to the cover – this happened in my care."

The professor was appalled. "You let this happen? My dear, your book is unique. It is a most unlikely survivor of a vanished age. You should guard it with your life."

"But I thought you said it was the work of recent generations..."

"Oh, no. No one has written in this book since it was bound two centuries ago. If *The Bullet-Catcher's Handbook* can be thought of as a family tree, then this copy belongs to a branch I would have thought long extinct. It is, in that sense, priceless."

CHAPTER 2
August 2009

As the mind expects, so will the eye perceive. This is the human condition. This is the conjurer's friend.

THE BULLET-CATCHER'S HANDBOOK

Exactly two weeks before my visit to the professor, I had been travelling east along the Grantham Canal, in my boat the *Harry*. With a crew of five, I could have steamed through the night, delivering my cargo in less than half the time. But my one helper was Tinker; a boy who, though loyal to a fault, had no use for schedules.

He'd hopped off the boat that morning and ducked behind the hedgerow, to relieve himself, I thought. When he didn't return, I went below and discovered his knife and a loop of snares had gone. I would see nothing more of him that day. Thus, when dusk came and I was obliged to tie up for the night, I was still a mile short of Skinners Lock.

Since the clocks went forward that spring, it had been my practice to sit out on the aft deck and watch the light fade, invisible to anyone beyond the boat. Each day the canal had found us at a different mooring place with new silhouettes to trick the eye.

I told myself that the purpose of my nightly vigil was to keep watch for thieves and bounty hunters. The fact that, in those quiet moments, an immense loneliness pressed in on me from every side – this I accepted as a bonus.

That evening, having cut a slice of sourdough loaf from the night before, I crept out to my usual place under the overhang of the cabin roof. The illusion of company is everywhere when the day is busy. Boats pass. People on the towpath wave. It is in quiet that loneliness can be fully savoured.

Whilst I navigated the canals of the Anglo-Scottish Republic, Julia, my friend and confidante, was far away studying law in the Kingdom of England and Southern Wales. Tinker, who, in want of a parent but against good reason, had adopted me, was as much company as any boy can be. We could never linger in one place for fear of being recognised. Rootless we wandered, carrying such cargo as would pay for the coal that kept the paddlewheels turning.

A movement in the hedgerow broke my reverie. I watched and waited. Hunting kept foxes rare in the countryside. It was more likely to be a badger. With a whisper of parting grass stems, a dark shape scrambled out of cover. It crossed the path in a hop and a jump, landing silently on the deck, where it resolved into the shape of a ragged boy. I felt sure there would have been a grin also, had it been light enough to see one. He held his day's work up by the ears for my approval, then dived down the steps into the cabin. There would be rabbit stew and two new furs to add to the pile.

Life was good.

I was about to follow him inside, but another movement made me pause. A shadow had shifted on the edge of my vision. It was too big to be a badger. A fallow deer perhaps. It could not have been a man. This I knew for certain because its stature had been too small.

Tinker had never been to school, but that did not mean he was without learning. He could forage food and kindling. He could set a fire without the use of matches. He could move with little sound, and hide where no one else would have found a hiding place. A drunken father had taught him that. Unwittingly. Tinker also had an instinct for sensing trouble before it came. It was an ability I never quite fathomed.

He was waiting for me when I abandoned my vigil and climbed down the steps into our small cabin, bathed in yellow light from the candle lantern. He had sloughed off his oversized coat and dropped the rabbits on the floor as if they were no longer of interest.

I perched myself on my narrow cot. There was little more than five foot of floor space in front of me. A bottle stove opposite provided the means of cooking. Next to it was a cupboard which also served as a bench.

The ornamental endplate of the engine had been left exposed in the aft wall. Cast in the form of a woman's torso, it leaned forwards, as if she might with another step emerge fully into the cabin, resplendent in her nakedness. Tinker studiously ignored her whenever I was near.

"Good hunting?" I asked him.

"Yes."

"Did you see anyone?"

He shook his head.

"Two rabbits?"

"Yes."

"Were there any deer tracks?"

"No."

"Then a dog perhaps? It would have been very large – like a wolfhound?"

He shook his head, then, tired of my questioning, grabbed the rabbits and his knife. "Light the fire," he said, before disappearing out of the hatch.

Without hunger, I slept more deeply that night than was usual. Otherwise I might have been disturbed by the tilt of the boat or the sound of movement in the cabin. As it was, my first awareness came with the feeling of a finger poking me in the cheek. It took several groggy seconds before I realised that it was not a finger but the muzzle of a gun. The squat figure of a dwarf loomed next to me in the near dark.

My cry woke Tinker, who sprang to his feet.

"Back off!"

I don't know if Tinker could see the gun or if it was something in the gruff command, but he did as he was told.

"No one do nothing!"

My head had cleared enough now to recognise the intruder's voice and form.

"Fabulo?" I asked.

"The same," growled the dwarf. "Now, tell the boy to light a lamp. And nothing stupid."

I heard the sound of a log being dropped. Tinker must have been holding it as a weapon. Then he opened the stove door. A dull glow bathed his face as he blew on the embers, coaxing a flame from a spill of twisted paper. In the yellow light I saw that Fabulo held a second pistol in his other hand. One was pointing at each of us. With the candle lantern lit he backed away and lowered himself onto the bench in the opposite corner.

"Come," I said, beckoning Tinker.

The boy clambered onto the cot next to me, his knees drawn up to his chest, more like a spider than a child.

"This is cosy," said Fabulo. Short limbed and stubby fingered, he was the opposite of Tinker. He rested the pistols on his knees. "Let me see – when was the last time we met?"

"You know the answer," I said.

"I'm just being polite. It's what old friends do, isn't it, when they get together – reminiscing? Do you remember your infernal machine? You fired a bolt of light from it and blinded Harry Timpson in one eye."

"It wasn't my machine."

"And that wasn't what I asked."

"Yes, I remember it! Too well. It was a hellish thing. I'm glad it's gone."

"But it's still there in your memory," he said.

"Is that why you've come? If you're here to avenge your master, it's your memory you should be worried about. He double crossed me. You both did. He would have killed me. Did you forget that bit?"

"No," said the dwarf with a sigh. "I'm sorry about that. Harry had a way of making things seem right. Even when they weren't."

"I never set out to hurt him."

"True enough," he said.

"Then we should be square."

"So we should."

"Then why stick a gun in my face?"

"Wanted to be sure, that's all. Didn't know if you might still hold a grudge."

"I'd find your visit a deal more pleasant if you'd put those pistols away."

He tapped his finger on the stock of one, as if weighing the risk, then placed them on the floor by his feet. "Better?"

They were still within his reach, I noted. And still cocked.

"Would you like some tea?" I asked

"I've brought my own." From inside his coat the dwarf slipped a metal flask.

I felt Tinker begin to relax. His strange life had left him more suspicious of a bar of soap than a flintlock. This might have seemed like old times to him. We'd all been part of the same circus troupe – me cleaning out the beast wagon, Tinker minding the horses and Fabulo performing under the Big Top.

Being a dwarf, Fabulo would always be a spectacle. But more than that, he'd been one of Harry Timpson's close advisors. And now something had driven him to seek me out again. I wanted to know what.

Tinker unfolded himself from the cot. I watched as he fed sticks into the stove. With a crackle and the smell of wood smoke he coaxed the fire back to life. Then he took the empty kettle and slipped out into the night.

Fabulo and I regarded each other. His eyes did not leave me as he swigged from the flask. "This is a pleasant reunion," he said, then looked around the cabin until his eyes lighted upon the casting of the naked woman. "I'll bet that shocks the Republicans!"

"She's called the Spirit of Freedom," I said.

"She's just like you then, eh? And just like me. I knew you wouldn't stay put in one place. We're travellers. We don't belong in the world of the country people."

"I have to travel," I said. "There's a reward posted for my capture. I'm sure you knew that."

"But there're many ways to hide. You took to the canals.

I can drink to that." This he did. "We'll always be outsiders, you and me. That's the truth. We've got to look out for each other. You didn't need to run from us. The circus would've taken you back."

It was a kind of truth. One that ignored the fact they'd tried to kill me.

"I thought the circus had folded," I said.

"Just because you don't see us, don't mean we're gone."

"What happened to the big top? The wagons?"

"Sold – most of it. Harry was in prison. The Great Harry Timpson! Who do they think they are to lock up a man like that? It was a sad thing. We needed the money for lawyers and bribes. In the end we got him a cell to himself. And food. And doctors. You know how old he was? One hundred and five. And knowledge you could never find in books. He died in that cell."

"Better than being hanged," I said.

Fabulo stared into the dark corner of the cabin, as if picturing the scene. "They'd have come to see that show! Tens of thousands. Hundreds of thousands. Can you imagine what tricks we might have pulled for a crowd like that?"

"You think he'd have escaped the gallows?"

"Escape? No. But we'd have given them a show, my friend. A fireball? A storm? Harry would have dreamed up something. The Greatest Show on Earth! They'd have been talking about it in a hundred years. He'd have been happy to go that way."

"Do you blame me for his death?" I asked.

He fixed his dark eyes on mine and said, "If I wanted to see you harmed, I could have pulled the trigger just now. Or I could have turned you in. Do you know how much the Duke of Northampton's offering for your capture? The man's obsessed with you. The price goes higher each month you're free. No, Elizabeth, I don't blame you for Harry Timpson's death."

I suppressed a shudder at the mention of the duke. The way Fabulo had delivered his speech made it sound rehearsed. I searched his face, but could detect neither sincerity nor lie. We had drawn closer to the purpose of his visit, I felt sure of that. But I still could not see where we were heading. There was something unsettlingly fey about his manner.

The moment was broken by a dull clanking and the padding of feet on the deck. Tinker hefted the full kettle back down the steps into the cabin. He knelt next to the stove, oblivious to the tension.

"What's your cargo?" Fabulo asked, as if making small talk.

"Furniture and small packages."

"They pay you well?"

"Enough."

"No pirates trying to steal your cargo?"

"None."

"So life's good."

"Yes," I said.

"And a new horizon every day." He raised the flask as a salute then took another swig. "What of winter?" he asked.

"We'll manage."

"There's always thieving. If it gets too bad."

"I'll not be doing that."

"Not even a thin chicken from a fat farmer?"

For a time neither of us spoke. I kept my eyes away from Fabulo's pistols, still cocked on the floor. My own pistol lay under the pillow next to me, loaded but not cocked. I shifted closer to it, as if making myself more comfortable.

There was a faint crackling from the stove and the smell of ardent spirits from Fabulo's breath. Tinker had curled up on the floor and seemed to be falling asleep. A pleasant domestic scene. The kettle began to rumble.

"I saw you last evening," I said. "You were watching from the hedgerow. I'd thought you were a deer. You should have come and introduced yourself."

"Would you have welcomed me?"

"I'd have wanted to know why you'd travelled all the way into Lincolnshire to see me."

"Ah. I was working round to that. But, since the pleasantries are out of the way, I may as well ask. There's an enterprise I'm engaged in that could do with a woman of your talents."

"You're offering me employment?"

"We'd be partners."

"I can't perform in a circus. You know that. There are bounty hunters looking for me."

"Not the circus. If all goes to plan, we'd not be seen. Not by anyone. There'd be payment at the end. Rich payment, at that."

"This is thieving then?"

"We'll take something, yes. But not from any person. None will be the poorer. You've no need to worry your pretty conscience. And there could be money upfront if you say yes. You could dump your cargo in the canal. Let it rot."

"If none's to be poorer, who'll you be stealing from?"

"That's the part you'll like the best," he said. "You'll be stealing from the International Patent Office."

Until then I'd thought him foolhardy. But as I heard this, I knew that he was mad. To steal from the Patent Office was certain death.

As he'd been speaking, I'd inched my hand under the pillow. Now I snatched the pistol and had it cocked before he could reach for his.

"Elizabeth?"

"Don't you know the risk you put me in – coming here and saying such things?"

"No one's listening!"

"You don't know what you're talking about!"

"The Patent Office ruined your life," he said. "I'm offering a way to get even."

"You're offering a noose and I want you gone! I'll give you this choice – I can pull the trigger here and now or you can promise to never come here again."

CHAPTER 3
September 2009

There is no better way to hide one truth than with another.

THE BULLET-CATCHER'S HANDBOOK

Two weeks after that unexpected meeting with Fabulo, I was sitting in Professor Ferdinand's office in the university. From the floorboards to the wall panels, the room seemed to glow in the late afternoon light. A century of beeswax and polishing might be needed to turn oak to such a colour. The desk had it too, on which lay my copy of *The Bullet-Catcher's Handbook* and the tea things, long cold.

I was trying to absorb the professor's revelation – that this gnarled volume of obscure aphorisms, which I had been carrying in secret through months of near poverty, might itself be priceless.

"Would you buy it then?" I asked.

The suggestion had a remarkable effect on the professor. His face flushed. He picked up a sheaf of papers and began to fan himself. For a moment he seemed overcome.

"The college is not so wealthy," he said. "Besides, a priceless thing cannot logically be bought."

"Then I'll offer it for what you can afford!"

"Why would you do such a thing? It would bring dishonour in the eyes of your people."

"I have no people."

"But your ancestors must have–"

"I need the money!"

He blinked rapidly on hearing my crude statement. Republicans like to believe their comfort comes from virtue. Reminding them of its true source is akin to mentioning bodily functions. He took a moment to compose himself.

"Are you not interested?" I asked.

He puffed out his cheeks. "I am tempted," he said. "Indubitably tempted. But there are steps that would need to be taken. Its sale would require the permission of the International Patent Office."

"It's a book," I said. "Not a machine."

"Have you not read it? It describes the construction of devices to be used in stage magic. Some of the entries are vague, to be sure. Yet others contain detail. The same laws cover this book as would cover the blueprints to an engine. If you would sell it, the Patent Office must first judge whether it's conducive to the wellbeing of the common man. As with any machine, they must pronounce it seemly before it can be sold. But once it has a patent mark – then I could consult the faculty. I would make the case but it's they who'd provide the funds."

At the name of the Patent Office, my stomach had twisted. Its agents were already searching for the book, though I couldn't admit that to the professor. One of their agents had shown particular interest. That was John Farthing – a man who always confused my emotions. He had traced it from its previous owner, but had not managed to prove that I'd received it. I didn't understand the nature of his interest, but had lied to keep it from him nonetheless.

My turmoil must have shown because the professor regarded me with new focus and said, "I fancy there's more you have to tell."

"I can't abide the Patent Office," I said, offering one part of the truth to hide another.

His frown smoothed. "Don't worry, my dear. I'm aware of the antipathy felt by your people for agents of the law." He leafed back through the vellum pages to the beginning of the book and read: *"There was once a line marked out by God through which were divided heaven and hell. The devil created lawyers to make amends. They argued the thickness of that line until there was room within it for all the sins of men to fit…"*

"…and all the sins of women too," I said, completing the quote from memory.

"There," he said. "We are like two old bullet-catchers meeting at the crossroads. I started the quote and you completed it, proving we're related. But only distantly because lines similar to these are found in every known version. It's the most ancient part of the text."

He sipped from his teacup, pulling a face that suggested he'd expected it still to be warm.

My purpose in seeking out the professor had been to sell the book. But now it seemed that avenue was being closed to me.

"How old is it?" I asked.

"This copy?" He stroked the gnarled leather of the back cover. "If I had to guess, I'd put it around 1810."

"But that was before the time of the Patent Office! Why would they be interested?"

"Are they?"

"You said as much."

After a pause long enough to make me feel uneasy he said, "Perhaps I did. But it's not my part to talk politics."

The frustration had been rising in me through our interview. Unable to contain the feeling any longer, I stood and paced away from him. There was a daybill framed on the wall, bearing Harry Timpson's famous profile. I wondered what that old rascal would have done in my place. For all his knowledge, the professor had given me little. He seemed to be leading me on a meandering path through the fog. From what he said, the book could not be sold. But somewhere in this landscape of confusion might be knowledge that could help me. I sensed as much. A tingling intuition whispered that it was near. I took one more look at Timpson's picture then turned.

"Perhaps I could lend you the book," I said. "The Patent Office wouldn't need to give permission for that."

He tilted his head. If his brain had been powered by cogs, I fancy I might have heard them whirring.

"Would you like to study it?" I asked.

"I would like that very much."

"You could hold it secure for me?"

"Yes, indeed!" His enthusiasm was growing with each exchange. At last I had something to bargain with. "I have a safe," he said. "It could be locked away. I would take the greatest care. I would–"

"But if not money," I said, cutting him short, "what then would you give me in return?"

"You said you would lend it."

"I merely raised the possibility. You might like to think of an incentive to offer. You would get a period of time in which to study the book. I would get, what? Some knowledge of yours, perhaps?"

"What kind of knowledge?"

"You said it's not your part to talk politics. That means you have something to say but are holding it back. If you'd just tell me what it is, I might be persuaded to let you borrow the book. For a few days. And afterwards – you'd tell me what your studies had revealed."

I sat down once more. But no sooner were we eye to eye than he was out of his chair, pacing as I had done. He came to a stop facing Harry Timpson's picture.

"Well?" I asked.

"You never told me your name," he said. "You have me at a disadvantage."

"Martha." It was the first name that came to mind. "Martha Morris."

"In certain cultures they believe that to know someone's name is to have magical power over them. What do you think of that, Martha Morris?"

"Fascinating."

"It must be their true name, of course."

His words hung in the air. I couldn't decide whether they were an innocent observation or if he was accusing me.

"It would be an honest exchange," I said.

He considered this. "It does seem that we each have something that the other desires. But I'd need two months with your book."

"How about ten days?"

He nodded readily, leaving me with the thought that I could have offered less.

"I accept your terms," he said.

"And the agreement will be a secret between us?"

"That suits me well."

"Then I'll leave my book in your care."

I found myself holding his gaze. The small intimacy of the trade had changed the nature of our relationship. It took a moment to adjust.

"What I have to tell you is… delicate. I must insist that you not speak of it. Not beyond this interview." He waited for my nod before continuing: "As an anthropologist, I'm interested in the development of culture. Not just from other parts of the world. Thus my research has taken me through the vast collections of books in the libraries of our own nation. I have counted them. I have made lists of numbers and dates. I've drawn charts in which a curious phenomenon is revealed. The number of books published each year over the centuries has inexorably risen. This with one exception. In the years 1810 to 1821 the trend was reversed. In particular, no one seemed to be writing about history and technology."

He was standing at the door now. I saw him turn the key and heard the lock click. He hardly seemed to notice himself doing it. Then he returned to the desk and sat once more.

"It was the Age of Revolution," I said. "I thought it was in times of change that histories were written."

"We might believe that now. From the Long Quiet we look back and think of them thus. But what did they think? Perhaps they were so immersed in history that they had no time to write?"

"I can't believe it."

"Nevertheless, these are the facts."

"But you said my book was from that time."

"Precisely!" He patted his hands together in an imitation of applause. "You are certainly attentive. I sometimes wonder what would happen to our universities if we followed the way of the Kingdom and admitted women as students. My colleagues hold that such a change would overturn all seemliness and order. But a little revolution isn't always a bad thing, don't you think? Within the bounds of moderation."

He opened the book and held it for me to see, as if I'd not already studied each page in fine detail.

"Your manuscript concerns technology and comes from the beginning of that period. What's more, it's been invisible from the record until now. We could regard it as having been untouched by the hand of the great censor. As such, it is doubly rare.

"It offers an intriguing possibility. In comparing this manuscript with versions that have been examined and passed as seemly, we may catch a unique glimpse of the mind of the Patent Office itself. And that in relation to the period of its establishment, when the founding fathers were still alive.

"Of course, this is only done to satisfy our curiosity. The results could no more be published than could any of the unseemly things the Patent Office chooses to expunge. And we must keep our voices to a whisper when we discuss it."

"Are you spied on?" I asked.

He spread his hands as if to encompass the university beyond his oak-panelled walls. "To listen, to remember and to repeat. Isn't that the very meaning of education?"

I leaned forwards and lowered my voice.

"What if we discovered bad thoughts in the mind of the Patent Office?"

The professor's laughter was a fraction too loud and a shade too forced. "Very good," he said. "A judicious joke from time to time is no bad thing."

"Like a little revolution?"

"Just so. I believe you would have made an excellent student, Miss Morris. It is your willingness to consider the unthinkable."

It did not seem unthinkable to me.

He stood and lifted a picture from its hanger on the wall behind his desk, revealing a safe, gunmetal grey. Positioning himself between me and the combination dial, he made some delicate manipulations and then hefted the door open. A stack of documents lay within. Lifting *The Bullet-Catcher's Handbook*, he showed it to me, as if to prove there was no trickery. Then he placed it on top of the pile.

"A little joke. A little revolution. Everything within the bounds of moderation. Curiosity does no harm among the educated classes, Miss Morris. Despite your dress, that is how I'd describe you. Moderate curiosity. What we discover will never be published, remember that. We will know it. That will be enough. I trust you understand, my dear, that anything the Patent Office does or has done – it is for our own good."

I was not so accomplished a liar as to completely hide the feelings that washed through me on hearing those words. A corrupt Patent Office agent had ruined my family. Another agent, John Farthing, had spied on me, lied to me and, worse, stirred me into a strange turbulence of feelings.

"The Patent Office," I said, echoing the name and tasting its familiar bitterness. But I also detected the flavour of a new possibility.

The first inkling of an idea tickled my mind. No – not an idea. That would suggest something more fully formed. This was but a spark, still hidden in the heart of the kindling. Two weeks before, Fabulo had asked that I league with him against the Patent Office. I'd believed him insane. Only a madman attacks the invincible. I'd sent him away with no good grace. The image of his disappointment flashed into my mind, for no reason that I could understand.

"We should meet somewhere away from the university," said the professor. "In view of the delicacy of the subject, it should be discreet. Perhaps you know Revolution Park?"

I nodded.

"Excellent," he said. "Let us meet there. Under the statue of Ned Ludd – that would seem most appropriate."

CHAPTER 4
August 2009

The eye is drawn to a thing if it is in the wrong place. But where it seems to belong, it may become invisible.

THE BULLET-CATCHER'S HANDBOOK

On the morning after Fabulo's midnight visit, I awoke to find Tinker vanished from the small cabin and the hatchway unlocked. It was not unusual. The boy would disappear for days at a time and then return as if no explanation were needed. It would not have surprised me if I'd learned that he lived on other boats as well, taking meals wherever a family would feed him.

I could handle the boat without him, but it made for even slower progress since it was impossible at one time to both stoke and steer. Whenever the boiler pressure faded, I was obliged to disengage the gears, leaving the paddle wheels to drag in the water, slowing us towards a stop. Then, having steered her to the bank and made fast, I would shovel coal, while boats properly crewed steamed past, rocking the *Harry* in their wake.

In this fashion, I limped east along the Grantham Canal to the wharf at Casthorpe Bridge, a sleepy mooring place inhabited by more ducks than people. At first no one would admit knowledge of my delivery. Eventually, on my request, the wharf keeper sent a boy to ask in the village. And at length, a cart arrived, driven by a man in a dented hat.

"I'm to take the cargo," he said.

"Have you brought payment?"

"That's for the master. I'm to load and carry."

"And when the master comes with money, I shall help you load."

He took off his hat and scratched at the back of his head, as if trying to dislodge a flea. I folded my arms and gave him what I hoped was an uncompromising stare. Presently he replaced his hat and climbed back on the cart, mumbling something about women and boat people and a deal more besides.

After an hour or so the wharf keeper approached and told me I would have to pay a mooring fee if I wanted to stay any longer. I told him to charge it to the master, whoever that was. He went away grumbling as well.

It was noon by the time a man in a high hat and tails rode up. I stood on the steering platform and he remained seated on his fine horse. Looking down at me he said, "You're late. The contract said Tuesday."

"There were delays," I said.

"Where's your husband? I need to talk business."

"He's been called away," I said.

"Well, it won't do! I'm told you refused to release my goods. When your husband hears, you'll surely get the belt."

"It was he who gave my instruction," I said. "I'm to take payment before letting the cargo off the boat."

"Well, you're a day late."

"Half a day. I was here at dawn. You've kept me waiting."

"Nevertheless – lateness must be paid for. I'll retain twenty percent of the fee."

"Very well," I said. "Then I'll retain twenty percent of the cargo. There are some chairs and a table that'll burn well enough in place of coal."

His neck and cheeks purpled. I turned and stepped back down into the cabin. Sitting on the cot, I inhaled deeply then held my breath and counted, doing the exercise my father had taught me to calm my heart before stepping onto the stage.

It was mid-afternoon before the cart returned. This time the man in the dented hat passed me an envelope containing banknotes to the correct sum. I undid the lacing and hauled back the tarpaulin to reveal the hold. There was little enough cargo. It took barely half an hour for me to pass each item up and watch it stowed on the cart.

When we had done, I offered my hand by way of reconciliation. He stared at it then swept his eye over the rest of me. "Goodbye, missus," he said. There was something reptilian about his smile.

When he had gone, I tried to put him and his master out of my mind. I had papers in hand for the collection of six crates of pottery. That might seem a petty cargo, but it would pay for the coal I'd burn getting back to the Trent.

"Will you help me load?" I asked the wharf keeper.

"Your cargo's not here," he said.

I could see it behind him, the crates stacked next to the wall of his cottage. I told him so.

"I'm sorry, missus." He removed his hat and hung his head. "That's what I'm to tell you. I'm sorry, but there'll be no loading today."

"And if I wait till tomorrow?"

"That's what the master said you're to do. Tie up on the quayside. It's sure to be here in the morning."

As he spoke the words, he shook his head. There was pleading in his eyes.

Only then, I understood that I'd pushed too far. I had overreached my station. Republican civility would not protect me if I stayed the night. Losing no time, I turned the *Harry* in the basin next to the bridge and steamed off west. Seven miles out, I found a mooring place between two bends. The boat nestled snug on the bank opposite the towpath, under the boughs of a row of willow trees. The branches dangled like a curtain, leafy tips trailing in the water. If I made sure the stove and lamps were out before nightfall, there would be no way for them to find me in the darkness.

My problem was coal. The trip along the Grantham Canal would have paid for itself. But a return journey with an empty hold would wipe out any profit. I'd first taken possession of the *Harry* in its present form early in the year. It had been six weeks before I'd developed the contacts to begin earning money carrying freight. Depending on the weather, I might get half a season of work before ice gave me no choice but to lay-to for the winter. The major routes would be kept open by icebreakers. But that business was dominated by fleets of large boats run by ruthless men. I wouldn't be able to compete – even had it been safe for me to try. My work would always be running errands on those little spurs and dead ends of the canal system that the large boats could not negotiate and the large fleets would not bother to travel.

There was a ballad popular among the canal folk, which

told of a boat iced in on the Leicester Summit. The family who lived on her ran out of food. Then, worse, they ran out of coal. They foraged for wood. And when all that was used up, they burnt what furniture they had. And then they froze to death. None of the country people who lived thereabouts would help them.

Through my years of being a fugitive, I'd felt as if I was also moving towards something – a place of security, perhaps around the very next bend. The hope of it had kept me going. But one by one, options were being stripped away. Perhaps I'd finally escape from the Duke of Northampton by freezing to death on some unseen spur of the canal. What would that feel like, I wondered – to fall asleep, knowing I'd never wake? The thought of it held me. It was an effort to break free.

Taking the shovel, I began to shift the coal from one side of the bunker to the back. On reaching the metal of the floor plate, I delved in with my hands, feeling blindly underneath nuggets of anthracite until my fingers found the tin box in which I kept my few valuables.

Having wiped it down and washed the black dust from my hands, I returned to the small cabin and laid it on the cot. There was no lock.

I laid out the contents: first my father's pistol with the turquoise emblem of a leaping hare inlaid into the hardwood stock, then a cloth purse, mostly empty, and finally an ancient copy of *The Bullet-Catcher's Handbook*, its leather cover gnarled and partly burned.

The woman who had given me the book was no longer alive. But her parting message had claimed it to have some hidden value. At first I'd set out to destroy it, to rid myself of the memory of its previous owner's death. But somehow the gift seemed sacred. At the last moment I changed my mind and snatched it back out of the fire.

Turning the pages of the book brought me pain. I might have left it hidden deep in the coal bunker, but for some reason I couldn't understand, the Patent Office had sent John Farthing to search for it. The insistence of his questioning made me believe that it did have a value, though I couldn't understand what. For that reason, it remained in my mind and from time to time I took it out to puzzle over.

Under the dappled light beneath the willow trees, I examined it once more, tracing the folded leather of each cover with my fingers. I had long assumed that the hidden value must lie in the information it contained. I had read it many times over, but found only obscure aphorisms and advice on the nature of illusion and conjuring. Useful, perhaps, to a stage magician. But nothing that I could convert into money.

Conjurors have a peculiar way of looking at the world. My father taught it to me from infancy. He encouraged me to turn things around so that I could look at them from a side that no one else would see. Wherever there was a statement, he would cast it as a question. There was nothing settled for him that could not become a puzzle if rearranged. Reading the book was like hearing his voice.

A flash of blue and orange beyond the willow curtain jolted me from my thoughts. A kingfisher had dropped into the water with a splash. Then it was up again, a speck of thrashing silver in its beak. It flitted away to land on the opposite bank. I watched as it beat the tiny fish against a stone. When the fish was still, the bird upended it and swallowed it whole.

The distraction had broken my chain of thought. When

I looked down to the book once more, it came to me that I had been blinded, such was the emotional intensity I felt when holding it. I had accepted it as a book when I should have been asking if it was one. I had opened it and read the words when I should have been turning it around and finding an angle to see it from that no one else would consider. I had avoided doing precisely what it and my father had urged.

The covers were thick and heavy. Thick enough, perhaps, for something to be concealed between the leather and the board. In a daze, I carried it below. Thoughts tumbled as I waited for the kettle to boil. There was room for a sheet of gold or platinum to be hidden. Yet it didn't feel heavy enough. Perhaps some forbidden technology could be slim enough to fit in such a space. If so, I could understand the Patent Office being bent on its recovery.

Water rumbled in the kettle. I held the front cover above the spout. At first the steam was only a wisp, but as the water began to boil, droplets condensed on the ancient leather and the glue that had held it in place began to soften. I grabbed a knife and started working it under the edge. The leather made a cracking sound as I peeled it back. More than once, I scalded my hand in the steam, but carried on through the pain, turning the book to unpeel the second side. I had got the knack of it now, and was quickly on to the final edge. Then the entire covering folded back, revealing a blackened board below. My pulse thudded in my ears as I held it up to the lamp, searching for a mechanism or hidden words or anything else that might carry the book's secret value. Seeing nothing, I turned it over, knocked my fingers against it, took it in both hands and flexed it. My fingers slid on the hot glue.

There was nothing. It remained as it had first seemed – a thin board, blackened with age.

I don't know how long I was standing there, but the trance was broken by the tilting of the boat and the padding of feet on the aft deck. The hatch opened and Tinker jumped down into the cabin, where he crouched, staring at me.

"Everything's well," I said, suddenly aware of how unwell it must look. Strands of my hair had worked free and now hung limp from the steam. My hands and one sleeve were smeared with black. And the book's cover dangled from my hand like a dead thing.

He wrinkled his nose. "It stinks."

"That's just the glue," I said.

"What is it?"

"A book. An old book."

This put the matter beyond his interest.

"Pour water for me," I said, holding out my blackened hands for him to see. He whistled tunelessly about the task, half filling the washing bowl from the jug then topping it up from the kettle. He was not usually so biddable.

The water clouded and my hands began to show pink once more. The dark mood that had gripped me was also beginning to recede. I took a brush to my fingernails but found my eyes returning to the boy, as if they had detected something out of place, though I had no idea what it might be.

"How has your day been?" I asked.

"Not bad."

"Did you follow the canal path?"

"Maybe."

"See any rabbits?"

"No."

"Did you talk to anyone? Any news of river thieves?

"No."

"Did you find anything to eat?"

He turned his head, as if hearing some sound beyond the boat, though it seemed to me that he was looking for a way out of my questioning. Those occasions when Tinker preferred silence were invariably the ones in which he wanted to hold some fact unsaid.

"Did you see anything I should know about?" I asked, drying my hands on a cloth.

"No!"

"Then did you find anything I should know about?"

He picked dirt from one of his fingernails in an unsuccessful attempt to appear casual. I held out my hand. He huffed and creased his brow into a frown that was clearly supposed to indicate displeasure but actually made him look rather sweet.

"Show me!"

Pouting now, he burrowed deep into his trouser pocket and withdrew something sparkling. A silver chain dropped onto my palm followed at last by a silver watch. I took it and pressed the button. It chimed one clear note for each hour, then twice more in a higher pitch for the quarters. Half past eight. It was clear from the widening of his eyes that Tinker was hearing its voice for the first time. His love for the object had turned to adoration.

"Did you steal it?"

"No!"

"You found it then?"

A nod.

"Where?"

"In the path."

I turned it over. A dark line of mud marked out the edge of the rear panel. The chain too had dirt caught in between the links. I now insisted that Tinker let me wash his clothes every two weeks, so it seemed unlikely the watch could have been so soiled from merely spending time in his pocket.

He held out his hand to take it back. It seemed the wrong moment to tell him that we might be forced to sell it.

"If you got caught with it, they'd not believe it was found."

"It's mine!"

"Then for keeping's sake, put it somewhere it won't get seen."

I dropped it back into his hand and was rewarded with a grin. Then he was on his knees, lifting a loose floor plank near the stove and secreting his treasure underneath. It would not stay hidden through a determined search. Least of all from me.

Not that I would steal from the boy. But I needed to assess its likely worth. Therefore, when he was next roaming, I returned to the stove and lifted the loose plank.

To sell a silver watch would be difficult. A jeweller might think it stolen. A fence would plan to melt it down and would pay less than its weight in silver, which was not great in any case. If winter found us in a desperate state, we might best trade it for coal.

I pressed my thumbnail into a dimple in the back. It clicked open, revealing the workings. A delicate wheel oscillated on a spring finer than a hair. I stepped to the lamp to read the copperplate inscription inside the casing.

Capt Bill "Lightning" Brooks
Thirty years at arms
From your battery brothers

The military rank of captain was peculiar to the Kingdom. This I knew. And no Republican would inscribe a nickname onto such a formal gift. But as to how the property of a red coated man-at-arms came to be found on a country path this far north of the border, I had no quiet thought.

CHAPTER 5
September 2009

A man may hold a belief or a belief may hold a man. Who is to judge which path is safer?

THE BULLET-CATCHER'S HANDBOOK

In the days following my visit to Professor Ferdinand in the university, I worked making deliveries within the county of Nottinghamshire. Short runs are bad business, since payment is made for distance rather than loading and unloading. But the thought of travelling further from my book made me somehow uneasy.

My savings were dwindling. In a couple of months, ice would spread over the surface of the canal. It would grip the hull of my boat, locking it in place. There'd be no more earning and no more coal. I knew what that would mean.

If *The Bullet Catcher's Handbook* yielded no good and it turned out I'd been chasing a phantom, then my stove would dwindle and I would freeze to death. In fey moments I pictured my own frost-covered body, curled on the cabin floor, the Duke of Northampton cheated of his prize. When that thought started to seem too much like a victory, I busied myself with chores, forcing my mind away.

At last, my time of waiting was complete. The day arrived and I steamed into the city, tying up the *Harry* on a quiet stretch of canal a mile from our agreed meeting place.

Last time, I had gone to the professor in the guise of a gypsy. To remain inconspicuous in a public park required a different costume. Therefore, I chose a stout grey skirt and jacket, pinning my dark hair under a plain straw hat. If anyone had cared to look as I advanced towards the rendezvous, they would have thought me a Republican of good character, though modest means.

On another day, I might have taken precautions along the way. I would have detoured along quiet streets, doubled back, stopped as if looking into shop windows, while stealing glances behind. But this was a day of hope and expectation. Driven by impatience, I strode directly to the meeting place, arriving early.

Revolution Park was created after the clearance of slums that once occupied the land. All the iron nails that had held together those ramshackle back-to-backs were collected, melted down and cast to make the grand ornamental gateway. So proclaimed a brass plaque attached to the gate itself. There was no mention of what had happened to the people who once lived there. But it did say that the park's famous statue had been paid for by public subscription.

The silver birches growing just inside the railings had been pruned to match each other as closely as nature would allow, giving them the kind of symmetry that a tree might have in a child's drawing. Geometric beds of white roses did little to soften the austere layout. At the very centre of the park, at the convergence point of four stoutly orthogonal paths, a sandstone plinth held aloft the heroic figure of Ned Ludd. Frozen in bronze, he held his hammer above his head, poised to start an uprising that would change the world.

I chose a bench on a path near the statue, only noticing after I had sat down that a baby's knitted shoe rested on the seat next to me. A clock chimed the hour somewhere to the north. Then there were other chimes around the city, one from the tower of a library adjacent to the park. As the last of them faded, I caught sight of the professor away to my left. After a few paces he looked back along the way he had come, though no one had followed him through the gate. Then after a few paces more he pulled his hat brim lower over his brow.

My heart kicked into a faster beat. Something had changed. He was a different man from the confident academic I had met in the university office.

"Good afternoon, professor," I said, when he'd drawn close enough.

"Hush!"

"There's no one to hear. And no one would give you a second glance if you weren't acting the very caricature of a spy."

"We should walk," he whispered. "It's not safe."

"You should lift the angle of your hat and turn your collar down," I said. "And sit. The bench is long. You can take the other end."

This he did, though tension was obvious in the angles of his body.

"This was a mistake. We could be arrested."

"For sitting on a bench?"

"For sedition."

"A grey-haired professor and a young woman meeting in a park – it's not sedition they'll be thinking of!"

We were both sitting stiffly upright, eyes fixed forward

like strangers, so I couldn't say whether he blushed at my remark.

"Tell me what's wrong," I said. "And where's my book?"

"You may come to the university to collect it."

"Why didn't you bring it?"

"It wasn't safe."

"But it was your suggestion we meet here!"

"That was another mistake. Forgive me. But I want done with it. There's to be a formal dinner tonight. You'll be able to come to my office unchallenged. All the staff will be in the Great Hall."

I recalled the image of him placing the book in the safe. There'd been a playfulness to his movements, despite the precautions. A glint of excitement in his eye, ignited by the possibility of new knowledge.

"You've had enough time to study it?" I asked.

"More than enough."

"Then tell me what you've learned."

"I've learned," he said, "that your name isn't Martha Morris."

Now it was my turn to glance around the paths and check that we were not overheard. A woman pushing a perambulator was approaching, but still at a fair distance.

"The text gave you away," he said. "I compared the book to other known manuscripts – a kind of genealogy in reverse. A family tree of books and bullet-catchers. The only person your volume could have belonged to was the Great Zoran, who passed away last year – survived by his daughter, who was then hanged. You alluded to it. But I didn't understand. The newspapers are lurid on the subject. And there's another young woman mentioned in the news story: twenty years of age, raised in a travelling show, the runaway property of a duke. You are Elizabeth Barnabus, I presume?"

The rattle of wheels was approaching. I looked to the woman with the perambulator and managed to put on a brief smile for her benefit. She averted her gaze. When she had passed far enough, I turned to the professor.

"Are you scared because I am a fugitive?"

"You should have told me. But no."

"Then what?"

"I came to tell you our agreement's at an end. That's all I'll say."

"Then you break your word!"

"You spoke falsely, woman!"

"Only my name. That has no bearing on what we agreed."

"You tempted me," he said. "You gave me no time to consider."

"You knew what you were doing and it served your curiosity well enough at the time. You entered the deal, eyes wide open. Now, tell me what's happened to scare you!"

Again he fell silent. This time I waited him out.

"You've changed my mind," he said at last. "About women and university. I didn't know what deceptive creatures you could be. If you are the product of education, then better we reserve our universities for men of virtue."

"If you can find any," I said.

"You'll come to my office tonight. You'll take possession of your book and we will never see each other again. Indeed, I wish we never had."

"Then you refuse to tell me?"

"That's my final word."

He had been holding himself upright through our interview but now sat back, as if his mission were complete. The woman with the perambulator had done a turn of the statue and was now heading back along the path towards us. I couldn't bring myself to smile at her this time. I'd invested what little hope I had in this meeting. She stole a glance at the professor and then at me as she approached. She would think I was his mistress. I might have blushed, but having lost so much, shame seemed of little consequence. The wheels of the perambulator murmured as they passed over the stones. I watched her go.

"A baby's shoe," said the professor, noticing the object between us on the bench. He picked it up.

How easily his mind had moved on. And how powerless it made me feel. Perhaps I was inspired by a perverse desire to see him discomforted once more, for that was the moment it came to me that I did have one power over him – my very desperation.

"Come to my office this evening," he said. "I'll make an excuse and absent myself from dinner. Seven o'clock should do well. Wait under the pergola until you see the light in my window. Can you remember that?"

"No."

"You can't remember?"

"I mean, no, I won't be there."

"Then the next day…"

"I'm not coming. You're correct about Zoran and his daughter. She sent the book to me. And you're right that the Patent Office have been trying to find it. They questioned me. I lied to them."

His body went rigid again. For a moment I thought he was going to be sick. But when his shoulders tipped forwards it was merely to spit out the words, "You lied… to them?"

"They know she sent the book from her cell. But they can't prove it came to me."

"My God," he whispered. It was a strange invocation for a Republican professor. "You've brought me poison!"

"Tell me what you discovered," I said.

"I will not!"

"Very well…" I stood and brushed down my skirts.

"Where are you going?"

"I'm going to the Patent Office. They have a building on High Pavement. It's but ten minutes' walk from here. I'm going to tell them about the book. And I'm going to tell them exactly where it is right now."

"You'd ruin us both!"

I fixed him with the hardest stare that such turmoil would allow me to conjure and said, "I'm as good as ruined anyway." Then I turned before my expression could crumble, and marched away, listening all the while for his footsteps or any sign that he was following.

Birds sang from the trees. The voices of playing children called from over on the other side of the park. For a moment, I caught the scent of the rose bushes.

All Professor Ferdinand needed to do was hurry back to the university and throw the book into the fire. So long as it was burned by the time the agents arrived, he would be safe. I imagined him running towards the park gates and hailing a hackney carriage. I itched to turn around and look.

Having skirted the base of the statue and marched the length of one of the paths, I arrived at a small gate in the perimeter fence. I reached out to open it and at last heard what I had been hoping for.

"Wait!" he called.

I pushed on at an increased pace, out to the roadway. He did not catch up with me until I was striding along past an arcade of shops.

"Please – give me a chance."

He was panting, his face blotched red.

"Very well," I said. "But hold back on me one more time and I'll be gone."

I took him across the road to a tea shop, selecting a table near the wall at the back. From the glances they gave us, the staff and the other patrons clearly believed our business to be no better than it seemed. A lady in a blue walking dress sitting at a nearby table went so far as to cup a hand to her ear, the better to eavesdrop.

Once the tea had been delivered and the waiter had withdrawn, I turned my back to the woman and leaned closer to the professor, who, overcome with the trauma of my threat, was oblivious to the scandal we were creating. He was mumbling into his cup, too quiet for anyone but me to hear. He would no longer meet my gaze.

"What have we come to? Oh, what have we come to?" he said. "And why did you choose my life to ruin?"

"The book," I prompted.

"The cursed book! Some knowledge is noxious. It will likely do you harm. But you leave me no choice now but to tell it." He took a moment to gather himself, then said, "It has lines I'd not seen before. I drew conclusions. Of course I did! Anyone familiar with the other manuscripts would have done the same. But it just wouldn't add up. It wouldn't do! What was it you said – consider the unthinkable?"

"You said that, not me."

"Well, there you have it."

"What do we have?"

"The other books had been altered. Parts removed." His eyes flicked up at me. There was fear in his expression. And resentment. "Why did you want to know? Why wouldn't you leave it alone?"

"No more riddles, professor!"

"I told you – the manuscripts are like a family tree. I said yours was from a forgotten branch. I was wrong. When you look at the pattern of young and old sayings, it's clear yours sits near the stem of a well-known lineage."

"But you said there are sayings in mine that are not in the others."

"Yes!" he exclaimed. "Yes. That's what I've been trying to tell you. The Patent Office is supposed to confiscate or destroy the unseemly. But these books – the other manuscripts – they've been forensically altered and then returned to the libraries as if nothing had happened. The anomalous phrases in your book have been removed from them. The changes are undocumented. They're invisible. They've hidden it all so well, only a genius could find it. And for the first time in my life, I wish I wasn't."

"But why remove references to conjuring tricks?"

"You have it wrong. The things they've removed are descriptions of guns. More specifically, they're references to the loading of guns."

"That's part of the trick," I said.

"Perhaps. But more than that as well. Do you know what happened in 1815?"

"Napoleon raised an army to threaten Europe. Every schoolboy knows that."

"And who won the war?"

"No one. There was a short battle. But the generals saw sense and agreed to pull their armies back. Why are you asking?"

"Because that's when your book was written. In that very

period in which no one seemed to be writing histories, yet it is a history about which every schoolboy knows. The Patent Office has gone to extraordinary lengths to hide something about guns written during that time. Do you not see where all this leads?"

"I'm sorry. But no."

"Do you remember this quote?" he asked. "*You may devise a switch, a gimmick tamping rod, a cunning barrel breech or any other plan…*"

"*…but also devise the means to double check before the gun is pointed at your head,*" I recited, completing it. My father had often repeated the same words. The last time was when he gave me the pistol. It had seemed a strange thing to say at such a solemn moment.

"What of it?" I asked.

"What is a barrel breech?"

"A hole, I suppose, in the side of the barrel. Something a bullet could be slipped in or out through."

"How would a gun be fired if there was a hole in the side of the barrel?"

"What has this to do with history?"

"This phrase – barrel breech – it occurs sixteen times in your copy of *The Bullet-Catcher's Handbook*. Those are the sixteen entries from yours that are missing in the others. They have been excised – all of them. Nor is there mention of *barrel breech* in any reference book I can find.

"The International Patent Office confiscate and destroy the unseemly. That's what the Great Accord allows them to do. They can also withhold permission to sell or manufacture. But it seems they've done more than that. They've expunged something from history. And they've hidden what they've done. That is not what they do. It's not what they're supposed to do."

"You're telling me they've broken the law?"

"The law is what a court decides. But no court has examined such a question. There is no law to cover it."

Thoughts ricocheted inside my head. The Patent Office was beholden only to the Great Accord and its amendments. Therein were the limits laid down by the founding fathers.

"What would happen if this were found out?" I asked.

He raised both his hands, palms towards me, as if signalling a speeding coach to stop, an expression of horror on his face. "That can never happen! Some knowledge is too much. We may fear the Patent Office, but it's all that stands between us and the chaos that lies beyond the Gas-Lit Empire."

"Who could bring them to account if they had broken the rules?" I asked. "Could a government do it?"

"Enough!" he said, suddenly loud. "That is enough!"

The woman in the walking dress gasped. Others turned to look.

"I've done everything you've asked. If you still wish to seek ruin, then go to the Patent Office and tell them what's been done. I can't stop you. But I have nothing more to say. Come tonight for your book, or I'll throw it in the fire. Our agreement is at an end."

CHAPTER 6
August 2009

*However many questions another may ask, you must always
ask more. That is the way of the illusionist.*

THE BULLET-CATCHER'S HANDBOOK

In the days following Tinker's discovery of the watch, which
was still more than a week before my first meeting with
Professor Ferdinand, I went back several times to lift the
loose board next to the stove. Each time I carried his silver
repeater to the light and examined the inscription, trying to
imagine what could have brought Captain Bill "Lightning"
Brooks north across the border and into Lincolnshire.

In retirement, he might have returned to settle in an
ancestral home. But few Royalists find life in the Republic
to their liking. Even as a child, I'd found the culture
oppressively austere. I thought it unlikely an old man
would be able to adapt. He could perhaps have come on a
short visit, though few tourists were brave enough to stray
beyond the highlights of the main cities.

There were two other possibilities. Either a Republican
had ventured into the Kingdom and brought the watch
back. Or the owner, a retired man-at-arms, had crossed on

a specific mission – to capture me and claim the reward.

Since the age of fourteen, I'd been running from the Duke of Northampton. He had plotted the ruin of my family, gathering our debts and bribing an agent of the Patent Office. All this he'd done with the design of owning my indentured servitude – of owning me.

The court gave him what he wanted, but I had fled. Each time I evaded capture, the duke offered a bigger reward. It was certainly enough to tempt an old soldier across the border. But I could think of no way he could have tracked me into Lincolnshire.

I was still immersed in these thoughts as I steamed back along the Trent towards Nottingham. Steering the boat had become so natural to me that I hardly needed to think about what I was doing. I stood with one hand on the tiller, gazing towards the next bend. On this day Tinker kept me company, sitting on the cabin roof, whittling away at a stick with his knife.

My thoughts were so far distant that at first I didn't notice the man waving to me from a narrow boat moored on the right bank.

"Ahoy there!" he called.

I waved back and was about to look to the distance once more when he beckoned.

"Are you the *Harry*?"

"Who wants to know?"

"If you've got an Elizabeth on board, I've a message for her."

I steered to the side and cut the engine. Tinker jumped down and quickly had us tied and secure. I turned a valve and a rush of steam vented into the air. It was not uncommon for messages to be passed boat to boat. Only the small community of the North Leicester wharf knew the name of my boat, so I should have been safe enough. But, as I approached the man who had hailed me, my senses were alert for danger.

"Are you Elizabeth?" he asked.

"I might be."

He held an envelope up for me to see. "It's to be put in her hand only."

"Then I'm she," I said. "Who gave it to you?"

"A barge on the Grand Union. Captain heard I was heading north and asked me to look out for you."

I took the envelope and read: *For Elizabeth on paddle boat the* Harry. The handwriting was unmistakeable. Julia, my friend and one-time student, had written it. I turned my back on the man and ripped it open.

July 18th 2009

My dear sister,

This is the seventh letter to you from my hand. As ever, I let it loose in the hope that it will find you, and find you well.

I am comfortably set up now in London, and am finding university studies to be just as fascinating as we imagined. Whilst I am learning the law of this country (they don't teach Republican law) much of it is rooted in the Great Accord, which is a foundation common to the legal systems of all civilised nations.

As you will understand, I do not wish to mention names or addresses in a letter dispatched in this way. But if you are able to write back, which is my ardent hope, do so via my parents' house. They would pass it on. Or, if you venture as far as this great city, you will find me every Tuesday and Friday afternoon with my fellow students watching cases argued in the courts of Fleet Street.

You are ever in my thoughts.

J

"Good news?" asked the man.

I folded the letter into my sleeve and turned to face him once more. "I'm in your debt for delivering it."

"Seeing a pretty girl smile is payment enough."

I looked at him closely for the first time. Pale blue eyes looked out from beneath a thatch of black hair, giving him a striking appearance. His cheeks and upper lip were shaved, but a beard hung down several inches from the point of his chin. I guessed him not much older than myself. Smoke rose from his boat's chimney and I could hear the hiss of steam from the engine, suggesting he was ready to be off.

"I've a pot of stew in the cabin if you'd eat with me."

I could smell it from the towpath. My stomach gurgled in protest. "Thank you, no," I said, not about to take the risk. "I don't want to hold you up."

"I'm not leaving just yet," he said. "And you've no need to worry. The boy can eat, too. I'm Zachary, by the way."

Tinker grabbed my arm and gave it a squeeze, to indicate the intensity of his hunger. Zachary stepped back and gestured with his hand. When we stepped up onto the deck, he flashed perfect white teeth in a smile that seemed genuine. Then he ducked through the hatch, saying, "Give me a moment to tidy."

I bent close to Tinker and whispered, "Give me your knife."

The boy seemed to understand and complied without hesitation. I tucked it into my other sleeve, ready to use, then followed the man inside where Zachary was in the process of bundling clothes into a drawer under the cot.

To a country person, one cabin might have seemed much the same as any other. The confined space left little room for variation. There were certain essential fixtures – a cot, a stove, a seat and built in cupboards. Perhaps because of this very sameness, each boat family strove to create differences: a display of china, embroidery and quilting, painted decoration of roses and castles. By this standard, Zachary's cabin felt starkly underdecorated.

"I told you to wait," he said, though he seemed pleased enough to see us.

A billhook and various other tools lay across the shelf where ornaments might have been displayed. Two pairs of men's boots lay next to the steps. Both muddy. The promised pot of stew sat on the floor next to the stove.

"The place wants a woman's touch," he said. And then, when we still hovered near the hatch, he gestured us to the cot to sit.

"What are you carrying?" I asked.

"I'm waiting for a load," he said. "They told me it'd be here yesterday. But you know how it is. I'm expecting it any time. What of yourself?"

"Packages."

"It's just you and the boy?"

"We manage."

"No doubt." He wiped out two bowls with a drab cloth and ladled stew into them. "There you go," he said, handing them to us.

Tinker raised his spoon. I put out a hand to stop him before the food got to his mouth.

"Won't you be eating?" I asked.

"Had mine already," he said. Then he lifted the ladle from the pot and took a mouthful straight from it. After he had swallowed, he said, "See? No poison."

I released Tinker's arm and he set to eating with purpose.

"Sorry," I said.

Zachary shrugged. "You're right to be careful these days."

The stew smelled better than it tasted. The chunks of meat were tough, yet the vegetables were somehow overdone. For all that, it was warm and filling and I felt grateful.

"Thank you," I said, when my bowl was scraped clean.

"You've got the reading then?" asked Zachary.

I nodded.

"But here you are, running packages. And hungry too."

"We get by."

"I'm sure you do."

Tinker had been licking out his bowl. Having extracted every bit of nourishment, he now put it to one side and rested back against the cabin wall.

"What's your delivery going to be?" I asked.

"Won't know till it gets here."

"You get by though. Just like us."

"I wasn't meaning no insult," he said. "It's just that you've got your boat. You can read contracts. Write them too, maybe? There'd be fleets as would love to have you. Or you could make your own."

"Why would I do that?"

"So you could eat steak all week and twice on Sunday."

"You're part of a fleet?" I asked.

"No."

"But there's meat in your cooking pot."

"I do alright."

"There you go then."

"Except that you were hungry," he said. "And I had stew." He winked.

Tinker turned to face the hatch. His muscles had tensed as if he expected someone to arrive. I'd heard nothing beyond the faint hiss of steam.

"The boy's jumpy," said Zachary.

"He's got good ears," I said, folding my hands on my lap, surreptitiously feeling the hasp of the knife.

Tinker stood.

"Perhaps he wants more stew. Hand me his bowl, will you?"

But the boy was off up the steps and gone. The hatch banged closed behind him. Zachary was smiling again, but I had caught a flicker of alarm on his face. I stood. He matched me. I took a step towards the hatch. He took two steps towards me.

"I really like you," he said. "Please don't go."

I let the knife slip half into my hand, but still concealed.

"I need to check on the boy," I said, then backed up the steps and pushed out onto the deck.

Immediately, I knew something was wrong. Tinker was sprinting back up the towpath towards the *Harry*. Then he was beyond it and I saw that a small launch was steaming away at speed. Understanding came to me all at once. I ran after him. The hatch of my boat gaped wide. The lock had been ripped away. Tinker had closed the gap on the launch, but it would be too far out into the water for him to reach. A man standing at the back of it waved to us, holding up stolen objects for us to see – my father's pistol and what I took to be Tinker's silver watch.

He shouted, "Thank you and goodbye!"

Though my feet were pounding the ground, the launch had started to pull away from me. Tinker was drawing level with it. Another man on the boat started throwing lumps of coal at him. The boy lost a yard every time he had to dodge.

The hoot of a steam whistle signalled a boat approaching from the opposite direction. Around the bend came a barge, wide beamed and taking up the middle of the canal.

Seeing what was about to happen, I shouted, "Stay back!"

But Tinker was hot on the chase and would not hear me.

The launch made a violent turn towards the bank to avoid being run down. Seizing his chance, Tinker leapt towards it. He cleared the water and landed half on the awning over the thieves' heads. The man with the pistol took aim. But Tinker had scrambled up and was a moving target. I saw a puff of smoke as the gun fired, then heard the crack of the shot. Tinker jumped or fell, I couldn't tell which. He was among them. Then the wash of the barge hit, tossing the small launch from side to side. I saw Tinker fall, hitting the water, his arms flailing. The launch continued on its way. In moments it was around the bend and out of view.

I ran till my lungs burned and kept running after that. At the place where Tinker had fallen, reeds fringed the edge. At first I could not see him. Then a splash called me further up the canal and I found him clambering out. He lay on his back, panting and black with mud. I took hold of him and rolled him over, searching for a bullet wound. He wriggled free of my grip and sat up.

"You could have been killed!"

He shook his head and held out what appeared to be a clump of water weed. When he placed it in my hand, I felt the shape and weight of my father's pistol.

"I got it back for you."

It came to me that he was unharmed, though another of his lives must surely have been used. I hugged him then, and kissed his cheeks, though the mud on him stank of sulphur. He had lunged for my gun and snatched it from them instead of going for his own precious watch. And he was alive. For that moment it seemed that I was the richest woman in the Gas-Lit Empire.

We could have run back and confronted Zachary. But there was no proof to present and no force that I could use to press my accusation. So we took time to wash away the mud as best we could before setting off back around the bend of the canal. By the time we reached the *Harry*, Zachary's boat had already steamed away.

The cabin was a mess. The drawers had been pulled out and emptied on the floor. Our hiding places had all been discovered. The money was gone. They had even taken the remaining sacks of coal. There wasn't enough left in the bunker for us to steam after them and alert the river police.

"Pirates and thieves," I said. "They must have stolen the letter from another boat. Probably they've a stack of others too."

"Sorry," said Tinker.

"Why?"

"I was hungry."

"No. You were perfect. I should have seen. There were signs, but I didn't read them."

Tinker frowned at the mention of reading.

"Two pairs of boots but bedding for only one. I should have asked myself where the other man was. I didn't think. And look what you did, you clever boy. You saved my gun. It's all we've got left. Though I'm loathe to sell it. My father gave it to me for a purpose."

"You can sell this as well," said Tinker, scooping *The Bullet-Catcher's Handbook* from under a pile of clothes. He held it out for me, the leather hanging limp from the board.

I turned it in my hand. It seemed the damage I'd done to the cover had been its protection. The thieves had seen it as worthless. But then, so would others.

"Who'd buy such a wrecked thing?" I asked.

"Someone who can read," said Tinker, cutting to the heart of the matter.

"We must collect firewood," I said. "Enough for us to steam back to Nottingham. Then I'll do as you say – find someone who can read. Someone who understands what it's worth. We'll see what they'll give us for it, eh? And then we'll eat. Sausage and mash and gravy till we can't eat anymore."

I don't know if it was the mention of food or if it was the delayed shock of facing death, but Tinker chose that moment to give me a hug. It was the first time he did so of his own accord.

CHAPTER 7
September 2009

There is no lie but what they discover. There is no truth but what you can make them believe.

THE BULLET-CATCHER'S HANDBOOK

Under scant moonlight, I picked my way through the gardens of the university. With a grand dinner underway, there was no one to challenge me. No need this time for me to carry a box on the pretence of making a delivery. The smell of roasting meat hung in the still air around the back door of the kitchens. I could hear the clatter of pans and a shouted order to plate up the puddings. Then I was through into the lawned quadrangle and quickly under the ink shadow of a pergola. All the windows of the ivy clad building were dark but one.

I had not yet knocked when the door opened and Professor Ferdinand drew me inside. His office felt different in lamplight. Objects that had been mere curiosities in the daytime now seemed menacing. Shadows made statues appear to lean forwards from their shelves.

The picture had been removed from the wall behind his desk. He stepped to the safe door and pulled it open, for it was already unlocked. I received the book.

"You tricked me into this," he said.

"You were keen enough to have it."

"It was still a trick."

"I'd like to be open," I said. "Lay my life bare for everyone to see. I just don't have that luxury."

"If you try to blackmail me again, I'll say I've never met you."

"So you do understand that the truth's a luxury."

"That's different!"

I let his words hang. The silence became uncomfortable. He looked down to the floor, ashamed, I thought. Perhaps it *was* different. I was well used to living on the ragged edge. For him the experience must have been a shock.

At last he said, "This isn't just dangerous for us. There are powerful men who'd use what I've told you if they knew it. People who'd rather the Great Accord had never been signed. You must burn the book. Please."

I found myself holding it more tightly to my chest. "You've given me what I asked. So our bargain has been honoured. I won't trouble you again."

I had turned and was reaching for the door handle when he called me back.

"Miss Barnabus. Your story – it reminded me of something I'd read. I traced it and... Well, it's here if you want it." He held out a white envelope. "Read it later. I only hope it'll bring more help than sorrow."

I had intended to wait until I was back on the boat before examining the professor's gift. But as I walked, a sense of foreboding grew, becoming unbearable. I speeded my step, hurrying to be home. Halfway there, I found that I had stopped. Then I was backtracking towards the sickly hiss of a streetlamp.

Under its yellow light, I ripped open the envelope and extracted two strips of paper pinned together. One was a newspaper article. The other, the banner from the top of the page, gave the publication date as two weeks before.

The newspaper article had been set out as a cautionary tale. The ingredients were familiar enough – a blacksmith who lived beyond his means, too ready to venture money on dogs or horses, empty gin bottles found by a reporter stacked at the back of the man's log store, gossip of profligacy among the neighbours. None of the blacksmith's debts were huge, to be sure. But when added together they amounted to a sum beyond his substance. This lifestyle he had maintained through an increasingly precarious feat of balance, borrowing from one creditor to pay off another.

I could have named any number of men and women about whom the same had been said. Few on workers' wages could afford to live without debt. A poor man never throws away a bottle. Gambling is merely hope by a different name. And were it not for hope, how could a poor man decide each day to live?

Yet the man was a wastrel, the newspaper said. His excesses might have remained unnoticed for a time yet, but for a vigilant agent of the International Patent Office. The blacksmith had made and sold some novel devices without a licence. The agent detected the breach and imposed a fine. Thus was the balance upset and the blacksmith toppled into bankruptcy.

His many creditors would surely have been injured by his inability to pay – themselves not wealthy men? However, a high-minded nobleman of that county saw their plight and bought up all the bad debts at a generous rate by way of service to the community.

The newspaper praised his actions. He knew he would suffer financial injury, yet pressed ahead for the common good. Naturally enough, he took the blacksmith to law in an attempt to recoup some of the loss. But once legal fees had been paid, even with the sale of the blacksmith's cottage, forge, and tools, there remained a shortfall of seven hundred and seventy-five guineas.

The blacksmith was locked in debtors' prison and his nineteen year-old daughter indentured to work in the nobleman's kitchens for a period of thirty-five years, or until the debt be otherwise paid.

The generous nobleman wished to remain anonymous, saying, "There is no virtue in a good deed proclaimed."

I became aware of a tacky feeling between my lips. And then a metallic taste. I spat onto the cobbles, my saliva bloody. I had been biting the side of my tongue while I read. I was breathing deeply, though I still couldn't seem to get enough air.

The story in the newspaper was my own retold. It came to me that the reporter had mistaken only the fine details – my father's profession, my age, the sum of the debt. Everything else fitted precisely with the nightmare that had rent my family. An agent had found a supposed violation in one of my father's devices, there was a fine, the gathering of debts, a trial, a verdict, indentured servitude.

And yet the date on the newspaper banner proved the article was recent. Either the banner came from a different paper or they were reviewing the news of six years before. I stared at the newsprint, no longer able to read the words.

There was a thought, puzzlingly out of focus and on the edge of my mind. It took the shape of a man riding towards me, his face yet too distant to discern. I could hear the hooves of his horse drumming the ground. But still his features were a blur. If I could but see clearly, I would be able to recognise him. Then I would understand. He had drawn so close now that he towered over me, impossibly tall. I found myself straining my neck to look up into the blinding yellow of his face. He reached down. I could see his gloved hand in every detail. Fine white leather. Stitches perfectly even. It extended towards my own hands, which cradled my face. Somehow I knew that if it took me, I would be lost. I wrenched my eyes from his hand and looked up to the face, forcing myself to see it.

A cruel gaze bore down on me, a face I had glimpsed but twice. It was the Duke of Northampton. But the story in the newspaper was not my own. It was happening again. To a different family. Another father had been ruined. Another daughter acquired.

I found myself kneeling, staring up at the spluttering gas lamp as understanding broke over me. I saw it all with vertiginous clarity. Then my stomach heaved. I braced myself, hands on the cold cobblestones and vomited.

When it was done – my hands no longer trembling and the sweat drying on my forehead, when I had got back to my feet, using the lamppost for support – it came to me that the duke had exercised the same monstrous practice before. And he would continue to repeat it until death toppled him.

But this time was different. This time I was watching. I had the means to identify the corrupt agent. What was more, I had a contact on the inside. John Farthing could walk the corridors of the Patent Office itself. He could investigate. For once, we could be fighting on the same side. And if the duke's corruption could be proved, I had at last the means to end him.

CHAPTER 8
September 2009

Take off the disguise and another is revealed beneath. Regard well the many people you must be. When the last layer is gone, there can be no more life.

THE BULLET-CATCHER'S HANDBOOK [2]

Of the many tangled threads in my life, the one I found hardest to describe was my relationship with the Patent Office agent, John Farthing. He lied to me the first time we met. And if I lied to him also, it later saved me from much trouble. I was the subject of his investigation and had since remained under his gaze.

On the occasion of our first meeting, I had been taken in by his charm. That was before his real identity had been revealed. At the time, I was attracted by his winning smile and his easy movement, which was so unlike that of a Republican. When he spoke, his American tongue gave familiar words a roundness that seemed enticingly exotic.

The truth was revealed on our second encounter, when he came armed and threatened me. For my part, I held the

---

[2] As recorded in the Great Zoran manuscript.

Patent Office responsible for the ruin of my family. From that day, I knew John Farthing and I must always be on opposite sides.

Every time we met thereafter, my confusion grew. His mere presence put me on edge. He did once offer to help me seek redress for the wrongs my family had suffered. But we'd both known such action would find no good conclusion. The Patent Office would do all it could to prove its agents' innocence. At the time, I hadn't sufficient evidence to force its hand.

I once used John Farthing to save my life. And in return I also once saved his. But our parting from that adventure had been the most painful and confused. I had never felt so angry or afraid. His last words to me had been these: "You need never look on me again."

It seemed that fate was about to prove him wrong.

The newspaper article had forced me to seek him out one more time. The Duke of Northampton had to be stopped or more young women would fall victim. Now armed with more evidence – a second case that matched my own in every detail – they would have no choice but to investigate.

Yet, as I stepped along Nottingham's High Pavement towards the building where John Farthing worked, I felt my usual resolve begin to curdle and my composure entirely disappear. My heart was beating heavy and irregular in my chest. I had reached his door, but found my feet carrying me on beyond it and away.

A thought – a ridiculous thought – had taken root in my mind. I had reasoned that the goal of my action was to confound the Duke of Northampton and enable my safe return to the Kingdom. But if the corrupt Patent Office official could be exposed and brought to book, could not also John Farthing and I be friends?

At the end of the row of townhouses I stopped and forced myself to breathe more slowly. I could not allow such foolishness in my mind. I would put it away entirely and go about my business as planned. Yet, when I turned and headed back, I realised that I was smiling. Indeed, I could not stop myself.

On my previous visit I had sent a boy into the building with a message. But this day I found myself opening the front door and stepping into an austerely furnished lobby. A young clerk stood behind a high wooden counter. On seeing me he folded away the newspaper he had been reading.

"May I help you?" he asked, in a voice that seemed older than his years.

"I wish to talk to an agent."

"You have an appointment?"

"I have not."

He slid a ledger across the desk, opened it at a black ribbon and traced his finger down a column of copperplate writing, too fine for me to read upside down.

"Could I suggest a week on Thursday?" he said. "Two thirty in the afternoon. Agent Blake could see you then."

"It's Agent Farthing I need to see. And I'd hoped he could see me directly."

"But without an appointment–"

"I believe he'll at least want to know I'm here."

The young clerk closed his ledger. "Your name?"

"Elizabeth."

"Your family name?"

"He'll know who I am."

I expected to be sent on my way, but he nodded towards a high-backed wooden chair opposite the entrance. "Please wait."

The chair seemed to have been constructed for someone with a different body shape to my own. Horizontal struts pressed against my spine and the seat was too high, so that only my toes touched the floor. But I did not mind. I wondered if John Farthing's office faced the front or the back of the building and what hours he kept.

A door opened close by, causing me to jump. But it was only another clerk, going about his business, a bunch of green cardboard files under one arm. He did not even glance at me in passing and was swiftly through the lobby and out the other side.

I could hear movement upstairs – the crisp tapping of hard soled shoes walking across a wooden floor. There were fainter sounds in the background. The creaking that every house makes. The flow of water in pipes.

Then the young clerk returned. I stood, ready.

"I'm sorry," he said.

"How so?"

"You cannot see the agent you requested."

"Is he not here?"

"He wishes you to know that he is unavoidably and permanently engaged."

I let the clerk book me an appointment with Agent Blake, giving my name as Elizabeth Underwood, an alias I had used before. He transcribed the time and date of the appointment onto a slip of stiff paper and passed it across the desk to me, though he was fastidious in avoiding contact with my hand. I thanked him and left.

I was no longer smiling.

Opposite the Patent Office building there was a library set back from and above the road. In the small garden at the front, under the shade of a tree, I waited and watched. Before the revolution the building would have been used for Christian worship and the grounds for burial. Always with one eye on the road, I strolled the perimeter, pretending to read the inscriptions on the gravestones, which had been arranged as a kind of ornamental boundary wall.

At half past five in the afternoon, the last patrons left the library and the great doors boomed closed behind them. Then, within minutes, people started to emerge from John Farthing's offices. There were young and old, but all were men and all dressed resolutely in grey. I observed a mixture of top hats and bowlers. And then among them I saw a centre-creased hat with a wide brim. It was the same one he had worn on our first meeting.

He was a man with an easy stride that looked out of place on a cobbled street in Nottingham. He never seemed to be hurrying, but as I set out to follow, I found myself having to throw in extra steps to keep him in sight.

I do not know if I was seen by any of the others who came out of that building. I do not know if anyone watched me or followed. I kept John Farthing in view all the way up Stoney Street and Warser Gate. Then he picked up speed and began to pull away. I lost view of him in Bottle Lane. Forgetting myself, I ran. I knew that people were staring. If I had thought about it, I would have known the risk. There were still fugitive posters bearing my likeness. If one person had recognised me, my life would have been over. But I kept running, turning right up Bridlesmith Gate for no reason but that it felt to be the way he would have gone.

Then I saw the grand columns of the Council House, and striding along beside it, John Farthing. I caught up with him on the wide plaza in front of the building. He must have heard my footsteps because he stopped and turned. I was out of breath.

"Miss Barnabus," he said, his voice strained by some emotion that I couldn't read.

"Mr Farthing."

"What possessed you to come to the office? Don't you know how dangerous it is for you?"

"It's the Duke... the Duke of Northampton. He's done the same thing... again. Another girl. Another family."

Farthing opened his mouth and closed it again.

"We must stop him," I gasped. "Don't you see? With this... A fresh trail. We can find the agent who did it. We can..." I faltered, tears running down my cheeks.

"No." He was shaking his head.

I stepped towards him, but he held up his hands, as if warning me away. People had stopped to stare.

"But you must help," I said. "Please."

He took a step backwards. "I'm sorry. But I have no more disguises from you. I loved you, Elizabeth. But that way is closed. I'm an agent of the Patent Office. You know what that means. Celibacy. For life. You shouldn't have come. We stand on opposite sides of a great breach. It is too much for me to bear. If we meet again, it will be as enemies. This is the end."

Some minutes after John Farthing had strode away, an elderly couple approached me and asked if I needed help. The woman took my hand. She wore a jet ring and pinched cuffs. Her fingers were very pale. I do not know why these details were important, but I noticed them. I seemed to see every wrinkle in her aged skin. The two of them looked so alike in face that I took them to be brother and sister.

Other people passed by in that busy square, making an art of looking the other way. A nurse pushing a perambulator, three students with battered satchels, two men carrying bags and carpenters' tools. The flagstones beneath my feet were worn smooth.

"My dear? Can we take you somewhere?"

The woman was still holding my hand.

"No. Thank you, no."

She unclipped her purse and withdrew a clean, white handkerchief. This she placed in my hand before guiding it to my cheek, drying the tear streaks. My nose was running. Suddenly I was aware of a plainly dressed woman standing alone on that wide plaza, in view of all, hundreds of eyes, surreptitiously stealing glances. The woman was me.

"I'd better go," I said, offering back the handkerchief.

"You keep it, dear." She closed my fingers around it with hers.

I should have liked to say thank you, but no more words would come. I turned and walked away.

I cannot say when the decision was made. Only that it was as I walked away from the Council House that I became aware of it. But, in truth, I seemed to have been making it for many years. Perhaps I had not been ready before then – my skills and resolve not fully honed. Or perhaps I just needed a big enough push. But I think it is more likely that until that moment there had always been some thread of hope. The illusion that my destiny could take any other course.

When I returned to the boat, Tinker was already asleep, curled up next to the stove. The candle lantern did not disturb him. I looked to the aft wall at the Spirit of Freedom. I had imagined her as many things. When she was first revealed to me, she had seemed the plaything of the sculptor. But her expression had suggested a different story – a woman more in control of the sculptor than the other way around. As I sailed the waterways of the Republic, she took on a different meaning, suggested by the name. Freedom. But now I saw her as she surely was – naked, stripped of every encumbrance. Supremely vulnerable. And thus, supremely dangerous.

I ate some food. It was a mechanical process. I tried to sleep. At three in the morning I gave up, and set wood and coal in the firebox. With the moon almost full, I could steam without a lookout on the prow.

By the time Tinker awoke, we were already on the Grand Union Canal heading south. He didn't ask where we were going. He sat with me on the steering platform, chewing on a hunk of bread. And when the boiler pressure grew low he hopped down and started shovelling coal.

By dawn we were approaching North Leicester. We passed the spur that would lead to the wharf on which I'd once lived. I did not look along it for fear of seeing someone from my previous life.

"Are you ill?" asked Tinker, blurting the question as if he'd been holding it back.

"No," I said.

He continued to stare at me. I turned my face away, towards the back gardens of houses that bordered the canal.

Soon there were factories on both sides and the sulphurous tang of coal smoke mixed with the smells from the warehouses – tar and hemp and bone meal and leather. The morning light touched the walls of terracotta brick but seemed to give them no colour.

Mine was not the only boat approaching the border crossing empty. It was common practice for captains to stop short and unload. Lines of porters were a familiar sight trotting through the backstreets of Leicester on the way to the many illegal crossing points. Each man would carry two great boxes, one on each side of him, dangling from a pole balanced across his shoulders. I had often been amazed by the loads thus carried, stout poles flexing under the weight of cargo.

Mathematics made the trade inevitable. The hiring of porters, fees paid to the owners of the illegal crossing points and the cost of lost time, when added together, amounted to less than the import duty thus avoided. Once on the other side of the border, the porters carried the cargo back to the boats for reloading. This industry, the only purpose of which was the avoidance of tax, had brought wealth to the city of Leicester.

The border came in sight – a high brick wall across the canal. I pulled the lever, disengaging the engine from the paddle wheels and let the *Harry* drift to a stop behind two other boats that were waiting their turn to cross. I could see the customs officers in their blue uniforms and flat caps talking to the captain of the foremost boat. He held a clipboard on which he wrote from time to time. Then I saw him shake the captain's hand and hop off onto the quayside. Two workmen in grey overalls then set to with boathooks until the vessel was in position. A steam whistle hooted. The crane swung around and, with a rattle of chain spooling over a drum, two giant mechanical grabbers descended, closing around the boat.

I had watched this process before and been amazed. But today I was merely impatient. In the background the rhythm of the steam engine changed. The chains went taut. The boat began to lift. Then the entire hull was visible and water was running from it, splashing down into the canal. It was like watching an airship rising from the ground. Though I could see the chains and understand the method, it seemed impossible – as if nature's laws were being contravened. The crane shifted and the boat floated forwards, smoke still issuing from its funnel, to descend beyond my view on the far side of the border wall.

While this had been happening, the customs officials had been inspecting the next boat in line. I watched the handshake, the positioning of the boat, the grabbers descending again.

"Good morning, missus," said the customs man. "Can I speak to your husband please?"

"I'm sorry," I said. "He's not here."

"Going by another route, is he?"

"Maybe."

While we were speaking, another man in uniform had unlaced the tarpaulin and peered into the hold. "She's empty," he called.

I handed over identification papers for myself, Tinker and the *Harry*. They were good forgeries and I had no worries that he would doubt them. He noted down details on his clipboard before returning them to me. Instead of shaking my hand he raised his hat. Then he stepped back to the quayside and the *Harry* was being positioned beneath the grabbers.

Tinker had not asked where we were going, even when he saw the border in front of us. It was only as we lifted from the water and I heard the hull creaking under the strain that I thought about the boy. Water splashed below us. The other boats seemed to have risen smoothly, but I could feel us swaying from front to back as we started to move forwards.

As the border wall passed below us, Tinker grabbed my hand. "We're up in the clouds," he said. "We're flying!"

CHAPTER 9
September 25th

> *To perform the impossible is elementary. It requires only that everything you are and everything you have learned be brought to focus in one moment, and at a place where no one else is looking.*
>
> THE BULLET-CATCHER'S HANDBOOK

At night and from a distance, the seat of the Duke of Northampton seemed less like a home, more a small town. From my hiding place, I could see over the perimeter wall, allowing me an unobstructed view of the front and one side of the buildings.

The main massing of stonework towered above a sprawl of outbuildings, workers' accommodation and the garrison that was home to his private army. The roofs were a chaos of pitched slate, skylights, balustrades and tall brick chimneys, each surmounted by a cluster of spiralled pots.

The only uncluttered aspect was the front, which was arranged symmetrically around a central portico. All was silver under the moonlight. A long drive bisected tiered gardens, descending terrace by terrace towards a gatehouse in the far distance.

As I watched, I found myself shivering. Caution had made our journey long. Sleeping in the boat we'd been warm enough. But my coat was now sodden from nights of stumbling through fields on a slow approach, and days of hiding, not daring to light a fire.

Tinker, however, seemed capable of sleeping anywhere. Within minutes of us bedding down he'd been away, his breath slow and even. The sleep of the innocent. I must myself have slept eventually, because at some time in the night I became aware that he had gone.

The first movement around the grand house and its outbuildings came before dawn. The moon had been obscured by cloud so there was no longer light enough to see, but I could hear the rattle of iron wheel rims on cobblestones – hand barrows, I assumed, since there was no sound of horses. Servants would be hauling food or coal from the storerooms, ready for the day ahead.

As the sky began to pale I counted six columns of smoke rising from among the forest of chimneypots. Farmers were already at work in the surrounding fields – all of which would be the property of the duke. I wondered how much of the Kingdom was run directly by the aristocrats. Every family for miles around would be in the service of the same man. It was less a household, more a seat of government.

At eight o'clock, with the sun already over the horizon, lighting the Cotswold stone of the buildings so that they glowed honey brown, a detachment of soldiers emerged from the barracks. Their red coats marked them out even at such distance. A small column of men marched with muskets shouldered, while two officers on horseback rode at the front. Out they went along the great drive. I tracked their progress until, two thirds of the way to the gatehouse, trees obscured the view.

But some minutes later, a column of men came marching back. They lacked the crisp energy of the first group. I wondered whether they were required to spend the night standing out in the cold or if there was a guardhouse where they could warm themselves from time to time.

One thing was certain: there were not enough of them to patrol the perimeter of that vast property. But why should they? There was no power to threaten the duke. Unless it be another duke. And for one aristocrat to make war against another would be unthinkable. Their families were tied together by countless marriages of allegiance.

At a quarter past ten in the morning, a white coach rolled up the drive, pulled by four white horses. From the head of each animal a plume of white ostrich feathers sprouted. The scene was dazzling in the morning sun. Footmen hurried to open the doors, whereupon two women emerged, dressed in outfits of yellow and green. It was a wonder that such a volume of skirts could have fit within the carriage. The women seemed young to be carrying such a weight of clothing.

They put their heads close together as if whispering, the rims of their hats brushing each other. The footmen followed them into the house, though at a discreet distance.

They were not long inside before a second coach arrived, this one black. Though it was smaller than the first, it was pulled by six horses. A mark of status, I thought, rather than the weight of the passenger. Each horse had been groomed to a shine almost as brilliant as the carriage itself.

Servants issued from the front of the mansion and lined up on either side of the door. Last out was an officer of the men-at-arms. It was he who opened the carriage door and offered his hand to the occupant.

The man who stepped out was almost as tall as the officer. I should have liked him to be corpulent or crooked. I wanted to see some outer sign of the corruption within. But his only physical defect was the slight hesitancy of movement that comes with age. Given that he had seen seventy years, he was wearing well.

He stepped down to the immaculate gravel and all the servants abased themselves, bowing from the hip or curtsying deep. There could be no doubt on whom I looked. It was the ruin of my family and others. It was the Duke of Northampton.

He turned his back on the bowing servants and stepped to the edge of the terrace, seeming to survey the garden. He straightened the hat on his head, took a few steps to the left, then a few to the right as if idling in thought. Then, on a moment, he wheeled and marched between the rows of servants, who still held themselves low. After he disappeared there was a second of stillness. Then, at some signal I did not catch, all were straightening themselves and hurrying away. They did not return via the front entrance as they had left. Instead they made their way around the building to a small doorway on the side.

I had seen the duke two times before, but never clearly.

On the first occasion I was standing on the stage of our travelling show, my family around me. My father had just completed his grand illusion. When you are focused on a trick, all the world fades. There is only yourself and the intricacy of learned movements. There is no fear that you will make a mistake because you have practised it a thousand times. It is a dance that carries you beyond thought.

In brief, the trick was this – my brother would be seen

to enter a cabinet to the left side of the stage. The audience would be called up to inspect. They would circle it. They would knock on its walls. They would get down on hands and knees to reach between its short legs and feel the sturdy wood of its base. The doors of the cabinet would be closed. And in those moments, the audience might catch a glimpse of me for the first time, mixing with the confusion of people on the stage, encouraging them to knock on wood panels, proving to them that there were no hidden doors.

Some volunteers were left to guard it. Others followed me across the stage to a second cabinet, open and empty. They examined it as thoroughly as they had examined the first. They circled around it until they pronounced themselves satisfied.

Then, centre stage, my father would be seen to summon the hidden powers of the universe. He would hold his hands out on either side of his body and they would burst into flame. The torches that lit the stage would change colour from yellow to ghostly blue. He would slap his hands together. In that instant, the flames would die and both cabinets would burst open. My brother would be seen to have been transported across from one to the other.

It was the finale of the show. No trick could follow without it being an anticlimax. The audience stood to applaud. They stamped their feet. My father would stand between the cabinets. For a moment they would see my brother standing with him, then the curtains would drop.

It was in those seconds, when the applause was at its loudest, that I would perform the most skilful part of the trick, changing back once more from boy to girl so when the curtain rose a few seconds later, I could step forwards and stand in line as the other facet of myself once more.

It must have been then that the duke fastened his eyes on me. I was not a great beauty. I still presented the innocence of childhood. I have the indistinct memory of seeing him, the one member of the audience still seated. I couldn't make out much against the lights, but I had the impression of the bright colours of his clothing.

The second time I saw him was a few days later. We had struck the tent, loaded the wagons and were already on the move when a black coach flanked by outriders came up behind, driving at speed.

I couldn't say how it came to be, but later that day the entire troupe was told to stand in line. Then each of us in turn was called to stand next to the black carriage until instructed to move on.

When it came to my turn, I stood on tiptoes, trying to see who might be observing from within. I caught sight of the sleeve and cuff of a dark jacket and behind that the suggestion of a face. Then the sun came out from behind a cloud and the glass became a mirror of the trees and sky. I waited to be waved on, but time seemed to slow. I found myself blushing in that way children do when they know they are observed. I glanced back to the line, but no one would meet my eyes. When at last the signal came, I ran, crying for a reason I couldn't explain.

I do not remember it in this ordered way. I had to piece the narrative together from scattered childhood memories. My father's tension. The debt collectors that seemed to follow us in the months after. Travelling to London for court cases. Then our flight, avoiding the main roads, often doubling back, making our way under cover of darkness.

We passed through Buckinghamshire into Oxfordshire and then struck north. I think my father intended to cross the border and make a new life in the Republic. But a travelling show is too big to hide.

The day that is clearest in my memory is the one where my father told me to grab my things and run. The duke's men-at-arms had found us and were on their way. It was the last day I saw him.

So deeply immersed was I in this memory that I didn't notice Tinker returning. He held a hunk of bread under my nose, making me startle. When at first I didn't take it, he moved it closer to my mouth, as if about to feed me.

"I'm not hungry," I said.

"Eat."

"And I'm not a child!"

The words came out sharper than I intended. He flinched. All at once I became aware of the responsibilities that I'd been carrying. They felt like a weight pressing down on my head. For everyone, I had to be a different person. A dutiful sister, a resourceful intelligence gatherer, a cheerful friend, a man, a woman. And now, unwontedly, a mother.

"Where did you get the bread? Did you steal it?"

"Didn't steal it!"

"Then where did you get the money to buy it?"

"Someone give it me."

"Who?"

He shook his head, mouth clamped closed. I realised that I was crying. I turned my face away from him whilst I wiped my cheeks.

"What is this place?" he asked.

"It doesn't matter," I said.

"Are you ill?"

It was the second time he had asked me that question.

I managed to put on a smile before turning to look at him again.

I took the bread. "Thank you."

It was a piece torn from a flat loaf. I could taste wood smoke in it. Wherever the boy had been, it had been cooked on a pan over an open fire. That made sense. There might be a camp of gypsies nearby. He would have been drawn to them. They would have reminded him of life in the travelling show.

"Tinker – there's something I need you to do."

On hearing these words, the anxious expression lifted from his face. He wriggled closer along the ground. I could smell the smoke of a campfire on his clothes.

"I want you to travel north. To the border. Head across to North Leicester. I want you to go back to the wharf. Speak to Mr Swain. I'll write a message for you to give him."

Tinker frowned in confusion as I rummaged in my haversack for paper and pencil. I didn't bother to hide the writing from him, since he'd never been taught to read.

My dear Mr Swain,

You have always been kind to me. And I have leaned on that kindness too often without giving back. So I do not ask this of you lightly, but am left with no other choice. I need someone to give food and shelter to this boy, whose name is Tinker. He will not need much looking after. Perhaps if you made up a bed for him in the workshop it would do. Mrs Swain will not want to let him into the house without a bath and a change of clothes – and these I fear would require all your powers of persuasion. He is bright, after his own fashion. And he is loyal to a degree you will seldom find. Indeed, I believe he is the most loyal person I have ever met. I am sorry to place this burden on you. But it will be the last time. This I promise. Please pass all my love to Julia.

I did not sign it. My name could only bring suffering. I folded the sheet of paper and placed it in Tinker's hand. He cocked his head, an expression of puzzlement on his face.

"Now?" he asked.

"Now."

He made to go, but I grabbed his arm and pulled him to me. He suffered the embrace in silence. Finally, I kissed the top of his head and pushed him away, turning so that he would not see that I was crying once more.

CHAPTER 10
September 25th

Worse than no plan is a plan half formed.

THE BULLET-CATCHER'S HANDBOOK

A strange kind of numbness worked its way into me as I kept watch on the seat of the Duke of Northampton. It had started as a physical sensation in my fingers and toes, a response to the cold, I thought. But after Tinker had gone it became something deeper, eating its way into the very core of me.

The duke emerged twice more before sunset. The first time was in the early afternoon. A servant followed behind him carrying a gun box. A second man scurried across to the low wall by the edge of the upper terrace. On this he placed a line of wine bottles. Then he ran to the side, as if the devil were after him. He was barely clear before the duke raised the first pistol, taking aim. There was a puff of smoke and I saw his hand recoil. A moment later I heard the boom of the gun. None of the bottles had been harmed.

The duke held the gun out to the side without looking. The first servant took it and placed a new pistol in his hand.

The duke took aim again. A second puff of smoke. One of the bottles exploded. I had thought them to be empty, but liquid burst from it, soaking the stones on which it had been standing.

After three hits and as many misses, the duke wheeled and marched back to the mansion. I watched the servants work for a long time afterwards, picking up fragments of glass and scrubbing down the stones with bucket after bucket of water.

His second excursion came with the sun low in the sky. Four mounted men-at-arms had ridden in at a canter. There was a flurry of activity – servants running to hold the reins of the steaming horses, orders barked. The duke emerged at a brisk march. From his body language I would have said he was awaiting news of some importance. But whatever they told him, he was unpleased by it.

One by one, lamps were lit at the front of the house, though the servants' windows remained dark. In the twilight I could just make out workers trudging towards their homes across the fields. As night took hold, a bank of cloud began rolling in from the west, blotting out the stars and then the moon. Nature was conspiring to help me in my endeavour, as if it wanted me to succeed.

It came to me that the numbness I had been feeling was a kind of peace. It had begun as a lack of physical sensation, but had grown into an unaccustomed stillness of thought.

I took my father's pistol from the haversack and turned it in my hand. I thought briefly about bringing spare powder and shot, but discounted the idea. From firing the gun, I would have but seconds. There would be no time or means to reload. Besides, one bullet would be sufficient. I stood and unbuttoned my coat, letting it drop. The night seemed warm enough and I would not be needing it anymore. Then I took my sheathed knife and secreted it in my sleeve.

The perimeter wall must have been eight feet high, but there were trees enough just outside and I easily found one that could be climbed. I waited in its branches until I felt sure no guards were near. Then I let myself down on the other side, hanging for a moment before dropping onto the soft earth of a flowerbed.

The depth of darkness did not allow me to see the lawn across which I walked, but I could feel it through the soles of my shoes. Perfectly flat and short cropped, it was more like a carpet than anything of nature. Then, without a break in the level of the ground, I was walking on flagstones. The side of the building loomed above me, a dark mass only broken by the reflection of stars in window glass. Trailing my right hand against the wall, I began to make my way towards the front. The first window I came to would have been too small to climb through. I guessed a serving corridor must lie behind it. Not the part of the house I wished to be found walking through.

The next window was many times the size – a latticework of diamond-shaped panes. I applied the point of my knife to a strip of lead holding two pieces together. With enough pressure, the soft metal began to bend. Soon I was able to work one sheet of glass free and place it on the ground.

It did not feel to me as if I was working quickly. Rather, I seemed to be watching myself from a distance and in slow motion as I picked away one strip of lead after another. But soon I had accumulated a pile of the small panes and made a hole big enough to climb through.

The air inside the drawing room – for that is what I seemed to have entered – smelled of roses and some kind of spice that I thought I recognised but could not name.

I was standing, trying to discern the layout of the room in almost complete darkness, when I became aware of a bright rectangle of light forming on the floor. I stood frozen, trying to resolve what I was seeing. Furniture and fittings were visible now – high backed chairs, a fireplace. I could even make out the edge of the carpet in front of me. Turning my head, I saw the garden through the windows that ran along the room's front aspect. All outside was shining. For a moment it seemed as if I had crossed the threshold into a magical world. Then I realised that a gap had opened in the clouds, revealing the face of the moon.

Nature had chosen to light me on my way through the house.

I unlaced my boots and stepped onto the carpet in stockinged feet. By the time I was at the door on the other side of the room, I had cast off my hat and was unbuttoning my blouse. Outside I found a wide gallery with a line of bay windows on the left and dark wood panelling on the right. I dropped the blouse in the shadow beneath a window and undid the ties on my waistband as I walked.

By the time I had reached the halfway point, I was stripped to my corset and chemise. Here the gallery opened out into an entrance hall. The front doors lay to my left, a wide staircase to my right. As I began to climb, I heard a cough behind me.

"Excuse me, miss?"

The words were spoken in a whisper.

I turned, holding the pistol and knife in one hand, which I let hang close to me, nestled into the loose folds of my chemise. A man-at-arms stood, sword in hand, blinking as if he had incompletely woken from sleep. He looked at me in puzzlement. His eyes ran down my body to my feet then back to my chest before he seemed to become aware of a mistake, at which point his gaze dropped to the floor between us.

"I'm lost," I whispered.

"But… uh… where are you going?"

"I was sleepwalking. I can't find my way back to his room."

"Oh… Up and to the right. Can you…"

"Thank you," I said. "I'll find my way now."

He bobbed his head in a shallow bow, then backed away into the shadows at the side of the staircase, where he might have been standing guard, or perhaps sitting.

Such was the softness of the carpet and the solidity of the stairs that I climbed making no sound. After one flight the stairs divided, each branch doubling back, climbing to a second grand gallery, directly above the one I had already traversed.

I turned right, wondering how I would recognise, out of so many, the one door that would lead to the duke's bedchambers. But then I saw it – larger than all the others, with a chair positioned next to the wall outside on which sat another man-at-arms, eyes closed, chin resting on his chest.

I might have laughed. A kind of lightness had come over me. I would have thought myself drunk, but for the dizzying clarity with which I saw everything.

The door was unlocked. Of course it was. You don't need

locks with a private army stationed on guard. The door handle turned, silently, the mechanism perfectly maintained and oiled. Such a mixture of efficiency and complacency. Had I known how easy it would be, I might have done it years before.

I pushed the door closed behind me, cutting out the moonlight, and saw that a candle burned on the far side of the room, dripping a stalactite of wax from its holder. The air was warm, though I could see no fireplace. I wriggled my toes against the carpet, realising that heat was rising from the floor itself. A pleasant luxury to have heating without ash or smoke.

Though the room was large, it was dominated by the duke's bed. Four carved posts supported a canopy. Between the drapes, I could make out the forms of two sleepers. My hand was sweating. I adjusted my grip on the knife handle. My feet carried me forwards. But when I reached the foot of the bed, with my eyes adjusting to the inconstant light of the candle, I saw that the sleepers were both young women. The covers had been half pulled back so that I could see one of them clearly. She might have been fifteen years old. Her hair was cropped short, as mine had once been. My mind jumped back to the two girls I had seen stepping out of the carriage.

There was a space between them where another person might have lain. I stared at it.

All was silent, but the skin on the back of my neck began to prickle. I turned, very slowly. And there, in the shadow towards the corner of the room, I saw him. A seated figure, a white nightshirt raised over his knees. It took me a fraction of a second to realise that he was sitting on a commode.

"Come here," he said, his voice neither loud nor quiet.

I found myself obeying.

"Which one are you?" he asked. "Have I had you before?"

"No, sir."

I was close now. My hands hung by my side, keeping the weapons out of his view.

"Are you from the kitchens?"

"No, sir."

"You look familiar. What is it about you?"

"I don't know."

He stood. "Well, what are you waiting for, girl? Clean me up and then we can get started."

I scarcely saw my own hand moving. In a blink the knife was at his throat. I felt his muscles go taut, but he had the presence of mind to not try to pull away.

He inhaled, as if about to speak, but I increased the pressure of the blade and he snapped his mouth closed again. I did not force it so hard as to cut him deep, but he would feel the sting of it.

I realised then that all I had to do was sit him back down and make a single swift movement to slice through. It would be no harder than butchering a joint of mutton. If I opened up his windpipe, he wouldn't be able to cry out. The girls might remain sleeping. And the guards. I could walk from the room, retrace my steps, collect my clothes and slip out into the night. I would be miles away by the time the murder was discovered.

Until that moment I'd planned to use the knife on him and the pistol on myself. My lightness of spirit had come from the knowledge that I would not have to walk away.

But in that moment, the spell was lifted.

"Elizabeth Barnabus," the duke whispered, as if amazed

by what he was saying.

"You killed my father."

"No."

"He died in debtors' prison."

"That wasn't me…"

I felt a jolt of pain across my chest so intense that, for a second, I thought I had been stabbed. It was my heart – beating fit to burst. All the feelings I had been numb to since crossing the border now rushed back at me. I tensed, ready to cut into his neck. It would be justice to kill him. It would be an execution that the law was impotent to perform. I had the means to set the balance right. I silently begged my arm to move, but my nature would not allow it.

"What happens now?" the duke asked, his voice too loud.

One of the girls shifted in her sleep.

I changed my grip on the knife, making it twitch against his skin, stepping around behind him so that my arm was hooked over his shoulder. If he tried to pull away, the blade would cut him and it would be his own fault.

"Move," I hissed, pushing him forwards.

At my instruction he opened the door. But having turned the handle full, he then released it so that it sprang back with a metallic click. As I shoved him out into the gallery, the guard next to the door was waking. He got out of the chair and fumbled with his musket.

I aimed my pistol at his head. "Make a noise and you both die."

The guard seemed not much older than the girls had been. His face was a mask of terror.

I started to back away towards the stairs, pulling the

duke with me. "Follow us," I said.

He did so, holding his musket across his body. When he began to raise it, I shook my head. His arms were trembling. So were mine.

We had reached the top of the stairs. I felt the duke's muscles tensing, as if readying himself to escape, so I pulled the knife more firmly to his flesh. He gasped.

The dampness of my grip was stickier than before. I had cut him, but not deeply. I began to back him down, one step at a time. He shifted his weight one way and then the other. He was doing all he could to make our progress difficult and noisy.

Escape had not been my intention. And certainly not kidnap. Thus I had no plan. All they had to do was make noise enough to wake the guard stationed below and I would be ended. I wouldn't be able to hold off the two of them.

I turned the bend in the stairs and started to back down the final flight. The duke was putting up more resistance, as if he sensed my weakness. The young guard had begun to tread more heavily. The sound of his footfalls reverberated.

"Stop that," I hissed. But too late.

There was a movement behind me and the metallic whisper of a sabre being drawn from its sheath. The young guard's expression changed. His eyes flicked across to look behind me. I sidestepped, pulling the duke with me so that I could half turn and see the danger. The guardsman who had challenged me earlier stood, sword extended, as if to run me through.

I tensed myself, ready for the inevitable. But instead, he opened his hand, releasing the sword to drop. It clanged and bounced, coming to rest between us.

Only then I became aware of two more figures standing behind him. The boy Tinker and a squat dwarf.

"You're going to get us all killed," said Fabulo. "I hope you know that."

CHAPTER 11
September 25th

They will applaud a horse for its wild gallop and an elephant for its size. Yet they will applaud only that man who can reach beyond his nature and theirs.

THE BULLET-CATCHER'S HANDBOOK

A strange picture we made, the six of us and our various weaponry arranged at levels down that grand staircase. Moonlight and stillness lent unreality to the scene, like Drummond light bathing a tableau vivant on a music hall stage.

Fabulo broke the stillness and the illusion, shifting around the guardsman, though keeping his knife poised at the man's kidney.

"Don't kill the duke," he said. "Not unless you have to. He's our ticket out of here."

Tinker rushed forwards and took the musket from the younger guard, who seemed eager to be relieved of it. Then we were moving again, crabwise down to the lower gallery and then at a march along it the way I had come. The men-at-arms led the way, with Fabulo immediately behind, encouraging them with the points of two daggers.

I pushed the duke on after them, with Tinker striding next to me.

"How did you find me?" I whispered.

Tinker stooped midstride to pick up my discarded petticoat. The skirt was a few paces further along.

"You left a trail of breadcrumbs," said Fabulo.

"But what are you even doing here?"

"You can thank the boy for that."

Tinker now had an armful of my clothes. The moonlight made a pool on the floor beneath each window. We entered the final room. Fabulo closed the door behind us then shifted me out of the way, one of his daggers taking the place of mine at the duke's throat.

"Clothe yourself," he said.

Tinker dropped my things and hurried to turn his back on me, as if seeing me dressing was somehow more intimate than having seen me in my undergarments. The younger guardsman stared at the floor. The older one was looking from person to person, as if calculating.

The duke had been silent as we walked the corridor, but now he spoke: "You don't all need to hang for this."

"No one's going to hang today," said Fabulo.

"The guards outside will see you. You can't run and take me with you. And you can't let me go or you'll be dead in seconds."

"Only one is going to die – and that will be you if you start to make a noise."

I heard the duke suck air through his teeth and guessed that Fabulo had given him another cut to be thinking about.

Having my clothes on well enough, I stepped to the window of unpicked panes. The lawns surrounding the mansion were now bathed in blue white. A party of six picking its way across the wide lawn would be visible for miles. Beyond that was the perimeter wall. It seemed the duke might be right.

"Climb out," said Fabulo.

I did as he instructed. My skirts hissed as the fabric pulled across the stone windowsill. Then I was standing in a narrow fringe of shadow next to the wall. The duke was the next one to clamber through, though he contrived to catch his elbow on the fragile edge, causing one of the diamond shaped panes of glass to drop free. My hand shot out as if of its own volition and I caught the glass a foot above the flagstones. Then my hand whipped back and was at his throat once more, this time with the edge of the glass pressed to his skin.

He came out quietly after that. Tinker was next. Then the two guardsmen. And finally Fabulo, who immediately set off along the edge of the building, heading towards the back.

There were shadows enough here, though if anyone had been looking out from one of the windows we passed, they would have seen us silhouetted. Howbeit, for all his private army, it seemed none of his men were watching.

Fabulo unbolted one of the stable doors and we all followed him inside. It was too dark to see, though I could hear movement in the stalls and I found my nose wrinkling to the smell of horses.

"I can't ride," said Tinker.

"All the gates are locked till morning," said the older of the guardsmen. "His Grace is right – there's no way out. But if you'd do a deal – some of you might be saved."

"I'll let one of you walk free," said the duke. "The dwarf or the boy. The other one gets whipped. And you'll leave little Lizzy with me."

"Get one of the horses," Fabulo hissed. There was venom in his voice. "Make it a mean one."

I walked blind towards the sound of a hoof scraping on stone, my arms out in front of me. The stall door was easy enough to find. Mercifully there was a halter hanging from the end post. But as I tried to get it straight in my hands, a horse pushed me with the side of its head, sending me stumbling.

A light flared behind me. Tinker had struck a lucifer. Now I could see the animal, which was reaching out from its stall, lips drawn back as if it might bite. I stepped in quickly so that I was next to it, out of reach of the teeth, and had the head piece around its neck in one swift move. It tried to back away, but I pushed my forearm down, forcing it to drop its head below the front of the stall door. The flame died, but I'd already got the noseband in place and was buckling it fast.

Another match flared. I turned to see Fabulo tying the duke's wrists behind his back. The rope was the end of a long coil hanging from a hook on the wall.

It took us five matches to get him up onto the horse's back. Fabulo didn't have the stature to help, so stood with the light in one hand and knife in the other, with which he pricked the backs of the guards.

On the third attempt, me standing on one side of the beast and Tinker on the other, we finally had the duke in place. Then, with the long trailing end of the rope, we tied him wrists to ankles below its belly.

"I'll give one hundred sovereigns and free passage to whoever kills the boy or the dwarf," he gasped, for most of the air was pushed out of his lungs.

Tinker struck another lucifer on the stable wall.

"There's no way to escape," said the older guard. "That horse is going to make one hell of a racket in the courtyard."

"Good," said Fabulo. He took a second coil of rope from a peg, resting it over his shoulder. Then he searched the floor for a moment before stooping and picking up something from among the straw.

He gestured to Tinker, who doused the flame.

Light slanted in as I pulled back the doors. Iron horseshoes clattered on the cobbles as we stepped out. The guard was right. We wouldn't get twenty paces before the alarm was raised. For a moment it seemed that Fabulo had come not to rescue me but to claim the reward, that this whole episode had been a sham. But then he held up the small object in his hand and I saw that it was the head of a thistle.

"This is going to prick," he hissed, in a tone of mock apology. Then he plunged his hand between the duke's trussed body and the horse's back. He had hardly pulled away before the animal reared up. I had to jump to escape its flailing hooves. It whinnied then kicked out at the back. We all of us retreated into the shadow of the stable wall. If there had been a moment for the guardsmen to escape, that would have been it. But they stood, open mouthed, stunned by the spectacle and the reversal of all the order they had known.

Lights were coming on in the great house. I heard footsteps approaching at a run. Someone swore on the other side of the courtyard. Then the duke began screaming his rage. The horse reared two more times then set off towards the gardens.

Three men-at-arms burst from the front doors of the

great house. The man on the other side of the courtyard was running after the horse, flapping his arms as if trying to communicate but unable to speak. Then at last he got three words out: "It's the duke!"

I heard shouts in the distance. Men-at-arms who had been on guard duty around the walls were rushing back to help.

"This way," whispered Fabulo, gesturing our captives along the line of shadow, taking them further from the chaos he'd created. I took a last glance back and saw the horse leaping a low hedge at a gallop, leaving the pursuing servants far behind. And all the while the duke screamed orders, incoherent with rage.

It took little time for us to reach the wall, which lay close in that direction. From the sound of shouting in the distance it was clear that they were no nearer to catching the horse.

Fabulo took the coil of rope from his shoulder and turned to the two guardsmen. "Stand back to back, gentlemen," he said.

They began to move, but I held out a hand to stop them. "You can't leave them here. What will the duke do to them?"

"In a couple of hours the whole county's going to be out looking for us," said Fabulo. "We can't take them with us."

"Please," said the older guardsman. "She's right. We're dead men if we stay. I won't slow you down. I'll give you my word on that. And I know the country hereabouts. I can help you find ways that won't be seen."

The dwarf swore under his breath.

"I'll not leave them," I said.

"What about you?" Fabulo growled. "You want to come too?"

The young guardsman shook his head. He held his wrists together behind his back and turned so that they could be tied, though he seemed very afraid.

CHAPTER 12
September 26th

If a cabinet has only six sides, then the trick will be found on its seventh.

THE BULLET-CATCHER'S HANDBOOK

We made our way as swiftly as we could in the darkness, first to the place where I'd lain watching the house. I picked up my coat and haversack, then followed Fabulo to the site of his own camp, not far distant, where he had hidden his travelling pack in the branches of a holly tree.

The miles that followed became a blur to me. But at last we came to the ruins of a labourer's cottage. The rotten wood of the door gave no resistance. Inside, thin weeds grew from the earth floor towards a large hole in the roof. Here we chose to rest out the day, sheltered from the wind, though not the damp.

The duke had surely known that I lived on a boat. His first action on rescue from the horse would have been to send out riders to search the canals and rivers of the county. Thus the *Harry* remained beyond our reach.

"Leave it where you moored it," Fabulo said, when I asked. "We'll send men to fetch it once we're safe."

I did not argue.

The man-at-arms who had chosen to accompany us had said little as we walked. Waiting out that first day, I watched him go about disguising his uniform. With the point of Tinker's pocket knife, he cut the stitches that held the braids and epaulettes in place. Once they were removed he dug a handful of clay from the overgrown garden and set to rubbing it into the scarlet broadcloth, softening the colour of the jacket to russet. The cut of it might still give him away, but from a distance he would look much like a working man.

"What's your name?" I asked.

"Fitzwilliam," he said, though he would not meet my eyes.

When night came we set off once more. Our new companion said he knew a safe track through woodland that would carry us east and south. Though it went against Fabulo's nature to trust this intelligence, all other options seemed worse. But whenever Fitzwilliam started to pull ahead that night, the dwarf would be after him, hand on knife hilt.

When the second day dawned we left the path and climbed to the crest of a hill where the trees were thinner. From this vantage point we could look out over a small town set below in a wide valley. Fitzwilliam lay down on his side and was soon asleep. I expected Tinker to do the same, but the boy sniffed the air and set off back down the slope.

I sat myself next to Fabulo, who kept watch, his back resting against a tree.

"That's a smart boy you've got," he said. "You shouldn't have sent him away."

"I wanted him safe."

"A boy like that don't want to be safe. It's belonging he needs more than anything. We all do in different ways. For him it's wanting to be with you."

I didn't answer. My thoughts had begun to clear through our long walk. But, despite the distance we had travelled, I had not moved beyond the darkness. A shadow still lay within me. Though I listened to the words that Fabulo spoke, I couldn't yet feel the truth of them.

"You weren't in your right mind," he said. "The boy could see it. You mustn't blame him. Sometime soon you're going to start thinking straight again and you're going to figure that I couldn't have found you without his help. That I've been following for a long time. And then maybe you're going to think of casting blame. But don't.

"Remember that night on the Grantham Canal when I came calling and you sent me away? The next day Tinker hunted me down at my camp. He came to tell me you weren't right in your mood. He's been looking out for you, that's what I'm saying. He's been telling me your plans as much as he knew. And where he didn't know, there was enough for me to guess."

"You fed him?" I asked.

"Food's as good as love for a boy like that."

"And you gave him the silver repeater."

Fabulo nodded.

"Where did you get it?"

"Picked it up in London with a few other pieces."

He reached across to his pack, extracted a shagreen jewellery box and passed it to me.

I turned it in my hands, feeling the weight of it, then popped the catch. Nineteen pocket watches lay inside on a bed of satin, each in its own shallow depression. There would have been twenty, but one place was empty. Gold gleamed. Small gems shone from some of the dials. Two of the cases I guessed were platinum. One was incongruously made of brass.

"It's our bank account," he said.

"You bribed Tinker?"

"That one was a trinket. It took his fancy so I gave it to him. But everything he did was just as he would have done anyway."

"You rubbed dirt into the watch," I said, feeling the pieces of an unsolved puzzle fitting together. "You made it look as if he could have found it in the path."

"You see, Elizabeth Barnabus – you're smart, too. But in a different way. At least the boy knows where his heart is."

I slept fitfully, waking with a start to find the sun high and the sound of galloping horses in the distance. Fabulo and Fitzwilliam were crouched, looking out towards the valley, keeping low behind the bracken that fringed the hilltop. Crawling to join them, I saw a detachment of men-at-arms heading along the road towards the small town.

"Tinker?" I whispered, in alarm.

"Been and gone," said Fabulo. "But don't you worry. He's safe enough. He said I should give you this." So saying he reached across to where a perfect red and green apple rested on the ground.

I took it, aware of the dwarf's eyes on me.

"Feeling better?" he asked.

Instead of answering, I put the apple close to my nose and inhaled. The skin felt cold and waxy.

The men-at-arms were riding out through the other side of the town. Trees by the roadside began to hide them from our view. The sound of them was almost gone. Fitzwilliam backed away from the edge.

"They'll be chasing a rumour," he said to Fabulo. "Else they'd have stopped and talked to the folk down there. He'll have heard a whisper from one of his spies. It's all to the good. That's thirty men and thirty horses not looking in any place that's going to find us."

"What was the other guard's name?" I asked.

"Reuben," he said, still not looking at me.

"And you fear for him?"

"Too late for that, miss. We're soldiers. There's no law for us but a court martial. And that with the duke as judge. Reuben will already be food for crows. It's bad enough to sleep on duty. But the duke himself being treated so... They'll put the body in the gibbet so everyone can see."

Bitterness dripped from his words. Still he faced away from me.

"You hold me to blame?" I asked, believing it was certain.

But he shook his head. "No." The word came without hesitation, as if it was a question he'd already considered.

"But the boy's gone. Why wouldn't you blame me?"

"You had cause to do what you've done. I've been in the duke's service ten years. So I've seen the way he is."

The full meaning of what he'd told me didn't reveal itself all at once. First I thought that ten years was a long time. I would have been a child when he joined. Then I thought that he must have been a soldier when I fled to the Republic. And then I began to wonder what he might himself have seen of my history. I'd been staring at the earth as these thoughts tumbled, at the scattering of fallen leaves, at the tree roots that spread like veins across the hilltop. When I raised my head, I found him looking directly at me for the first time.

"Ten years?" I asked.

"Yes, miss."

"But that means... Were you... Did you..."

"I've seen you before, miss, if that's what you're asking. Six years ago. You weren't full grown. I was there with the duke that day."

"You saw our show?"

"It was a marvel, and that's no lie. To see that boy magicked across from one cabinet to the other. To tell the truth, you weren't much on my mind, what with all the conjuring on stage. I hope you don't mind me saying it.

"But after, when we were back at the Hall, the duke was changed – skittish, like a horse before a race. He couldn't settle. And he was asking about you. Soon enough he was back in his coach, with me riding escort. We tracked back to where the circus had been pitched. On finding it gone, we were off again, following any gossip we could find, until we caught up with the wagons. But you'll know the rest."

Thoughts were coming to me so fast that I couldn't order them. But that strange numbness of feeling was still on me. "I want to hear you tell it," I said.

"Well, the duke spoke with your father. Asked to see the cast of the show again, every one of them. He'd give a purse of silver if all could be lined up and brought before his coach. So it was done just like that. That's when I mostly remember you from. I was standing next to the coach when you came up. Everyone else, he'd seen and sent away. But you, he kept standing there. Even when you started to cry. I thought it a shame that he should treat a child so.

"After all that was done, he went to see your father again. Said what a bright girl you were. Asked how much he'd need to compensate to have the pleasure of you living in his household, a companion for the other children, he said. You'd be well fed and clothed.

"But your father wouldn't have it. Said he needed you for his conjuring show. To which the duke countered that he'd pay a thousand guineas. But your father must have seen his real intent, because he said he wouldn't be parted with you for any price. At which the duke said there was a price for everything, though it might not be to your father's liking."

A strange thing was happening to Fitzwilliam as he told my story. The soldier's composure, which he'd worn so naturally through our journey, was crumbling. Or perhaps it had gone already and I hadn't noticed because of the way he'd avoided my gaze. There was a hollowness about his cheeks and the skin sagged below his eyes.

"You know these things already," he said. "Why must I say them? Isn't it enough that there's no blame on you? The duke's a man of evil passions, and that's all there is to it."

"I could have left you there," I said. "Tied and gagged with Reuben. You owe me this."

I glanced over to where Fabulo sat, looking out at the valley. He was listening to every word.

"Did your master do such things before?" I asked.

Fitzwilliam rubbed his hands over his face, as if trying to wake himself up after a bad dream. "The duke is a man who gets what he wants. He was always that way. Whether it's a painting or a horse, he puts down the money and that's it. Or a girl. But you were different, miss, begging your pardon."

"Different how?"

"Just different. He liked pretty girls before."

"I wasn't pretty?"

"I'm not saying that, though you weren't dressed up in frills and satin. The thing was, you had a way about you different from his usual girls. When the men came up on stage to see the cabinets, you looked them straight in the eye. You acted so sure of yourself. It got him all fired up somehow. Then your father denied him. That was different too.

"No one's ever made him angry like you did. Three times he's thought he had you. But you got away. And each time it's made him worse. He's been mad with anger. I mean mad like he's fit for the asylum. It's not your fault. You did nothing to make him what he is. Except you got away. None of the others ever did.

"After you, there were girls he set out to get in the exact same way. Buying debts. Bribing judges. But each time it was like he was trying to stage a show. He was going through the self-same act. Like each girl was a stand-in. But none of them was you.

"That's how I know Reuben's dead. That's why I couldn't stay. It's not just that the duke was brought low. But it was you that did it. You got past all of us. You put a knife to his throat. You, of all the people in the world. Every guard from that night will be flogged till there's no skin on their backs.

"I'm sorry, miss, for my part in it. Sorry to you. Sorry to them. And to Reuben."

I lay down again to rest, now knowing why he had been avoiding my gaze. It had been shame, not malice. For when he looked at me, it was his own sins that he saw.

The tiredness just came up and took me after that. I slept with no sense that time was passing. When I woke, the trees above me were lit up in the last sun of the day and the sky between the branches was pale.

The wind blew, causing a few leaves to fall. I fixed on one and watched it drifting down to the forest floor. All those years I had lived in exile, dwelling on the way one aristocrat had ruined my life and destroyed my family. Now it seemed that the disruption had worked both ways. It would never have occurred to me that the duke's obsession could be corrosive to his life as well as mine.

Fitzwilliam was up and seemed to be readying himself to leave.

"What will you do?" I asked.

"I'll need to steal clothes first. Then I'll keep on east. I've family in Norfolk. Farmers. Good people. They can hide me till it all dies down. After that… soldiering is all I know. I might try my hand in the navy. Or on a whaling boat. They don't ask where you've come from."

I believe Fabulo would not have trusted him to go, but that had changed with the recounting of his tale. Before he slipped away, the two men shook hands. No words were said between them.

Having crossed the county boundary, we stopped in a copse near a river. There we found charred logs and ashes from a recent camp. Fabulo, who didn't get on well with a diet of fruit and raw vegetables, said he was willing to take the risk if the result was a proper meal. So he sent Tinker out to buy food, whilst I gathered the driest sticks I could find and lit a fire.

Later, when I bedded down, it was with the smell of wood smoke in my hair and an unaccustomed sense of fullness in my stomach. My body relaxed into the soft moss. The side of my face nearest the fire felt warm. Tinker had curled up near me and was fast asleep. Fabulo sat, gnawing the last of the meat from a rib bone.

"Did you have a plan?" he asked. "For after you killed the duke? And what happened about that, by the way? You had him under your knife."

Fabulo hadn't spoken of anything but practicalities since Fitzwilliam left us, but the food had animated him and he seemed more himself. I considered the question before answering.

"I couldn't do it," I said.

"By all that's sacred, girl, you should have thought of that before you set out!"

"I did. In my imagination it seemed a natural thing. Someone told me once that I wasn't a killer. But that man I watched die, doing nothing to save him. So I thought... you know."

"Not saving someone isn't the same as killing them," said Fabulo. "Least of all with a knife. You might get a philosopher to say it is, or a lawyer. But only if he'd never had to stick someone himself."

"Have you ever killed?" I asked.

He gave me a sideways glance. "Well, isn't this cosy? We're like two old lovers and this is our pillow talk, eh? Well, forgive me, Elizabeth Barnabus, but I don't feel like sharing that kind of story."

"I didn't mean to put you in danger," I said. "I wasn't looking for rescue."

"You're crazy – you know that? The duke's got a private army and you've got... what? A knife and that antique pistol. He ruined your family, that I know. But he's an aristocrat. His kind have been doing the same for a thousand years. You're not the only one to suffer it. What makes you so special that you need to have your own private revolution?"

"I wasn't going to come back," I said.

He was quiet after that.

I had been looking up at the tree branches but now turned so that my back was to the fire and to Fabulo. Cloud shadows moved over the fields beyond the copse. The afternoon slipped away. The sun grew low enough for its rays to reach under the trees and touch us.

I had remained silent for so long that, when I spoke again, it was with no confidence that my voice would sound. "Why did you come to rescue me?"

"The boy asked it."

"Before that. You were trailing me for weeks."

"You've got something I need," he said. "If you go to the gallows, I lose my only chance to get it."

"What something?"

"That's a thing I don't feel like talking about right now. I'm not sure I trust you enough."

This was a puzzle I should have been able to solve. I had few enough possessions, and only three of them unique – my father's pistol, my boat the *Harry* and *The Bullet-Catcher's Handbook*. But the pistol he'd spoken of disparagingly and the boat he could have taken by force if he'd a mind to. He'd pressed his gun to my head that night. It would have been easy.

As for the book – he could know nothing of the dangerous power it contained. Professor Ferdinand had believed it a poison that might eat into the vitals of the Gas-Lit Empire. Fabulo had his own reasons for hating the Patent Office. I wondered if he'd use that power if it came into his hands. I still hadn't decided what I would do with it.

I turned over to look at him. The firelight reflected in his dark eyes.

"Can you at least tell me your goal?" I asked.

"Now you're asking the right kind of question," he said. "When I came to you before and asked if you'd help me steal from the Patent Office, you said no. Well, I'm going to ask you again."

"What makes you think I'll change my mind?"

"We've travelled a fair few miles since then, don't you think? And had a cosy pillow chat today. Seems like we understand each other better now. I thought you were mad to try to kill the duke. But then I heard Fitzwilliam's story. And today I heard more of yours.

"I still think you're mad. But it's the kind of mad that I can't argue with. You were going to your death. That's an honour thing. I'm not one to stand in the way of a man who's got a debt to pay."

"I'm not a man," I said.

He laughed then. It started as a chuckle and built until he was rolling on his back with his knees pulled to his chest.

"You'll bring the constables on us with that noise!" I said, when he'd calmed enough to hear me.

He sat up and wiped his eyes with a handkerchief. "Not a man! You've got bigger balls than most every man I ever met."

"Is that supposed to make me feel good?"

"Yes, girl! Now will you listen to me? I asked before if you'd help. You said no because you were scared. And there's no shame in that. You'd have to be mad to steal from them, right? But now you are mad. And you know it. You're as mad as me. What have you got to lose that they haven't already taken?"

"What do you want me to do?"

"Like I said, help me steal something."

"Steal what?"

"That's a secret."

"Then tell me how you'll do it."

"I'll do it with your help. But you're asking the wrong questions again. What you should be asking is this – what will *you* get out of it if we win?"

"There's nothing I want," I said. "Nothing that can be stolen, anyway."

"Then how about this? You can have all the secrets of the International Patent Office. All the devices they've hidden away in a hundred and ninety years. Enough power to bring down your duke and a hundred like him."

"Enough power to bring down the Patent Office?" I asked.

He laughed again. "You couldn't stick a knife into a man who deserved it, Elizabeth. You're not going to pull down the pillars of the Gas-Lit Empire."

While I was still thinking, he said, "Stand up."

I did as he instructed.

"Elizabeth Barnabus, will you join company with me and put that madness of yours to good use?"

"Yes," I said.

He spat on his palm and held it out to me. I did the same and our handshake sealed it.

Sleeping in ditches and under hedgerows, I'd thought my clothes couldn't become more soiled. But rolling into London on the back of a wagon, I found a different kind of dirt. Oily, metallic and sulphurous, it insinuated itself through the air, coating every surface. And, by stages, it worked its way into the very pores of my skin.

Our conversation had been sporadic on the journey,

but passing through the suburbs of the great metropolis it dropped away to almost nothing. After the carter dropped us off, I found Tinker staying close by my side. Fabulo adjusted the canvas bag he carried over his back, retying the straps so they could not be slyly undone.

I didn't recognise any of the streets through which we passed, though once, between houses and through smog, I saw the dome of St Paul's Cathedral, pale as the moon in the daytime. It was enough for me that Fabulo knew where we were going. It suited my mood to let him lead.

He kept us to the smaller streets and the poorer parts of town. Gradually the houses became more tightly packed and the stink of the river filled the air. At first people had stared at us because of our filthy clothes. Then we began to blend in. But, as we progressed along what a signpost proclaimed to be Commercial Road East, I noticed that we were being stared at once more. We were no more or less dirty than the population, but our clothes didn't hang from us in rags.

"Listen," Fabulo said, beckoning us closer. "We'll soon be into the rookery of St John's. Constables don't much go there, so we're safe from that. But that don't mean they don't have a law. It's just a different kind. So don't go looking them in the face. Just walk. And if they stop you, it's me that does the talking."

He looked to each of us, as if searching for assurance that we understood. Then he set off again and at the next junction turned right onto a road far narrower than the thoroughfare. The name Grove Street had been stencilled high on the wall of the first house in the row. There was no traffic. Indeed, none could have passed, such was the number of people milling about. Some sat on doorsteps, others huddled in groups in the roadway, their backs turned outwards like a wall. I kept my eyes downcast as Fabulo had instructed. Conversations dropped away as we approached and started again in our wake. I could feel their eyes on me.

There were more women than men. And too many children to count – most running barefoot with the dogs. A man turned to gob on the ground in front of me. To my right, a woman shouted something about dwarfs, at which others laughed. We carried on walking. A little girl burst from a doorway and pinched Tinker on the arm before running away again. He flinched, but didn't break stride.

Then we turned left onto a yet narrower alleyway. This one sloped inwards from the close-packed houses on either side to an open drain running along the very centre. There were fewer people here, and they had no time to form an opinion of us before we were turning off again. The words Samuel Street had been daubed on a wall. The way was so narrow it seemed strange it had been named at all.

A dead dog lay on the ground, blocking the drain. A pool of black water had formed behind it. Fabulo stopped in his tracks and I thought he was recoiling from the putrefying animal. Then I looked and saw that he was gesturing for us to follow him into the open doorway of a tenement.

We stepped after him into a dark corridor then up a narrow flight of steps to a landing where he unlocked a door. We shuffled through into a bare room in which no angle was square. The entire contents were two beds, a limp curtain hanging half over a skewed window and a chamber pot lying next to the wall.

"Well done," whispered Fabulo.

"What is this place?" I asked. "And why have you brought us here?"

He spread his arms in a flourish as if revealing some marvellous trick. "This is your new home. The duke'll never find you here. Safest place in London. And as to why we're in the great city – that I'll show you tomorrow."

I woke with a jolt, not knowing where I was. Then I saw the dwarf, pacing wall to wall in the small room. The whites of his eyes seemed unnaturally bright in the darkened room. With each pass, the floorboard near the door creaked under his weight. Tinker lay snoring in the other bed.

"This is London," I said, as the memory came to me.

He didn't answer. Then I must have been asleep again because when I next opened my eyes he had gone. So had the boy.

CHAPTER 13
September 30th

Cut a second into a hundred pieces and put your bullet inside one. Though it is in full view of the audience, it will never be seen.

THE BULLET-CATCHER'S HANDBOOK

London. A crawling mass of humanity. A paradise for gamblers, lawyers, beggars, bankers and royals. For every church it was said you could find a pub. And for every gin house, a museum or university. It was, in short, the fairest, foulest, safest and most dangerous metropolis in the entire span of the Gas-Lit Empire – depending on who you were talking to.

With so much chaos and lawlessness it might have seemed an unlikely place to find evidence of the Patent Office. But in a twist of perversity, or perhaps genius, it was here that the architects of that all-powerful institution had chosen to place their most conspicuous structure. Even from a distance, it dominated the skyline.

"You're not taking us there!" I said.

"Keep walking," said Fabulo.

I drew closer to him and whispered, "When you said

you were going for *them*, I didn't think… That is, I didn't imagine…"

My words dried up.

He winked at me.

I'd yet to ask him about his midnight wanderings. When I'd woken in the hour before dawn, he and Tinker had both been sitting on the other bed, eating bread and taking turns to drink water from a wine bottle.

"Rise and shine," he'd said. "The sun waits for no man."

Later, when the memory of the empty room came back to me, it became just one more in a list of questions that the dwarf seemed in no hurry to provide answers for.

He pressed on along Fleet Street, leading us past the doors of the Royal Courts of Justice, whose curved towers and turrets lay under the shadow of the great monolith that was the International Patent Court.

The sacrilegious thought of stealing from the Patent Office had been enough for me. I hadn't worried about practical concerns. When Fabulo had spoken of the theft, I'd imagined him breaking into a discreet building tucked away in a side street. I had been picturing the office on High Pavement, not the tallest building on the continent of Europe.

Tinker, walking beside me, had never before been to the great city. He slowed as we approached the wide plaza before the court, his head tilting back to take in the columns, the high portico, the cliff face of grey granite behind it, the rows of identical windows, fading into the smoggy air.

I caught his elbow and pulled him along.

"Those soldiers," he said, meaning the swordsmen in yellow silk standing to each side of the great entrance.

"Don't stare," I whispered.

"Stare all you like," said Fabulo. "Everyone else is."

"Where're they from?" the boy asked.

"These ones are Chinese," said Fabulo. "Tomorrow it might be Prussian or Crow or Nigerian. It's an honour thing. Only the best soldiers get to guard it."

"But if they're the best…"

I squeezed Tinker's arm. "Hush! We'll talk later." Though I'd been thinking the same thing. The greatest bastion of the Patent Office, guarded by elite fighters from around the world – it seemed impossible that anyone could break in and get away with their lives.

"Men-at-arms," Fabulo said, pointing to a kiosk between us and the court. It was a structure of glass and wood, bigger than the ones next to the border crossing in Leicester. Through its windows, I could make out eight guards, all wearing the scarlet uniforms of the Kingdom.

They had not looked in our direction. I was about to hurry away before they could see us, but Fabulo had set off towards them with Tinker by his side. He strode out with such brash confidence that I found myself following.

In this grand setting, I felt conspicuous, though no one seemed to be looking. Alarmingly, Fabulo had stopped right next to the guard kiosk. He looked back and gestured for me to hurry up.

"Are you mad?" I hissed, when I was close enough.

"Look at the grand building," he said out loud, playing the tourist.

I forced my tight muscles into a smile. Fabulo's eyes flicked down to the paving slabs below our feet. I followed his gaze and saw the regular pattern of flagstones was cut by a line of yellow bricks immediately in front of us. It ran parallel to the road as far as I could see in either direction.

The guard kiosk was just on the road side of the line, as were we. On the far side was another stretch of plaza, then a flight of low stairs rising towards the doors of the Patent Court.

A few paces further down the line, a young man hovered, trying to catch our attention. A vending tray hung from a strap around his shoulders. When Fabulo beckoned, he hurried over.

"Maps, guides, histories, court proceedings." His accent sounded Eastern European.

Fabulo dropped some coins on the tray and gathered up one pamphlet from each of four piles. The man grinned, then hurried off towards a party of scholars in uniform, who were standing further down the brick line. "Maps, guides, histories, court proceedings," he called.

"He has to stay this side of the line," said Fabulo. "So do the red coats."

"Why?" asked Tinker, for whom any strangeness could become homely if the ones he trusted were relaxed.

"This side, we're in the Kingdom of England and Southern Wales. That side you're in no country. Kingdom soldiers can't go there. Nor can anything be sold or bought."

Then he stepped across the yellow bricks and turned to look back at us. Holding out the pamphlets to me, he said, "You should read this stuff. You'd be amazed."

I hesitated.

"Come on," he said. "We've travelled a long way to be here."

"A long way," I said, stepping after him, pulling Tinker with me.

"We're tourists," Fabulo said.

I took the pamphlets. One was a map, which I handed to

Tinker. "Open it up," I whispered. "Pretend you can read."

For myself I leafed through *The International Patent Court: A Visitor's Guide*. It was a flimsy object – six sheets of poor quality paper, folded down the middle and held together with stitching. The print was smudged and uneven. Illustrations of the building were printed in ink of a different shade.

"What are we doing here?" I asked.

"Casing the joint," said Fabulo.

"Why not speak louder?" I said. "I don't think everybody heard."

He laughed at that. "No one cares. You've been too long in the Republic, girl. This is London. Full of strange people. The louder you speak, the less they listen. If you really want to be ignored, wear a bright red jacket and juggle pineapples."

"But if you want to get someone's attention, you say you're going to steal from them."

"Perhaps," he conceded. "If they're a fruit seller. Or a jeweller. Or a bank, maybe. But this..." He spread his hands, palms raised, and craned his neck. "This is beyond theft. Beyond any dream of it. You've been saying as much yourself. You could walk up to one of those guards and tell them you're going to break in next Thursday and they wouldn't even twitch."

Noticing that Tinker had the map opened upside down, I turned it and gave it back to him.

"Is it a picture?" he asked.

"It's like a picture," I said. "It shows where things are. Like the road and the buildings."

He shot me a disbelieving glance. I'd seen him use the same betrayed expression on those occasions when I'd forced him to have a bath.

"What time is it?" Fabulo asked.

I looked up at the clock mounted at the centre of the portico. "Half past eight," I said.

Sure enough, the half hour began to chime. Perfectly on cue, four new guards in yellow silk came marching up the steps, swinging their arms in synchrony, an exaggerated but precise movement from hip to chest and back. We were not the only onlookers. Other tourists stood watching the ceremony. The party of scholars stood nearby, gawping. And there were other people watching, from all over the plaza, Londoners and visitors from all over the Gas-Lit Empire. The chimes had not finished when the changing of the guard commenced. Once the new soldiers were in place, the relieved guards marched away, their movements just as crisp, though they must have spent hours standing frozen. I'd seen the ceremony once before. That time the soldiers had been German, wearing blue uniforms and helmets capped with a spike.

With a creak and an echoing boom, the great doors of the Patent Court swung inwards. A queue of civilians had been waiting under the portico. They now began to shuffle forwards into the building. Among them would be claimants, plaintiffs and lawyers – all cast of the morning's court cases. I thought for a moment about Julia. In her letter she had said she came to the courts hereabouts on Tuesday and Friday afternoons. I had assumed she meant the Royal Courts, but now realised that she could equally have meant the International Patent Court. So confusing had been recent events that I didn't even know the day of the week.

"You notice anything strange?" asked Fabulo.

"Give me a clue," I said.

"The time."

"Half past eight," I said. "Always prompt and punctual."

"You think so?"

Tinker knelt down on the lowest step and unfolded the map. Once again, he was looking at it askew. I tried to shift it around but he resisted, putting it back to the odd angle he had chosen before.

"That's the Patent Court," I said, tapping the blocked out region of the map. "And that's the road."

He tilted his head first one way and then the other. A look of fierce concentration had taken up residence on his brow.

"It's not really quite a picture," I said, trying to think of a way to explain cartography to an illiterate boy.

"It is," he said. Then he pointed into the sky where, high above the rooftops, three red kites were circling, their wing feathers spread like fingers.

"The birds?" I asked.

He nodded.

"What of them?"

"It's a picture like they drew it."

My first thought was to correct him. But then I realised that, in a manner of speaking, he had it exactly right. I was about to ask him about the angle he had chosen to position the map on the ground when the clocks around the city began to chime the half hour. I listened, puzzled. The clock on the wall of the Patent Court put the time at nine minutes past the half hour.

"How about that?" said Fabulo, triumphant.

"Then it's nine minutes fast?"

"Nine minutes and twenty-one seconds, to be precise.

Though more rightly speaking it's the other clocks that are late."

"I don't understand," I said.

"Then you should read the pamphlet."

So I did, scanning the pages until I came to the heading *Timekeeping and the International Patent Court*:

Londoners know it as the Patent Court Clock. But the timepiece with its display on the high portico is more properly designated ICN2, so named because of its place within the International Chronological Network.

Another name for it that you may hear mentioned on your visit is the Fast Clock. The reason will become obvious when you compare it to other public clocks in the city which, if they are keeping good time, trail behind ICN2 by exactly nine minutes and twenty-one seconds.

Please be aware: These differences are not a subject to be joked about when in the Kingdom. For many Royalists it is a touchstone that reminds them of grievances remaining from their accession to the Great Accord. With the signing of the Twelfth Amendment, all other nations adopted the metric system and the Paris Meridian for the fixing of longitude and the setting of clocks. Alone in the Gas-Lit Empire, the Kingdom secured an exemption to this standardisation. Thus, it still uses the Greenwich Meridian and Greenwich Mean Time. But, because the International Patent Court exists within its own jurisdiction, its clock is set according to the international standard.

Geography may have forced London's clocks to trail behind ICN2. But in the shift to and from Daylight Saving Time, the Kingdom chose to be twenty-four hours ahead (4am on the second Saturday in March and October respectively.)

In securing its exemption, the Kingdom burdened itself with perpetual confusion in international dealings. Visitors, not knowing the history, may find these irregularities perverse. But the Kingdom's stance is a matter of considerable local pride.

It would be a serious faux pas to ask why the clocks in the Kingdom are running slow. For Londoners it is quite the other way about.

Reaching the end of the section, I closed the pamphlet. The grievance it mentioned was a powerful force in the politics of the Kingdom. I thought again about what Professor Ferdinand had told me, wondering what Fabulo would do with that knowledge. I looked down and saw that he'd been staring at me.

"Well?" he asked.

"It's curious."

"Curious indeed."

"But I thought you were bringing us here to show how we could... you know."

"Break in," he said, voicing the words I still felt too afraid to say. His voice had grown more serious now, and mercifully quieter.

"Are you saying the clock running fast is important?"

"It's more than important," he said. "That nine minutes and twenty-one seconds is a crack that we're going to climb through. Right into the heart of that mighty fortress. And then we're going to help ourselves from the treasure house."

CHAPTER 14
October 1st

To hide an elephant is easy. Simply put it where they are not looking.

THE BULLET-CATCHER'S HANDBOOK

I woke to the sense of shaking and opened my eyes to see Tinker leaning over me. He was gripping my shoulders. A lantern rested on the floor. It hadn't been there when I went to sleep. I was about to say something, but he put his fingers over my mouth. Then I heard shouting in the street outside.

I was out of bed in one movement. The boy turned the other way as I pulled on clothes over the chemise in which I'd been sleeping. Fabulo was nowhere to be seen. I could hear fists pounding on a door in the street below. Heavy footsteps.

"Open it or I break it down!"

I grabbed stockings, shoes and shawl. Tinker turned the wick down and the lantern went out. I stepped to the side of the window, pulled the thin curtain an inch and looked down to the street.

A troop of red coats were moving house to house. A man in a nightshirt was rolling on the ground, legs in the open drain, hands holding his face. A woman knelt next to him, wailing. Further down, I could see a carriage standing waiting, its horses pawing the ground where they stood.

I felt a tug on my sleeve. Tinker was pulling me in the direction of the door. He jabbed a finger towards the ceiling. I thought of the skylight on the landing above. I was about to follow him there when an even louder banging made me freeze. Footsteps sounded in the hall below. Soldiers were in the building, trying to get into one of the ground floor rooms. Wherever Fabulo had gone, he had left his travelling pack on the other bed. My haversack lay open on the floor.

Breaking free from Tinker's grip, I heaped my loose clothes into it. Tinker saw what I was doing and went to grab his own meagre possessions. I shook my head and pointed to Fabulo's bag. If we were the object of the search, we couldn't leave the clothes of a young woman and dwarf for them to find.

Bolts were being snapped back below. Booted feet crashed. I ran up the stairs towards the top landing, hoping the noise of our escape would be swallowed by the violence of their entry.

The roof angled low across the top landing. Low enough for me to push at the skylight. I had escaped across rooftops before. This time all we needed was to get out quietly and hide on the slates. But the skylight would not lift. I tried again, pressing harder. The frame bent and creaked, but the wood seemed to have swollen, anchoring it closed.

Doors slammed. I could feel the vibration of each act of violence through the rickety banister rail.

"Let us in or we force it!"

A door opened below. There was a scuffle. A man cried out in pain. There were but two rooms on the ground floor.

In seconds the soldiers would be climbing the stairs where they'd find our room empty. But the lamp would still be hot if they thought to feel it. And the beds.

Tinker grabbed my wrist and pulled, as if trying to get me away from the top of the stairs.

Booted feet were climbing the stairs. I heaved at the skylight again, increasing the upward force. The frame shifted suddenly with an ear splitting shriek. A crack arced across the pane of glass above my head.

I froze. The footsteps had stopped. In the sudden silence I could hear the beating of my own heart. Tinker heaved on my arm again. This time I stepped after him along the small landing towards a single door at the end.

Everything in the building seemed to be holding its breath, but I could hear the raid continuing outside. There were shouts of impotent rage from the denizens of St John's. A door was kicked in further down the street. Dogs barked. Quieter but much closer a step creaked on the flight immediately below us. We were backed up against a door and they were coming.

Then, all in the same moment, two things happened. I felt the movement of the air on the back of my neck as if something had shifted behind me. And the cracked glass detached itself from the skylight and fell. Half of it shattered on the landing. The other half crashed on the stairs. Out of instinct, I pressed back away from the destruction, expecting a door behind me, finding only air. I started to fall into the darkness, but was caught by unseen hands. Then the door was closing after me. I could hear the soldiers hammering up the stairs.

"After them!"

Glass crunched under their boots on the landing. There

were two men, I judged. They swore as they clambered up through the empty skylight. Whatever they said after that was in whispers. But I could hear their feet on the slates of the roof above my head as they made their way up the slope. Only when I was sure they had set out along the apex of the roof did I turn to look at my rescuers.

But the room in which I found myself was without windows. The darkness was complete.

"Thank you," I whispered.

A match flared in the air in front of me, and then a candle was lit, illuminating Fabulo's face. There were others behind him, but the light wasn't enough for me to see them clearly. I was about to ask for an explanation, but the dwarf shook his head, putting a finger to his mouth. Then, gesturing for me to follow, he began to pick his way across the attic room, which I now realised was only partially boarded.

Ducking under a roof beam, I followed him along a narrow path of floorboards, themselves resting on joists that looked too thin to take our weight. I was aware of Tinker just behind me. And behind him followed the others, whoever they were.

Questions tumbled in my mind. But, before any of them could take form, I found myself facing the end wall of the attic, at the bottom of which a small hole had been knocked through. It was only three bricks across and low enough that even Fabulo had to get down on hands and knees to pass.

I hesitated and Tinker slipped through ahead of me, negotiating the hole with the confidence of one who had made the same journey many times before. I followed, clambering through to what must have been the attic of the next house in the row. As I got to my feet, the others were crawling through after me. The last one pulled the floorboards we'd crawled over through after him, as if it was a drawbridge being raised. Then they were filling the hole with bricks. It was all done with a quiet efficiency that spoke of practice. Finally a sheet of wood was placed over the remade wall, to stop light escaping through the cracks, I guessed.

Tinker took my hand and led me to where Fabulo was lighting lanterns from the candle.

"What is happening?" I hissed.

"Men-at-arms," he said. "Searching the rookery for something."

"For what?"

"No way to tell."

"You said we were safe here!"

"And so we are."

"But… what is this place? And…"

"It's a refuge."

"And who are these people?"

Instead of answering he gestured for me to turn around. I did so, seeing their faces in the light for the first time. There were three of them – two young women and a giant of a man with a forked beard. I blinked as recognition hit me.

"You might remember them," said Fabulo. "They were your comrades in the travelling show."

"Ellie, Lara and Yan," I said, reciting their names.

"Good," said the dwarf. "No need for introductions."

"What – are – they – doing – here?"

"The same as you."

All three of them looked at their feet, shamefaced, as well they might be. The last time we were together they'd been storming my boat, hellbent on burning me from my home.

"I would have told you sooner," said Fabulo. "But..." He shrugged.

"But we needed to make sure which side you were on!" growled Yan, his long beard quivering as he spoke.

He stepped towards me and I saw the unevenness of his stride, a slight drag of his left foot along the floorboards.

"We've been through this already," said Fabulo. "What went before is over."

"Might be over for you, little man. But it wasn't you got shot."

"You were attacking her boat, Yan. Remember that. She had a right to defend herself."

"No warning shot," he grumbled.

"It was night time," I said. "No light to see you by. I didn't know who was coming for me. I didn't know how many."

"What if you *had* known?"

"Does it hurt?" I asked.

"Yes."

Fabulo was trying to catch my eye. He shook his head as if to warn me off the subject. Since the giant and I seemed to both be part of his plan, I could understand his desire to soothe our meeting.

"I knew a trick rider once," I said. "She was part of the circus where I grew up. One day she fell off her horse and broke her collarbone. It healed in a month. But she said it still hurt at night. Then one day – it was two years later – she was washing and found the lump in her shoulder where the bone had healed. And that was when she realised she'd forgotten all about it. The pain had stopped. That's what she said."

Yan nodded. "Night time it does hurt worse."

"What's it been?" I asked. "Not yet a year?"

"Then do you think it will stop?" he asked.

"I hope so. I think so. But even if I knew it'd hurt you for the rest of your life, I'd still have shot you."

He flinched as if I'd slapped him. "You would?"

"What choice did you give me? I'm sorry. But people who break into the homes of others in the middle of the night – they do tend to get shot at."

I waited for his reaction, knowing it could go either way. If good, there'd be one problem less to think about. If bad, it'd be better to see things for what they were than to let the wound be hidden.

Fabulo stood next to me, tensed as if ready to leap forwards and get between us, though nothing could have stopped the big man if he charged.

Everyone seemed frozen. Then Yan's shoulders dropped. I allowed myself to breathe again. Lara stepped up and took his arm. Then Ellie was at his other side. Together they guided him to an upturned tea chest on which he sat.

"She's right," said Lara. "I'd have done the same."

"You would?"

"We all would," said Ellie.

"I know that," he said, after a pause. "Thing is, I could blame her before. But now she's here, I can only blame myself. Truth is, I liked it better the other way."

Fabulo puffed out his cheeks, firing me a glance that suggested the stress of our meeting was costing him. "Glad we've got that out of the way," he said.

"So this is it?" I asked. "Or do you have more surprises hidden away in a cupboard somewhere?"

"This is it."

"In which case, please tell me how you plan to do it. If the International Patent Court has a treasure house, it must be the best protected in the world. You must have found a weakness – something no one else has seen. Otherwise you wouldn't be thinking of it. But if there is a weakness, you would have broken in already. So you must still be missing something or someone. I want to know what or who that is!"

Everyone was looking at me. I had the sudden feeling that I'd missed something obvious.

"That's too many questions all at once," said Fabulo. "And definitely too many for this time of night. But I'll give you one answer now. You're right – I didn't do it before, 'coz I was missing someone."

"Who?"

"You," he said. "I was waiting for you. You've been gone somewhere I couldn't reach. But to judge by what I've just seen, I think you're really back."

CHAPTER 15
October 1st

All luck is illusion. Few illusions are luck.

THE BULLET-CATCHER'S HANDBOOK

On the morning after the raid, I woke gently to find my senses alive in a way they hadn't been since before I set out to kill the duke. It wasn't that I'd been unaware of my surroundings. Every detail of the journey was clear in my memory. But my feelings had been in some other place and without them all sensation seemed dull.

I opened my eyes and saw a thread of cochineal silk snagged by a splinter in the rough bed frame. I'd noted it on the previous day, though with little interest. Now I marvelled at the intensity of its colour.

I sat up and looked at the room afresh. Motes of dust drifted in bars of light that entered around the edges of the ill-fitting curtain. Lara and Ellie were still sleeping, lying top to toe in the other bed. After the soldiers had left, Fabulo sent us downstairs together. He and Yan were sharing the hidden attic.

I swung my feet to the floor. The bed frame creaked, a single low note that seemed almost musical.

Lara stretched out an arm and yawned.

"What time it is?" she whispered.

"The clocks have chimed for half past six," I said.

She smiled sleepily, making a dimple in her cheek. "It's good to have you back, Lizzy. As one of us, I mean. Didn't sit right having you on the outside."

"What do you know of Fabulo's plan?" I asked.

She closed her eyes again and sighed. "Near as much nothing. You know what dwarfs are like. But whatever he's got up his sleeve, I'll bet it's you who'll know before the rest of us."

The rookery of St John's once provided manpower for the rope makers of Cable Street. But, with the coming of flight, this industry gave way to the fabrication of the skins of airships. On streets where hemp had once been twisted, animal guts were now cleaned and stretched – they being the only material to hold in the gases that kept the leviathans airborne.

Perhaps the wind had changed, but the stench of the slaughterhouses and tanneries seemed stronger that morning than before. I felt my eyes stinging as I followed Fabulo through the rookery. Here and there were wrecked doors, remnants of the night's excitement. I could make out no pattern to the destruction. It was as if the soldiers had chosen their targets without thought or plan.

The people milling in the roadway were less hostile than on the previous day.

"I've spoken to someone," explained Fabulo, running his thumb over the fingers of his upturned hand, suggesting that money had been involved. "We'll have no more trouble from these folk."

"And the men-at-arms?"

"It was just a raid. It happens. A toff gets his purse lifted. The papers make a big story of it. Doors are going to get kicked in. Then there'll be nothing for half a year. We were unlucky. That's all."

As we turned onto the main thoroughfare, I said, "My father used to tell me there's no such thing as bad luck, only bad skill."

"In cards, maybe," said Fabulo. "But this was just one of them things that happen. Don't worry about what you can't control."

"Then what do you worry about?"

"Everything else," he said. "We're going to do this thing. But that don't make it easy. You just have to pick at it one worry at a time."

"I could help if only you'd tell me the details of the plan."

"I will do," he said.

"Then why not now?"

Instead of answering, he pointed to a crossroads ahead. There stood a pub with a hanging signboard showing a crown and a dolphin. "There's one more of our crew you've yet to meet. He's a stranger, so there'll be no surprises for you."

"He can be trusted?"

"More or less. He's our locksmith."

"More or less?" I said, somewhat alarmed.

"More," said Fabulo.

"Well, there are other locksmiths if you're not sure."

"He's one of a kind. It was Harry who found him. Or one of Harry's spies. That was the very beginning of the plan. He can't be replaced any more than you can."

I stopped dead. Fabulo carried on a couple of paces before

turning to face me.

"Harry Timpson made this plan?"

"You see?" he said. "You always want to know more. Whatever I tell you, it's never enough. Yes, Harry Timpson made the plan. And that's why it's going to work."

"And Harry wanted me to be part of it?"

"If I answer that, will you promise to ask no more?"

"No!"

"Then you may as well go back and wait with the others. I'm not having it."

He turned on his heel and marched off. When he was halfway to the pub, curiosity got the better of my pride and I set off after him, catching up just in time to hold the door open. The familiar pub smells of beer, tobacco and hashish wafted out at us.

The dwarf glared up at me. "Yes, you were part of Harry's plan," he said. "And that's why you're here!" Then he stomped through and I followed him inside, where I found myself walking on a layer of freshly strewn sawdust.

There were few patrons at that time in the morning, but I saw no glances of particular interest. The barman was busy polishing a glass case on the rear wall. As we stepped closer, I saw that it contained what appeared to be a human skull. I was trying to read the inscription, but the barman had nodded Fabulo through to the back and I had to hurry to keep up. After a short corridor and a flight of creaky stairs we came to a dim landing.

"The locksmith is going to be viewing you," Fabulo whispered. "That's the way it's got to seem. Not the other way around. So play it sweet. If we get to the end of this and he's happy, it'll have been a good day's work. One more worry scratched off the list."

"What do you mean, *play it sweet*?"

"I guess there're people might say you're pretty. So flutter your eyes at him. And no mention of last night's fun and games. He's a jumpy one."

The dwarf was off again before I could protest. He opened the third door along.

"Jeremiah," he said, smiling. "My good friend! Have we kept you waiting? Wine – I should call for more wine."

"No more wine," came a voice from within. "Are you alone?"

"No indeed," said Fabulo, beckoning me through.

I stepped into what appeared to be a private dining room.

"Jeremiah, this is Elizabeth. Elizabeth, Jeremiah – the finest locksmith you'll ever meet."

He was a large man, his features flattened and indistinct. He frowned on seeing me, but extended a hand, which I took. My own was engulfed, feeling as if it had been plunged into a bowl of warm dough.

His cufflinks and cravat were pale blue to match his eyes – which were the only clearly defined feature in his clean shaven face. His shirt had oil stains on one cuff and had not recently been near an iron, though I judged it must have once been an expensive garment.

"Elizabeth is one of us," said Fabulo.

Jeremiah released my hand and turned to the dwarf. "You said we'd be a small crew."

"And so we are."

"Yet here's one more."

"She'll be the last."

"But why have her?"

"Elizabeth has special skills."

Jeremiah made a *harrumph* sound, as if to say that the

special skills of young women could only be worthy of reproach. "What've you told her about me?" he asked.

"I've been told little enough!" I snapped, irritated at being talked about as if I wasn't present.

"Good," he said.

"I vouch for her," said Fabulo, glaring at me again.

We all sat. I found myself looking at Jeremiah's hands, which were folded on the table in front of him. It seemed impossible that they could manipulate something as fine as a lockpick.

"Tell her the story," said Fabulo.

"You've vouched for her," said Jeremiah. "But a man can make mistakes. That's all I'm saying. And with more people in the circle... it gets dangerous. All it takes is one too many glasses of wine and someone blabbering. Then it gets in the wrong ear and we're all riding a horse sired by an acorn."

"What does he mean?" I asked.

"He means the gallows," said Fabulo. "But that's not going to happen. With this one, you have to trust me." He folded his arms across his barrel chest. "Now tell her the story!"

The skin of Jeremiah's forehead rippled into a frown of concern. "So be it. But if she goes talking to one of those Patent Office bastards – then you'll be the one to deal with it, Mr Dwarf. You'll cut her throat and drop her in the river. Agreed?"

All the while he said this, he had been holding my gaze. I stared right back at him. My knife was in my boot. I could feel it pressed snug against my ankle.

"Agreed," said Fabulo.

Jeremiah nodded and subsided back into his chair. His frown melted into the dough of his face.

"Very well," he said. "I'll tell it again. But know what it costs me. I'm breaking every vow I made to the Guild of Locksmiths. Once this business is done, once we've gone our ways, most like I'll never be able to work again."

He took a moment to rub the side of his face with the flat of his hand. His eyes were downcast. I wanted to ask why he would choose to do anything if the cost were so great. I glanced at Fabulo, who made a shaking of his head so slight it seemed like the movement of a watch spring. I clamped my mouth tightly closed and waited.

"Have you been inside the Patent Court?" he asked. "Such a work, it is. How much it cost to build is beyond the counting of men like me. They had money back then. If the Gas-Lit Empire had a government, it would be the Patent Office and if they had a palace it would be that court – what with them being lawyers. They made it so big that a king would feel small if he went there. That's what it's for.

"But it's made of stone and mortar and iron just like any other building. Even the mighty Patent Court bows down before King Time. They put it here in London so as to cow the Royalists. But London won't be cowed. Every winter the smog gets deeper into it. Have you seen what smog does to iron? A hundred years of smog would rot the whole city to the ground – if the people didn't keep fixing the metalwork and mortar.

"So every ten years the guild is bound to send in trusted craftsmen to inspect. And repair if it be needed."

"Is bound?"

I had voiced my question without thinking and became aware that I was sitting forwards, my shoulders over the edge of the table. Fabulo glowered at me for interrupting the flow of the story, but Jeremiah seemed hardly to notice.

"Bound is right," he said. "Though I've never seen it

written. It gets told to you…" He sighed as if saying the words caused him pain. "There are ceremonies. You don't need to know of them. These are secrets of the locksmiths' guild. They're like examinations. If you pass them, you move on up. If you fail, then that's the level you've reached. With each step, you're told more secrets.

"When the ten years last came round, I was at a rank high enough, so it was my turn to do it. That's how I came to be inside and see the Patent Court storerooms. Leastways, I didn't see into the rooms. But I walked the corridors and I cared for the locks and the keys."

"How can you inspect a lock without opening the door?" I asked.

"I did open the doors. But they'd hung drapes behind, so I couldn't look beyond. But I can tell you this – there's ventilation. For I could feel the draught flowing out of each room. And when I used my hammer to re-seat the lock, I heard the echo come back from inside. These are no small rooms. They're great halls, I'd say. Big enough to have voices of their own."

He closed his eyes and slumped even lower in the chair, as if exhausted from the effort of betraying his oaths.

"None of that will help us," I said. "Even if you had all the keys to the building. There are guards standing outside it – the elite soldiers of the Gas-Lit Empire. Don't you think they'll notice when you stroll up and start unlocking doors right in front of them?"

"You're thinking the wrong way around," said Fabulo. "It's not the front doors we need to worry about. Tell her the rest, Jeremiah."

The locksmith opened his eyes. "The little man's right. The storerooms are there in the building. But you couldn't get to them through the front door. They're all underneath. It's a labyrinth of passages and tunnels down there. The entrance we need to get through is away at the back. Near the Inns of Court."

"There you have it," said Fabulo, now focused on me. "We have the knowledge. We can get in."

"Then why do we need her?" the locksmith asked.

A silence followed, during which the question grew heavier in my mind. Fabulo looked from the locksmith to me and back. Then he drew in breath and said, "Before I tell you that, I have to ask if you're with us? Are you going to do this thing?"

Jeremiah put his sausage-like fingers onto the edge of the table and heaved himself onto his feet. "I've said I'll do it!"

"And you, Elizabeth?"

"I agreed already," I snapped.

"So you say. But I've had complaints and questions all morning from both of you. And I don't need the trouble! I do not need it! So I'm going to ask you to say it once more. In front of each other this time. You can back out now, or we can go forward together.

"Jeremiah – are you in or out?"

"In," he said.

"Elizabeth – look me in the eye and tell me."

I stood up, pushing my chair back. It screeched on the floorboards. The dwarf tensed. He dropped one arm below the table. He had no gun with him, but I imagined he'd positioned his hand on the hilt of his knife. I looked down at him. My intention had been to meet his eye and say my words of agreement just as he'd asked. But, as I was about to speak, I realised that I hadn't decided. Not really. A plan to break into the International Patent Court had seemed beyond sanity when he first asked me, so I had rejected him. Then, when I'd been beyond sanity myself, it had been easy to agree. But now... now I was not the same person.

"Well?" he asked.

"This is real, isn't it?"

"It's real if we make it real."

There had been few choices for me in the shaping of my life. I didn't choose to be born into a travelling show, nor to be alluring to a corrupt aristocrat. Exile had been my only road. All my volition had been expressed in such tiny gaps as fate had allowed. But this time I did have a choice. The hairs on the back of my neck prickled.

"I want to do this," I said.

Fabulo exhaled. Jeremiah whistled. I hadn't noticed that they'd both been leaning forwards. I felt lightheaded.

"This calls for a drink!" Fabulo said. The locksmith nodded and lumbered off down to the bar.

"What would you have done if I'd said no?" I asked.

"It didn't happen."

I began to laugh, though nothing funny had been said. It started as a giggle but then Fabulo was laughing also and I couldn't stop myself. There were tears running down my cheeks and his by the time Jeremiah returned with a bottle and three glasses.

"Tell me the joke," he said.

It was a rich Armenian wine. We all stood around the table making toasts and drinking. Fabulo stood on his chair. At first I drank too quickly, enjoying the fruity flavours filling my mouth.

"Here's to success," said Fabulo, draining his glass.

Jeremiah moved the bottle around again. Though we

were becoming unsteady, he didn't let one drop spill. "To locks that open for us and confound our enemies," he said.

We echoed the toast. They both looked at me. My head was swimming – partly from the wine and partly from the enormity of what I'd agreed to do.

"To being alive," I said, raising my glass.

"And death to all agents of the Patent Office," said Fabulo.

I watched them drink, then found myself sitting back down with a bump.

"She's had too much," said Jeremiah.

"You didn't answer his question," I said.

"What question?" asked Fabulo.

"She's right," said Jeremiah. "You were going to tell me how Elizabeth can help us in our endeavour. What's her special skill?"

Fabulo climbed down from his chair. He reached inside his jacket and pulled out a document which he then unfolded on the table.

"There was a case heard in the Patent Court this year," he said. "It was the confiscation of a machine that created 'a light of marvellous intensity'. It was the machine you used, Elizabeth, when you blinded the great Harry Timpson. We both lost something that day, so we're square. I'm not raking up old dirt. But we have to talk about it now. This…" he slid the paper across the table, "…is the judgement of the court from that case."

I looked at the paper. Jeremiah moved closer to read it over my shoulder. It had been written in an immaculate copperplate.

"How did you get it?" I asked.

Fabulo waved his hand in the air, as if dismissing the matter as trivial. "Harry's lawyers did it. They asked it be sequestered as part of his defence – though we never got that far as it turned out. It was a capital case, so they had no option but to supply it. Go on – read."

Case number: KESW 157,319
Date: January 28th 2009
Category: Arcane technology
Subject: The late Duke of Bletchley

Description: An investigation was initiated in August 2008 following reports from informant **REDACTED**. The existence was suspected of a machine for the production of a beam of light, perfectly focused and of marvellous intensity. Paperwork subsequently acquired has linked formal ownership to the late Duke of Bletchley. Since leaving his collection, the machine is thought to have passed through the hands of several individuals. These include: **REDACTED**, **REDACTED** and Harry Timpson.

The machine came into the hands of the International Patent Office on the night of REDACTED. It was on that evening that the aforementioned Harry Timpson was blinded as a result of contact with the machine.

A supply of chemicals designed to fuel the machine was subsequently discovered following information given by **REDACTED**.

Judgement: The machine is judged likely to be detrimental to the wellbeing of the common man. The machine and chemicals will therefore be confiscated by officers of the International Patent Office.

Action: Completed.
Location reference: IPC XI XXVI III DXIV
Signed: John Farthing

Reading John Farthing's name so disturbed my thoughts that I had to go through the document a second time to absorb its meaning. I became aware that Fabulo was watching me intently.

"We can guess that final redacted name," he said. "I wasn't of a mind to think about it at the time. But I took it you'd been thrown into whatever pit the Patent Office holds for renegades like us. But then you turned up again, alive and well in the Republic. And with money enough to buy that hulk of a canal boat.

"Harry may have been in prison, but we still had spies abroad. I watched and wondered. Then this came to my hand."

He took back the document and folded it away in his pocket.

"You cut a deal, Elizabeth. That agent John Farthing seemed like a bright young man. With initiative, I'd say. You told him where to find the chemicals if he'd let you go."

It hadn't happened that way. But I nodded, not knowing how to explain to a man who hated the Patent Office as much as I did that Farthing had let me go of his own accord. And that I had, afterwards, told him where the chemicals could be found. As to why I'd given the information without inducement, I was now at a loss to explain. At the time it had seemed to me that, for the good of all, the chemicals should be put beyond use. If there had been more to it – an attraction to John Farthing, perhaps – that now seemed like a cruel joke.

"I don't blame you," said Fabulo. "I might have done the same myself. Even though it was dealing with the enemy. But now... what you did has become pure providence."

I stared at him, confused, trying to read meaning from

the smile that grew on his face. Way back at the start of this, when he'd stolen onto my boat in the middle of the night and kept me at bay with his pistols, he'd asked if I remembered the machine. At the time I'd thought he was blaming me for the damage it did, but now I began to see a different significance in the question.

"What do you suppose those letters and numbers mean?" he asked. "Location reference: IPC XI XXVI III DXIV?" He recited the code from memory.

"A filing system?" I asked.

"It's Harry that saw the obvious. IPC must be…"

With thoughts of the building still fresh in my mind, the answer came easily. "The International Patent Court."

Fabulo nodded. "That told us there was an archive in the building. The Roman numbers that follow – a storage code. So we started to ask questions, looking for anyone who might know the layout of the building inside. That's how we came to find Jeremiah."

On hearing his name the big man nodded slowly. "The storerooms are under the building, like I said. Each has a Roman number above the door. I was to service the locks from ten through to sixteen."

"That's X through to XVI," said Fabulo. "Jeremiah worked on the door of room XI, which is where your machine is stored."

"It's not my machine," I said.

Jeremiah was staring into the distance, as if remembering. "If I'd reached a higher level in the guild, I'd have been working further in," he said. "But there was a door beyond which I couldn't go. I tell you now, I could open any of the doors to that point. I've seen the locks inside and out. And I've had the keys in my hands. But then we get to that last door that my rank wouldn't let me through. Whatever lies beyond it, I never got to see. Maybe I could open some of them. But I never had the chance to try."

All the time Jeremiah had been speaking, my mind had been snagged on what Fabulo had just said. "You still want the machine?" I made no attempt to hide the disgust in my voice. "After all you saw? After all that happened? How many lives must that thing cost before someone sees fit to smash it?"

"I don't want it," said the dwarf. "I need it."

"It drove Timpson mad," I said. "All because of what he believed it could do. For once I do think the Patent Office had it right. That machine brought nothing but misery."

Fabulo had folded his arms while I gave vent to my incredulity and disdain. When I had finished he stepped up to my chair. With me seated and him standing our eyes were on a level. He held up his hand, palm towards me, stubby fingers spread. I knew the machine had damaged his hand. But I'd never seen the injury so clearly displayed. A neat hole had been drilled in the skin between his thumb and first finger – perfectly circular, almost big enough to slip a pencil through. The beam of light had cut it and cauterised it in the same instant. I had also seen the place where its beam had cut a hole through a cast iron gatepost.

"I know it's a thing of devilry," Fabulo said. "But we'll be leaving it there in the International Patent Court. We only need to use it once or twice. Jeremiah's lockpicking may only take us so far. But that machine – it can melt through any lock. Once we've got it in our hands, we can go into their storerooms as deep as we like. Think of it – all the machines they've taken in a century and a half."

He put his damaged hand on mine. He leaned forwards,

fixing my eyes with his. "All the documents of the International Patent Office. That means the records of the court case that ruined your family. Everything is there if we can get through those doors."

"But why do you need me?" I asked.

"Because," he said, "you're the only person alive who knows how to use that cursed machine."

CHAPTER 16
October 2nd

The illusion must be one story hidden and one story shown.
Without the first, there will be no trick. Without the second,
they will discover the first. For no mind will accept a thing
unless it sees a reason.

THE BULLET-CATCHER'S HANDBOOK

The next morning I woke late and groggy to find Lara and
Ellie gone. I felt no nausea, but the effort of climbing the
stairs set my head thumping. They put out the boards for
me and I crawled through the hole into the hidden attic
room. The others had already assembled. The place smelled
of body odour. Jeremiah was sitting upright on a tea chest,
his hands lying on his lap.

I sat on the floor next to Lara.

"Too much wine," she whispered, getting up to fetch me
a cup of water.

I sipped, pulling a face at the metallic taste, but finishing
it all the same. She'd been right about the wine. I'd stayed
late in the Crown and Dolphin, listening to the dwarf and
the locksmith exchanging stories. They'd toasted each other
and the enterprise. With each emptied glass they'd been

better friends. But to judge by the faces in the attic room, the tension had returned.

Fabulo coughed loudly. "Are you quite ready? May we continue?"

There were nods around the circle.

"Sorry I'm late," I said. "What are you discussing?"

Fabulo radiated impatience. "We must borrow a key without it being known, so that Jeremiah may copy it. But the man who holds the key he's met once before."

"Why not have someone else do the borrowing?"

"It must all be done there and then," explained Lara. "The key taken, pressed into wax and returned, all in a minute."

"Then could you teach one of us to do it?"

"Perhaps I could," said Jeremiah. "If you've seven years to spend on the learning of it."

"You're making this harder than it is," growled Fabulo.

"Well, you should have planned better," Jeremiah fired back.

Fabulo folded his arms. "It's simple enough. I know people who can disguise you. Theatre folk. I take you to them. They do their magic. You'll be recognised by no one."

Jeremiah wagged his finger in Fabulo's direction. "I told you already – it's got to be a small crew. But every day you bring in more! It's a shambles, is what it is."

"They won't be part of the crew! They won't know where we're staying. Nor what we're doing. You can tell them it's a costume party, if you want. They get their money. They keep quiet."

"It's too many people!"

"The theatre's miles from here!" Fabulo's voice had grown louder. "And it's miles from the Patent Court. There's nothing to connect us to anything!"

"They'll ask questions."

"Then we'll tell them lies!"

"They'll see my face. I do not like it."

"Excuse me?" I said. "If Jeremiah needs to be disguised, why don't we do it ourselves?"

"Because it's got to be done right!" said Fabulo.

Jeremiah nodded. It seemed there was something they agreed on, after all.

"I can do it right," I said.

Everyone turned to look at me.

"This isn't a job for amateurs!" said Fabulo, sending a drop of spit flying. It landed on the boards between us.

I got to my feet, somewhat shakily, then cleared my throat and announced, "An amateur, I am not!"

Disguise was my father's speciality, the key to his grand illusions. We played games with it from when I was very small, in which he would make me up to appear as someone else. Or sometimes he played it the other way around. The first time a stranger came up to me and spoke with his voice, I cried. Later I learned to enjoy his attempts to fool me, though he succeeded less and less.

By the time I started appearing on stage, disguise had already become natural to me. By then I applied my own makeup. I came to do it better, he said, than he could have done.

After I fled to the Kingdom, I discovered another use for my skill. Places that the Republic would not allow a woman to go, I could access if they thought me a young man. And legal documents were accepted when I signed in my brother's name.

I'd even used disguise to hide from Fabulo and the others

in the circus, though they didn't know it. Ignorant of this history, they would not at first accept my claim. Except for Tinker, who knew the secret of my other identity.

"She'll do it good," the boy said, pride in his voice.

Their doubts softened when I wrote a small list of makeup supplies to be purchased.

"Spirit gum, crepe hair, skin pigment," read Lara. "You really have done this before."

"I have," I said. "I once walked right past you and you didn't know me from Eve."

"When?"

"That's my secret."

"Well, you wouldn't have fooled me," said Yan.

I smiled at him, remembering that on the day I'd fooled Lara once, I'd fooled him twice.

With the supplies in hand, I set to demonstrating what could be achieved. The very blandness of Jeremiah's face made him easy to work with. I darkened his chin, adding shadows that suggested the protrusion of cheekbones. Then I brushed on the adhesive and began working in the hair, building a beard from the bottom to the top.

When the process had only just begun, Fabulo let out a snort and said, "You don't know what you're doing!"

This made Jeremiah twitch with embarrassment, which multiplied the trouble of my work.

"Out!" I said, pointing to the hole in the wall.

I made faster progress once they were gone and presently it was done to my satisfaction. I trimmed down the false beard to the cut known as a "doorknocker". Then, for good measure, I painted a line of latex and pale pigment on his left cheek, forming the likeness of a scar.

The change in his appearance was dramatic. But my main problem was his very stature. A tall man with broad shoulders will always draw the eye. So I set about teaching him to move like a different person. Since he had an upright stance, I told him to walk around the attic with a bent back and rolling gait. This he managed, so long as he was not distracted. But the moment I asked him a question, he would revert to his normal posture.

Therefore I took a length of twine and tied it to his trousers front and back, so that it looped over his right shoulder.

"It's cutting into me!" he said, when he tried to stand tall.

"Then hunch forwards."

This he did and the result was better than I could have hoped. Not only did the cruel twine change his posture, but when he walked around the attic it was with a pronounced limp.

"Who is the man you're hiding from?" I asked.

"A key holder," said Jeremiah. "Appointed by the Council of Aristocrats."

"When did you meet him?"

"Four years ago."

"Then he'll not know you! Trust me. We shouldn't even be worrying about this. You won't be in his mind."

Jeremiah looked at the floorboards, seeming more miserable than ever. "I might be," he said. "Three months back, I stopped going to the guild. I couldn't face them since joining with this plan. There are duties for one of my rank, which I've left untended. A month ago the Guild Masters sent for me. I wrote back to say I was ill. I don't know if they believed it. But if they've been asking around – this key holder might have been one of the people they spoke to."

This news alarmed me. "Then go to the guild!" I said. "You must allay their suspicions."

He shook his head. "They'd read trouble in my face. I'm not one who can hide such things." He paused for a moment before adding, "There's no need to mention this to the dwarf."

I found myself disquieted by the revelation, but continued with my work. We borrowed a jacket and flat cap to dress him and called the others back.

"That's a marvel," said Ellie.

"They're my clothes!" said Yan.

"It'll do," said Fabulo, though the way he regarded me afterwards gave me to believe that he'd been favourably impressed.

Later, when the others had gone, he asked, "Why are you so quiet today?"

"Just a headache," I said.

It takes money to be a successful beggar in London. Organised gangs control the best pitches. Their bosses may once have been beggars themselves. But having risen through the ranks to claim a busy street or a popular landmark, they live lives of luxury, idle but for intervals of violence when their authority is challenged.

"How did you get permission to work here?" I asked Fabulo, as we surveyed the grassy square of Lincoln's Inn Fields.

It might not have been as busy as the Strand or Fleet Street on the other side of the International Patent Court, but wealth flowed through those leafy paths. Lawyers crossed it to move between the chambers of the Inns of Court, also those wealthy enough to afford their services.

"I sold some more of those watches," said Fabulo, stony-faced. "Paid for one day on the park and on the road bounding it. Just to present the show. We'll not be driven off."

"But where did you get a bear and a barrel organ?" I asked, voicing the question that had been on my mind all afternoon.

"I know a man who knows a man…"

"And were we to need a giraffe, would you know a man for that also?"

"We don't need a giraffe."

I'd given the bear a wide berth since Yan arrived, holding its chain. In truth, the Dutchman was the taller of the two, even when the creature reared on its hind legs. And fiercer looking. But for sheer bulk I judged the bear could have taken him easily enough, had it a mind to.

Yan had cared for the lions of the travelling show. They'd been like kittens to him. I hoped the bear would be as biddable.

Following behind the bear, I took turns with Lara and Ellie, pushing the barrel organ, or turning its handle to work the bellows and make the music sound. Its narrow wheels ran smoothly enough over paving slabs but quickly bogged down when we cut a corner and tried to cross a stretch of grass.

Jeremiah did not offer to help. Rather, he trailed behind, limping along with an entirely un-circus like expression of misery on his face. I reflected that I had perhaps cut the twine a trifle too short.

"How are you going to get the key?" I asked Fabulo as we walked.

He winked at me. "The key holder has a certain weakness."

I glanced back at Lara and Ellie who followed behind. On

catching my eye, they waved.

"Only two kinds of people can be conned," recited Fabulo. "Those with vices and those without."

"And which one is the key holder?"

He winked at me. "Getting the key off him – that's the easy part. The problem is, soon as it's gone missing, the lock gets changed and they double the guard. We end up worse off than we started."

"And a bear helps how?"

"Be patient. You'll see."

I had worked to disguise the locksmith but not myself. Thus I felt exposed walking in the open with Fabulo beside me. The raid on the rookery could have been aimed at us. That would mean the duke's spies had found some scent of us in the capital. After the humiliation we'd meted out to him, I didn't even like to think how he might respond. Or the resources he'd dedicate to our capture.

Few passersby paid us attention, however. All eyes were drawn to Ellie and Laura, who were dressed in their showgirl costumes from the circus. Their skirts hung to a respectable length at the back. But at the front, the hemlines climbed to reveal the high reaches of their thighs. To each man who stopped to stare, Lara would wave and Ellie would blow a kiss. Indeed, the bear seemed superfluous, though Yan was enjoying its company.

We first set up our pitch on the northeast corner of the square. I turned the handle of the barrel organ, causing it to play a tune of breathy notes. Yan lifted his hand, on which signal the bear reared up and shuffled on its back feet as if dancing. Lara and Ellie encouraged passing lawyers to come closer, whereupon Fabulo approached them, offering his upturned hat, into which more often than not they dropped money.

From time to time one or other of our benefactors came close enough to whisper some proposition in the ear of whichever woman had caught his fancy. But in every case Lara and Ellie skilfully evaded, even when the men got out their wallets.

Fabulo was all smiles as he approached the public. But whenever he turned away I saw a frown of concentration return to his face. Often he consulted a brass pocket watch, which I recognised from the shagreen box.

All the while, Jeremiah loitered in our midst.

As the afternoon progressed we relocated further south along the edge of the park. Then, at a quarter before five o'clock we moved again, setting up on the edge of the park facing the rear of the International Patent Court.

Immediately on the other side of the road from us, a wall surmounted by iron railings formed a barrier, controlling access to a plaza. Beyond that rose the grey masonry of the patent court itself, doubly austere on this, the rear of the building.

Fabulo drew close. I bent low so he could whisper in my ear.

"See them railings? They were made by the Kingdom." He nodded towards a heraldic device woven into the ironwork. I didn't recognise it, though it was surely not the work of the Patent Office.

"I thought the Kingdom could have nothing to do with guarding the Patent Court," I said.

"You're right," he said. "You remember that line of yellow bricks at the front? This wall, these railings, it's just outside that line. Kingdom soldiers can't go beyond it. But they can make themselves awkward – which is what this wall is here for. Whichever soldiers come to guard the Patent Court, they must first be allowed through by permission of the Kingdom."

Lara and Ellie had drawn closer to listen, though Yan was obliged to keep back by at least the length of the chain on which he held the bear. I noticed him dip into his pocket before stroking the bear on the muzzle. Each time he did this, the bear licked his hand.

"Time to move," said Fabulo, loud enough for passersby to hear.

I stopped turning the handle of the organ and wheeled it once more. This time I did not have far to push. Fabulo clapped his hands and we stopped to resume our show. Immediately opposite us was a gate in the wall and railings. Were it unlocked, one might access the rear plaza of the Patent Court.

Jeremiah, I noted, had turned his back on the building, from which I guessed that he expected the key holder to soon appear.

In the distance I heard the Patent Court clock began to strike the hour. As if on cue, the doors of a coach parked nearby opened up and out climbed six soldiers in Turkish uniform. They straightened their tarboosh hats and formed themselves into a line. At the same moment, another group of six soldiers, identically dressed, began marching across the plaza within the railings. The two groups converged at the locked gate from opposite sides in perfect synchrony.

There passed a second in which nothing happened. Then, just as the chimes reached their end, I became aware of a small man wearing an unusually tall stovepipe hat. He had been strolling along next to the road. As he arrived at the gate, he paused to extract a key from inside his jacket. With this he unlocked the gate. The six Turkish soldiers behind the railings were now allowed through to the street. I was expecting to see the group outside marching in. But before they could do so, the small man – our key holder – had closed the gate and locked it once more. I watched as the six soldiers who had just come off their guard duty marched to the waiting coach and climbed aboard.

The key holder stood facing the foremost soldier. He clasped his hands behind his back and rocked on his heels in time with the barrel organ. Then he began whistling along to the tune – lazily so – slurring from one note to the next like a schoolboy.

The soldiers did not move. Nor did they return his gaze, but continued to stand in rigid line.

Perhaps bored by their lack of reaction, he cast around, his eyes passing over our little band of circus folk and sweeping beyond us before snapping back towards where we stood just in front of the bear.

His whistling stopped. He stared, brazenly, drinking in the scene. I felt myself blushing on Lara and Ellie's behalf. Fabulo had told me our target had a weakness, but I had not expected it to be so openly displayed.

Then, after he had remained unblinking for longer than I would have thought possible, he turned his attention back to the Turkish soldiers.

Even with his hat, he was shorter than them by perhaps half a foot. He resumed his whistling and started to stroll around the line, giving the impression of a general who had arrived to inspect the troops, still drunk from the night before. The soldiers stared towards the horizon over the top of his hat.

It came to me that I was looking at a performance. It

was ritual humiliation delivered by a specialist. Here they were, these elite soldiers. And here was he – a small, round man keeping them waiting in his outrageous hat. Their movements had been crisp and military, his were casual and unwaveringly insolent.

Then other clocks began to chime the hour, close and far around the great city of London.

The key holder got out his key, which I now saw was attached to the inside of his jacket by a loop of thin chain. As the chimes rang out, he seemed to examine it. He scratched at it with a thumbnail, as if removing a speck of dirt. Then he blew on it and looked at it again. Only as the chimes were ending did he put it into the lock and turn. Nine minutes and twenty-one seconds must have elapsed since the chiming of the clock on the Patent Court.

The soldiers had played their part in the drama by remaining aloof. The lead soldier shouted something – in Turkish, I assumed. As one, they marched through the gate that was then relocked behind them.

"Now," said Fabulo, and strode away along a path into the park, beckoning us to follow.

Yan was first to move, followed by the bear, Lara, Ellie and Jeremiah in that order. I brought up the rear, pushing the barrel organ.

I was thinking that Fabulo had made a mistake. Though the sight of Lara and Ellie, or rather their legs, had attracted him, I did not think that showgirls would be unknown in the metropolis. The key holder could not be relied on to follow. But then I heard his voice, calling from behind me.

"Hi! Good people!"

Fabulo continued to lead us further into the park, though he must have heard.

"Please wait!"

I listened to the slap of the small man's feet on the path as he ran to catch up. At last he overtook me and I expected him to go straight to the women. But he overtook them also, circling Yan and the bear at a safe distance before coming to a stop in front of them.

"It is… a fine… bear," he said, through gasps, for he was out of breath.

"Why, thank you," said Yan, bowing.

"You like him then?" asked Fabulo, reaching up to give the key holder a friendly pat on the shoulder. When he withdrew his hand, I noticed a smear of syrupy liquid had been left behind.

"Indeed, yes," enthused our target. "He is a black bear, I can see that. But from what part of the world?"

"Formosa," said Fabulo.

"Formosa? How singular. Indeed, how very singular! How, may I ask, did he come to be brought back over the border into the Gas-Lit Empire?"

"I don't rightly know," said Fabulo. "But that's what I was told when he came to me."

Now, I am not an expert with animals. But it seemed to me that the bear was displaying more than a passing interest in the key holder. The two of them leaned towards each other, the bear held back by the chain and the man held back, presumably, by a sense of self-preservation.

"I have a certain interest in exotic mammals. Indeed, I'm proud to be on the board of trustees of the London Zoological Park, bears being my speciality. We have several specimens of *Ursus thibetanus*, that is the black bear, but none I believe of *Ursus thibetanus formosanus*. I don't suppose you would be interested in selling?"

Fabulo put a hand to his chin and frowned as if contemplating the suggestion. But whatever he had in mind to say was cut short by the sound of running feet. Then several things happened in the same instant. Tinker sprinted through the middle of our group careening off the key holder, who fell to the floor, spilling his hat. The bear lunged forwards as if to attack the sprawling man.

"Stop him!" bellowed Fabulo. "Stop the thief!"

Ellie launched herself after Tinker, who had continued to run. Unencumbered by skirts at the front she moved with surprising speed. Yan heaved on the chain, trying to pull back the bear. I saw now that it was not attacking. Rather, it was intent on licking the key holder's jacket where Fabulo had touched.

"Get it off me!" wailed the man.

Lara bent low and, getting her hands underneath his armpits, began to pull him along the ground away from the animal. There was so much noise and confusion that I almost missed the moment when it happened. As the bear was hauled in one direction and the man in the other, Lara dipped her hand inside his jacket. I saw the key on its chain. Then Fabulo was helping him back to his feet. I did not see any cutters used but a moment later the key was gone and the chain was hanging limp by his side.

"My goodness!" he gasped, looking at the animal in horror.

"I'm so sorry," said Lara, fussing over him. She had already passed the key to Fabulo, who had passed it to Jeremiah who stood behind, out of the man's eyeline.

"He's never done that before," said Yan.

The man patted himself down and found the dangling chain. "I've been robbed!"

All eyes now turned to Ellie in the distance as she tackled Tinker, bringing him to the ground.

"What's he taken?" asked Lara.

"My key! I must have it back!"

As they watched the woman and the boy, I watched Jeremiah standing just behind them, pressing the key into a wax pad, making two impressions of each side and then two more of the end.

The drama in the distance seemed to have resolved itself. Ellie had Tinker on his feet and was dragging him back towards us by his ear. Holding her free hand aloft she showed us what she had won from him, though it was too small and distant to see.

"Bravo," said the key holder. "She shall have a reward. And the boy shall be punished."

Jeremiah closed up the wax tablet and slipped it inside his tunic. He passed the key to Fabulo, who passed it to Lara.

"I'll whip the boy myself," said Fabulo.

Ellie was halfway back when Tinker made his move. He barged his hip sideways, knocking her to the floor then made off at great speed. Lara ran, as if to her friend's assistance.

"My key!" cried the man.

"She still has it," said Fabulo.

And indeed, so it proved. For when the two women returned, there it was in Ellie's hand, a short length of chain still dangling.

As soon as the man had it back, he clutched it to his heart. "I don't know how to thank you! You have no idea the trouble it would have put me to. Even had it been out of my sight for a minute."

So saying he tucked it deep into his jacket pocket and

drew out a wallet, from which he extracted a silver shilling. This he placed in Ellie's hand. "Thank you, my dear," he said. And then addressing all of us: "I would be grateful if you kept this event to yourselves."

Fabulo nodded and held out his own upturned hand. "I can be as discreet as the next man," he said, and received a shilling of his own.

We watched him hurrying away, the bear forgotten, his jacket slightly muddier than before, the stovepipe hat askew.

When he was out of earshot, Ellie said, "One shilling? Why, the ungrateful little sod!"

CHAPTER 17
October 6th

Comfortable seats make for a better trick.

THE BULLET-CATCHER'S HANDBOOK

Two days after we returned the bear to its keeper, the wind backed southerly and the city began to bake, though October was already begun.

That afternoon, Jeremiah moved in with a suitcase of clothes and possessions, taking up residence in our tenement on Samuel Street. Each coming and each going brought risk, Fabulo said. Therefore it was better for all of us to be hidden away together until the crime was done. Thus, a third sleeping roll was laid out in the hidden attic room.

Jeremiah had not been idle in those two days. He brought with him a blank key, made by a blacksmith he knew and trusted, whose forge lay ten miles south of the river. Far enough away to have no thought of the International Patent Court or its locks.

I had caught only a glimpse of the original key, and that while it was half pressed into the wax block. The colour had been silver. The handle, which Jeremiah said should more rightly be called *the bow*, had been intricately filled with ornamental wirework. I had the impression that perhaps pale yellow gems had been embedded in the design.

The blank key was entirely different to my eye. The shaft, which Jeremiah called *the stock*, was a plain iron bar. The bow, a plain iron loop.

"None of that matters," he said. "It's *the bit* we must consider. That's the business end."

The bit was that rectangle of iron, projecting from the stock, which gave the key its distinctive shape. Examining the wax block, I could make out the impression of a fine lattice of cuts in the bit.

I'd assumed the new key would be produced by some method of casting. But to my amazement I now saw Jeremiah unfold a leather tool bag and place a dozen files on the upturned tea chest. Each was different in shape and size. None of them were longer than the palm of my hand. The finest was no thicker than a fingernail. With these, and a drill of similar scale, he began to work, cutting slots into the metal to match the imprint.

I had marvelled that those great sausage-like fingers might manipulate something so fine as a lock pick. But that was as nothing to my amazement at seeing his work with a file.

Through the afternoon the sun baked the roof, which radiated its heat down into the attic space. Yan managed to extract some of the slates from near the apex, so that hot air could find its way out, but the atmosphere remained oppressive and our tempers thinned.

Lara, Ellie, Tinker and Yan all found errands to run outside. But Fabulo had been unsettled by the raid and said that he and I should remain indoors for fear of being recognised by one of the duke's spies.

When the attic became too uncomfortable, I retreated to the downstairs room to sit on my own. But my mind was hungry for interest and staring at the blank walls was setting my nerves on edge.

The next morning, I returned to the attic and found Fabulo sitting with the shagreen jewellery box open on his knee. He stroked the brass watch, as if it was his favourite. Then, becoming aware that I was looking, he snapped the lid closed. I'd already glimpsed two lines of empty depressions in the satin. Half the watches had gone.

Jeremiah seemed hardly to have moved from his work place since my last visit. Iron filings had accumulated on the tea chest and on the floor around it. The key had developed. The end of the bit was now shaped into a series of castellations.

"Each one pushes up a lever inside the barrel of the lock," he explained when I asked. "The lever must be raised to a certain height. Then the central drum of the lock will be free to turn."

"What about all those other patterns?" I asked, meaning the lines and crosses cut into the body of the thing.

"Inside the lock will be wards – that is to say, sills of metal that would block the turning of the key were it not for these slots. Some of the patterns may be ornamental. Some may be needed. We can't tell which is which."

"Then why not hollow out all the metal in the middle of the bit?"

All this conversation had been carried out whilst he worked, his eyes fixed on the emerging key, accompanied by the rhythmic scraping of the file. But on hearing my question he stopped and looked me in the eye.

"You're a quick one," he said. "I had an apprentice work

three months for me before asking that. For most warded locks you'd be right. We could hollow out the bit and leave no metal there to be blocked by any of the wards inside. That'd be called a skeleton key. It's why warded locks aren't secure."

"So, why aren't you doing it that way?" I asked.

"Because the locksmith who worked on that gate was no dolt. Things won't be as simple as they seem. Maybe these patterns are needed. What if we got there and tried a skeleton key and it didn't work? Or, worse, it could be a detector lock – one that knows when you use the wrong key and sets itself to stop working altogether."

"Let the man make his key!" snapped Fabulo, whose brow was already glistening with sweat.

It was not just the heat that began to press in on us. As London warmed, its smells became more intense. The tanneries, the drains, the river and a million sweating bodies – with no breeze, their exhalations hung over the city. Yan had removed more slates since the previous day. When I looked directly up through the gaps, I saw a blue sky, but it grew sepia above the roofscape. Chimneys faded with distance.

"How much longer?" Fabulo asked.

"It can't be hurried," said Jeremiah.

"I didn't ask you to hurry."

"No locksmith could do it quicker."

"I asked when it would be finished."

"It'll be done when it's done!"

Jeremiah's fingertips were black with iron dust. There was a dark streak across his brow where he must have wiped a hand. Fabulo was doubly oppressed, I thought. Once from such physical discomfort as the weather had brought and once from the burden of directing his strange crew. We'd none of us been so biddable.

I sighed. "When will the weather break? That's what I want to know."

"It's still London Summer Time," growled the dwarf.

In the early afternoon, with little shade to be found, the people of St John's retreated into their houses and the streets grew quieter. Having been enclosed for two days, I chose to ignore Fabulo's warning and ventured out to the water pump at the end of the road, where I set about washing those few spare clothes I'd brought from the boat. I soaked them then rubbed soap into the weave before beating them against the cobblestones, which had here been worn smooth.

The water on the ground dried as I watched.

From time to time I saw eyes peering from dark windows and wondered how much the dwarf had paid for us to remain unmolested. I feared it would not be as much as the duke would pay to know the location of our hiding place.

It was late afternoon when I climbed again to the hidden attic. I found Fabulo pacing like a wolf caged in a zoo. With his short stature, he could walk close to the eaves without stooping, making it a dozen of his paces from sloping roof to sloping roof.

Jeremiah now wore a leather band around his forehead from which sprouted various lenses of different magnification. Positioning one of these in front of his right eye, he examined the key next to the wax block, then took the smallest file and brushed it against the metal.

I knelt next to the tea chest. "Are you almost done?" I asked.

"There is no almost! A fraction off and he won't work."

"The key must be so precise?"

"A key will try many locks. But the lock – she'll allow only one key."

"You speak of them like people."

"And so they are. Imagine the one you love. If he were a fraction off, you'd know him for an imposter."

The image of John Farthing swam unwanted in my mind. I got to my feet in an attempt to hide my reaction.

Fabulo stopped pacing. "Will you let the man work!"

But Jeremiah stood and held up the key, turning it so the bright metal caught the light. "It's done," he said.

The dwarf accepted it with two hands, as if it were a thing of great value, which indeed it was. I watched as he took it to a gap in the slates and examined each surface in the sunlight.

"Indeed it's a thing of beauty," he said.

"Thank you."

"Will it do the job?"

Jeremiah seemed less than pleased by this question. "Probably," he said.

Fabulo appeared to be satisfied with this, though it seemed scant assurance to me.

"Could it be tested?" I asked.

This went down even worse than had Fabulo's question.

"I'll have my tools with me," said Jeremiah. "If it won't turn the first time, I can make adjustments."

Fabulo listened to the exchange, as if weighing up the risks. But, before he could speak, a creaking sound from beyond the end wall of the attic room made us turn our heads.

Fabulo dropped the key into his trouser pocket. I saw him reach for a knife. But then we heard a knocking – three light taps followed by a pause and then two heavier knocks. It was a code that had become familiar to me over the last few days. Everyone relaxed. Fabulo rapped his knuckle on a beam of the roof, repeating the signal.

I stepped to the partition wall, where I removed the layers to reveal the entrance hole. Ellie and Lara stood in the attic on the other side. Once I had slid the two floorboards out across the bare joists, the women ducked through into the refuge. But, even as I pulled the boards back again, I knew something was wrong. They were out of breath, their eyes wide.

"They're searching," gasped Lara.

"The soldiers," said Ellie.

"They're searching over again," said Lara. "Now, I mean. They're doing it now."

"Not here," said Ellie. "The other side of St John's." She pointed towards the rear of the house. "Back Church Lane. Six streets over."

"Slow down," I said. "What did you see? Was it the same as the other night – men-at-arms and a carriage?"

"Yes," said Ellie.

"What do you mean?" asked Jeremiah. "What carriage? What men?"

Fabulo groaned. "Nothing," he said. "Nothing. We had a raid, is all it was."

"It is the same as the other night," said Lara. "But different also. They're taking their time. Then it was all of a race. Now they're working slow. And they've got men just watching – spread up the street like gunmen waiting for a hare to bolt."

Men-at-arms were bound to aristocratic houses. There would have been a coat of arms emblazoned on the coach. But to ask after such a detail would have revealed too much of my fears.

"We didn't run," said Ellie. "We wanted to. But we didn't."

Fabulo jabbed the point of his knife into the roof beam and left it quivering there while he paced. "How long have they been searching?" he asked.

"Since noon," Lara said. "We walked right past them, down to the end of the street they'd already searched. Everyone was out watching. So we asked when it had started."

"That's good work," said Fabulo, though his face was grim. "How many houses have they done?"

"Only a dozen," said Lara.

"Twelve in five hours? They must be going through every room!"

"And every cupboard," said Ellie. "That's what folk are saying."

"Hold on a minute!" said Jeremiah. "When were you thinking of telling me you'd been raided?"

"It wasn't important," Fabulo growled.

"You say I've got to move here to do my work in an attic hotter than a bread oven. All because it's safer, you said. And after two days of hell you let slip you've been raided!"

"And I'd do the same again. It is safer with us here, all together."

"So, Mr Dwarf, what is it you think they're looking for?"

"It could be anything. A pickpocket. A runaway bride."

"Or us?"

Fabulo shook his head. "That's the one thing we know

for sure. Those as know who we are, don't know we're here. And those as know we're here, don't know who we are. They're not looking for us."

Jeremiah fixed me with his eyes. I tried to swallow, but the movement caught in my throat.

"What if someone blabbed?" he demanded.

I remembered the Duke of Northampton's impotent rage as we bound him on the horse's back. If men-at-arms were searching the rookery, I had little doubt it was me they were after.

Fabulo pulled his knife from the roof beam. "No one's blabbed. Nor will they." He sheathed the blade. "Besides – from what the girls say, the trouble's over the other side of the parish. That's all to the good. We know where they are – that's six streets away. Which means they're not here."

Jeremiah beat a hand against his own chest. "Someone's talked!"

The abrupt change in his mood made me step back.

"Keep your voice down," growled Fabulo.

Jeremiah pointed at me. "It'll be the girl."

Fabulo's face had reddened. "It is not!"

"Can't you see it, little man? She's too pretty for you to think straight!"

Fabulo bared his teeth. "You're the one putting us in danger with your noise!"

"I've done all the work! And now you're accusing me?"

"There's been more work done than you know!"

"By the King's hand! I could do this thing alone for all the help you've been."

"You can shut your mouth right now!" Fabulo growled. "Or you can get out!"

"Good," said Jeremiah. "I was waiting for that. I was

hoping for it! You can rot in a Patent Office prison for all I care. You can all hang! But you'll not be seeing me again."

I believe Jeremiah would have crashed through the wall if he'd had the strength to do it. But as things were, he was obliged to go down on hands and knees to crawl through the low hole. There was no dignity in his leaving. I was thinking that from such a parting it would be hard for a proud man to return.

Then Fabulo, beside himself with rage, shouted after the departing locksmith, "You're slithering away like a coward!"

I heard the crash of Jeremiah's foot going through the unboarded floor of the attic room beyond. He cursed under his breath as he pulled it free. Then he was away like a departing storm. I listened to the slam of the door beyond and the stamping of his feet down the stairs.

"That could have gone better," I said.

CHAPTER 18
October 7th

There is truth to be found in the mouths of liars, and lies in the mouths of truthful men, though they set out only to deceive themselves.

THE BULLET-CATCHER'S HANDBOOK

Fabulo's anger quickly turned to remorse. Seeing the intensity of his emotion, I sent the others away.

"Would you like me to go also?" I asked.

"Go," he said. And then, "What am I to do?"

"You'll think of something."

"It can't be done without the locksmith."

"You have the key," I said.

"That would get us through the gate. But then we'd just be stuck in an empty plaza, waiting for the soldiers to come and get us."

"Then you must go to Jeremiah and apologise."

"I will not!" he snapped.

We were both outsiders, Fabulo and I. But the difference that set me apart from polite society could be disguised. For him, it would always be the first and last thing that anyone saw. I supposed he grew his armour to deflect the glances that saw him as something less than human. His prickly temper. His immunity to insult. His indifference to emotion. He had always seemed indestructible to me. But in that, perhaps I, too, had been blind to his humanity. How many cares can one pair of shoulders carry? One worry at a time was the way he had described his role in leading our enterprise.

He sat on his bedroll. Then he lay down and turned over so that his face was pressed into the blanket.

I didn't bother to cover the hole in the wall when I left. In the room downstairs I found Lara, Ellie, Yan and Tinker sitting on the two beds, their faces long.

"Do we have wine?" I asked.

"I'll get some," said Ellie, jumping to her feet.

"Let me do it," said Yan.

"You can all go. And what else does he like? Tobacco? Hashish?"

Lara shook her head. "He's careful with his lungs."

I beckoned her out of the room so that I could speak to her alone and unheard by the others. "Does he like anything else in particular? I mean to say, if we had money enough, there might be women in these parts who could… cheer him up."

"I don't think so," she whispered. "He'll flirt if the humour takes him. But I've never seen him… you know. There's once we boarded in a knocking house. He had the money. But he never did."

Having bought four bottles of wine and gathered all the gossip they could pick up, the crew returned to the tenement. The information was little enough. I should have liked to talk to whoever it was had been paid to secure our safety. But none of us except Fabulo knew the name. And he hadn't been in a mood to answer questions.

In brief the news was this: the men-at-arms who'd been terrorising Back Church Lane had left when night fell. During daylight, they'd worked their way from the thoroughfare of Cable Street up to the junction with Ellen Street. No one could say what they'd been searching for. But two men had been beaten senseless for resisting and a quantity of untaxed gin had been seized. No one had been charged with excise fraud, so the locals thought the drink not so much destined for the pound as the soldiers' stomachs.

None of the residents could remember such a raid. One woman said it was a good thing the soldiers had gone before dark, since some lads had been talking about getting a gun. And if one hothead took a pot shot, they'd have every door in the parish kicked in. But another said that seeing as the doors were being kicked in anyway, it might make sense to spill some blood. The soldiers needed to be told it wasn't them that ruled St John's. There had to be raids, everyone agreed. But those raids should be for show, so that the wealthy and the powerful of London could go on believing they were in control.

"That's it?" I asked.

"That's it," said Lara.

"It's not enough."

"How's the dwarf?" asked Yan.

"That's what I'm going to find out," I said, taking two drinking glasses and placing them over the top of two of the bottles, one of which had been opened already and was missing a couple of inches of wine.

Lara, Ellie, Yan and Tinker were all looking up at me. There was relief in their expressions, just as there'd been panic before, when their leader had shown his weakness. It gave me an uncomfortable feeling.

We were like a ship wallowing in heavy seas. We'd surely sink if we didn't move forward. They might think of me as a substitute captain, but it was a job I couldn't do. Half the soldiers in the Kingdom were searching for me and I didn't even know what Fabulo had planned.

"Have a bottle for yourselves," I said. "You've earned it. But not too much for the boy."

There was no answer to my knock as I approached the attic room. The silence set the skin on the back of my neck tingling. Placing the bottles on the floor, I got down on my hands and knees and crawled through. The room would have been pitch black but for the missing slates, which allowed beams of blue-white moonlight to lance down to the floorboards.

"Hello?" I spoke the word softly.

At first I'd been certain that our endeavour was a work of madness. But, as the aspects of the plan had been revealed, I'd started to see it as logical, and then as possible. In that moment of silence, as I contemplated an empty attic room, a terrible thought came to me. The man who had brought us together had chosen now to walk away. I could not lead the others. The endeavour would be over. And my future would be blank again.

"Hello?" I called again, louder this time.

The glasses clinked against their bottles as I advanced.

"Go away," came a gruff voice from the darkness.

"I've brought wine."

Fabulo's shape sat up from his sleeping roll.

Feeling a wash of relief, I knelt near him and poured two half glasses. He accepted his only after I'd placed it in his hand and wrapped his fingers around it. Then he lay back against his bag, which kept him propped high enough to drink.

I raised my glass. "To Harry Timpson."

I wet my lips but didn't swallow. Fabulo sipped and coughed.

I toasted again: "To all his tricks and dreams."

This time Fabulo drained the glass and I refilled it.

"What would that old rascal think if he saw us here?" I asked.

"He wasn't a rascal."

"No?"

"No." Then, after taking another drink, he said, "He'd have known what to do."

I raised my glass again. "Here's to knowing what to do."

He downed his in one. This time he sat up and gestured for me to give him more. I emptied the bottle into his glass.

"This was Harry's dream," he said. "What have I done? We'll not get back from here. Locksmiths! They think they're so…" He drained his glass. "All that secret knowledge makes them proud. And then there's me – can't hold my temper."

Picking up the other bottle, I realised my mistake. "The corkscrew's downstairs."

"You're useless!" he grumbled.

"No more than you!"

"Pah!"

He lurched up onto his feet and grabbed the bottle from me. I saw him silhouetted against a beam of light, wobbling slightly. He unsheathed his knife, held it out level with the bottle, as if comparing the two unlike objects. Then he swiped. There was a crack of breaking glass and the neck fell to the floor, complete with cork still in place. Then he lifted the bottle above his head and poured a stream of wine from the jagged end directly into his open mouth.

After he'd swallowed a goodly amount, he belched and said, "Never try that yourself, Elizabeth."

It was an act so perfectly characteristic of the man that I laughed.

This time I allowed the wine to pass my own lips. It was vinegary and strong. I winced as I swallowed. "It's good to have you back," I said.

"I was never gone."

That was a lie, but I let it pass.

"So," I said. "The locksmith – do you think we should go and talk to him?"

The morning came, and with it the heat and stink returned. None of which was pleasant through the fog of a hangover, or so it seemed to judge by the reactions of the others. I'd drunk only the half glass, and was feeling as fresh as any Londoner could. The worst of us was Tinker, despite my admonition for him not to be given too much. Yan seemed not so bad, perhaps due to his size. As for Fabulo, who was smallest and had drunk the most, only the pallor gave him away.

"I'm going to get Jeremiah," he announced.

"We should come," said Ellie.

Though she and Lara had complained of nausea, they'd cheered up on seeing their leader back on his feet.

"It's me and Lizzy on this trip," Fabulo said. "You keep an eye on those men-at-arms. Careful, though. I don't want no trouble."

•••

Tower Bridge was raised when we reached the river, so we were obliged to wait. I watched as a flotilla of tall cargo steamers passed beneath. Fabulo leaned his back against the parapet and stared in the other direction.

Out of nothing, he remarked, "Thanks for the wine."

"It was more like vinegar," I said.

"It was sweetly given."

I glanced down at him. "How are we going to persuade our locksmith back?"

"Don't know."

"Will you apologise?"

"I'd kiss his filthy boots if it'd help, but I don't think it will."

"You may have to."

An engine clattered into gear within the nearest tower of the bridge and the two sections of roadway began to swing down once more.

"You should watch this," I said. "It's good."

"I might if I could see over the damn wall!"

From the bridge we continued south for a mile or so. As the heat grew, Fabulo declared himself gripped by a powerful thirst, so we stopped in a public house on the Walworth Road. Fabulo's temper was tested again when the landlord attempted a joke by serving him a half and me a pint. But once I'd swapped and the drink was in his belly, a more sanguine humour returned.

The landlord waved to us as we left. "Good day to you."

Fabulo grumbled under his breath. "If I'd a shilling for every time someone's thought that funny…"

"You will be tactful when we talk to Jeremiah," I said.

"Tact is my middle name!"

•••

We approached the locksmith's home via a yard lying behind a row of terraced houses on Cambria Road. Wheel ruts in the flagstones suggested centuries of wear. Accommodation seemed to be upstairs, with a workshop on the ground level. A giant key hung on chains below a bracket on the wall, announcing his trade to anyone who didn't already know.

The workshop doors being closed and the downstairs windows shuttered, Fabulo knocked and we stood back to wait.

"Maybe he's out on a call," I said.

Fabulo knocked again. "Maybe he doesn't want to talk."

"Well, if a locksmith wants to keep us out, there'll be no way…" I pulled on the handle and the door swung outwards.

Fabulo glanced over his shoulder and then stepped inside. I followed, peering into the dark corners of the workshop. The air felt stuffy and smelled powerfully of machine oil. I could make out a small steam engine from which belts ran to a lathe and a pillar drill. Row upon row of keys hung from a rack on the wall. Stepping closer I could see that each of the bits was a blank rectangle of metal.

"Why get our key specially forged when he had all these ready?" I asked.

"He just wanted to sound clever," said Fabulo.

"I expect he had good reason."

A creaking floorboard made me jump and turn. Jeremiah stood, framed in a doorway on the other side of the room.

"I know why you're here," he said, "but you've wasted your journey."

"Hear us out first," said Fabulo.

"I did hear you, Mr Dwarf. I had the key forged to sound clever, did I? You came all this way to flatter me?"

"You should've locked your door."

"And why would I do that?"

"You're a locksmith. A locksmith should lock his own house!"

"Well, that's how little you know!"

"Look," said Fabulo. "Arguing is for fools – of which I'll admit I'm one."

Jeremiah sighed and stepped into the room. "Maybe that's the both of us."

"Will you not talk? Away from that stinking attic, I mean."

"I'll talk. But it won't change nothing. "

Jeremiah pushed back a window shutter. Light spilled onto an uneven workbench surrounded by high stools. We all sat.

"It's the heat made us quarrel," said Fabulo.

Jeremiah stared down at the wood of the workbench, which was scratched and grooved. "Maybe you're right," he said.

"In a day or two, it'll pass. Things'll look different. It was a mistake having you make the key away from your workshop, I can see that now. But it's done. The key you made – it's a fine thing.

"You know how long Harry Timpson spent planning this? The last ten years of his life he was thinking of it. Then Elizabeth's machine comes to us. We see it make a beam of light hot enough to cut through iron. But it was only later, after they took it and we found out where it had been stored – that's when Harry sees what can be done.

"And then we find you, Jeremiah. The finest locksmith in the land – and with the knowledge of that place. I tell you, even in his prison cell, he was happy. And why? Because of what treasures are hidden there. He knew we could get to them. All we have to do is take your key and Elizabeth here and you, with all your skills. It'll all be ours, my friend. All those treasures will belong to you and me."

Jeremiah shook his head. "Have the men-at-arms stopped searching St John's?"

"Didn't see them this morning," said Fabulo.

"That's not an answer."

"Are you scared then?"

"I shouldn't have said those things about Elizabeth last night. I'm sorry for that. But the meat of it hasn't changed. All it takes is a word in the wrong ear and you're all of you swinging on the end of a rope. Am I scared? Yes. Are you not?"

"You knew all that before you agreed," said Fabulo. "What's changed?"

"Too many people," he said.

"I trust every one of them," said Fabulo.

"But my share's being cut with every new one you bring into the circle."

"You're worried about money?"

"There's only a handful of locksmiths could do it. If I was still here after it's done, the guild will come asking questions of me. Or I could go into hiding. Either way I couldn't be working again. Not in this trade. I'd need money enough to last. And with six of us, you're cutting the cake too thin."

"So, is it the money or the risk?" Fabulo asked.

"It's the money."

"Then you can have a bigger cut. Yes, that'd be fair. We couldn't do it without you. I see that now. Instead of a sixth share, you can have a fifth."

But Jeremiah was shaking his head. "It's not enough."

"There's going to be fortunes for all of us!"

"You're asking me to give up my craft."

"Then we'll make it more," said Fabulo, though his eyes had narrowed and his voice had dropped to a rumble. "A quarter share. I'll talk the others round."

"I want a half," said the locksmith, getting to his feet.

"A half!" Fabulo didn't hide his outrage.

"I'll take that and no less!"

"You think your neck worth more than mine? Than Elizabeth's?"

"I think you can't do it without me!"

"Nor Elizabeth! Nor me! Nor any of us!"

"Take it or leave it, dwarf!"

The stool fell as Fabulo climbed off it. Then he kicked out at the one Jeremiah had been sitting on, sending it clattering. He was reaching for his knife when I pulled him back.

"I hope you burn in hell!" he growled.

"Get out!" shouted the locksmith.

The door to the workshop clattered closed behind us as we marched out into the yard.

The first mile of our journey back we walked at double speed, driven by Fabulo's mood.

"We'll get another locksmith," he said.

"I thought you spent ten years looking for this one."

"Once we've got your machine in our hands, we can melt through any of the doors."

"Could we use gunpowder?" I asked.

"But think of the guards! They'd hear us."

By the time we caught sight of Tower Bridge, our mood and our pace had dropped. Fabulo had remembered something that he and Timpson had once mooted. A mixture of concentrated acids dripped into the lock might eat it away from within.

"If that would work, why use a locksmith at all?"

"Because… the lock may be needed to pull back the bolt. If we leave it in ruins, the door may open, or it may be locked forever."

"So this is no answer at all," I said.

"But we only need to get through two doors! Then we'll have your machine. It's a risk. Maybe…"

"If it's true for acid, it's true for the light machine. Unless you know what you're doing, we could be locking the doors forever rather than opening them."

"You're not being helpful," he growled.

After he'd been silent for a time, I asked, "Did you believe him?"

"Believe what?"

"That he wants money."

"Everyone wants money."

"So that's why you're doing this?"

"Yes."

The towers of the bridge loomed above us in the hazy air. A thought had come to me and was growing in my mind. I slowed as we started to cross the first section. At first Fabulo pulled ahead. But at the midpoint he stopped and turned, waiting for me.

"I don't believe you either," I said. "You're not doing this for money."

"You've done things for gold," he said. "Taken risks, I mean. Put your life in fate's hands."

"No. I've taken risks for what gold could buy. But that's different. Jeremiah can earn money. He's in a guild. He has a job. It's the other way around. He said this would stop him earning."

Fabulo spat over the parapet. "You're thinking too much."

"Give me some money," I said.

"There you go!" He brushed his hands against each other, as if I'd proved his point and the argument was over.

"I mean give me a few shillings. I've got a long walk to do and I'll need to eat later."

"You're not thinking of going back!"

I held out my hand, palm upwards. Fabulo let out a growl of irritation. But he dug coins from his pocket nonetheless.

"Thank you."

"Don't make things worse!"

"I'll try to be as tactful as you, shall I?"

He pulled a face. "Be careful. Feels as if the weather's going to turn."

Fabulo was right. Heat still radiated from the paving stones, but my shadow had become indistinct. A haze of cloud had turned the sun into a pale disc. At one point on my walk I thought I felt a heavy raindrop landing on my arm. I found myself looking up into the sky, hoping the weather would break. But the cloying air pressed in on me with even greater intensity.

The streets began to empty. A few coaches and steamcars rattled past at speed, as if hurrying to be somewhere else. It's easy to be unseen in a crowd. But I was now the only person walking that stretch of road.

The duke was pouring his resources into the hunt. I risked capture each time I stepped out of the tenement. But with soldiers searching the rookery, staying put wasn't an option. Neither was running. I hadn't even the money to buy lunch without begging it from Fabulo. My only hope was to get our mad enterprise rolling once more. And for that, I needed the locksmith.

By the time I reached Cambria Street, I could see no other pedestrians. My legs ached from the miles and my inner garments were sodden with sweat.

Jeremiah's workshop seemed untenanted as before. Though this time the main door had been left a few inches ajar. I called through into the darkened room: "Are you there? It's me, Elizabeth."

I waited and presently heard the creak of someone descending wooden stairs. Jeremiah's face appeared at the door.

"I'm alone," I said.

He stepped aside to let me through. "The weather's going to turn," he said.

At first I thought he was going to take me back to the workbench where we'd spoken earlier. Indeed, he paused there before leading me on through a doorway and up to the floor above.

The room that we entered showed no sign of order. Clothes lay draped over the furniture. Empty beer bottles clustered on the floor near the fire. Jeremiah scooped up some shirts and long johns from one leather armchair and laid them on another.

"Please sit," he said.

"Did you never marry?" I asked.

"The dwarf sent you to propose?"

"I'm just trying to understand."

"Maybe I don't want to be understood."

The armchair was firm and comfortable. It must once have been expensive, though there were signs of wear. My finger found a small burn mark on the right armrest. Jeremiah cleared a wooden chair for himself, dragging it so that he could sit directly opposite me. The legs screeched on the floorboards.

"Fabulo didn't send me. I came back so you could tell me the truth. I thought it might be easier without him listening in."

A patter of soot falling from the chimney into the fireplace made me turn my head. The temperature in the room had dropped.

"I need to get it swept," he said.

"Great craftsmen don't make great housekeepers," I said. "I've seen that before. They put so much into their work, there's nothing left for taking bottles back to the shop. Seeing you make the key – it was a thing of beauty."

He sighed. "I had a wife used to arrange things. I don't even know which sweep she used. She died last year. She was a little whirlwind with her cleaning and her sorting. And never sick. The rest of London might be coughing up their lungs but nothing ever touched her. Then I come up here and find her sitting perfectly still. And just like that she's gone."

"You could get someone in," I said.

"You're not the first to say it. And I will. I just don't feel ready."

We were both quiet after that. I couldn't think of what to say next and he seemed content to stare into the empty fireplace. Before, I had thought he'd been lying to us. But now it seemed that perhaps he had been lying to himself.

One of the window shutters swung free and clattered against the wall outside. A breath of rain-scented air wafted into the room. Jeremiah heaved himself out of the chair and went to hook the shutter in place. For a moment he leaned his arms on the windowsill and stared out.

"Is that enough?" he asked. "Do you understand me now?"

"How's your business faring?"

"There's work if I want to take it. But I can't get interested."

"You're an artist."

"I used to be."

"There are paintings in the National Gallery less works of art than that key you made us."

"Well, thank you for that."

"You see," I said, "that's my problem. I've never known an artist do anything for money. That's why I don't believe you're telling the truth when you say you need a half share or you won't help."

The world beyond Jeremiah's room had grown still as we spoke. London's bee-swarm-hum, never noticed because it's always present, had dropped away. Into the new quiet, a dog began to bark. As if the sky were responding to the call, a growl of thunder formed in the far distance, boomed then faded.

Jeremiah glanced back over his shoulder at me. "If I tell you the truth, will you go away?" When I didn't answer he said, "I'd better go secure the doors downstairs. This is going to be a big one."

Off he went. I listened to the sounds of him moving

around – the clack of bolts being slotted home on the shutters. The front door clattered. From the window, I could see him in the yard, working the pump to fill a bucket, which he carried back inside. The daylight had a sickly hue. Thunder rumbled around the horizon once more.

"Filth gets in the water when it floods," he said, returning with the bucket, which he placed near the wall.

"Will it flood?"

"Maybe. We'll see soon enough."

He joined me at the window. The sky in the distance was streaked with falling rain.

"I hate politics," he said. "What I mean to say is, I'm no good at it. In the guild, if you want to get on, you have to have friends. That means doing stuff for people higher up. And then if they like you, you'll get put forward for the examinations. That's when your skill is supposed to show. Four candidates go for each examination. Only one gets through. And once you get through, you're into the next circle. And the further in towards the middle you are, the bigger the presents you get from them further out. The one in the centre – the Grand Master – he'd never need to work again if he didn't want.

"I've been slow to progress. Too much time greasing locks and not enough time greasing palms. That's what my wife used to say. She said any other locksmith with my skill would have gone faster."

"Did she mind that?"

"She said it would've been better if we were further in. But she said that wasn't the man she married. And she didn't want any other."

A sudden breeze shifted my hair. I inhaled the smell of the rain and heard it hissing towards us, a grey veil sweeping across the courtyard. In an instant everything outside was wet. Lightning flashed. I counted twelve seconds until the thunder. The wind was blowing the rain inside. I stepped back from the window, into the dry, but Jeremiah remained.

"Did you pass examinations?" I asked.

"Many. In the first few years it was easy. Your master puts you through the first, at the end of your apprenticeship. And there are plenty enough places in the outer circles of the guild. But once you get further in – a master locksmith – each circle has less seats than the last. And one Grand Master appoints the next. They say big money changes hands for that. Or it's a family member who gets the place.

"So I've been in my circle three years and no chance of sitting an examination. Then one of the High Masters comes to me – came to my very workshop – and he says there's a chance he can get me examined in the autumn. One of the candidates had withdrawn. I thought my life was about to change. One circle further in and it would be me people came to for advancement. So I agreed. He had the papers with him, which I signed there and then.

"After he left, my wife came rushing down to the workshop to ask whose coach it had been in the courtyard. I told her. She kissed me and said that it seemed justice was to be done and how proud she was.

"A locksmith should always be looking for false keyholes. You can see a hundred locks and they'll all be simple. Then one comes along that looks as if it was bought for three shillings. But when you try to pick it, you find, underneath the cheap iron, a thing of craft and cunning. Maybe it sets off a time lock or an alarm, or a knife springs out to cut your hand.

"Three days after I signed the papers, a friend comes to me and says did I know the High Master's nephew is to be examined in the autumn. None of the other candidates would have a chance, he said. Then I saw what he'd done, that High Master. Because only one candidate goes through. And at this level, once you're examined, if you fail you can never be examined again. The test would be fixed. The High Master's nephew couldn't be allowed to fail."

The rain had been falling fast and heavy. It gurgled in the gutters. It rushed, white, from the bottom of the downpipes, bubbling onto the cobblestones and away into drains. Jeremiah's sleeves dripped. The floorboards under the window had darkened. Thunder rumbled around the city and the clouds flickered with lightning.

"Hadn't you better close the shutters?" I asked.

"I want to see it," he said.

Abruptly, the rain intensified. Water began to cascade directly from the roof. I could no longer see the cobblestones in the yard. All was a mass of dancing water. The scene flickered brilliant white and for a blink Jeremiah became a silhouette. The house shook with the impact of the thunder.

"Come away from the window!"

I pulled at his arm, dragging him back so that he was standing on the dry floorboards. More flashes lit the window. I unhooked the shutters and swung them closed, then led him to the armchair. He sat, but only when I pushed him back.

"I'm angry," he said, his voice soft.

"And with good reason – if they marked his paper unfairly."

"There is no paper. Only locks to be opened."

"Then they gave the easiest lock to him?"

Jeremiah shook his head. "They're all the same. The first candidate to complete the task is the one who passes to the next circle."

"Then how was the contest fixed?"

"They would have shown him the locks beforehand. He would have been schooled in them. I was cheated and now must remain outside."

"Then your motive is revenge?" I asked.

"What use are oaths sworn to people who have no honour?"

I became aware of water dripping on the floor next to my foot. The slates were letting the rain through. The roof space would be sodden.

"You have your answer," said Jeremiah. "Now go. Tell the dwarf if you must. But no one else."

I found two more leaks on my way to the stairs. Water was pooling on the stone floor of the workshop, though I couldn't see where it was coming from. I started to push the door open and felt the storm battering it back. Rain lashed at my face through the gap. Water lapped over my shoes. I looked down and saw that it was flooding in from the courtyard. Stepping out, I found myself ankle deep. After two paces it was up to my calf muscles. I jumped back inside and closed the door. Water still flowed in underneath, though not as fast.

Retreating, I sat on the lowest stair. My hair and sleeves dripped. If inches of water stood in the yard, it would surely be deeper on the road, which lay below it. I shivered, partly from the cold and partly from the thought of the filth that must be rising from the sewers.

Water was inching over the flagstones. I backed up another couple of steps and watched as it crept towards me.

In half an hour the entire floor would be covered. Yet such was Jeremiah's distress, I didn't want to go back up to him. Therefore, I climbed to the turn of the stairs, where there was more room, and curled up as best I could.

Since I could not sleep, I thought about the story Jeremiah had told me. It was the undoubted truth. Money would never be sufficient motive for such an artist to give up on his craft. But the guild had betrayed him. That he would turn against them was no surprise. He had taken his oaths believing the guild to be a thing of high ideals. When he discovered the truth, how sour those oaths would have tasted.

There was corruption in the guild and corruption also in the Patent Office. The two institutions had become deeply intertwined.

The Patent Office had rewritten history. In doing so, they'd created secrets that would become more toxic the longer they were held. I remembered the fear in Professor Ferdinand's eyes as he told me what he'd discovered. A little revolution isn't always a bad thing, he'd said. But if these secrets escaped, it could trigger a revolution that might sweep away the order of the world.

The biggest secrets require the best locks and the most skilled of locksmiths. But what happens when one of those locksmiths believes himself betrayed?

Fabulo's offer must have seemed like the perfect opportunity to Jeremiah. The only way the court building could be broken into would be with the guild's secret knowledge. The Patent Office would know that. Whatever special privileges the locksmiths had enjoyed might well be pulled away.

A satisfying revenge.

One niggling doubt remained. I didn't understand why Jeremiah had held back his true story from Fabulo. With that question on my mind, I slipped into a fitful sleep.

I awoke in near darkness, aware that something had changed outside. Thunder still rumbled, but it was distant. The shutters no longer rattled. The steady rhythm of dripping water inside the house sounded louder than before. Realising that I was sitting in water, panic touched me. But looking down, I could make out the flood level in the workshop, not much deeper than it had been. The puddle at the top of the stairs must have over-spilled and cascaded down to where I slept.

It was as I stood, dripping, that the answer to the question came to me. I found myself climbing the stairs.

The shutters had been opened. Moonlight caught the side of Jeremiah's face as he stared out. He did not turn as I stepped across to join him. Stars shone in half the sky.

"I couldn't get through the flood," I said.

"I know."

He pointed towards the south where a column of smoke was rising. "Lightning strike."

"Will the fire spread?"

"I doubt it."

"Your workshop's flooded. And your roof leaks."

"I do know that."

"When will the water go down?" I asked.

"It's going down already. Might be a couple of hours before you can get through."

For a minute we stood in silence. Perhaps he was thinking of his lost wife. It would surely have been her who arranged for such details as the fixing of roofs.

I had a question to ask. It had come to me out of nothing. Perhaps I'd dreamed it. But I could see no way of phrasing it that wouldn't cause him pain.

"I think your story about the examination was true," I said.

He did glance at me then, annoyed. "Well, thank you!"

"But you were still deceiving."

"I was not!"

"I think you've been deceiving yourself."

"I think you'd better go!"

"I will. But first tell me why you hid your real motive from Fabulo. You say you wanted revenge on the guild? Revenge should be made of stronger stuff."

He flinched. "I just didn't want him to know."

"You told me you were angry the High Master cheated, that he helped his nephew win."

"Yes!"

"I think it's the other way around. Somewhere deep in your mind you're afraid he didn't cheat. Because if the test was fair, it'd mean you just weren't good enough to pass it."

Jeremiah shook his head, but didn't speak. The annoyance on his face had turned to pain.

I pressed on, though it felt cruel. "The thought that you'd failed in a fair test was so terrible, you couldn't admit it. And you couldn't talk to Fabulo about the examination, because it was too close to the real truth."

"You're wrong," he said, but with no conviction.

"It was easy for you to agree to the plan when it seemed impossible. But with each barrier that's been removed, it's become more real to you. And that fear, which you can't admit to – it's grown stronger. It wasn't the men-at-arms that frightened you off. It was the bit of you that thinks you're not good enough to crack the locks we'll find once we get inside."

"Why... why are you saying this?"

"To remind you of the reason that made you agree in the first place. If you *could* break into the International Patent Court, if you cracked the locks that your rank in the guild hasn't let you see – it'd prove you *were* good enough to pass the exam. And that would prove they cheated."

"You're taunting me."

"No. I'm trying to save you. I've been running from a monster since as long as I can remember. I kept running because there was always somewhere I might escape to. But the faster I went, the closer he followed. Then – it was a few days ago – I needed to run and there were no more roads. So I turned to face him. That was when I started to understand. I'd been carrying him around in my head all those years. The fear of him. That's why I could never escape. But when I looked him square in the face, he wasn't inside me anymore.

"He's still a monster. And he's still chasing. More than ever. I'd be a fool if I wasn't afraid. But I feel lighter because I'm not carrying him with me.

"You have it the same, but worse. Because your fear's different. There's always going to be another road for you to run down. That means you'll carry it with you to your grave. Unless you turn around and stare it in the face."

It seemed he had aged ten years as I'd been speaking. "So-be-it," he said. "Now please go. I want to be alone."

The walk back to St John's was long. Mud and slime coated the cobblestones, making every step a challenge. Several times I had to detour to avoid roads still flooded.

The sun rose into a sky washed clear. The oppressive heat had mercifully gone with the storm, but there was warmth enough for my clothes to dry on me. Mud began to cake on my shoes and ankles. My feet seemed twice their size and more than twice their weight.

Wanting to delay my meeting with the others, I found a cafe in which to spend my coins. The ground floor was thick with filth, but the upper storey was open. I sat for an hour, nursing a pot of Ceylon tea. The scones were stale and there was no cream to go with them, because of the flood, the manager said. But I hadn't eaten since the previous morning so they tasted delicious, particularly when heaped with strawberry preserve.

The direct route being closed to me, I crossed the river at London Bridge and then cut east along Lower Thames Street until I was back on familiar ground. With heavy feet, I climbed the steps of our tenement. The bedroom was empty, so I continued up to the attic where I knocked on a roof beam, two times light and three times heavy. The answering knock came back. Light shone from the hole in the end wall. Ellie and Lara came scrambling out and took turns to throw their arms around me.

"You're safe!"

"We worried for you, Lizzy!"

"When the rain came… we were all aflood."

"Them holes we'd made in the roof!"

"We put the slates back, but still it came!"

"And we thought you'd be drowned for sure!"

"I need to talk to Fabulo," I said, extricating myself from their embrace.

"He's inside," said Lara. "Talking to the locksmith."

"You've found a new locksmith?" I asked.

"Whyever would we do that?"

At which point I turned and saw Jeremiah crawling out through the hole in the wall.

"You took your time," he said.

CHAPTER 19
October 8th

If the catcher of the bullet chooses the moment, it is called conjuring. If the shooter chooses the moment, it is called murder. Never let them rush you ahead of your plan.

THE BULLET-CATCHER'S HANDBOOK

Fabulo called the meeting to order by rapping his knuckle on the upturned tea chest. There was no need for him to do it. We had been seated in a loose circle on the floor, watching as he paced the attic room, waiting for him to start. But something felt right about the formality of it nonetheless. For the first time, it seemed to me, we were all of us together. All focused on the same goal.

"This is it, comrades," he said. "Some of you have been with me on this for longer than others. But here we are. The number's complete. And it's been decided between Jeremiah and me that we're all going to be equal partners. Whatever comes of this enterprise, we each get the same share. That's because the danger's the same for all. And what we've put up front in risk – that's been equal too.

"We're going where none but those Patent Office bastards have gone. We're going to see what not even the Grand

Master of your guild has seen, Jeremiah. Isn't that right?"

"That's right," said the locksmith, his face grave.

Fabulo looked around the circle, meeting everyone's eyes, mine last because I was sitting next to where he stood. "There's going to be machines in there. We don't know what it is they'll do. But there's going to be marvels. That much I can promise. And there's going to be documents and books – things the Patent Office don't want no one to see. We'll be the first to see them.

"From all these treasures we get to choose which bits to take. It'll only be what we can carry, but that should be enough. Then we ride away and we don't look back. Not ever. They're going to know they've been robbed. And they're going to know what's been taken. But not who did it.

"What will happen after that? I can't tell you. Depends on what we've found. We know there's a machine there can punch a hole through metal like a bullet through wax. Lizzy – you tell them."

"It's true," I said. "I've seen it."

"She's more than seen it," said Fabulo. "She's used it."

"Does it make a fire?" asked Lara.

"No fire," I said. "It mixes chemicals and water to make a beam of light. There are tubes and mirrors. I don't understand it, but I know how to make it work."

"It's a marvel," said Fabulo. "And there's going to be other marvels besides. Maybe there's a machine that makes you invisible. Or one to make you fly without an airship. Or breathe underwater. Or one to let you whisper across a thousand miles. We can't know till we get there. But, whatever it is, we can use it to make our fortunes."

Lara put up a hand. "How can we use it if the Patent

Office won't let it be used?"

"They can never know," said Fabulo. "Whatever we do with what we take, it's got to be a secret thing. It's got to be out of sight from the law. What we do now makes us criminals forever. But we were always that."

Jeremiah sat up straighter. "I wasn't," he said.

I tensed, fearing another argument would break out between them. But then the locksmith sighed and his doughy frame subsided once more. "I'm content with it, little man. Don't worry. As soon as I told you the secrets of the guild, I put myself on the other side. It's done already. It's what I want."

Fabulo nodded as if he'd never had a doubt about Jeremiah's dedication to the cause, though I knew him well enough now to recognise relief from the sloping of his shoulders.

"Good," he said, then turned towards Lara and Ellie. "You've been keeping watch on the men-at-arms?"

"Yes," said Ellie.

"Since the storm they've started searching again," said Lara. "They've got as far as Mary Anne Street."

Not recognising the name, I looked around the circle, searching for a reaction. Tinker, Yan and Jeremiah seemed as confused as I. But Fabulo had tensed.

"Good work," he said, with a forced smile.

"How close is that?" I asked.

"Three streets across," said Ellie, gesturing with her thumb towards the back of the tenement.

All of us who hadn't known inhaled in the same moment. "Only three streets?" said Yan. "But…"

"They've got quicker," said Lara. "And there are more of them. There are two carriages where there was one before."

"How soon before they reach us?" I asked.

"Depends which streets they do first," she said.

"What's the shortest time – if they move directly here?"

"Maybe five days."

"Five?" blurted Yan, alarm in his voice.

"They'll never reach us!" barked Fabulo. "In five days we'll be gone from London forever."

It took a second for the meaning of his words to unfold in my mind. "When are you planning to break into the Patent Court?"

"Just as soon as everything's ready," he said. "That'll be in four days' time."

"As most of you know, we're going to break in at the back of the court, which is the north side of the building. It's like the wall of a castle back there. No windows near the ground. Buttresses to keep it strong. Enough grey stone to block out half the sky. There's just one door, which is towards the east side of the plaza. It leads down to the cellars, which is where we're going.

"But first we have to get past the railings. These the Kingdom built just to irritate our lords and masters in the Patent Office. There's but one way through, which is via a gate. You saw the key holder there, making a nuisance of himself, keeping the Turkish soldiers waiting. The Kingdom built it to be about as inconvenient as possible, putting it over towards the west side of the plaza, giving the soldiers a good long march. I've timed it at one minute. Regular as a clock."

He fished in his waistcoat pocket and extracted the key that Jeremiah had crafted. Everyone stared at that small object as Fabulo placed it on the tea chest. I nodded to the locksmith, who managed to return a smile, despite the tension in the room.

"This will open the gate," said Fabulo.

"It's simple enough when you have the knowing," said Jeremiah.

"But we'll be seen," said Yan. "Even at night."

"True," said Fabulo. "There's lights around the Inns of Court. They're far enough from the gate to be feeble. But the soldiers guarding the door would see us – if they were looking in the right direction. That's where Ellie comes in."

She beamed at the mention of her name. Lara reached over and squeezed her hand.

"Ellie has a way with the horses, so she's the one in charge of the carriage to take us there and get us away at the end. At twenty minutes to eleven, she drives it up the road and stops in just such a place as will cast its shadow on the gate. The soldiers guarding the door will see it in silhouette, but they won't be able to see us opening the gate and getting inside. The carriage can't stay more than a few seconds, or they'll send one of their number to check. Once we're through and the gate's closed, Ellie drives on and away."

"But we haven't got a carriage," said Tinker.

"We will have in four days' time," said Fabulo. "It's being made for us. With hidden compartments for the most precious of the marvels, in case we get searched."

"Won't the soldiers see us as soon as Ellie drives off?" I asked.

"Not if we keep low. The railings sit on three foot of wall. We can make it most of the way in shadow."

"Easy for a dwarf," growled Yan.

"It's sixty yards from the railings to the wall of the Patent

Court. You can crawl that far. We'll have time enough to do it. You can crawl on your belly like a worm if you like. And you won't be seen once you're in the shadow of the buttresses, even if it's an owl doing the looking.

"That's the way it's going to work. We sneak into one of them corners and wait. When the Patent Court clock starts to strike eleven, we'll see the soldiers marching away towards the gate. As soon as they've passed us, we can walk along next to the Patent Court wall. We'll see them if they walk between us and the gas lamps. But even if they look back, all they'll see will be grey walls and shadows.

"From the moment the key holder lets them through, we'll have nine minutes and twenty-one seconds. Plus another sixty seconds for the new guards to march from gate to door. Jeremiah – will that be enough for you to pick the lock and let us into the building?"

"That door's easy. It's a simple warded lock. I could teach any of you to pick it."

"Why a simple lock?" I asked, suspicious of anything so easy.

"Because the door's always guarded."

"They're complacent," said Fabulo. "It's their weakness. No one's ever tried to break in."

"How do you know?"

"We'd have heard about it."

That seemed unlikely to me, but I could see my questioning was disturbing the others so I let it lie.

"Once inside, we'll see a corridor ahead, sloping down. After thirty paces there'll be doors to right and left. Jeremiah has seen this with his own eyes. He can open them. But further in, there's a door blocking the way that he can't."

The locksmith stirred. "That's not right," he said. "I might open it. Or I might not. I never had a chance to try. If I'd been higher in the guild, I'd have gone through it to whatever lies beyond. But…" He spread his hands in resignation.

"But one door you can get through contains Elizabeth's machine."

"It's not mine," I said.

"But you know how to work it. You can use it to cut holes through the door that blocks our way. Once we have the machine in our hands, there'll be no lock or door that can stop us. We will find our way to the innermost heart of the Patent Court and take whatever we wish."

"How do we get out?" asked Lara.

"By the same route. We wait until the guard is due to be changed. Then we slip out onto the plaza and hide in the shadow of a buttress. Once the new guards are in place, we'll crawl back across the ground to the gate. At ten minutes past the hour after every guard change, Ellie will drive to the gate. If we're there, she'll stop the carriage to shield us as we leave."

"When do the guards change?" asked Lara.

"The front of the building is different. But at the back there's a guard change every two hours on the hour. We get in at eleven o'clock. That leaves us the guard changes at one o'clock and three o'clock to get out. By five o'clock there'll be too many people around on the street. The clocks will have gone back by then, so the sky will be getting light."

"And how will we know when we've found enough treasure to leave?" I asked.

"Ah, well," said Fabulo. "There's one room we need to get to. It's why this enterprise got started in the first place. It was Harry Timpson that found out about it. There's a room where all the most valuable things are kept. And just outside it, there's a guard."

"A guard?" said Yan.

"It's nothing," said Fabulo. "A ceremonial post. He'll be an old man, I expect. But we have you and your knives to help us, whatever his skills turn out to be. The one thing we know about him is his title. And that's why we know we have to pass him. He's called the Custodian of Marvels."

CHAPTER 20
October 9th

Declare a thing unknown and they will share in your wonderment. Declare it a secret and they will consider it a challenge.

THE BULLET-CATCHER'S HANDBOOK

Although Julia's letter lay on my boat, sixty miles to the north, I had read it so many times that there was no chance of forgetting even a word. In the course of her studies she went on Tuesdays and Fridays in the afternoon to observe cases being tried. Thus it was that I started waiting at midday just inside the entrance of the Royal Courts of Justice.

Had I access to my boat and its contents, I might have chosen to come disguised as a man. Through years of practising, such a presentation was my second nature. It seemed no more unusual for me to wrap the binding cloth over my breasts than it was to tighten the laces of a corset. But, deprived of my wardrobe, I made such small adjustments to my appearance as I thought sufficient to protect me in the teeming city. A pair of wire-rimmed reading glasses and a leather satchel gave me a studious appearance. A straw hat was also useful, its brim wide enough to hide most of my face beneath.

These items I purchased from a second hand shop on Cable Street, using a few coins I'd managed to save from petty cash. I'd no intention of telling Fabulo about my journey, it being a risk he wouldn't approve for a purpose I couldn't admit.

My disguise proved only partly successful. There were many bookish undergraduates in the lobby of the Royal Courts of Justice. But those of the most studious appearance were all men. The scattering of young women were dressed with conspicuous glamour. Happily, I was ignored for the most part, though three different gentlemen did pause to raise their hats to me.

At half past one in the afternoon, being somewhat after I'd grown tired of sitting on a hard wooden bench, a new party of law students arrived, led by a gentleman wearing a barrister's wig and silks. He stopped and faced them, waiting until they were all quiet before issuing his instructions.

"Wait here. I'll fetch the list of cases being heard. Then you can choose. But I want no more than three of you in each court."

As he strode away to grab the sleeve of a clerk who happened to be hurrying past, I approached one of the women students on the outer fringe of the group.

"Excuse me," I said.

"Yes?"

She turned towards me and I was surprised to see how much makeup she wore. Her lips shone with a deep gloss, her eyes had been outlined with kohl and her cheeks blushed with rouge.

"Are you from the University of London?" I asked.

She looked me up and down.

"Yes, indeed," she said. "What about you?"

"I'm not a student. But I'm looking for a friend who is. She's in her first year of studies."

"That'll be Julia Swain, right?"

"How did you know?" I asked, amazed.

"If there's something different, it's always going to be Julia. I mean, you can tell she's a Republican. Not that there's anything wrong with her." A thought seemed to strike her. She covered her mouth with her hand and said, "Oh no! You're not one as well, are you? I didn't mean anything by it."

"I'm not," I said.

"I wouldn't have minded. I'm not prejudiced or anything. I mean, I'm sure there are some very nice Republicans. It's not their fault where they were born, right? And Julia – she's really kind and everything. But she's just… different. I mean, she really studies. Like the men."

This I did not understand, but put my confusion to one side. "Where might I find her?"

"The other place," said the woman, pointing.

It took me a moment to realise that she didn't mean the wall of the lobby, but what lay beyond it. "You mean the International Patent Court?"

"Oh my God! You shouldn't say its name. It's bad luck to say it in here. Are you sure you're not a Republican?"

Craning my neck, I took in the extraordinary height of the building I'd been told not to name. I could understand why the "Fast Clock" had become a sensitive issue for the people of the metropolis. Precisely out of step, it was the perfect symbol of a conflicted relationship.

The Kingdom couldn't have flourished outside the Gas-

Lit Empire. But Royalists still resented being within it. The Patent Office's decision to plant the towering court building in the heart of London might have been a stroke of brilliance. But it would surely turn to folly if proof of their lawbreaking was ever uncovered.

I joined a small queue, shuffling forwards under the portico. Within a minute, I was through the doors and into a high, marble hallway. A rope partition guided the line towards a reception desk, beyond which lay corridors and staircases. I knew from my previous visit that these led to court rooms and offices. A different Greek letter had been carved into the stone above each entranceway.

An austerely suited man, surely an agent, marched past the line and into the lobby. I wondered if there might be others, less conspicuous, milling with the crowds.

"Next," called a tall clerk behind the desk.

Jolted from my private thoughts, I stepped forwards.

"Your name?"

"Elizabeth Underwood."

He wrote my alias in his ledger.

"Your business?"

"Student."

He peered at me over his glasses. "Which case will you be observing?"

"I don't know," I said. "It's my first time. An interesting case, please."

"Interesting?" The word seemed distasteful to him. "I have no table showing how *interesting* each case might be to you!"

"Then which cases have other students gone to observe?"

He sniffed as if affronted, but ran a finger down the ledger nonetheless. "There's a maritime case being heard."

"Then that will be the one for me," I said.

"Very well. Do you have on your person any firearms, blades, impact weapons, projectiles, pointed weapons, black powder or corrosive chemicals?"

"No."

"And do you agree to submit, whilst in this building, to all instructions given by officers of this courthouse, under the powers and penalties of the International Patent Office, even in such cases as these instructions conflict with the laws of the Kingdom or any other nation?"

"I do."

"Then by the power of the International Patent Office, I grant you entry. Staircase Gamma. All the way along the corridor. Doorway at the end." Then he leaned forward over the desk and dropped his voice. "The court's in session so bow to the judge when you go in and don't sit till he bows back."

On my previous visit I had been struck by the extraordinary size of the building. It contained numerous courtrooms and conducted business relating to many parts of the world, yet it seemed sparsely populated. I followed the directions I'd been given, passing only one person on the staircase and none in the long corridor. Where the entrance hall had echoed, here each footstep was muffled by a carpet soft as moss.

The doors to the courtroom were closed. Stealing myself, I turned the handle and stepped through.

I found myself standing in a tiered observers' gallery, above and to the back of the main courtroom. Three judges occupied throne-like chairs on a dais at the focus of the room. The face of the central judge was so deeply wrinkled that he seemed more corpse than man. The other two, men of middle age, were arranged symmetrically, one to each side of him and slightly lower. To the right, a seated witness was being questioned by a barrister. Other men of law sat facing them, stacks of papers piled on desks before them. The gallery contained a scatter of observers. Students and reporters for the most part, though I guessed a family group sitting at the front had personal business with the case.

I might have had to try many different courts, but for once, luck was running with me. I saw Julia immediately, sitting apart from the other students. She was bent over her desk and writing at speed. I sidled along the row until I was next to her then bowed towards the judges. The one on the left nodded his head in my direction and I sat.

Only then did Julia turn to look at me. Her gasp of shocked recognition was thankfully masked by a loud interjection from the judge on the right, who had taken exception to something in the proceedings. But one of the seated barristers had heard and turned to glance at us.

Julia took possession of my hand and squeezed it. I watched as her bewilderment melted into happiness and found myself smiling in response. In a world of constantly shifting suspicions, Julia had always been as fixed as the pole star. Her friendship had no layers of hidden motivation. But that did not make it shallow.

She flipped over a new sheet on her legal pad and let go of my hand to write: *I have been worried about you!!! Where have you been? Why are you here?*

I prised the pen from her grip: *To see you, of course. And I'm so proud to see you here.*

She read my words then turned her head away from me, pulling a handkerchief from her sleeve and dabbing it to her face. When she turned back to me, her eyes were still glistening.

I got a letter from you, I wrote.

Only one? But I sent so many!

How are your studies?

There is too much to learn. I'll never pass the exams.

Others do. You shall also.

Not all others bother to try!!! She jabbed the pen at the point of each exclamation mark with such force that I thought the nib might snap.

There was a whooshing sound in the courtroom below us. The barrister who had looked at us before, now got up from his chair and stepped to the side of the room, where several brass pipes ran from floor to ceiling. He pulled a wall-mounted lever and a section of one of the pipes hinged open with a pop, revealing a canister within. This he opened, unscrewing the lid and extracting a sheet of rolled paper. Then he replaced the canister and closed the pipe again.

I watched him carry the paper to the senior judge, unrolling it on the way. Stepping back to his desk, he stared at us again, an expression of suspicion on his face. I was puzzling on these events when it came to me that I had seen the man before.

Luck was indeed on my side.

I took the pen from Julia and wrote: *How is your lawyer friend?* For I now understood why she had chosen to observe this case in particular, rather than staying across the way with her classmates.

Her blush confirmed it. And from the barrister's concerned expression, I took it that the interest went both ways.

Feeling a pang of loneliness, I wrote: *I'm happy for you.*

She took back the pen. *He wants to marry me.*

And you him?

Yes. But I don't want to end my studies.

I don't understand.

University is not for married women.

Is this a rule?

Not exactly. But it is understood that every woman student who marries will then leave. The university would not let me stay.

I thought about the woman I'd seen in the Royal Courts of Justice. She'd been made up as if to go to a debutantes' ball. I hadn't understood when she said that Julia was different. Those vehement exclamation marks that my friend had jabbed into the paper now made perfect sense.

We had many times discussed the liberality of the Kingdom in permitting women to study the law. Compared to our lives in the Republic, we thought it a Promised Land of sexual equality. But we had misread the signs. The purpose of a woman in the Kingdom signing up to study the law was not to, it seemed, become a barrister. It was to find a barrister for a husband. In permitting a woman to study, the university was merely lining up a potential wife for one of its graduates. I cast my eye across the judges' bench and then along the line of seated lawyers. All were men.

I wrote: *What do the other women students think of this?*

She took the pen. *They all hate me.*

I think not!

They certainly do! Without trying, I have a proposal from a handsome and successful lawyer. The thing they want most.

Then let them try harder! I jabbed the pen at the exclamation mark as hard as she had done.

She wrote: *They think it unfair.*

Nothing could be fairer. He wants you because of the content of your heart.

She turned away from me again and dabbed at her face with the handkerchief before taking the pen and writing. *I did not try to win him. Not like they try. And now he has proposed, but I do not want to lose all that I have studied towards. What shall I do, Elizabeth?*

Do you love him?

You know I do!

Then marry him.

But the university will throw me out.

Let them try! You'll have a husband who can take them to law.

I had not been paying attention to the court, so was surprised to hear the people around us getting to their feet. We stood, a second behind them. The elderly judge was already shuffling out of a doorway behind the line of thrones. As soon as the door was closed behind him, everyone else in the room started talking. The barristers shook hands with each other. Papers were being squared off and tied in bundles.

Julia and I sat, allowing others to pass along the row and out. Presently we were alone in the gallery. Below us, the barristers were leaving in twos and threes. But Julia's intended, the man who'd kept watch on us, gathered his documents and climbed the stairs. Such a smile he gave to Julia as warmed my heart, but towards me he cast a look of icy politeness.

"We've met before," he said, not offering his hand.

Julia stood and moved close enough to him to whisper. He nodded at whatever it was she said. Then she was by my side again.

"You shouldn't have come here," he said. "It puts Miss Swain in danger. She can't be associating with…"

Julia took my hand. "Don't say that! She's your ally, though you don't know it."

He'd doubtless seen that steely gleam in Julia's eyes before. And must have known what it meant because, instead of pressing his case, he sighed and nodded. "Then perhaps we should be properly introduced."

Julia beamed. "Elizabeth, I'd like you to meet Richard da Silva, QC, my particular friend. And Richard, I'd like you to meet Elizabeth… Underwood, my teacher and mentor."

"Julia's spoken much about you." He glanced over his shoulder at the empty courtroom before adding, "And I've read of your… exploits. In the newspapers."

"Did you win your case today?" I asked.

"I did."

"Then maybe I'll be able to read of your exploits also. In the newspapers."

"*Touché*. But my activities aren't so spectacular. The Duke of Northampton has the Kingdom in uproar – what with the fortune he's offering for the capture of a certain fugitive. They say men-at-arms from seven different dukedoms have been tearing up the rookeries of London. If it wasn't beyond reason, I'd say the old duke was calling in all his debts and favours to find you."

"Madness needs no reason," I said.

"Yet it may have a cause."

"You think I bring trouble?"

"I know it!"

I held his gaze. Neither of us blinked.

Then Julia's exasperation broke. "Will you two please be nice to each other? Elizabeth – this man has brought me a kind of happiness I'd never known. And Richard – without this woman's help and encouragement, I'd not have come to London. Without her we'd never even have met!"

He rubbed his hand over his face, as one suddenly overwhelmed by fatigue. "Forgive me. I'm indeed in your debt, Elizabeth. And I'm sorry to you, my dear Julia. But if you see caution in me, it's for a reason. Last week I was taken in for questioning by two agents of the Patent Office. They were looking for your friend."

Julia's mouth opened and closed twice before she managed to speak. "Why question you?"

"They… that is… they know me from my work here."

"But you never told me!"

I squeezed her hand. "You'd never betray me," I said. "They know that. Asking others to keep watch – it's the kind of thing they do."

Julia fixed him with a look sharp enough to skewer a wild boar. "Is this true, Richard? You were spying on me?"

"Heavens, no! I'd not do that! The only reason I didn't speak of it was to keep you from alarm." He turned to me, his expression imploring.

"If he was a spy, he wouldn't be telling you all this," I reasoned.

Julia's expression twisted from suspicion to concern. "What do they want with Elizabeth?"

"They didn't say. Except that there was a band of circus folk who she'd once known, and I should also be on my guard for them. The ringleader is a dwarf from the freak show. He's the most dangerous of all, despite his stature."

Fabulo's name hovered just behind my tongue. I kept my mouth closed.

Richard seemed to read my hesitation. "The less you tell me, the better," he said.

"Where's your boat moored?" Julia asked.

But Richard shook his head. "Don't say."

"But we need to help her!"

"What can we do? The duke's claim on her is unassailable. And the agents – unless they make a case of law against Elizabeth, there's no action we could take."

"We could hide her!"

"With the Patent Office searching? And half the aristocrats in the Kingdom?"

"I don't care."

"I can't let you not care."

"You don't have the power to stop me!"

Their romance might have ended in that courtroom, with Richard da Silva, QC, finding himself on the wrong side of Julia's sense of loyalty and justice. Although, remembering their first meeting, I guessed it was this very nature that had first attracted him to her. It was resolve, not curlers and kohl, that the women of the law school needed to apply if they were to follow her example.

"Stop!" I said.

They both looked at me.

"I'm the most wanted woman in the Kingdom. Even if I'd let you take the risk, hiding with you would be the worst thing I could do. Your homes are the very places they'll have set a watch. I'd be risking my own life as well as yours."

"Then why did you come here?" he asked.

"She came to see me!" said Julia.

"Yes. I came to see you. But someone else as well."

A flicker of hurt crossed her face as I turned to Richard.

"Me?" he said, in surprise.

"I didn't know who else to ask. I'm sorry. I have two questions about the Patent Court."

"Then I'll do my best to answer."

"First, I need to know where the records of cases and investigations are kept. Where would I go to see them?"

"I'm afraid you can't see them. They could only be accessed by a barrister or a judge."

"You're a barrister. Where would you go?"

"I wouldn't go anywhere. The records would come to me." He pointed to the brass tubes from which I'd earlier seen him withdraw a canister. "I'd write my request, saying which room I'm in. Then I'd load it into that machine and pull the lever. It's a pneumatic system. The request shoots away. And when you hear the compressed air rushing back through the tubes, it means the reply is waiting."

"Where do the pipes run from?"

"They're everywhere in the building – here in the courts, also the judges' chambers and the barristers' mess. I don't know where they start. But I'll tell you this, it must be a warehouse of enormous size. The records of this place go back over a hundred years."

"Whatever you request is found?"

"Indeed. And swiftly."

This was the confirmation I'd come to hear. The records of my case were in the building. From everything Fabulo and Jeremiah had told me, the warehouse of enormous size must indeed be in the basement level, accessible only from the rear of the building. The pneumatic messaging system conveyed the records back and forth. I wondered at the number of workers who would be required to service a great archive with such speed and efficiency.

"Thank you," I said. "That answers my first question."

But Julia reached out and took his hand. "Could you request a record now?" she asked.

●●●

Close up, the brass tubes were more substantial than they'd appeared from the gallery. Touching the metal, I felt my fingers tingle with a slight vibration. A thought had come to me: this piece of metal ran all the way to a room in which lay the records of my family's ruin.

On a small shelf next to the pipe lay three of the canisters and a small pile of blank cards.

"Do you know a case number?" Richard da Silva asked, taking one of the cards.

Momentarily unable to speak, I shook my head.

"Does that matter?" asked Julia.

"There are different ways to search. We might put in the name of the judge, the name of the defendant, the place where the case was filed, the date it was filed, the date of the court case. The more we know, the fewer records they'll have to search."

"Gulliver Barnabus," I said, giving voice to my father's name for the first time in years.

"That's the defendant?" Richard asked, having transcribed the name.

I nodded.

"Place?"

"The case was lodged in Northamptonshire," I said. "It came to court on the twelfth of June, 2003."

He wrote the place and date. "That should be enough. I'm requesting the judgement. That'll give us the case number. Then we can go for the documents of investigation. That's where the real information is."

He printed his name at the bottom of the card, before slipping it inside one of the canisters. I watched as he screwed on the lid.

"How will they know where to send the answer?" asked Julia.

"The cards have the court number printed on them," he said. Then, turning to me, "Would you like to do the honours?"

I pulled the lever and a section of the pipe opened with a sigh of escaping air. He slotted the canister in place and nodded. I pushed the lever back, resealing the tube.

"Now what?" I asked.

But before he could answer there was a whooshing sound and I heard what I imagined was the canister rattling away downwards inside the pipe.

"Now we wait," he said. "It'll be twenty minutes or so."

So we waited and I talked about the storm and the heat before it and the food in London and the extraordinary mix of nationalities and races mingling in the streets. I talked about anything, in fact, that would avoid what I was really thinking about.

If I could access, with Richard's help, all the records of my father's case and all the records of the blacksmith's case which so resembled mine, then I might get everything I needed without ever breaking into the storerooms beneath the Patent Court. The prospect thrilled me. But, in a corner of my mind, I felt also an inexplicable disappointment.

Five minutes had passed. Julia took my hand and stroked it. Richard told me how well she was progressing in her studies and how proud he was of her. And such was the love in his eyes that I decided I wouldn't mind so very much if he did marry her, though the thought shot another pang of loneliness through my chest.

He had just begun to ask about the practicalities of life on a houseboat when he was interrupted by a rumble and a whoosh of air. Only seven minutes had passed. He pulled the lever and extracted the canister, which he handed to me.

"How do we know it's the right one?" I asked.

He pointed to a small glass window in the canister, through which his name could be read.

I twisted the lid, which unscrewed smoothly. But instead of a rolled court document, inside I found another card.

Gulliver Barnabus
Northampton
12 June 2004
Court Judgement Restricted

"What does it mean?" asked Julia, who had taken the card from my hand and passed it to Richard.

"It means the documents are there, but, as a barrister, I can't get access."

"Could a judge?" I asked.

"Perhaps. There are different levels of restriction."

Julia hugged me. "Oh, Elizabeth. I'm so sorry."

But, just as I'd felt a pang of disappointment before, I now experienced excitement. I would break into the storerooms, after all. And it came to me that something of Fabulo's compulsion had infected me. I wanted to see the secrets of the Patent Office laid bare before my eyes.

"It doesn't matter," I said, extricating myself from Julia's embrace. "Thank you for trying, Mr da Silva. You've been very kind."

"It was nothing," he said. "But you said there were two questions. What's the other one?"

This was the question that had driven me to take the risk of seeking him out. It would surely provoke his suspicion. "There's an official of the Patent Office that I want to learn more about," I said. "Could you tell me everything you know of the Custodian of Marvels?"

But Richard da Silva stared blankly back at me. "I'm sorry," he said. "But I've never heard of him."

We agreed that I should leave first and they would follow ten minutes later. I stepped out of the courtroom and began walking down the long corridor, which was eerily empty. Then a single figure came into view at the very end. He began walking towards me, as I was walking towards him. Time seemed to congeal around me. It was not his features, which I could not discern at that distance. Nor was it his clothing, which seemed little more than a silhouette. It was his movement – that easy, open stride, so unlike a British man.

We had closed the distance to perhaps half the corridor's length. He slowed, then stopped. I continued to walk towards him, recognition washing through me – fear and sorrow mixed with a pang of affection that I neither wanted nor knew how to control.

"John Farthing," I said. "Please... I..."

But, instead of answering, he turned and hurried back the way he had come, first walking and then breaking into a run.

CHAPTER 21
October 9th

Choose a comely face from the thousand and address that one alone. When the lights go up and all the faces disappear, still picture that one in your mind.

THE BULLET-CATCHER'S HANDBOOK

John Farthing's appearance and disappearance had each been so unexpected that for a moment I stared along the empty corridor, doubting he'd been there at all. Then I remembered the words he'd spoken to me in Nottingham: *If we meet again, it will be as enemies.*

I ran.

My feet made hardly a sound on the thick carpet as I pelted back towards the stairs. Whatever Agent Farthing was doing at that moment, I needed to get away or bad things would happen.

Rushing down the marble steps that led to the entrance hall, my footsteps echoed and reverberated. People below turned to look. Immediately I slowed, only speeding up again once I'd reached the floor of the hall. My shoulders bumped one visitor after another. An African woman in a green and gold dress called out angrily. But in the midst of the crowds I was hidden to some extent.

Away behind me, almost masked by the hubbub of movement, I heard heavy footsteps advancing at speed. Jinking past a party of schoolchildren, I stepped out through the giant doorway and into the sunlight. Instead of running directly away from the building down the stairs to the plaza, I jagged left and tucked myself behind a group of Chinese tourists, who were being directed to look up at the portico above our heads.

"Note the Doric capitals," said the tour guide, "and the false perspective given by the tapering columns."

Two men burst from the building and were immediately searching. Advancing to the top of the steps, they looked down on the crowds arrayed below them. One raised a hand to shield his eyes as he scanned. I knew they were agents from the crisp focus of their every movement, the dour grey of their suits, and the appalling sense of authority and entitlement that they radiated.

I sidestepped behind the base of one of the giant columns and counted to ten under my breath. Then I set off directly away from where they'd been standing, hoping I'd be shielded for long enough to get away.

I chose a family group that was descending the steps and followed close behind so that it might seem I belonged. But three quarters of the way down, they stopped in their tracks to consult a map. I bumped into one of the children, stumbled and continued on my way, alone and exposed.

Then I was heading across the plaza towards the line of yellow bricks, beyond which street vendors made the crowd thicker. I glanced towards the court one final time to assure myself I was not being followed. But when I turned back I was confronted by a man of dark complexion, dressed in the same austere grey.

He spread his arms, as if to stop me trying to break past him. "Miss Barnabus," he said. "Would you be so good as to accompany me?"

I did not try to escape. The agent stood too close for that, as he escorted me across the road and along the other side of Fleet Street. From his accent and appearance, I guessed his home to be on the Indian subcontinent. At all times he was polite and attentive – though it seemed to me his attention was readiness against the event that I should run.

From the outside, the building appeared to be like any other Georgian townhouse. That this was an illusion became apparent once we were inside and through the entrance hall. There were no pictures, no patterned wallpaper, no lampshades. Thick walls and bare corridors gave the impression of a fortress. The room into which I was pushed was unmistakably a prison cell.

There being no window, all light came from six wall-mounted lamps. The walls themselves were plain and whitewashed. The floor was tiled. The only break in this monotony was a mirror, some three feet along the base and two feet high. This had been built into the wall itself, arranged so that it left no overhang. The furniture consisted of a table, topped with silvery metal, and three white painted wooden chairs.

It was a room that offered no relief for the eye and no distraction from fear.

John Farthing may have said we would be enemies, but he had no reason in law to detain me. None that I knew. The Patent Office was bound to remain aloof from any legal case beyond its jurisdiction. He could not deliver me into the custody of the Duke of Northampton's army. But, staring at my reflection in the mirror, I wondered if he might be so bent on my injury as to let the duke know the place and time of my release.

I worked to dismiss this thought with reason. He had no cause to be vindictive. Conflict of loyalties had riven his feelings. But it was hard to believe he would place me in active harm. I became aware that my heart was drumming and my skin had become clammy with sweat.

I chose one of the white chairs and sat, waiting for him to appear. I wondered whether he would be alone to confront me. The image of his face came to my mind, unbidden. Which, I wondered, would hurt me more – for him to shout and rage or to be questioned without emotion?

Coming upon him so unexpectedly, I'd assumed our meeting had been by chance. I'd been in the International Patent Court – a place I would expect him to frequent. But, sitting in that white cell, my racing mind seized upon another possibility. One agent had already questioned Richard da Silva about me. Farthing could have been on his way to do the same. Then a more terrifying thought struck. I'd asked for the records of my father's trial. If that had triggered some alarm, which had called Farthing to investigate, it would have brought Richard da Silva to the attention of the Patent Office once more. And then, by implication, my dear friend Julia.

My thoughts began to tumble, uncontrolled.

I took a deep breath, closed my eyes, folded my arms on the table and rested my head on top of them. Farthing's image was hard to banish, so I focused on my boat, the *Harry*, picturing it moored on the canal bank somewhere deep in the Northamptonshire countryside.

In my mind, I walked the length of the hull from prow to tiller. Then I stepped up onto the steering platform and ran my hand over the edge of the roof. Stepping down past the engine I entered the small cabin. Then, starting with the cot, I moved around the space, touching each item until I was facing the Spirit of Freedom statue. As ever, she leaned from the metal plate, powerful in her nakedness. I was reaching out to stroke her hair when a loud clunk jolted me back to the present.

I sat up in time to see the door swinging open. Two agents stepped through and took the seats on the other side of the table. One was the Indian man who'd brought me to the room. The other was a tall and pale man with high cheekbones and clear grey eyes. He might have been handsome if he'd smiled.

"Elizabeth Barnabus," he said, speaking my name as if it were a distasteful thing.

"Your name please?" I asked.

"You're in a lot of trouble," he said, ignoring my question. "How much trouble is up to you. So don't play cocky. You don't even know how bad this is going to get. What are you doing in London?"

"Sightseeing," I said.

The Indian agent, shorter in stature and rounder of face, was leaning back in his chair, his eyes downcast as if embarrassed to look directly at what was happening.

"What are you doing in London?" Grey Eyes asked again.

I stared right back at him and repeated my answer: "Sightseeing."

He moved so quickly that I wasn't prepared for the impact. One moment he was sitting, bending forwards over the table. Then his hand shot out and slapped me. He was back in his place so quickly that, but for the stinging heat in my left cheek, I would hardly have believed it had happened.

"What are you doing in London?" he asked once more, a trace of a smile on his face, as if encouraging me to try my luck.

"Would you prefer me to lie?" I asked.

This time I was braced for the slap and my head did not flick around with the impact. I kept my gaze directly on him. He drew back his hand again, but this time the other agent touched his arm. The two men put their heads close together, the Indian man whispering. Grey Eyes nodded. He got to his feet, letting the chair legs scrape over the tiles. He knocked once on the door and it was opened from outside.

"May I apologise for my colleague?" said the other, when we were alone. "He's within his rights. But that was uncalled for, in my opinion. If you say you're sightseeing, then I'm sure that must be part of the truth. There's more, of course. No one does anything for just one reason. For example, from the ledger at the sign-in desk, we know that your friend was observing a case at the International Patent Court this morning. Miss Julia Swain. It would seem an impossible coincidence that you just happened to be sightseeing in the same place as her.

"Now, my colleague is of the opinion that Miss Swain should be brought in for questioning also. I imagine he would ask her if she'd seen you recently. She would naturally deny it – since you're wanted by the law of the Kingdom... I'm sure you can imagine how he would behave."

The impact of these words was greater than the physical assault had been. I found myself answering, though I'd intended to keep my mouth closed. "Please don't."

"Believe me, I don't want her brought in. What purpose would it serve? But you must give me something or it'll be out of my hands."

"I did meet her."

"And what did you talk about?"

"Her law studies. The other students. Her hopes for the future."

"Old friends catching up? That's nice. And what does she think of the other students?"

"She thinks they aren't all really studying," I said.

He chuckled. "And her?"

"She'll confound every expectation."

"You're proud of her. She's lucky to have such a loyal friend. What other friends do you have here in the capital?"

Though I understood what the two agents had been doing – one playing rough, the other gentle – the effect was hard to resist. I found myself wanting to tell this man the answers to his questions. "There are some," I said. "But you'll understand, I don't want to say their names."

"Of course," he said. "You're loyal. I understand. I wouldn't expect anything less from you. But this is nothing to do with the law of the Kingdom. These friends may be harbouring you, a fugitive. But that's nothing to do with our investigation."

"What is your investigation?" I asked.

He spread his hands, palms raised. "Alas, I cannot tell you."

"Then it seems you'll have to bring your colleague back."

"But he may hit you again."

"I'm expecting it." I sat back in my chair and folded my arms.

"I'm very sorry," he said, then got up and left the room.

When Grey Eyes didn't immediately return, I tried again to picture my boat. This time I imagined her as she had been when I first lived on her. She'd been called *Bessie* then. There had been two cabins and a galley, but no cargo hold. This was before she'd been disguised as a working craft. But, however hard I tried, I couldn't bring the detail to my mind.

The lights in the room seemed brighter than ever, the whiteness of the walls giving me no relief. The mirror reflected the white of the ceiling.

I stared at it.

Some of my father's tricks had employed half-silvered glass that would either be transparent or throw back a reflection, depending on the lighting and the angle. The thought came to me that perhaps this mirror could be a window – that an observer might be standing on the other side, watching me. I was just about to get up and investigate when the door opened again.

Grey Eyes entered and sat facing me.

"Who are your accomplices?"

I remained silent, braced ready for violence.

"Have you been in contact with any circus folk whilst in London?"

"No."

"When did you last see the dwarf known as Fabulo?"

My mind twisted at the mention of the name. I couldn't deny knowledge. I'd seen the court record that linked us. "Last winter," I said.

He must have picked up my slight hesitation, because that cruel smile curled the corners of his mouth again.

"You're lying. When did you see him?"

"Why do you want to know?"

His hand moved faster than I could react. The slap

sounded loud in the bare room. The shock of the pain made me gasp.

"When did you last see the dwarf?"

"Last winter."

The second slap hit me further back on the side of my face, leaving a high-pitched whistle in my ear. I looked past my interrogator to the mirror and found myself imagining a man standing in darkness behind the glass.

"Tell me the truth!"

"Hit me again," I said.

He did. And I welcomed the sting of it. We were performers. I understood that now. And with this knowledge, I could take the punishment he was going to give.

"When did you see the dwarf?"

"I've told you already."

"Then tell me about the locksmith Jeremiah Cavendish. When did you last see him?"

I hadn't been prepared for the change of question. The surprise must have shown on my face. The uncertainty.

"I don't know anything," I said.

Grey Eyes swung his arm. I watched it coming, registering too late that it was a fist, not the flat of his hand. The blow connected with the side of my head. I saw lights flashing. I didn't even know that I was falling until my shoulder hit the tiles.

He was on his feet and around the table. I saw his mouth moving, but could hear nothing beyond the steamsaw cutting wood inside my head. His mouth moved again. He clenched his fist and drew it back, but something stopped him.

He turned to look back over his shoulder, though there was no one else in the room. He straightened himself. He looked directly at the mirror. There was a pause. Then he marched away.

At first, I couldn't get up. I lay on my side, concentrating on breathing in and out. As my hearing began to return, I clambered onto hands and knees, and then to my feet. I swayed, staring at the mirror, as Grey Eyes had done.

I sensed the presence of someone watching. I lurched towards it. There was a sound behind the wall – the opening of a door. I put my face close to the glass and cupped my hands to blank out the light. And there it was – ghostly on the other side, a hidden room, small, blank and dark, but for the crack of light streaming in through a door that was slowly swinging closed.

The attic room smelled of roasted meat and garlic. As I crawled through the hole in the end wall, Ellie, Jeremiah and Fabulo looked up from their meal of sausages wrapped in slices of bread.

"What happened to your face?"

The question had been voiced by Ellie, but they were all asking it with their eyes. I hadn't yet seen myself in a mirror, but I'd known it must be bad from the look on the face of the agent who'd come to escort me from the cell.

"Would you believe I walked into a lamp post?"

"Who did it?" demanded Fabulo.

I told them, in a roundabout way, omitting my visit to Julia and Richard da Silva. Stepping into the Patent Court would have seemed like reckless stupidity to Fabulo. I couldn't explain my reason for taking the risk without admitting I hadn't trusted him. So I said I'd been walking along Cable Street when John Farthing spotted me.

"He must have been searching for you!"

"No," I said. "He was as surprised as I."

"Look what he did to your beautiful mouth," said Ellie, dabbing a wet cloth against my swollen lip. Each time she dipped it in the bucket, I saw threads of my blood spreading through the water.

"That Farthing's a bastard like the rest of them!" said Fabulo.

"What did you tell him?" asked Jeremiah.

Ellie rounded on him. "She wouldn't say nothing! Just look at her face."

"Then why did they let her go?"

"'Coz she wouldn't talk!"

"If she hadn't talked, she'd still be there!"

"No, she wouldn't!"

"That's enough," snapped Fabulo. "Tell them, Elizabeth."

"I didn't give them anything! But they gave me something – though they didn't mean to. They asked about you, Fabulo. Wanted to know when I'd seen you last."

"What stupid thing have you gone and done, little man?" growled Jeremiah.

"I've done nothing!"

"You must have. The Patent Office are after you!"

"I have not!"

"That wasn't all," I cut in, before their tempers could heat up further. "You should let me finish. They also wanted to know about a man called Jeremiah Cavendish. That *is* you, I suppose?"

The locksmith sat down on the tea chest with a bump.

"But you're right in what you said. If they'd been after me, I'd still be locked in that cell. They grabbed me because they have court records connecting me to Fabulo. But what do they know that connects Fabulo to Jeremiah?"

"Nothing."

There was a silence. Then the locksmith cleared his throat. "There is something," he said. "When you took me to see Harry Timpson in prison, there was a register. We had to give our names. It was a Kingdom prison. But Timpson's case was mixed up with the Patent Office. We were both on that visitor list together."

Fabulo put aside his bread and sausage, as if it had lost its flavour. "Connection or no, why are the bastards after finding us?"

I looked to Jeremiah, who was staring fixedly at a weevil crawling across the floorboards between his boots.

"I think you'd better explain about your duties to the Guild of Locksmiths," I said.

A deep frown was growing on Fabulo's forehead. "What has he gone and done?"

"It's more what he hasn't done. He can't face his old colleagues. He's dropped out of circulation. I think perhaps they've noticed."

Ellie had finished tending my face. She dropped the cloth into the bucket and sat back on her heels. "Why would they be bothered that he's missing?"

"Jeremiah," I said. "How many people know what you know about the locks of the International Patent Court? "

He looked up and met my eye. "Five," he said. "Including me."

Fabulo groaned. "That looks like a good enough reason."

CHAPTER 22
October 10th

Regard the lie of the liar as the shadow of a truth. Study a shadow and the position of the sun will be revealed.

THE BULLET-CATCHER'S HANDBOOK

From his title, I'd assumed the Grand Master of the Guild of Locksmiths would have a larger and more palatial residence. It turned out to be a half-timbered structure, the upper storey of which overhung the road.

An entranceway wide enough for a small coach to pass gave access to a brick courtyard. Standing inside, hidden by a stack of barrels, I could see the red evening sky reflected in the leaded glass of the upper windows. Below them was a door that seemed to access the residence. A low range of workshops faced it from the opposite side of the courtyard.

"I can't do it," whispered Jeremiah.

"You can and you will."

"I can't lie," he said, slurring the words.

"Then keep your mouth closed. I shall do enough lying for us both."

Before we'd set out, Ellie had prepared a pipe for him to smoke. "To calm him," she'd said. The smoke had been cloying and sweet. At first he complained. But, after a couple of breaths, he relaxed into his task. And, after a few more, he'd been reluctant to let her take the pipe from his hand. "That's enough," she'd said.

But now, standing in the Grand Master's courtyard, the danger had grown more real.

I took his hand and led him to the door of the residence. "Trust me," I said.

I pulled the cord and a bell rang somewhere inside, followed by voices calling within and then approaching footsteps.

It was an elderly woman who opened the door.

"It's guild business," I said. "My uncle needs to see the Grand Master."

She curtsied towards Jeremiah, who I could see she recognised. But then she dithered on the threshold, caught by indecision.

"May we come in?" I asked, putting my foot on the doorstep.

This tipped the balance. She beckoned us inside, escorting us along a crooked wood-panelled passage to an equally crooked drawing room. Here she lighted the lamps and told us to wait.

The house gave the impression of having been in a state of gradual collapse and remedial maintenance since some time in the middle ages. I perused the spines of a row of leather bound volumes. None were on the subject of locks. The shelves leaned at such an angle, it was a wonder that any of the books stayed upright.

"Jeremiah Cavendish," crackled a voice in the doorway.

I turned to see a grey-bearded man, wearing a Lincoln green smoking jacket and cap. He stood bent to the left, resting his weight on a walking cane.

"Grand Master," said Jeremiah, bowing unsteadily.

"What a pleasant surprise," the man said.

I coughed to attract his attention.

"And who might this be?" he asked, with a look and a smile that I didn't find comfortable.

I answered, though the question had been addressed to Jeremiah. "My name's Elizabeth. Mr Cavendish is my uncle."

"Ah? How charming."

"It's me persuaded him to come."

"That was thoughtful of you," said the Grand Master, his eyes still directed away from me. "We've missed you, Jeremiah. Not in a good way, you understand."

Jeremiah was looking at the floor. "I'm… sorry."

"We should adjourn to another room. Your niece can remain here. There are things we need to discuss. In private."

He was turning as if to leave when I said, "I can't let you do that."

"What did you say?"

"My uncle's ill. I can't let you take him from my side."

"He can walk, can't he?"

"Yes."

"He isn't knocking on death's door?"

"No."

"Then, young lady, take a seat and wait for the return of your elders and betters."

"His illness isn't of the body." This I said in a whisper.

The Grand Master stepped laboriously towards Jeremiah, the metal tip of his cane clacking against the ancient floorboards. Such was the height difference between the two men that when he came close he had to crane his neck to peer up into the other man's eyes. He sniffed to the left and right of Jeremiah's jacket.

"Have you been using opium?"

"It's the only thing that keeps him calm, sir," I said.

"I didn't ask you, girl!"

"Yet I must be the one to answer."

The Grand Master wheeled and scuttled towards me, his speed driven by anger.

"You've been drugging him? No wonder he forgets his duties."

"Without it, he raves."

"You insolent girl! I'd have you whipped, but I see I'd not be the first!" He prodded a finger against my swollen lower lip.

I recoiled, from shock rather than pain, for his hand was a prosthesis of metal.

"Now leave us. Go home!"

"I will not," I said.

"*Will* not?"

"I'm sorry, sir."

"You've drugged him to this piteous state. That makes you responsible for the trouble in which he finds himself!"

"His beloved wife died," I said. "At first he showed a stoic face to the world. But he was crumbling from within. You don't know how he ranted! He was driven mad from grief. If you'd seen, you'd not blame me for giving him this little comfort. I would've kept him away from all gazes, but then I heard that he'd been missed. So I came here. To you. Did I do wrong?"

The Grand Master half-turned and seemed to be examining Jeremiah. My face had flushed during our exchange. If he'd been able to hear my heartbeat, as I could, thumping in my ears, he'd have known my words for lies.

He ran the tip of his tongue over his thin upper lip, calculating, I thought. "Perhaps I've misjudged you," he said. "And I've been remiss in not offering refreshment. Would you sit while I have something brought?"

"There's no need."

"For you, maybe. But I'm an old man, dry in the throat. And to share a pot of tea might soothe your uncle's ill humour. I fancy it's just what he needs. Make him as comfortable as he may be. And you yourself as well, my dear." Then he tapped his way from the room, saying, "I'll need to raise a servant."

Like Jeremiah, the Grand Master was not a proficient liar. His abrupt conversion to our wellbeing was transparently false. We'd come to soothe the suspicions of the guild. But it seemed things had already slipped too far for that. Our appearance at his door, indeed everything I'd said and done, had made matters worse.

I listened until I could no longer hear his walking stick. Then I took Jeremiah's hand. It felt clammy.

"Come," I whispered.

He stumbled after me. "Where to?"

"I think he's telling the Patent Office you're here. He may have sent for them already – when we first arrived. We must go. Now."

I retraced our path, along the crooked passage to the front door, which I found unlocked. Jeremiah dragged his feet as he walked, his boots making a scuffing sound against the bricks of the courtyard. It had grown dark whilst we'd been inside.

I left him standing in the shadow of the barrels and went

to check the road. At first glance all seemed safe. But then I caught the scent of tobacco smoke on the air and saw the profile of a man standing in the recess of a doorway some yards up the street. He was thickset and wore a coat so long it almost reached his ankles. I watched as he raised a pipe to his mouth.

Back in the courtyard, I found Jeremiah sitting on the edge of one of the barrels.

"I want to sleep," he said.

"Could you run if pressed?"

He stared blankly at me.

"Then could you open a lock for us so we could hide?"

He held out his fat hands and examined them, front and back, as if they were unfamiliar objects. "Maybe," he said.

I grabbed his arm and guided him to the door of the workshop. A model of a key hung from a bracket projecting above our heads. I'd seen the same arrangement at Jeremiah's house.

"Open this one for me," I said.

I expected him to extract a set of lockpicks from his pocket. Instead he put his hand on the door and pushed. It swung inwards.

"Don't you people ever lock your own homes?"

"No," he said.

We were inside now. I closed the door behind us, shutting out what little light there had been.

"You're locksmiths," I hissed. "Why not lock up?"

"A locked door gets broken down. Setting traps is better."

"There were traps in your workshop?"

"It's alright," he mumbled. "You didn't try to steal."

I put that thought to the side and said, "We need light."

There was a whisper of cloth, then a distinctive rattle and

a strike. Light flared from a lucifer to my right. Jeremiah angled it down to let the flame grow, then held it above his head. My eyes darted around the walls, locating windows. All were shuttered from within. Then I began to take in the room itself. It was of similar size to Jeremiah's workshop. Indeed, the only differences I could see were in the arrangement of the working space and the tool racks. Jeremiah's benches and tables had been set around the edge of the room. The Grand Master had gathered his together to form a single large surface in the centre.

The match died. When, after a pause, nothing had happened, I reached out and gave Jeremiah a prod in the ribs.

"What?" he mumbled.

"More light!"

"Oh. Sorry."

Another flame spluttered to life, revealing his face. His pupils were like black saucers. This time I found an oil lantern, hanging on a hook near the door. A third match had it lit, though I kept the wick turned low. It wouldn't do to have cracks of light showing in the courtyard.

"Are you awake?" I asked, prodding him again.

He jerked upright and opened his eyes. "Wide awake."

"We need to get away from here. One of those windows should let us out at the side of the house," I pointed.

"Mmm."

"Might it have traps?"

"Maybe."

"What will the traps look like?"

He shuffled towards the tables in the middle of the room. I followed, holding the lantern high. He stopped half a pace short and wobbled slightly. There were rectangles of brass on a sheet of paper on the bench nearest us. They reminded me of pieces of cloth laid out on a dress pattern. Jeremiah took the lantern from me and moved it left to right.

"There," he said, pointing to nothing that I could see.

"What?"

"A wire."

He shifted the lantern again and this time I caught a glint as fine as a thread of spider's silk stretched across the air in front of me.

"What does it do?"

"Dunno. But don't snag it."

He sidestepped, maintaining his distance from the edge of the bench. Near the corner, he stopped and got down on his knees. I crouched to see what he was seeing, bringing my eyes level with the surface.

"There," he said, and yawned.

In front of us were what appeared to be the innards of a clock. I moved my head across closer to his and then back, but could see no wires in the air.

"Down there," he said, pointing to the base, which sat a fraction higher from the bench at one corner.

"Spring trigger," he said.

I straightened myself, choosing not to ask what might have happened if we'd moved it. Jeremiah remained on his knees, staring at the clockwork. I was about to prod him once more, but the rigidity of his posture made me hold back. He lowered the lamp towards the bench and inched it forwards, rotating it slightly so that more light fell on the cogs. His lips moved, but no words came out. The bizarre thought came to me that he might be praying. But then I caught a word and realized he was counting under his breath.

When he was easing back from the mechanism, I asked, "What did you see?"

"A pendulum spring." He pointed one of his sausage-like fingers. "And there's an escapement. Then a train of cogs. It's a timer."

"But what were you counting?"

"The teeth on the cogs."

"We need to be gone," I said, taking his hand.

"Divide if it's gearing down. Multiply if it's gearing up." His words were still slurred, but there'd been more focus about him since we entered the workshop.

I led him around towards windows that would face the side of the building, making sure I held myself back from the benches, as he had done.

"Focus on the shutters," I said. "Tell me if there are wires or springs or anything like that."

He held up the lantern in front of a window and moved it around. He angled his head to look into the cracks between the shutters and the frame. "There's just that wire," he said at last, drawing a line in the air.

I could see nothing.

He prodded at the blackness with his finger.

"It's slack," he said.

"Meaning?"

"We can just unhook it."

He reached to the left of the window and made some small manipulation. Only when he held the thing over his palm could I see that there was indeed a wire with a neat loop at the end.

"Douse the light," I said, then, holding my breath, I swung the shutter inwards.

No bell chimed and no gun fired. I breathed again and

opened the other shutter.

Jeremiah was growing sharper by the minute. His examination of the sash window was quicker. On his nod, I hefted it up. It slid smoothly on its counterweights. I climbed out and found myself in the alley to the side of the Grand Master's residence. There being no watchers that I could see, I beckoned Jeremiah, who clambered out to join me. Then he reached back in and reset the wire. I watched as he pulled the inside shutters back into place.

"It was a fine clock," he whispered.

Having lowered the window, I took his hand and started leading him towards the rear of the building. Keeping to the backstreets would be safest at first. But once we'd put some distance between ourselves and the Grand Master, we'd be less conspicuous mingling with other evening walkers on the main thoroughfares.

"A fine clock," Jeremiah said again, his voice sharper.

"Good," I said.

"It belongs in a timer lock."

We had turned the corner of the building. Light streamed from a row of windows on the other side of the alley. I led Jeremiah along next to the wall.

"I counted the teeth on the cogs," he said.

"I saw you do it."

"So I know how long the timer runs for."

We crossed the street, entering another alleyway. Every step now took us further from the Patent Office agents that I feared had been summoned.

"The escapement allows one click for a second."

"That's interesting," I said, though I had no sense of what he was really trying to tell me.

"I counted the teeth on the cogs, so I know the number of

seconds. It'll run for six hundred and twenty-one of them."

We turned another corner and came under the glow of a line of streetlamps. I began to open my stride.

"So, you're telling me that he's building a lock that stays shut for exactly that time?"

"Yes."

"And how much time does that make?"

"It makes ten minutes and twenty-one seconds," he said. "I just thought you should know."

CHAPTER 23
October 10th

To solve a mystery you must ask the right question. To keep a mystery you must have them ask the wrong one.

THE BULLET-CATCHER'S HANDBOOK

We didn't go back directly to the tenement. Our first stop was the Crown and Dolphin on Cable Street. I sat Jeremiah in a private booth and ordered wine for myself and strong coffee for him. Then, once my heartbeat had slowed and his had speeded, I set off back to the rookery.

Tinker was playing by the yellow light spilling from a doorway, kicking a bladder with some other boys. On seeing me, he ran to my side, whereupon I gave him a message to carry, then headed back to the public house. Fabulo must have sprinted all the way after me, because I was scarcely back in the booth with Jeremiah before he burst into the saloon bar.

He clambered up onto the bench, out of breath and with a smell of fresh sweat on him. "Is it done?"

"It's done," said Jeremiah.

"But it's not good," I said. "There was too much suspicion for anything I could have said to make things right. We can never go back there. The Grand Master wanted to hand us over to the Patent Office. He didn't say it, but I'm certain. And the fact that we ran away will put him doubly on guard."

"Then stay away we shall!" said Fabulo. "In a few days we'll have quit London forever." He looked first at Jeremiah, then at me. "But there's more bad news in your eyes. Damn it all to Hell! Tell it to me straight."

So I told him of our escape through the workshop and of the clock mechanism laid out on the bench. Then Jeremiah filled in the detail of what he'd seen – the number of cogs, the number of teeth, the escapement and the spring. I wondered how many men in England could have made the same diagnosis from such a fleeting look.

"There's only one place they're going to use it," he said. "I'm sorry, little man. You found a weakness in the Patent Court. Nine minutes and twenty-one seconds between the clocks. And another minute for the guards to march from the gate. But they're not so stupid. And now they've made a new lock to put on the door for when the guards aren't there."

"But why must they do it now?"

Jeremiah looked down at his hands. "It's my fault."

Fabulo shook his head, as if trying to clear water from his ears. He was usually quick to make connections. But these were connections he didn't want to make.

"There's no fault," I said. "But there is a cause. By not attending to his duties in the guild, Jeremiah raised their concern. As far as they knew, he'd disappeared. And him knowing the secrets he knows. So they told the Patent Office, who began searching. When they didn't find him, they looked for any of his known contacts. Even me. And for all they know, I'm just a contact of a contact. It's a serious matter for them. Serious enough to increase the security. So they commissioned a new lock. One that can't be picked."

"Can't be picked?" Fabulo seemed unable to accept the evident truth. "You're a master locksmith! You wouldn't tell me it's impossible."

"It's a lock with no key," said Jeremiah. "There's nothing to open it but time itself. All you can do is wait for six hundred and twenty-one seconds. Then it springs open. But by then, our time's used up."

"You said the lock is sitting in the Grand Master's workshop. That means it's not on the door yet."

Jeremiah was shaking his head. "The clock was assembled. And he'd the casing ready. He'd have fitted it soon enough. But with me showing myself and then running... It'll be on the door by tomorrow. It may be there tonight."

Every question Fabulo presented to Jeremiah, I'd already asked on our long walk back. I knew the answers before they came. And with each, Fabulo crumpled a little further.

"There must be a way!" This was no more a question. He was pleading with the actuality. "We've spent most everything," he said.

Jeremiah slid himself out of the booth. "I'll get him a glass."

I put my hand on Fabulo's. "It was better we found it this way – before risking our necks."

"But what am I to tell the others?"

"The truth."

"It'll kill them."

"It was a good plan," I said. "But that was never the reason they followed you. Now the plan's broken, they're not going to leave you either."

"They'd have been better never to have known me!"

"You told me once that Tinker needed to belong and that I'm the one he belongs to. Well, it's the same for Lara and Ellie. And Yan. Except they belonged to the circus. That was never the big top. You know that. It wasn't the beast wagons. It's the people."

"It was Harry."

"It's a family, not one person. Lara and Ellie and Yan and you. And now Tinker and me."

"You're wrong," he said, the words escaping from deep in his chest like a sob. "It's Harry himself they want to follow. This plan – it was the last thing they had of him. We all clung to it like a log. Like we'd drown if we let go. But the ship's sunk and here we are. And now the log's sunk too. We've got nothing left."

I might have argued, but I wasn't his audience. He was purposefully coaxing himself deeper into a place where the light couldn't reach. There were no words I could say that would change the truth. The plan was dead and there was nothing that would ever replace it.

Perhaps it'd been the lingering effects of the opium that caused Jeremiah not to rage. Acceptance had grown in him with the gradual inevitability of a rising flood. Lara and Ellie responded with tears, and then with concern for Fabulo, rubbing his back and stroking his hair, as a mother might comfort a poorly child.

It was Yan, usually the quiet one, who needed someone to blame. First he shouted at Jeremiah, accusing him of betrayal. And when our locksmith didn't rise to the bait, he turned on Fabulo.

"You said we should trust you. And now this! What plan

have you got for this? Don't say you haven't got one. We went along with you. Trusted you! How much have we spent? Chasing a crazy dream?"

"I never said it was going to be easy," said Fabulo.

"When have things ever been easy? How much money have we got left?"

"Enough to get us out of here."

"And how much is that? We had treasure once. Remember that? When Harry was here. He knew how to treat us. Show me what we've got now. Go on! Get out the watches. Let's see what we've spent."

If Fabulo had been at his best he might have talked his way out of it. But the fight had gone from him. At first he refused. But Yan took hold of his collar and began to shake him. I would have stepped forwards to intervene, but Lara grabbed my hand. I let her hold me back. Perhaps the fight had gone out of all of us.

When Yan let go, Fabulo fell to the floor. Instead of springing back and confronting the giant, he crawled on hands and knees to the small pile of his possessions, from among which he pulled the shagreen box. Yan snatched it from his hand and popped the catch. I watched as the bristling anger on his face collapsed into despair.

"This is it? All the others sold?"

He turned the box for us all to see. Of the twenty shallow depressions in the satin lining, nineteen were now empty. A single watch remained – the brass chronometer of which Fabulo had been unaccountably fond. All the gold and platinum treasures had been sold. All the diamonds and rubies.

"This? This worthless thing? Why did it have to be this one we've got left?"

"I was keeping it for us to use," said Fabulo, his voice quiet.

"But that's typical! It's gold for everyone else and tin for us." He plucked the watch from its place in the box, shook it and held it to his ear. "It doesn't even keep time!"

Fabulo got up off his knees. "It's the best one of all. That's why I didn't sell it. We would have used it when we were in the Patent Court."

"Can't you even get that right? It's an hour fast if it's a minute."

"It keeps perfect time!"

I pulled my hand away from Lara and I stepped between the two men. "Give it to me," I said.

I put it to my ear, as Yan had done. The ticking was clear and regular. I examined the dial. It showed twenty minutes short of eight o'clock. "What makes you say it's wrong?" I asked.

"The bell of St John's church last struck for six."

"Men will argue over nothing," said Lara. "We're all alive. What else matters?"

She took the watch, laid it back in its place and snapped the box closed. "We stole those watches. We can steal more. If the locksmith wants to join us, there'll be no shortage of treasure we can have. Maybe we start small again. Yan juggling knives and axes. Fabulo with cartwheels and clowning. Let's go to France or Italy. I've heard it's always sunny there."

Yan's shoulders slumped. Fabulo nodded. Ellie stood, took the giant's hand and kissed it.

"She's right," said Fabulo. "Lizzy, could your boat make it across the channel to France?"

"I don't know," I said. "If it was very calm, perhaps."

Each of them looked at the others. I could see no disagreement. Just like that, it seemed a new plan was resolving out of their despair. But for me there could be no such resolution. The duke would never give up his search. One day his agents would find me. My only hope lay in the records of my father's trial, which lay in the storerooms under that mighty court building.

Yan cocked his head. I realised he was listening to the chiming of a distant clock. It was the three quarter hour. I counted the strikes and saw that Fabulo was doing the same. After six strikes it fell silent.

"There!" said Yan in triumph. "A quarter to seven, not a quarter to eight!"

"Impossible!" said Fabulo, snatching the shagreen box from Lara's hand. He took out the watch and examined it. "But it's always kept perfect time."

"It still keeps perfect time," said Ellie. "You forgot to change it when the clocks went back."

Fabulo slapped his forehead with the palm of his hand. "I'm an idiot," he said, twisting the knob to turn the hands by an hour. He clipped the box closed again and slipped it among his possessions on the floor. The others were already turning away.

"What's the date?" I asked.

The urgency in my voice made the others stop in their tracks.

"What does it matter?" asked Lara.

"Just tell me!"

"It's the tenth of October," she said.

Understanding rushed in at me with such intensity that I felt dizzy. I held onto the roof beam to steady myself. "We can still do it!" I cried. "Don't you see? It's the end of summer. This morning the clocks went back. But only in the Kingdom. It'll be tomorrow morning at four when they go back in the Republic. And everywhere else in the Gas-Lit Empire. That includes the International Patent Court!"

Fabulo's eyes bulged. His mouth fell open. He was trying to speak, but could only blow air.

"I don't understand," said Yan.

"You could knock me down with a sparrow's wing!" said Jeremiah. "The girl's right!"

"I don't understand either," said Ellie.

"It means," I said, "that the guards aren't going to be held back from the door of the Patent Court for just nine minutes and twenty one seconds. Tonight they're going to be standing around outside for that and a whole extra hour."

"So… we can…" Now it was Yan's turn to lose the power of speech.

"We can do it!" said Jeremiah.

"So the old plan's going to work?" asked Ellie.

"Yes," I said. "And no. We were going to do it in three days' time. But there's only one night in the year when the clocks have gone back here and the Patent Court's not yet followed. That's tonight. We have to do it now."

They celebrated then, with hugs and handshakes and back slapping and beaming smiles. Everyone except Ellie. It was her voice that broke the spell.

"We can't do it tonight," she said. "We haven't got the carriage yet. If we don't have a carriage to block the light, you're going to be seen opening the gate. There's no other way."

Fabulo's face had charted such a journey of emotions in the last hour that I wouldn't have been surprised if he'd suffered an apoplectic fit. A groan escaped from somewhere deep in his chest. We all turned to look at him.

"Three hours!" he cried. "We have but three hours! And every jot must be prepared! Get to it!"

"But the carriage?" said Ellie. "We've no money to buy one!"

"We don't need money," he shouted. "Nor horses. Just get me a brush and a tin of black paint. Do it now. And run!"

CHAPTER 24
October 10th

They will beg to be told the secrets of your illusion. But you must know them better than they know themselves. The truth will disappoint.

THE BULLET-CATCHER'S HANDBOOK

Paint is everywhere in a city – on every door and window frame, on walls and coaches. You'd think it would be easy to find a can of the stuff. But nothing is easy when you have no time.

I ran from the rookery and started out along Commercial Road East. A night market was setting up further along the street and many of the settled traders had stayed open to take advantage of the crowds. I looked in through shop windows, searching for any that might sell decorating supplies.

Bumping shoulders in the crowd, I drew shouts of annoyance. So much attention is a dangerous thing. Any one of the people staring at me might have seen a fugitive poster with my description. But there are times to spend such luck as is one's portion.

There were pubs, butcher's, cobblers and druggists. There

were lamp sellers and glove makers. Then I was into the street market itself, with fruit and vegetables laid out on tarpaulin sheets on the road, all lit by oil lamps laid here and there.

I almost missed the ironmongery shop, since it was half hidden behind a canopy that one of the street traders was setting up.

"Paint? Do you sell paint?"

At first, I thought the ironmonger's assistant was confused by my question, but his expression was one of concern.

"Are you well, miss?"

"Well?"

"You're… perspiring."

There was a display of mirrors on the wall next to the counter. I glanced at my reflection and understood his reaction. My lip was still swollen. Strands of dark hair had escaped from under my hat and were stuck to my skin by a slick of sweat. My cheeks were blotched red.

I took a breath and let it out as slowly as I could manage, then started again. "I'm quite well, thank you. I need black paint. Please."

He nodded, then fetched a set of wooden steps from the back of the shop, which he climbed to reach a paint tin on the topmost shelf. His progress was unbearably slow. "We've Benson's in stock, but I could order some of Cartwright's Gloss if you prefer it?"

I grabbed a paint brush from a rack display and the tin from his hand.

"I'll get your change," he said, when I threw the money on the counter.

But I was already on my way to the door.

More market stalls were setting up when I emerged

back onto Commercial Road. Pedestrians who might have walked on the roadway were now being squeezed in along a narrow path next to the shops. I tried to push ahead, but tempers were rising in the crush. I'd got past an overlarge woman, trailing children and a wheeled shopping basket, and was shouldering through a knot of workmen when a hand grabbed my arm. I pulled free and was stepping away, but a voice I knew called out from behind me.

"Stand where you are!"

It was John Farthing again.

There was no room to run forwards along the pavement, so I lurched towards the roadway, jumping a tarpaulin piled with fruit. I must have caught him unprepared because I'd already set off at a run before I heard him crashing through the fruit stall in pursuit. There were shouts of outrage and the sounds of a scuffle. I glanced back and saw apples scattered over the road and the stallholder grappling with Farthing, trying to haul him back.

In that moment, it seemed I would get away. But the breath was knocked out of my lungs, for I had run headlong into the clutches of another man. Farthing freed himself, shouting his rank to cow the stallholder. Then he was looking down at me, his face severe.

"Miss Barnabus, please accompany me to my carriage."

The man who'd caught me gripped my wrist and twisted it, sending a jolt of pain up my arm. "Walk," he growled.

From the outside I'd not noticed the curtains covering the carriage windows. A sliver of streetlight found its way in around the edge. But not enough for me to make out the details of the interior. Farthing sat opposite, a deeper dark than the upholstery of the wall behind him. Only the side of his hat and one shoulder had any definition, being edged with grey.

"What are you doing in London?" he asked.

The abruptness of my abduction and the sudden change from lamplight to gloom had left me disorientated. But it was the cold precision of his presence that robbed me of speech. Being with him had always cast me into confusion. The effect had grown over the months of our acquaintance. Once it had disturbed only my thoughts. Now it gripped my body like an illness. I found myself pushing my hands down against the padded leather underneath me, bracing hard against the back of the seat as I tried to push myself away from him.

"Refusing to answer may constitute deliberate obstruction," he said. Then he reached up and gave the roof of the carriage three brisk knocks. Somewhere above me, the man who'd grabbed me now sat on the driver's bench. I heard him calling, "Walk on!"

There was a rattle of horseshoes on cobblestones and we lurched forwards. The curtain shifted and for a heartbeat there was enough light to see Farthing's blank face. Then we were rolling steadily and the blackness returned.

I managed to say, "Where are you taking me?"

This he ignored.

"Why did you cross the border?"

"Am I to be locked up again?"

"Refusing to answer may constitute..."

"Or am I to be beaten?"

I blurted the words, trying to stop him. But he would not be stopped.

"...may constitute deliberate obstruction. As a result of which, I, a sworn and commissioned agent of the

International Patent Office, am empowered to detain you pending resolution of the case under investigation."

"You'd quote the law at me?"

"It's your right to be informed."

"Then inform me – what happens when *you* break the law?"

"What are you doing with this paint and brush?" he asked.

"I'm going to be an artist!"

"Don't joke with me! Don't you know the danger you're facing? Baiting me isn't going to make things better."

His voice, so controlled at first, had grown louder. The coach slowed and I found myself thrown to the left as we turned a corner.

"Answer the question," he growled. "Why did you cross the border?"

"I came to seek justice."

"Don't lie to me!"

"Will everything I say be a lie until you hear what you want to hear? I crossed the border to make things right – since a sworn and commissioned agent of the Patent Office told me he'd no interest in justice!"

Again the carriage slowed and cornered – the other way this time. The curtain shifted and I caught another glimpse. This time his face was turned away from me and away from the light.

"What's the penalty for bribing someone like you?" I asked. "Death, isn't it? A man who did that would be hanged. But that would mean admitting the Patent Office makes mistakes."

"I offered to investigate," Farthing snapped.

"That was before we had enough evidence."

"There are agents to look into it! If you wish to—"

"How many agents were hanged this year? How many have ever been hanged?"

"That's not the point!"

"It's exactly the point! Who'd lock you up if you broke the law? No one! Because if the Patent Office broke the law, the Gas-Lit Empire would come crashing down!"

I was leaning forwards now, my voice harsh.

"The International Patent Office—"

"Is corrupt!" I shouted it into the dark, towards the place where his face had been.

"That's not true!"

"Yet here I am," I said. "Forced to cross into the Kingdom to make my own justice. Where at any moment I could be taken as the property of a man you chose not to pursue. You asked me why I crossed the border. I've told you the truth. But you're so blinded by faith that you can't accept it."

We lurched as a wheel dipped into a pothole. For a heartbeat, the interior of the carriage was lit and I could see his expression. Then the curtain had fallen back. But the afterimage remained – Farthing's face close to mine, since each of us was leaning forwards, his teeth bared, his face racked in what could have been anger or pain.

I sensed him shifting back in his seat. I did the same, wondering what emotion my own face might have betrayed in that same moment. I found myself breathing deeply.

"Why did you cross the border?" His voice was level once more.

"I came to kill His Grace the Duke of Northampton," I said. "Since you'd refused to do it by legal means, I would do it by murder."

"I simply don't believe you! The duke has an army at his

call. You know it couldn't be done. Even if you could have got in range and pulled the trigger – you'd be dead before you drew another breath. It makes no sense."

"You'd be right," I said. "If I'd wished to survive the act. But you must believe me, John Farthing, when I tell you that the last hope had been ripped from me. Living was never part of my plan. Nor was it my desire."

I waited for his response, but none came. The carriage turned once more but without the curtain shifting. As in a dream, I had no sense of what time had passed. Nor could I guess how far we'd come or in what direction we were now heading. There was little to hear outside beyond the sound of the horses and carriage wheels. Gradually my mind calmed and, as it did, a question crystallized. I should have thought of it as soon as I saw him on the street.

"How did you find me?"

Instead of answering, he reached up and rapped his knuckle on the roof boards. Inertia pulled me forwards as the coach abruptly slowed. I found myself sliding on the smooth leather, inching closer to him. Then we had stopped. I heard the driver clambering down and felt the carriage sway. The door opened with a click and gaslight flooded in.

The driver's face appeared. He held the paint and brush in one hand. "All done?" he asked.

Farthing nodded.

I took my things and stepped out, disorientated. Crowds mingled around street market stalls. In front of me three African men sat on stools, leather goods laid out on a cloth in front of them. We'd travelled in a circle. The ironmonger's shop was barely yards away.

I turned to confront Farthing, but the door had already closed. The driver was climbing back to his place. I shifted my head, trying to peer in through the carriage window, for it seemed the curtain might have been raised. But all I could see was the reflection of the streetlamp in the black glass.

The question of how Farthing had found me tumbled in my head as I ran back towards the rookery. We might have walked for a hundred years in that vast metropolis without our paths ever crossing by chance. Had he known the precise location of the tenement, we would have been overrun by agents of the Patent Office. More likely he'd some evidence we'd been lodging in St John's. He might have followed us back from the Grand Master's house. Or one of the duke's spies had been paid twice for the same intelligence.

Fearing I might lead him straight back to the others, I ducked down a cut between two low buildings, emerging after fifty paces in the next street. No one followed.

But approaching our tenement, I found the roadway packed with the ragged denizens of the rookery, who were pouring out of doorways and pressing up towards James Street. All were stirred up in angry excitement. I would not have dreamed so many bodies could have lived in such a small space.

Ellie was in the hallway waiting for me.

I had to shout to make myself heard over the uproar outside. "What's happening?"

"It's a fight," she cried, then took my hand.

But instead of climbing up to our rooms, she dragged me along a narrow passage, which issued out onto the street at the back, where more crowds were pushing past. There, we set off against the tide.

When the main mass of them had passed, I leaned in close and whispered, "I must know what's happened!"

"Have you got the paint?" she asked.

I held it up for her to see, whereupon she pulled me across the road and through a gateway to a tiny courtyard, filled almost entirely with a black carriage and four horses.

I opened my mouth to ask where it had come from, but then saw the emblem on the side-panel. Within a shield was a green oak tree, to one side of which three white stars hung, forming a triangle in a blue sky. It was the crest of the Duke of Northampton.

Yan was moving from horse to horse, whispering to each, calming them. Lara ran over to me.

"We were frightened for you," she said. "What happened?"

But before I could decide how or if to answer, Fabulo emerged from behind the coach. He grabbed the tin and brush from me and handed them to Lara, who was immediately at work, prising off the lid. I watched as she started to paint over the duke's emblem.

"You took it from the men-at-arms!" I said, aghast.

"They were busy kicking in doors," said Fabulo, excitement in his eyes. "Ellie's a smart driver. She had it turned and would have been away without them seeing, but the folk on the street started cheering her."

"There's a fight going on out there," I said.

"That there is, girl! Luck's running with us for once. The duke's men got rough with the crowd – thought they were in on the theft. That was the last straw. St John's has put up with enough already. Someone called riot and now everyone's on the street."

"It's the Duke of Northampton's carriage."

Fabulo grinned. "He was after finding you so bad. And now he's given us horses and a coach. And a riot! Everything we needed. It's poetry, that's what it is!"

Lara had worked her way around each side of the coach. She returned with the paint and brush. "It's done," she said. "It'll pass. From a distance."

The coach door opened and Jeremiah clambered out, followed by Tinker.

"All ready?" asked the locksmith.

"Ready," said Lara.

"And the riot?"

"It's the perfect misdirection," said Fabulo. "Everyone's looking the other way."

"You're certain of that, Mr Dwarf? We're going to be safe?"

"We've planned for how to pass the guards. And we're armed, ready for the Custodian of Marvels. We're as safe as may be."

He cleared his throat and the others turned to look at him. "In a minute, we're going to ride out of here and do what we've been fixing to do. After we start there'll be no turning back. So if anyone knows of a danger they haven't yet said, now's the time to tell it."

Thoughts churned inside my head as he swung his gaze around the courtyard. Too many thoughts for me to know the balance of them. He met my eyes last of all. I nodded, readying myself to admit that I'd been followed. But he just nodded back at me and his gaze moved on. And in that moment I was glad I hadn't put a stop to it.

"You see?" he said to Jeremiah. "The gods of chance play for us tonight."

CHAPTER 25
October 10th

A thing may be hidden in plain sight if only the audience does not want to see it.

THE BULLET-CATCHER'S HANDBOOK

We ran back to strip out everything from the tenement that could have been used to identify us. In the deserted roadway we made a pile of papers and other oddments, to which Yan set a match. Fabulo slipped the brass watch into his waistcoat pocket and tossed the empty Shagreen box on top of the fire.

The light from the flames made an eerie sight, our shadows dancing off walls and cobblestones. Hearing the sound of the riot in the distance, I found myself shivering. But the others seemed to see none of these omens. Buoyed up in mood by the sudden urgency, they set off back to the small courtyard.

Ellie draped herself in Jeremiah's coat and took her place up top on the driver's bench. With a bowler hat on her head she looked the part well enough. She would pass a first glance at least. And few people looked up at the drivers of carriages. The rest of us took our places inside.

Then I remembered something and felt my stomach clench in panic. "We forgot the water!" I cried. "The light machine won't work without it."

"It's here," said Yan, holding up a wine bottle.

"And here," said Lara, doing the same.

"And here," said Fabulo, showing me a third. "You see – nothing's forgotten. We've done our planning well. It's time to go."

He rapped his knuckle on the woodwork and we lurched forwards, turning sharply out of the gate and away.

At every turn, Fabulo leaned forwards to look out of the window. And each time he sat back it was to take out the brass watch, though sometimes only seconds had passed since he'd checked it.

"It's going to be tight," he muttered.

Outside, I heard the whip snapping in the air, as if Ellie had sensed his thoughts. We were picking up speed. I caught glimpses of St Paul's Cathedral and then the Guild Church of St Martin as we rattled down Ludgate.

"You're all ready?" Fabulo asked.

"We are," said Yan. "And won't be more ready from fretting."

"You have your lockpicks?"

Jeremiah nodded. "Yes – for the tenth time this hour!"

I put my arm around Tinker's shoulder and pulled him closer, wanting to send him away but knowing he'd follow me, whatever order I gave. Fabulo had told me the boy didn't want to be safe. He only wanted to belong. He might one day repent of such foolishness, if he lived long enough.

The coach slowed and we swayed into a tight right turn. I didn't recognise the buildings outside, but knew we must be cutting north, looping around towards Lincoln's Inn Fields and the back of the International Patent Court.

Fabulo was staring at the brass pocket watch, as if willing the second hand to move more slowly. My heart was beating at such speed Tinker must have felt it, us being pressed close together on the seat. He tilted his head to rest it on my shoulder. The carriage turned left then right. Though I couldn't see the great tower of the Patent Court, its shadow lay over the streets and buildings, making the darkness more complete. The carriage tilted on its springs as we turned once more and, through the window, I saw the silhouettes of trees and, far behind them, the lamps of the Inns of Court.

"We're here," said Jeremiah.

"We're late," said Fabulo. "The guards'll roll up in three minutes."

The carriage slowed, then jerked forwards again as Ellie aimed for the few yards of road that would give us the cover we needed. We stopped with a jolt.

Immediately Lara had the door open on the side facing the Patent Court. Jeremiah was out first, then Lara, Fabulo, Yan and Tinker. I followed in time to see the locksmith using the key he'd made. The click was so quiet I could have missed it from two paces. Then the gate was open and we were passing through into the expanse of the plaza beyond. Jeremiah locked the gate and we all looked to Fabulo, who gestured towards the ground. We dropped to hands and knees and began crawling towards the great building.

Behind us, Ellie made a clicking sound with her tongue. The horses responded and the carriage began to roll away.

The flagstones felt unnaturally smooth under my palms. I glanced back. The low wall below the railings blocked out the lights from the Inns of Court. We were in shadow,

just as Fabulo had said we would be when he explained
the plan. But something was different. Another coach was
rolling up outside the gate. From away in the darkness I
could make out the stamp of boots. The guards at the rear
door were forming up, ready to march. I'd crawled only a
quarter of the way. Then the Patent Court clock began to
chime the hour.

I could barely make out Fabulo in the darkness up ahead,
but sensed the movement of his arm waving. I crawled
faster, my knees hitting the stones with painful force.

The bootfalls of the soldiers echoed off the buttressed
wall that loomed ahead. And there were men marching
behind us now, the new guard arriving to relieve the old,
taking up their place just outside the gate.

A hand reached out of the darkness and pushed down on
my shoulders. It was Yan. I dropped flat to the stones. The
whisper of our crawling had stopped. I twisted my neck and
saw that the others had done the same. We were marooned
halfway across with no cover but the shadow and our own
stillness.

I could hear the breath ebbing and flowing through my
nostrils. But louder now were the marching boots. From
that low angle, I could see the double line of soldiers
approaching, the faint light touching their upper bodies.
Each carried a shouldered musket.

Closer now, I caught the glint from their bayonets. I held
my breath, for it seemed their march would bring them
directly over us. I closed my eyes for fear the whites would
show.

The noise of their marching grew, seeming impossibly
loud. And then it was receding. I looked and saw that
they had passed close to our left. They reached the gate

and stamped to attention. Immediately outside their replacements did the same.

And now I could see another figure – a short man in a ridiculously tall hat making casual progress along the road. The key holder was arriving to play his part. The hour chimes were sounding. I counted them. On the eleventh stroke, the gate swung open and the guard marched out. There was a clang as the gate closed again.

"Now," hissed Fabulo, his voice no more than a breath. He began to crawl and one by one we got back to our hands and knees and followed. Every few yards, I found myself glancing back. This would not be the usual nine minutes of humiliation. On this one day in the year, the key holder had over an hour to taunt the representatives of the Patent Office.

With twenty yards to go, we passed beyond the shadow of the low wall. Looking back, I could make out the lamps of the Inns of Court, but they were so far distant now that we would only have been seen had the guards been staring directly at us.

Then the shadow of a mighty buttress swallowed us. I climbed to my feet, my knees stinging from the punishment they'd taken.

"That was the hardest part," Fabulo whispered.

"So are all the other parts," replied Jeremiah.

I felt rather than heard Lara suppressing a laugh. It was relief, I guessed.

"Are you ready?" asked Fabulo.

We all nodded.

"Go slow. Go steady. And go silent."

So saying, he led the way out from the shadow and along next to the wall. The building was like a cliff face above us.

Looking up at it made my stomach lurch, so I focused on the ground in front of me, concentrating on placing each foot in silence.

But a movement beyond the railings caught my eye. Another figure was advancing along the road outside the perimeter. I could tell it was a man, though he was too distant to see in any detail. There were no others about. Only the key holder and the troop of guards waiting outside the gate. And this one man, who now had my attention so caught that I hardly noticed the others had stopped. We had reached the door that the soldiers would guard. Fabulo was getting everyone to lie on the ground next to the wall, except for Jeremiah, who knelt next to the door itself.

He was unrolling a leather bundle on the slabs, revealing an array of picks and torsion bars. From these he selected three items, the shapes of which I couldn't make out. I saw now that as well as a keyhole, the door had a padlock. Though I hadn't seen it assembled, I recognised the shapes of metal I'd seen laid out in the Grand Master's workshop. There could be no doubting that this was the timer lock, just as Jeremiah had described it. I could even hear the ticking of the mechanism within.

Fabulo poked me on the leg and I got down onto the stones like the others. The man outside the railings had passed us and was advancing towards the soldiers at the gate, so I turned my attention back to Jeremiah, who was probing in the keyhole with the picks, two of them in one hand and one in the other. Such was the delicacy of his control, he seemed more a musician than a locksmith.

Then the clocks of London began to chime the hour. From near and far came the tolling of bells. On any other night of the year, the new guard would be allowed in. But with the clocks going back, there was still an hour for them to wait. If we'd figured it all correctly.

The last bells finished chiming. The key holder had not moved to open the gate, instead, he set off ambling around the group of soldiers. I let out a breath I hadn't realised I'd been holding.

With a sharp metallic double *clack*, the timer lock sprung open. The sound echoed back at us from the low wall.

The lone figure on the road had stopped in his tracks. I watched him turn. Then he was hurrying back towards the place outside the railings nearest to us. And seeing him run with that powerful, open stride, my heart seemed to stop.

There was another sound, much softer this time. Jeremiah turned the handle of the door and pushed it open.

The locksmith was first inside. Then Lara, Yan and Tinker. Fabulo beckoned for me to follow.

I pointed to where Farthing stood, a clear silhouette. Fabulo grabbed my hand and pulled.

"We're seen!" I hissed.

But Fabulo shook his head, as if rejecting the evidence of his eyes. Then he grabbed my hand and hauled me inside. The door closed behind us and all was black.

CHAPTER 26
10.03pm

The plan that no one else has thought of may be genius or
delusion. Time alone will reveal which.

THE BULLET-CATCHER'S HANDBOOK

There was camphor somewhere nearby and the space in
which we stood stretched out ahead of me. I knew this
before anything else, before even a light had been struck.
As I sniffed the air, I heard a click from the door behind us.
Then a lucifer fizzed to life and oil lamps were being lit and
I saw that Jeremiah had pulled a handle on the door.

"Locked it," he said. "Even with a key it won't open from
outside now."

Yan held one of the oil lamps close to the ceiling and
I saw that we stood at the end of a downward sloping
corridor, square in cross section. The walls were brick,
though painted white. The floor had been laid with the
same grey flagstones we'd crawled over in the plaza.
The ceiling was grey also, though I couldn't guess what
it might be made of. Set into it every few yards were
circles of glass, which reminded me of portholes – though
if they'd been portholes the ship would have been lying

on its side. I found myself shivering.

"Lead the way," said Fabulo.

At which, the locksmith set off and the others followed. I grabbed Fabulo's shoulder and held him back until we had a few yards of privacy. Then I bent low and whispered in his ear.

"Are you mad?"

He batted my hand away. "I'm doing what we planned!"

"But we've been seen!"

"He was no one."

"It was John Farthing!"

That stopped him in his tracks.

"What?"

"It was Agent Farthing. We could have given ourselves up. Out there, we'd only broken a Kingdom law. But now…"

"Are you certain?"

"It was him."

"Then how did he find us?"

I looked away. Fabulo grabbed my wrist. "What aren't you saying?"

Then Lara turned to look back at us. "Is all well? Lizzy?"

Fabulo gave my wrist a warning squeeze.

"It's all good," I said, then hurried after her.

Within thirty paces, the slope of the corridor levelled off and we came to the first of the doors, one on each side of the corridor. The Roman numeral "I" had been carved into the stone lintel above the one on the right. The lintel on the left bore the numerals "II".

"Rooms one and two," said Fabulo.

"Can you open them?" asked Yan.

"I can and I will," said Jeremiah.

"Not today," said Fabulo.

"But that's what we came for," said Yan.

"Find the door marked XI. That's where we start."

None of them liked it. Nor could Fabulo explain the reason for the sudden urgency with which he drove them forward. Only I knew.

When I'd seen the man outside the railings, I'd been certain it was Farthing. But doubt had started to grow in me. Perhaps my feelings for the man had warped my perception. And even if it had been, he might not have been able to see us. Indeed, when we had been outside the railings, I hadn't been able to make out the base of the wall.

But, one way or the other, there was nothing now that could be done. We would be hanged for breaking into the building. There could be no greater punishment for pressing on.

"A penny for your thoughts," said Lara.

I hadn't noticed her drawing close as we walked.

"We're doing it," I said, trying to hide my disquiet. "All that planning and here we are."

I had the feeling she was about to press me further. But, in front of us, Jeremiah had come to a stop in front of a door. "This is it," he said, pointing to the lintel stone, on which the letters "XI" had been carved.

He knelt and unwrapped his leather bundle on the floor, choosing a torsion bar with a thin, springy arm. This he fitted in the keyhole, resting his little finger on the end. It flexed under the pressure. The pick itself was unlike any I'd seen before. Instead of a single spike of metal, it forked halfway along. He had to push the two tines together before they would fit into the hole.

"Light!" he snapped. "More light."

Fabulo grabbed a lamp from Tinker and held it close to where Jeremiah worked.

"And must you crowd me, little man?"

"I must if you'll have light!"

I eased the lamp from Fabulo's hand and held it close to the door, but above the locksmith's head, out of his line of sight. Yan did the same with the other lamp.

Jeremiah didn't jiggle the pick in and out of the keyhole in that random way that I might have tried. His sausage-like fingers moved with such delicacy that it was clear he knew exactly what he was feeling for. He whispered numbers under his breath.

"Eight. Nine. Ten."

Then the torsion bar dropped with a hollow sounding click.

"Done," he said.

"What did I tell you?" said Fabulo, to no one or to everyone. "The man's an artist."

It was Fabulo who turned the handle and opened the door. A breath issued from the room, like a sigh. The smell of camphor was suddenly more intense. We followed him inside and saw rank upon rank of storage shelves stretching off into the distance beyond the reach of our raised lamps. On each shelf rested wooden crates beyond my counting. They were plain, except for code numbers stencilled onto the face of each.

The ceiling was not high. At first I marvelled that such a span could stand without supporting pillars. But then I saw that there were iron columns built into the shelving and that they must be taking the weight of whatever lay above.

"What's that?" asked Tinker, pointing to a small lever on

the wall next to the door.

"Don't touch…" began Fabulo.

But Yan had already reached out and was pulling the lever down. There was a soft popping sound and in that instant the entire room became flooded with white light. The effect was so dramatic and unexpected that all of us ducked. Then, having come to no harm, we looked up and saw that the light was shining from behind the glass circles.

"Windows," whispered Yan.

"Not unless the sun's risen in the night," said Jeremiah.

"They're lamps," I said, for I'd made out some of the detail behind the glass. Each circle had a niche behind it and within that was a centre of brightness.

"If they were lamps, we'd hear the hissing of the gas."

"I told you we'd see marvels," said Fabulo. "This is the first of many. But we've no time to gawp. Lizzy's machine lies at this code…" He pulled the court record from his pocket and unfolded it: "*IPC XI XXVI III DXIV.* The first three letters are the building. The second three are this room. So go search for the others."

We spread out left and right, but for Tinker who, not being able to read, stayed close by my side. There were more roman numerals stencilled on the end of each rack of shelving. And the shelves were themselves numbered from "I" on the lowest level to "VI" just under the ceiling.

The numbering system proved more complex than it had seemed. I was acutely aware of our precious time slipping away as we searched, my frustration and fear building with every minute. Then Lara shouted from the far end of the room. We all ran to where she stood, pointing to a box on the third shelf up.

Yan took it down and placed it on the ground before me.

The lid hinged back and there inside was the machine I'd hoped never to see again – an assemblage of tubes, flasks and mirrors. And next to it lay two demijohns of liquid, the reagents that would cause it to create a ray of intense light.

"That can never damage metal," said Lara, incredulous. "It's little more than glass!"

I reached into the crate and lifted it out. "This little machine can punch a hole clean through an iron gatepost. And that from a mile away."

Fabulo eased it from my hands, which I now saw were trembling. "We'd best not drop it then," he said.

Yan reached up to the topmost shelf and began taking down other crates, placing them on the floor. Lara opened one and pulled a glass flask from a bed of cotton wool. Its end was capped with silvery metal. She held it up for us to see. Within it, fine filaments of wire were suspended.

"What does it do?" asked Tinker.

Lara handed it to Jeremiah, who shrugged and passed it to Yan.

The next crate contained more flasks, these nearly spherical in shape. The filaments within were curled rather than straight. Yan was trying to unscrew the metal cap from one. It came away suddenly with a pop and a crunch of breaking glass. He sucked air over his teeth. There was a drop of blood on his hand.

"I've broken it," he said.

"But what do they do?" asked Lara, taking down yet another crate.

"Stop!" said Fabulo. "We must move on."

"I don't see why," grumbled Yan, who was sucking his finger. "We have the time. And a treasury, you said. Marvels beyond count."

"Treasure there is. But the greatest of it all will be further in."

Scowling his defiance, Yan opened three more boxes. I tried to peer inside, but Fabulo slammed the lids closed.

"We go!"

Yan looked ready to make trouble. But Jeremiah said, "The dwarf is right." Then he started back between the shelves and everyone followed.

I don't know what Fabulo thought about the help he was getting from a man who usually argued, but I knew his real reason. The locks themselves were Jeremiah's treasure. Or, rather, the opening of them. For only by cracking locks he'd never been shown could he find the peace he desired.

Back in the corridor, I searched for and found another of the small levers on the wall. Not asking Fabulo's permission, I pulled it down. Light flooded in from the niches in the ceiling. So bright was the corridor that our lamps hardly seemed lit.

"All this time we thought they put unseemly science out of use," said Fabulo. "Now we see they hoard the best things for themselves."

"How can light be unseemly?" asked Lara.

"They think it too good for us!" said Yan.

Jeremiah had been standing still as a gatepost since the lights came on, staring towards a door that blocked the end of the passage ahead. Abruptly he lurched towards it, striding so fast that I was obliged to run to keep up.

The door's surface was made of riveted metal. He placed his hand on it. I watched as he leaned his weight against it, shifting his head left and right as he did so, as if searching for tiny movements.

He went down on his knees and was putting his eye to

a keyhole as the others caught up. Then he shifted lower and peered in through a second keyhole. I watched as he unwrapped the leather bundle and selected a probe with a tiny round mirror attached to the end. He had to turn it to the vertical to get it inside the lock, but once there it had freedom to rotate. He dipped into a pocket and pulled out an optical device, which fitted like a monocle over one eye, yet projected like a camera lens.

Fabulo consulted his brass watch and seemed about to speak. I put a finger to my lips and gestured for all to back away. The locksmith now shifted his mirror and lenses to the other keyhole. Fabulo turned the watch towards me. Only twenty minutes remained before the soldiers could return to their place outside the door. Farthing also – if it had been him, and if he had seen us. He would surely bring an army of agents to track us down.

But there was another question in my mind. When I'd been interrogated, had John Farthing been watching through the half silvered mirror? Something had stopped the interrogator from beating me to unconsciousness. His arm had been drawn back ready to strike. Then he'd looked towards the mirror and walked out as if called away. If it was Farthing who'd stopped the beating, if he couldn't bear to see a fist smashing at my face, then how would he react to the prospect of a noose being placed around my neck? If he simply turned around and pretended to have seen nothing, the authorities would never find out.

I might almost have convinced myself that, when the time elapsed, there would be no agents following us inside. But my judgement had been twisted by longing.

"Here and here," said Jeremiah, scratching two crosses on the metal door, one near each keyhole.

"What?"

"Place your machine back twenty yards. Then aim its light where I marked."

Fabulo was already on the move, carrying the machine back. Jeremiah nodded and he laid it on the floor. "Now, Lizzy," he said. "Time to earn your share."

Lara had been carrying the two demijohns. These she placed next to the machine, while Tinker laid down a bottle of water. Everyone was looking at me.

I stepped to the machine and knelt, trying to remember the sequence of actions. There were two reservoirs. These I unscrewed, almost filling each with water. Then I decanted a few drops from the demijohns so that each reservoir took a different liquid.

With each step, my memory crystallized and I became more confident. There was a small lever, almost hidden within the maze of glassware. I depressed it and the two reservoirs drained, filling a central tube. The final step was to turn a handle on the side. A faint whirring issued from the machine and a beam of light, pencil thin, hung in the air before my face.

"There," I said.

"I see nothing," said Jeremiah.

So I twisted the mirror mounted into the machine, angling the light lower, sending it lancing along the corridor to paint a single spot on the door near where he'd marked a cross.

They all saw it then, and crowded in closer.

"This is just to find our aim," I said.

"Then move it left three inches."

It took me several minutes to find the spot exactly, for the slightest touch would make the spot of light jump.

When Jeremiah pronounced himself satisfied, I let the liquid drain and refilled the flasks, but this time with a far greater concentration of the reagents.

"Everyone stand clear," I said.

With one hand braced on the machine to stop it shifting, I began to turn the handle. I had only turned it three times when there was a sharp report from the door, like the firing of a pistol.

I'd seen nothing, but knew that all the energy of the reagents had been consumed in a span so short that no eye could have detected it.

Jeremiah approached the lock and reached out a finger with the caution of one stealing cheese from a mousetrap. "She's done it," he said.

The second cross took just as long to hit. Again I turned the handle. Again we heard that sharp crack. Then Jeremiah inserted a torsion bar into each keyhole and twisted them. Fabulo pushed and the door that had barred our way swung open.

"We're in!"

Lara, Yan and Tinker all grinned with their excitement. But Jeremiah frowned, running his hand over the edge of the door. Fabulo consulted the watch. He was also frowning. I met his eye. He made the smallest nod and I knew our time had gone.

Lara and Tinker carried the machine and its flasks of liquid through the doorway. As we followed, Fabulo asked Jeremiah, "Can you lock it behind us?"

"I could," the locksmith replied. "But why would I want to?"

Before Fabulo could answer, a low boom reverberated in the throat of the corridor. I felt it through my feet as much as my ears. We all looked back in the direction of the entrance.

"What was that?" asked Lara.

A second boom followed, louder than the first.

"I think they're trying to break down the door," said Fabulo. "Now, can we lock this one please? In some way that they won't open it from the other side."

CHAPTER 27
11.15pm

Misdirect the eye to create illusion. Misdirect expectation to create amazement. Illusion without surprise is nothing.

THE BULLET-CATCHER'S HANDBOOK

I counted ten seconds before another boom reverberated from the walls. The outer door had been made of iron, banded and studded for strength, but if they had a battering ram it wouldn't stand for long.

I searched for and found another small lever on the wall. Pulling it caused white light to shine down at us from the ceiling. This time none of us ducked. How quickly the miraculous had become commonplace.

Instead of a corridor ahead, the light revealed a flight of stairs spiralling down.

Having unscrewed a small panel in the edge of the door, Jeremiah was poking around inside the lock mechanism. He inserted a pair of narrow nosed pliers and snipped twice. Each time, I heard the twang of a wire being cut.

"That'll do it," he said, pushing the door closed and turning the torsion bar in the keyholes. "I've disconnected the drum of the locks. No key will open it from that side."

"Quick then," said Fabulo. "Down the stairs."

But Jeremiah planted his feet. "You knew we were being followed," he said.

"I did not."

"You asked me if I could lock the door. That was before you heard…"

The door rattled with another distant impact.

"It was a precaution," said Fabulo.

"Saying that don't cut it, Mr Dwarf. You knew!"

"I feared."

"Yet chose not to tell?"

"If I told you half the fears I carry, you'd lie down and weep!"

"If there was a risk, I'd the right to know. We all had!"

"Well, you know it now!"

Another tremor reverberated around us. Both men looked back towards the door. Jeremiah drew in breath, as if to speak.

"Argue later," I said, cutting in.

"Lizzy's right," said Lara. "We've no time."

Jeremiah's shoulders dropped, though his face remained grim.

The stairs wound clockwise as we descended. I counted three and a half turns before we reached a new corridor. By my reckoning it would lead us back along the same line we'd been walking, but several fathoms deeper in the earth.

Lara found the control for the lights and flicked them on. Ten paces ahead another metal door barred our way.

"I'm going to pick this one," said Jeremiah.

"Will that be quicker than the machine?" asked Fabulo.

The locksmith wouldn't answer.

"Then the machine it is!"

"I'm going to pick it!"

Without waiting for approval he got down on his knees, unrolled his bundle of tools and set to work. Fabulo began to pace, clenching and unclenching his fists. I sat on the lowest step and listened. The boom of the outermost door being rammed had grown quieter as we descended. I had to focus to detect it. But there it was. It had been ten seconds between impacts when it started. Now it was eight.

Tinker came and sat on the step. "Will it all work out?" he asked.

"Yes," I said, trying to make the lie sound true.

"Good," he said, and I felt the warmth of him as he rested his slight body against me.

"Sometimes things happen though," I said, after a pause. "Things we don't expect."

"I know that," he said, and sighed.

I was about to say more, but Fabulo exclaimed, "You're no closer to cracking it!"

"It'll be done when it's done," growled Jeremiah.

"We could have been through already with the machine!"

"I must have a chance to pick one of them. That's my price for helping you!"

"So you're giving away your share?"

"There will be no share! The deeper we go, the more trapped we are!"

Lara had been sitting on the floor all this time, with her back resting against the white painted bricks. I saw her body stiffen. Then she jumped up and cried, "Hush, all of you!"

Everybody listened. It was so quiet that I could hear the ticking of Fabulo's brass watch. I counted under my breath until I could be sure. "They've stopped," I said.

Lara tilted her head. "Have they given up?"

But Fabulo had grabbed the machine and was hefting it towards me. "They've broken through," he said. "That's why they've stopped. There's no more time for picking!"

Practice made me quicker about my work. I set it up on the third step, giving a level aim at the spot Jeremiah marked. Then I fuelled it with the concentrated reagents and turned the handle. With a loud crack, a pencil thin hole appeared in the metal. Jeremiah poked a hook through it and extracted a loop of fine wire. With one firm pull the latch clicked and the lock was undone.

Fabulo punched the air with his stubby fist. The locksmith scowled.

Then a new noise began – a machine noise, high pitched, teeth jarring and unbearably loud. It screamed down at us from the corridor above. We all covered our ears against the pain of it.

Jeremiah hauled back the door and we dived through into a new stretch of corridor. Lights blinked on, though I didn't see who'd pulled the lever. Yan started to heave the door closed.

"Wait!" I shouted. "We must know what we're facing."

Fingers wedged in my ears, I slipped back out. But, as I began to climb the spiral stairs, the sound cut to nothing. In the silence that followed, it felt as if I could still hear the mechanical scream inside my head.

I rounded the final bend, fearing I might see the door already breached, but it stood. On first sight I thought it just as we'd left it. I stepped closer. There was a vertical line next to the lock. Another step and I saw it was not a line, but a cut of several inches in length. I pulled the lever on the wall, turning off the ceiling lights. The crack shone in the new darkness. Light was seeping through it from the other side of the door.

I was reaching out to touch it, when the light dimmed. A toothed blade poked through, like the circular saw of a wood mill.

Then the blade began to turn, screeching against the metal, accelerating, its cry becoming higher and louder. Some hand on the other side must have hefted it forwards. The blade bit into the door and the banshee scream began again. Sparks of hot metal showered out towards me.

I jumped back, then ran.

The door at the base of the stairs was ajar. Fabulo beckoned me through. They slammed it behind me.

"Locked," said Jeremiah.

"It won't hold long," I said, still shouting though the scream was muffled now. "They've some devilish machine. It's biting through the metal."

So we gathered up our things and hauled them as fast as we could along the length of the passage, ignoring doors to left and right. Though the volume dropped as we increased our distance, it remained frightful and unearthly.

Each time it stopped, I found myself dreading it starting again. And dreading it not starting, also. For that would mean the lock had been cut from the door and they would be after us down the spiral stairs.

Lara flipped a wall lever, illuminating the next stretch of passageway, revealing another door in our way. Jeremiah set off towards it in a loping run. Fabulo followed, but he was already wheezing and panting and couldn't keep up.

"Wait!" shouted Yan. "Stop!"

They did.

He beat a hand against his wide chest. Distress racked his face. "Is there even a plan?"

"We keep going," said Fabulo.

"Is that it? You think the tunnels go on forever?"

"I know what I'm doing! We go deeper."

"That's no plan at all!"

"You have something better?" asked Lara.

"I do," said Yan, nodding vigorously, his forked beard waving beneath his chin. "We break into one of these side rooms. We find something to fight with. Must be guns here somewhere. Then we face them."

"You want to kill them?" shouted Fabulo.

"If we must!"

"How many? They'll bring an army. You going to kill them all? No. There's only one way out of here. We go on. We get to the Custodian and take him hostage. Then we can bargain our way free."

Yan stared at him. "So you did have a plan? You should have told us."

"I couldn't," said Fabulo. "I've only just thought it up."

The cutting machine went quiet as Jeremiah inspected the lock of the next door. After half a minute, we were all listening for it to start up again. After a minute of silence, I knew they must have broken through. Then the metallic screaming began again, closer and louder.

This time Jeremiah did not try to argue for picking. It took me little time to set up the machine and punch a hole where he indicated. Through this he poked his tools. So loud was the cutting machine, I didn't hear the click of the lock as it opened.

Once more we gathered up our things and hurried

through, putting another door between us and our pursuers. I found the lever for the lights and flicked it on, revealing a short stretch of passage and another flight of spiral stairs leading deeper into the earth. It was identical to the previous set. Indeed, it could have been the same place, but for a smell of cooked meat.

Tinker raised his nose and sniffed the air. He moved his head from side to side. Then he scampered off, down the stairs. I followed around the spiral, lagging behind.

"Slow down," I called.

But he was away from me, his feet quicker on the stones. I tried to go faster, but slipped and had to steady myself with a hand on the wall. As I took a breath to recover from my near disaster, I heard a sound from below, a scrape of fabric on stone as if the boy had fallen, but no cry followed.

I leapt down the stairs, rounding the final turn to see a man pinning Tinker to the wall, holding a knife to his neck.

He was more bull than man – broad shouldered and carrying so much muscle that his arms were as thick as thighs. He was dressed in black from hat to shoes, but not in the way of a hired thug. The tailoring was fine, the silk of his top hat shining in the light from the ceiling niches. As was the blade of his knife.

Lara was next around the stairs. She cried out, whereupon the others came charging down. They pulled up short next to me.

"Give up or I cut his throat," said the bull man.

"Hurt him and we kill you," growled Fabulo.

The metal cutter had been quiet for the last few seconds. Now it started up again.

The bull man nodded. "We'll see who can wait longest," he said.

Yan unbuttoned his jacket and opened it wide, displaying a line of knives, each snug in its own pocket. He drew out three, and held them up, gripping the blades together between finger and thumb.

"Just a warning," said Fabulo.

Yan nodded. In one movement, he tossed all three knives in an arc, as if he would juggle them. But instead he snatched them from the air, one after the other. The bull man braced himself for attack, switching his grip.

That was his mistake. Or perhaps it saved him. Yan's arm shot out. The knife that had been at Tinker's throat jumped as if it were alive. It clattered to the floor. Then everyone rushed forwards and all was reversed. Yah held a blade to the bull man's throat. Tinker broke free and ran to my side. He wrapped his arms around me and buried his face in my breast. His every limb was shaking. I pulled him closer, feeling a pang of emotion so strong that my heart put in a double beat.

The bull man's knife lay on the floor, the tip of one of Yan's blades embedded in its hilt.

I felt the boy's muscles begin to loosen.

"Told you we'd be fine," I whispered.

"Search him," Fabulo barked.

Lara jumped to it. While Yan's knife held him motionless, she patted around his huge shoulders and down his jacket, inside and out. She handed his pocket watch and handkerchief to Fabulo, then a bunch of keys, which Jeremiah took and began to examine in minute detail. Lara moved down to the bull man's trousers. She frisked none too gently up the inside of his leg, the impact of her hand making him suck air through his teeth. Finally she yanked up his right trouser leg to reveal a sheath strapped to the calf, in which rested a second knife. This Yan took, testing its balance by tossing it from hand to hand.

Lara stood back and nodded.

"What's your name?" said Fabulo.

The man's eyes flicked from person to person, as if considering his options. "Chronis," he said.

"Mr Chronis?"

"Agent Chronis."

"What were you doing here?"

"Eating lunch."

"It's midnight," said Fabulo.

"That's when I have lunch."

"He's a night worker," I said.

Chronis nodded. "Do you know you're going to die?"

Jeremiah held up the bunch of keys. "What doors do they open?"

"I've given you my name," said Chronis. "But I'll not give more."

"I could kill you right here," growled Yan.

"If you must. But I won't betray my vows."

Fabulo made a shake of the head. "One more thing," he said. "Are you the Custodian of Marvels?"

Chronis blinked rapidly, as if the question had caught him off guard. He closed his eyes and swallowed. I thought he was about to confess that he was, but instead he smiled.

Fabulo's anger burst out in a shout. "Answer me!"

"My name is Agent Chronis," he said.

Through this exchange, Jeremiah had been kneeling at the next door that barred our way. Now he stood and turned the handle. It opened onto another stretch of passageway. I was about to ask if he'd picked the lock, but saw him withdrawing one of the keys.

Once more we gathered our things and filed through, but slower this time because Yan had to manoeuvre Chronis through. Though unarmed, I didn't doubt his capacity for destruction should he break free.

Jeremiah set to work unscrewing the end plate of the lock and disabling it as before. The machine noise had stopped. However fast we went, they'd been able to match us. I braced myself for it to start again, nearer and louder.

Instead, I heard a brittle hiss issuing from somewhere close by. Everyone but the locksmith stopped. I turned my head, trying to locate the sound. It was issuing from a small grille in the wall. My eye had passed over similar grilles in the corridors above. I'd taken them to be the covers of ventilation ducts.

I edged closer. The noise had been akin to dry sand being stirred. Now it changed to a sharp crackling, like gravel being ground under a boot. Then a man's voice barked: "Attention Jeremiah Cavendish. Attention the performer known as Fabulo. Attention Elizabeth Barnabus. This is Agent John Farthing. You are instructed to lay down your weapons and surrender."

CHAPTER 28
11.55pm

Alone among craftsmen, the bullet catcher must hide his skill. For, once glimpsed, the illusion would be gone forever.

The Bullet-Catcher's Handbook

No magic could have amazed me so completely as Farthing's voice issuing from the wall. In volume and immediacy he sounded close. Yet this impression jarred with the thin, metallic quality of the sound.

Fabulo's eyes were wide. Lara held both hands in front of her mouth. Tinker pulled himself tighter against me. All were waiting for new words to break through the dry crackling.

"Best do what he says," said Agent Chronis, his voice a dry whisper. Yan's knife was still tight against his windpipe.

Jeremiah bent to bring his face close to the metal grille. His finger found the screws that seemed to hold it in place. But there was another detail I hadn't noticed before – a button no bigger than a threepenny bit, flush with the rim and made of the same dull metal.

He was tracing the edge of it when the crackling changed and Farthing's voice again barked from the wall.

"Attention, intruders. This is Agent Farthing. You *must* lay down your weapons. Failure to comply will result in lethal force being authorised."

"It's a speaking tube," said Jeremiah. "Like on a ship. But with something else at work. Perhaps a fan to carry the words more perfectly."

"And what of the lamps?" said Fabulo. "Do they work through tubes also? No. There are marvels here we've been denied. The Patent Office have been hoarding for their own good comfort!"

Farthing's voice crackled through the grille: "Attention. Be aware that failure to respond will be taken as refusal. You have one minute."

Fabulo spat at the wall. "Lethal force?" he shouted. "I'll give you lethal force!"

"He can't hear you," said Chronis.

"Then how, by all the powers, does he expect us to respond!"

"You have to use the button."

I prised myself free from Tinker's arms. Fabulo nodded and I pressed it. The dry noise ceased.

"This is Elizabeth Barnabus," I said.

I pulled my finger back and the crackling returned. Seconds passed, agonisingly slow.

"We'll move on to the next door," said Fabulo. "The bastard's just trying to hold us up."

"I'll stay a while longer," I said. "Lara, you've watched me. Could you work the machine if it's needed?"

She nodded, grim-faced.

"You be careful, girl," said Fabulo.

"I will."

As they started away, I put my finger on the button again.

"Attention Agent Farthing. This is Elizabeth Barnabus. Please respond."

In my mind's eye, I saw him standing next to a wall just as I was, his head bowed. He had said that we would meet as enemies, and here we were, the criminal and the agent of law. Yet there was something else. Behind and below the awful inevitability of the roles we were playing out, he was in pain. I'd heard it in his voice through the machine just as I'd felt it before in the darkened carriage. But, until now, I'd not understood his love for me with such blinding clarity.

There was a bitter irony in our situation. I found myself laughing.

Then his voice came through the grille. "This is John Farthing." It sounded more intimate than before, as if he was whispering from very close. "Elizabeth? Are you still there?"

I pressed the button. "I'm here. And I'm alone."

"Oh, what have you done!" he said. From the desperation in his voice, I knew he was alone also.

"I've done what I had to."

"You must give up."

"To be hanged?"

"At least that way there's a chance."

"It's no chance at all."

"Death penalties can be commuted, if you show good will. Persuade the others, or... or come back and unlock the door."

"So they can be hanged and I can spend the rest of my life in a prison?"

"It would be something!"

"Are you so desperate to save me that you'd have me betray my friends?"

He didn't answer. In the distance I heard a door opening. There'd been no time for Lara to use the light machine, so one of the keys must have worked. If I didn't follow soon, I'd be left behind.

I pressed the button again. "We have a prisoner," I said. "Agent Chronis. I could persuade the others not to kill him, but you'll have to let us run free."

Seconds passed before he answered. "You have less to bargain with than you think." His voice had returned to cold formality. "We have a prisoner also. I can authorise an exchange. But no more than that."

"Who?" I asked, dreading the answer, for I already knew what it must be.

"She hasn't told us her name, but she was driving the carriage that brought you."

On hearing the news, Lara's face whitened to ash. Fabulo was first to her side, doing his best to hold her upright, despite his stature. Then I took her other arm. Together we lowered her to the floor. She sat, face in hands, shoulders rigid, breathing too fast. I looked to Fabulo and knew that her reaction had been no surprise to him.

"His life must be worth more to them than that," said Yan.

"They can't bargain," said Chronis.

"They'll soon bargain if I leave them your ears to find!"

There was fear in the agent's eyes. Enough fear for me to know he spoke the truth.

"It's the law," he said. "An agent's life can't be traded. They can only swap me for her because it's not letting her go. There's no way for you to get out."

I looked to where Lara sat, bent forwards. Fabulo was rubbing her back and her breathing had slowed. "Let's take the trade," I said.

"Why?" asked Yan. "If there's no way out?"

"We've got a bunch of keys," I said. "While I'm holding them up negotiating, you can be pressing on ahead. In this place, who knows what you might find?"

Jeremiah let me through. "Good luck," he said, then wedged the door ajar. Feeling intensely alone, I began to retrace my way along the passage.

All I'd said to the others had been true. By negotiating, I could slow our pursuers. They might try to grab me. That was a risk. But if they really believed we had no way out, there was nothing for them to lose in trading honourably. They would surely want to save the life of Agent Chronis.

All the minutes I occupied talking to them would be time my comrades could use. If we could find our way to the very end of the tunnels, we'd be in a stronger position. It was against the law for them to let us free in exchange for one of their own. The same might not be true to save the Custodian.

I had reached the door barring the passage ahead. The speaking grille was silent. I pressed the button.

"Attention, Agent Farthing. This is Elizabeth Barnabus. Please respond. We want to trade."

I could feel my heart beating faster as I waited. Though my logic was faultless, that alone would not have been reason enough for me to take the risk.

The grille crackled.

"This is Agent Farthing. What do you propose?"

"You'll have cut through to the next section soon enough. I want you to step through alone. I'll do the same and we can parley."

•••

I turned the torsion bar in the lock, as Jeremiah had showed me and heard it click open. The noise of the cutting machine was suddenly louder as I stepped through. He'd also given me a sliver of wood, which I used to wedge the door.

"Don't let it shut with you on the wrong side," he'd said.

I advanced down the passage towards the noise. I could see sparks fountaining from the door ahead. Threads of smoke drifted close to the ceiling and there was an acrid smell in the air. With one final shriek, the machine pulled back. The engine noise subsided. Then there was a sharp impact and a rectangle of metal fell to the floor.

I stopped, feeling the queasiness of fear and excitement.

The door swung half open and John Farthing stepped through. There were other faces crowding behind him, but he turned and pushed the door closed again, shutting them out. Then he scooped up the rectangle of cut metal and fitted it back in the hole.

I'd intended to wait for him so we could meet halfway. But, as he closed the distance and I began to see the pain in his expression, my feet began to carry me forwards, one step after another. It was he that started running first. We threw ourselves into each other's arms.

He held me.

For a moment, I knew nothing but the touch of his cheek against mine, the heat of him and the scent of his skin. I closed my eyes and pressed myself more firmly against his body.

"Elizabeth." My name burst from his mouth.

"John," I whispered back.

"I'm so sorry," he said. "It should never have been like this."

I don't know how long we stood entwined. It may have been only seconds. The effort of will it took for me to pull away was like nothing I'd experienced before. We held each other at arm's length. His eyes, his beautiful eyes, locked with mine. I stepped back.

"Remember," I said. "Whatever happens next, what we just felt was real."

He nodded, then looked down to the ground between us and would no more meet my eyes.

"It's time to make the bargain," I said, though speaking the words felt like driving nails into my own flesh.

"We have your driver," he said. "You have Agent Chronis. Do you still wish to exchange?"

"Yes."

"How do you wish to do it?"

"Can you control your men?"

"I can."

"Then it'll work. We each go back to our own side. You'll send your prisoner walking towards us. When she passes the halfway point, we'll send ours. But if he tries to grab her or if any of your men do anything stupid, then things will turn out bad. Do you understand?

"I do."

"And do you agree?"

"I do. And I…" His words faltered. He was breathing heavily.

"What?"

"I must ask once more for you and your collaborators to put down your weapons and surrender. If you fail to do so, I'll be obliged… be obliged to authorise lethal force."

"I thought you'd done that already," I said, then turned and walked away, though my legs and heart seemed made of lead.

CHAPTER 29
12.40am

The novice learns through ear, eye and mind. But to be a master is to weave your craft into muscle, sinew and bone.

THE BULLET-CATCHER'S HANDBOOK

Yan held his throwing knives at the ready as we watched the exchange. Only when Agent Chronis had passed Ellie did he slip them back into their pockets. We pulled her through the gap and slammed the door closed.

"You're safe now," I said.

But Ellie was weeping and wouldn't be consoled.

"I'm sorry," she said. "So sorry."

We ran back along the passage then down yet another flight of spiral stairs, passing through three more doors on the way. Only one of them had been damaged by the light machine. It seemed that Chronis's keys had speeded our progress. Each door had been wedged by Jeremiah. Once we pushed them closed behind us, he turned the torsion bar and they were locked.

When the others saw us, Lara ran and gathered her friend in her arms.

"I didn't mean to be caught," Ellie sobbed.

"It wasn't your fault."

"I've ruined everything!"

"It's the other way round. We were seen first. You were caught because of us."

As they held each other, Fabulo beckoned me towards one of the side doors. "You'd better see this," he said.

I followed him through to another vast storeroom. Ceiling lights illuminated rack upon rack of shelves, receding into the distance. It was similar to the first storeroom, but the shelves were more closely packed one above the other. And where those shelves bore wooden crates, these were stacked with muskets.

The sheer scale of what I was seeing didn't hit me all at once. I began to walk along the edge of the room, counting the racks. After ten paces, I gave up.

"Close your mouth or you'll swallow a fly," said Fabulo, his voice a whisper.

"How many?" I whispered back. Somehow it felt wrong to let my voice disturb the air.

"Don't know. Two hundred thousand? Three?"

"It feels like… a graveyard."

"You got that too?"

He stepped across to the nearest rack and hefted one of the guns from its place. Dust drifted as he dropped it into my hands. "Your old man was a bullet-catcher," he said. "What do you make of that?"

I rubbed my sleeve across the stock. It came away smeared black. Beneath the dust, the wood had a dull shine. The metal too. I could see no corrosion. "It was oiled before they stored it here," I said. "I'd say it's old. But the design's strange to me."

Fabulo turned it over in my hands. "What's that?" he asked, tapping the barrel where it met the stock. A small catch projected from the gun. I pushed it and a section of metal sprung out, like a trapdoor, exposing a slot beneath.

"It's a barrel breech," I said, remembering what Professor Ferdinand had said. The phrase occurred sixteen times in my copy of *The Bullet-Catcher's Handbook*. But he'd found it nowhere else, not in any book in any library.

"What's a barrel breech?" asked Fabulo.

"It's something the Patent Office have written out of history."

"I mean, what does it do?"

"This gun wouldn't be loaded through the muzzle," I said. "It's not like an ordinary musket. The bullet and charge must be slotted in here. Then the cover clicks back over it and they can fire."

"It can't fire," he said. "There's no flint in the hammer. And no pan for the powder."

The extraordinary scale of the room was sinking in. "All these guns – so many. A million, I'd say. They were made to fire. No matter that we haven't seen how. But what did they fire? Where are the bullets to go with them?"

"Ah," he said. "That I can show you."

I took the strange gun with me, resting it across my arms, and followed him out of the room. He opened the door on the opposite side of the passage and led me through. This time I was expecting the scale of what I would see, but it still brought me up short.

Fabulo hefted down a small box from the nearest shelf. It clinked as he laid it in front of me. Crouching, I pulled back the lid and found a layer of metal cartridges resting on hessian. A ball of lead projected from each. Below the fabric were more layers. If the other room held a million guns, this one must hold a hundred million bullets.

I flipped open the trapdoor on the gun and slotted one of the cartridges in place. The fit was perfect. The breech snapped closed with a click.

"It can't work without a flint," said Fabulo again.

I stood, pulled back the strange hammer, took aim down the length of the room and braced myself. Fabulo stuck fingers in his ears. The recoil when it fired felt like being punched in the shoulder.

Yan and Tinker came running.

Fabulo batted smoke from before his face. "Why load a gun through a barrel breech?" he asked.

I sprung the trapdoor and the spent cartridge flew out. Then I stooped to take a fresh one from the box and had it quickly slotted into place. The hammer clicked back and I fired again.

This time Fabulo had no time to protect his ears. He was not best pleased. "Why did you do that?"

"How long did it take me?"

"I didn't time you!"

"Ten seconds? Less? It takes me three times that to load my pistol through the muzzle. And this you could load lying flat. Can you think what it would mean in a battle? A hundred men dug in might hold back an advance of ten thousand!"

"What did you mean, the Patent Office have written it out of history?" Fabulo asked, as if the importance of my words had only just hit him.

"They've broken their own law," I said.

Fabulo slapped a hand on his own forehead. "You mean all this…"

"It's part of a secret big enough to bring them down."

"Then they'll kill us here tonight for sure! They won't

risk us going to trial. Not after we've seen this."

I was about to answer, when Lara rushed in, leading Ellie by the hand. "Jeremiah sent us," she gasped. "You need to come."

Yan took the gun from me. As we left, I saw him lifting two more boxes of cartridges from the shelf.

Our locksmith had not been idle. We passed through three more wedged doors before reaching him. He was sitting on the ground facing our approach, his back leaning against what seemed to be a huge mirror blocking off the passage. At the centre of it, a Greek letter had been etched.

I'd once seen the same design tattooed on John Farthing's skin.

"This is the end," said Jeremiah.

"The end of what?"

"The end of us. I can't get you through."

Yan was bringing up the rear, labouring under a load of cartridge boxes and guns. He knelt to lay them down. "Can the boy shoot?" he asked me.

"Course I can shoot," chimed in Tinker.

"No one's going to shoot," I said.

"You keep thinking that. I'm going back for more."

He loped off the way we'd come.

"This can't be the end," said Fabulo. "We haven't found the Custodian."

"We've found him," said Jeremiah, pointing to the stone above the mirror. "We just can't get to him."

I looked up and saw the stone was a lintel. Where Roman numerals might have been carved was the inscription: *Hall of the Custodian*.

Only then did I understand the nature of the mirrored surface behind him. "It's a door?"

"We tried your machine," said Lara. "The light just bounced off. It burned a hole in the roof."

Jeremiah's head dropped. He pulled a handkerchief from his pocket and pressed it to his eyes.

"If you can't help open it, get out of the way," growled Fabulo. "We'll blast through if we have to."

Jeremiah didn't get up, but hauled himself over the stones until his back was propped against the side wall.

Fabulo hammered his fist against the door and shouted, "You can't hide in there forever!"

Each impact made the dullest of thuds.

There was a small rectangle in the mirror. I'd not noticed it before. It had been hidden behind Jeremiah's head. I tapped my knuckle against it. Hearing the hollowness, I began picking at the edge with my fingernails.

"You have to push," said the locksmith.

I did, and was rewarded with a crisp click. When I pulled away, a hatch swung out, revealing a cavity behind. I had to lower my head to see inside. At the end, perhaps a foot deep, was a small keyhole.

When I made to reach inside, Jeremiah shouted, "No!"

"What is it?"

"It's a guillotine lock. I've seen schematics, but never before the real thing."

"It has a keyhole. You must be able to pick it."

"I'd have to reach inside. Both hands. *These* hands."

He held them up. They were twice the size of mine. He'd barely have room to get them in, let alone manipulate the picks.

"The lock's fitted with a hair trigger. There are blades inside. They cut in from all directions. And with great force."

"Open up!" shouted Fabulo, heaving his shoulder against the door. It didn't even vibrate. "We'll blast you out!" He turned to Lara. "Run back to Yan. The cartridges are full of black powder. If we empty enough of them... we could fill one of the boxes, pack it tight..."

Lara stood her ground.

"It won't work," said Jeremiah. "You can see the depth of metal before you even reach the keyhole. If you set off enough black powder to crack it, you'd bring the whole Patent Court down on our heads!"

"There must be a way!"

Jeremiah shook his head. "I'm sorry."

"We'll die here if we can't get to him!"

"Then we've lost."

Yan returned along the passage, a cluster of guns strung over one shoulder and four of the cartridge boxes balanced between his hands and chin. "They've cut through another door," he said, unloading. "There's time for one more trip. After that we'll have to lock ourselves out from the hall of guns. Help me, won't you?"

He made off without waiting for an answer.

I looked at Jeremiah, slouched on the floor, then at the guillotine lock. It was a diabolical device. The skill of the locksmith, all the years of training, all that put at risk if he would even reach towards the keyhole.

I turned to the others and said, "Go and help Yan."

"I thought there wasn't going to be any shooting," said Fabulo.

"Do it. Please." Then I bent to his ear and whispered, "Buy me a minute alone with our locksmith."

Fabulo met my eyes. A second passed before he nodded. Then he snapped his fingers. "You heard the lady. We've work to do!"

Once they were gone, I stepped across to sit next to Jeremiah. He looked at me. I saw a broken man.

"Have you proved yourself?" I asked.

"Proved?"

"Have you picked the secret locks of this place?"

"You know I haven't! The dwarf wouldn't let me. First there was your cursed machine. Then we had keys."

"But not the key to this lock?"

He shook his head. "The hole's too small for any of them."

"So you'll never know the answer. The examination they failed you on – was it fixed or was it not?"

"You want me to reach into a trap?"

"Yes. But that's not the important thing. All that matters is that *you* want to do it."

He held out his hands. "These are everything I have."

"I know."

"You're going to tell me I'm going to the gallows anyway, so it's worth the risk."

"They won't hang us," I said. "They'll shoot us here. Unless we can get through that door and take the Custodian hostage."

"I'd rather die with my hands than live without them. I know that won't make sense to you."

"It makes perfect sense. Your hands are who you are."

"So how could I do it?"

"Because it might not be so bad dying if you knew you were the finest locksmith of the age."

"If I could pick that lock, I'd be one of the finest, for sure."

"You'd be better than the Grand Master," I said.

"How?"

"Did you never wonder how it is he's got a metal hand?"

Jeremiah didn't answer. He stared at the guillotine lock. A shiver passed through his body. It was as if two great forces pushed him, one towards it and one away. He lurched forwards onto hands and knees and crawled. He peered inside the hole, then covered his eyes with his hands like a frightened child.

"Imagine it's done," I said. "How would you feel?"

"Like the greatest locksmith of the age," he said, his words barely a whisper. Then he unrolled the bundle of picks on the floor.

CHAPTER 30
1.10am

It is sweet and fitting to live for your art. But die for it and you will be remembered forever.

THE BULLET-CATCHER'S HANDBOOK

The last load brought it to fourteen boxes of cartridges and seven guns. The noise of the machine cutter had stopped some minutes before and then resumed louder and closer.

From where I sat, there were but three paces to the guillotine lock, before which Jeremiah was laying out his tools, and twenty paces back down the passage to the last of the doors he had opened for us. That would be our final line of defence. Yan had wedged it a foot open and tied his jacket across the gap by its sleeves so that it formed a half-curtain. It would not stop a bullet, but it would make it harder for them to aim.

Fabulo and Tinker came running back along the passage. Yan lifted the jacket and they edged through underneath.

"That's another door breached," said Fabulo. "Two more and they'll be in our sights."

Jeremiah shot back a fiery glare. "Will you keep quiet, Mr Dwarf? I'm trying to work!"

Fabulo seemed ready to shout something in return, but caught my warning glance and retreated to where Yan was getting the others to practise loading and unloading.

Jeremiah laid down his jacket and rolled his shirt sleeves high. He selected a torsion bar and a simple hook-ended pick, then stood facing the door, adjusting the spread of his legs, bringing himself an inch lower, aligning his arms with the hole. I saw now how unnatural his body position must be to reach inside the guillotine lock. He brought his elbows close together, paused for a second, then eased his hands into the hole, shuffling his feet forwards, bringing his face close to its reflection.

He closed his eyes and his body became still. His breathing slowed until I could no longer see it. His forehead was glistening under the ceiling lights. A drop of sweat broke free and ran down the side of his face.

The machine cutter had stopped again. I'd been so focused on Jeremiah that I hadn't noticed the moment it happened. The others were no longer loading and unloading. They stood, holding their guns still, listening. I forced myself to breathe and focused on the locksmith. Though his body seemed frozen, there was a slight rippling under the skin of his forearm, betraying the shifting of muscles.

A metallic scream sliced through the stillness. The machine cutter had started again. I clenched my teeth against the noise. Jeremiah pulled back from the lock and stumbled away from the mirror. Dark patches of sweat showed under his arms and at the top of his chest.

"I can't do it!" he shouted.

Flinging down his tools, he stormed away and grabbed the gun from Tinker's hands. I leapt up to follow. For a heartbeat, I thought he was going to try to use it on himself, but he took aim over the tied jacket and fired down the passage. Sparks flew from the door up the other end. But, as the ringing in my ears began to subside, the sparks grew more intense, becoming a fountain.

The machine had cut through.

Ellie fired next, then Lara, each report so loud it felt like a slap across the ears. Fabulo waved his arms. His mouth opened and closed.

Spent cartridges jumped free from the guns and all were reloading. Lara fumbled and dropped her bullet.

Then Fabulo's words reached me through the whistling of tinnitus. "Stop firing! Stop firing!"

Ellie looked around, wide eyed, as if startled by her own actions.

"There'll be time enough for shooting once they're through," said Yan.

"Please don't," I said.

"And why not?"

"It'll make no difference in the end. Except more will be dead."

"We'll be dead anyway," he growled. "I'm not waiting for the gallows. I'm not going alone!"

The air in the passage smelled acrid and sulphurous. I walked back to the mirrored door and rested my forehead against its cold metal, wondering how much the Custodian would have heard. He might be standing on the other side, his ear pressed to the metal. Though that would put him within touching distance, he may as well have been a thousand miles away.

I'd known this would be the end, most likely. It wasn't so long ago that I'd flung myself at death's feet. But the memory felt alien, as if I had been a different person. Now

I wanted to live. And, more than that, I wanted to save the others from harm.

"Here we are then," said Fabulo, his voice quiet and close.

"If only I could save Tinker," I said.

He leaned his back against the door and sighed. "Sorry about that."

The others were huddled around Yan's flimsy barricade, too far away to hear our conversation.

"Don't be sorry," I said. "I've lived again in the last few weeks. I mean, really lived, like I haven't for a long time. You gave me that."

But he shook his head. "It's been a selfish thing I've done."

"We were all of us selfish. It's just we were all after different things. Different goals."

"But I never told you mine," he said. "Not really. This was Harry's plan. It was all I had left of him. So I couldn't give it up."

"You *did* tell me that."

"But I didn't say the other thing. Somehow I can't tell the rest of them. But I want you to know that I loved Harry."

Way back when Fabulo first approached me with his plan, I'd thought it was madness speaking. Then later, when I saw that it *could* be done, I'd put that notion aside and tried to understand what was driving him. I'd never found the answer. But, by that time, I'd become caught up in the excitement of it all and his motivation seemed unimportant.

I'd understood the motives of everyone else. Jeremiah was in the tunnels, trying to regain his self-esteem by breaking locks that no one else in the world could break. I'd set out to take hold of the reins of my own destiny. Tinker was here because he wanted to belong, and I was the person he'd chosen. Lara and Ellie and Yan were a home for each other, and together they'd judged the spoils worth the risk.

But Fabulo himself – I now saw *had* been mad all along. It was the first and deepest of all madness.

"Did he love you too?" I asked.

Fabulo nodded. "He used to say it was only because his eyes were shot that he could feel that way. Pug ugly, he used to call me. But that was never the truth of it. I think it's 'coz he'd spent all those years looking at conjuring tricks and seeing past the obvious to what was happening underneath. When he looked at me – even that first time – he didn't see what everyone else saw."

I felt a twinge of guilt. It had taken me too long to get past the simple illusion of his stature.

"I think maybe Tania sensed it, but only because she was a fortune teller. The rest of them never knew. It was easy enough to hide – what with Harry keeping himself locked away in that wagon. We could be together there with no one else to see it.

"There's a story Harry picked up on his travels out east somewhere. It's about this man who gets down on the ground outside his house and starts sifting the dust. A friend comes over to ask what's happening. I lost my ring, says the man. It's gold and it's got a ruby, big as a cherry on it. So the friend gets down in the dirt to help. But after an hour they haven't found it and the sun's getting hot. So the friend asks if he's sure he lost the ring just there. The man shakes his head. No, he says. I lost it in my house. But the light inside is too bad for me to search."

"That's a good story," I said.

"Harry liked it. But then he was always searching for

things. I liked it because he did. But now here I am, trapped under this damn building. And the truth is, it's him I'm looking for. We both know I'm not going to find him. But if I stopped looking it would be like saying I'd never be with him again. Even though this is the most crazy place in the whole Gas-Lit Empire to be. And it's going to get us killed. It was his plan and that's all I've got left of him. I'd rather be here searching than be anywhere else without hope."

"And the light's better down here," I said, pointing to the ceiling.

"Exactly! Do you think Harry told me that story so many times so I'd remember it after he was gone – so I'd understand?"

"No. I think he told it because it's a good story. If he were here now, what do you think he'd say?"

"He'd tell us to stop moping and find a way out."

"I think you're right."

Jeremiah at first refused to return to the guillotine lock. I took one of his doughy hands and eased him forwards until we were standing before it.

"I need you to try," I said.

"To pick a lock, you… you put your mind inside it. But all I'm thinking about… All I can think about… it's those blades."

"We'll all die if you don't."

"I know it. But I can't put my hands back in there… unless…" His reflection met my eyes. "Unless… you could… end me. Shoot me clean if I spring the trap."

I remembered holding the knife to the duke's throat, being unable to kill him. "We can get Yan to do it," I said.

"No."

"But I'm not a killer."

"It's mercy, not murder. In *that* I trust you more than any of the others. Yan could do it. But he might not."

My feet felt heavy as I walked back to the guns. I took one and loaded it. The trapdoor in the barrel snapped shut over the cartridge.

"Promise me," whispered Jeremiah, when I was close enough to hear. "A clean shot. And quick. I don't want time to know what's happened."

"I promise," I said.

"With this lock, I'll only get one chance. One way or the other it's not going to take long."

He took up his tools and positioned himself as before, his wrists together as if they were bound. He edged forward and they disappeared inside the mouth of the guillotine. Adjusting my stance, I raised the gun. He watched me in the mirror. Only when I'd aimed at the back of his head did he close his eyes.

Then the scream of the metal cutter stopped. There was a moment of terrible silence followed by the harsh clang of the lock smashed with a hammer.

I braced myself, forcing my focus to stay on Jeremiah.

At the other end of the passage, a piece of metal clanged to the floor. Then the shooting started. Five shots from close behind me. I couldn't hear the reloading. I would be deaf to the snap of the guillotine lock if it sprang.

Then came the reply from the other end of the passage. A stream of bullets smashing into the door. Not sporadic as ours had been, but a drumbeat, perfectly regular, inhumanly rapid, followed by silence and then another burst.

A scream of pain whispered through my deafness. It was one of the women. I couldn't turn to see who. A fog of gun smoke seethed in the gap between my gun barrel and Jeremiah's head. I forced myself to focus on the muscles of his arm.

Three more shots fired close behind me.

Jeremiah's eyes snapped open. His arm made a sudden twist. My finger flicked from the trigger guard to the trigger itself. He lurched back. I took a breath. Then he turned, amazement on his face and his hands held before him, unharmed.

The mirrored door had begun to swing away from us, inch by inch.

"It's open!" I shouted, snapping around, searching for Yan, who would surely lead the charge.

But he lay on his back, unblinking, a small bullet hole in his cheek, a spreading halo of blood on the stones. Lara knelt next to him, clutching her own bloodied forearm. Fabulo, Ellie and Tinker were taking cover.

I beckoned to them. "To the Custodian! Bring the guns!"

The great door had swung deep enough to clear its frame, revealing darkness in the room beyond.

There was no time to weigh the danger. We were running, diving through the widening crack into the clean air of the newly opened room. Fabulo was the last through.

I put my back against the huge door and pushed. The others joined me. It slowed and stopped. Then it begin to inch the other way, accelerating until it came up hard against its housing. The boom of it closing echoed back from distant walls.

The blackness was sudden and complete. I was aware of movement next to me. Jeremiah's hand pushed me aside. I could hear him working along the width of the door.

A match flared, revealing Tinker's face. He reached out to the wall next to him. There was a faint pop and white light flooded down from the ceiling.

Fabulo cocked his gun. "Come out!" he shouted.

I turned to look where he was aiming and saw the vastness of the room for the first time. It was filled with a maze of grey cabinets, connected here and there by what looked like grey shelves. I knew instantly that it was a machine, though unlike anything I'd encountered before. There was no engine, no firebox or funnel, no regulators or valves. One thing only in the room was familiar – a mass of brass pipes on the wall, identical to the ones Richard da Silva had shown me in the courtroom far above. There, I'd seen but two pipes. These were more than I could take in at a single glance.

"Show yourself!" shouted Fabulo, his voice echoing back from the room.

No one emerged.

I glanced back to the others. Jeremiah had been fitting wedges of wood under the door and up its side, hammering them in place with the butt of his musket. "I've no other way to lock it," he shouted.

I nodded to show him that I'd heard and that the gunfire deafness was leaving me.

Ellie was ripping strips from her own skirt to bandage Lara's arm. Tinker stared blankly over the machines. We all knew that Yan was lying dead on the other side of the door. But none would speak of it. Not yet.

As in a trance I stepped towards an indent in the nearest of the grey cabinets, where buttons were set out like the keys of a stenotype. Behind and above them, embossed on a grey metal plate, I read the letters *C.O.M.*

"This is it," I said. "The Custodian of Marvels is a machine."

CHAPTER 31
1.25am

There are two powers in every secret: that others do not know it and that others may be told.

THE BULLET-CATCHER'S HANDBOOK

Fabulo had walked off in a daze. He meandered between the grey cabinets, ducking under the connecting shelves, finding his way gradually deeper into that vast room. His flimsy plan had collapsed. There was no person to be held hostage. John Farthing would be outside the mirrored door already. Wooden wedges would not hold them back for long.

Each of the stenotype keys had been printed with a letter of the alphabet or a number. To one side of the recess was a hopper, containing a great stack of cards. I took the topmost, examined both sides, which proved blank, and flexed it. It was perhaps nine inches by four and no more stiff than a playing card.

Jeremiah came to stand beside me. "I want to thank you," he said.

"You'll be hanged because of me," I told him. "If they don't shoot us all first."

"I picked that lock. It's the greatest thing I ever did. You were right in what you said before. I would have been running forever. But this way I'll die knowing…"

"…you're the greatest locksmith of the age."

He chuckled. "Maybe I am."

"Then tell me," I said. "What does this machine do?"

I handed him the card. He examined it as I had done, then stepped to the side and held it against a slot in the machine. The width of the card matched perfectly.

"The cards move through here," he said. "If you look at a low angle, you can see small wheels. They're rubber coated for better grip. They shoot the cards along. See those shelves between the cabinets? They're about the same width. I'm betting the cards will travel through them."

"But why? And where's the engine to power it?"

"I'm stronger on the how than the why," he said, then pointed to a small lever on the machine, next to the *C.O.M.* nameplate. "Doesn't that look familiar?"

It was of the same design as the wall-mounted levers that had operated the lights. I reached out and flipped it down.

The lights in the room dimmed for a moment and a low whirring noise began. It emanated from the cabinet in front of us, but also from other cabinets around. The entire room was humming with it. I had barely time to react before the hopper juddered and a card whisked along the slot, where it came to an abrupt halt. A vent in the metal was blowing air against my leg.

Fabulo was running back between the cabinets. The others stepped closer, fearfully, as if they were approaching a bomb.

"What does it do?" asked Lara.

"Shall we find out?"

I pressed the stenotype key marked "E". A chatter and thud from the slot made us all jump. A neat rectangular hole had been punched in the card, and the letter "E" had been printed, though I'd not seen it happen.

Fabulo reached us, panting for breath.

I pressed the keys: L I Z A B E T H B A R N A B U S. On each press, an arm sprang out and stamped the letter. And each time another hole had been punched in the card. I could make no sense of the pattern.

We all stared.

"What now?" asked Fabulo.

"What do you think that might do?" asked Jeremiah, indicating a button set apart from the others. Rather than a letter, it was marked with a word: *SEND*.

I pressed it. Immediately, the card shot away along the slot, disappearing into the machine. There were new sounds now. A rattling and a whirring that started close, but moved quickly on to the next cabinet, and the cabinet beyond. Then an answering chatter began somewhere deep in the room, rushing back towards us, hopping from machine to machine. With a click, two new cards shot out of a slot nearby, coming to rest in a shallow tray.

Ellie picked them up and passed them to me.

They were pale blue, but the same size as the card we'd sent. And they were punched with holes, much as it had been. But these were printed with type front and back.

Subject: Elizabeth Barnabus
Category: Person
Date of Birth: Unknown
Year of Birth: 1989
Family: Gulliver Barnabus, Father. Felicia Barnabus, Mother.
    Edwin Barnabus, Twin.
Class: Informer and Suspect
Status: Wanted for Questioning

I turned the cards, scanning the text, finding lists of names – my friends and people I'd associated with. Finding also a great list of case numbers, among them surely the reference to the court case that had ruined my family, killed my father and sent me over the border in exile. Against each case was a filing reference. All began with IPC. All had Roman numerals – references to the rooms we'd passed, the doors we'd not opened.

"It's a filing machine," I said. "An index."

Fabulo snatched the cards from my hand. "But if it's the Custodian of Marvels…"

"Don't you see? We're talking about the Patent Office. For them that's just what this is. They're not interested in the things themselves. They're fixed always on the knowing. On who knows and who isn't allowed to know. This machine – this great index – it gives access to knowledge. It is the custodian."

So focused had we been on the cards and the machine that, for minutes, none of us had turned to look at the great door. And under the whirring of the machine, small sounds were lost.

"Elizabeth Barnabus!" barked Agent Chronis, behind us.

I froze, expecting a bullet, my guts clenching.

Fabulo raised his hands above his head. Lara followed his lead. But Tinker turned to face the door.

"Attention, Elizabeth Barnabus!"

Tinker tugged at my sleeve. "It's the speaking tube," he said.

We all turned then and found the door wedged closed as we left it. "Someone go speak to him," I said. "Buy us time."

Lara was the first to move. She ran to a grille on the wall. I hadn't noticed it before.

"Who are you?" she asked, pressing the button.

"You know who I am!"

"But I'm not sure I do."

Knowing we were in good hands, I turned to the machine once more, trying to filter out Chronis's angry questions. Jeremiah had taken some of the cards from Fabulo.

"It talks about me," he said.

I nodded. "They know we're associates. They've been following us."

"Give the machine my name," he said.

"No," said Fabulo. "Ask it about Harry Timpson."

"For what? There'll just be more references to files in rooms we can't get to!"

Chronis's voice barked behind us. "We know the door is unlocked. We will be able to force it open. Remove whatever is blocking it."

"Why would we do that?" asked Lara.

"If you fail to comply, we will use lethal force once inside."

"You've done that already," she said, her voice bitter.

I bent over the stenotype and started pressing keys. A blank card shot through and the hole punch chattered.

B A R R E L B R E E C H

I pressed SEND and the card shot away. I listened to the humming and clicking of its progress. Then, as before, the sound rushed back from across the room and a card shot out into the tray.

Subject: Barrel Breech
Category: Terminology
Class: Restricted. Agents only
Operation Code Name: Clean Start

There was a great list of case numbers that spilled over onto the other side. My hands were back on the stenotype keys.

CLEANSTART

As I sent the new card shooting off into the machine, a terrible creaking noise began behind me. The door shuddered.

"Keep it closed," I shouted.

They all ran to lean against it, bracing themselves.

"Just give me time!"

The answering card shot out into the tray.

Subject: Clean Start
Category: Operation Code
Class: Restricted. Agents Only
Related Terms: Napoleonic Weapons. Breech Loader Musket.
    Converter Musket. Battle of Waterloo.

My fingers flew across the keys, printing each of the phrases. This time I didn't wait for a return card before sending out the next. The noise of the machine grew. But louder still was the grinding and creaking of the door beginning to open, fraction by fraction, forcing the wooden wedges to scrape across the floor.

A response card shot into the tray, others following rapidly after it. I picked out the top one and read:

Subject: Waterloo
Category: Historic Battle
Class: Expunged from History. Agents Only

Date: 18th June to 20th December 1815
Casualties: 3.19 million
Combatants: France. Prussia. Belgium. Netherlands. Britain.
   Russia.

The list went on over to the other side and to three more cards after it. I stared at them, trying to comprehend the magnitude of the revelation. The great halls of guns and ammunition suddenly made sense. There had been a terrible conflagration. A battle of a scale beyond understanding. Many people dead for each of the guns we'd seen in that vast storeroom. And all of it had been wiped from history. Expunged by the Patent Office.

I remembered Professor Ferdinand's terror, not at the thought of history being changed, but at the possibility of proof existing. The Patent Office had gone beyond its authority, beyond the provisions of the Great Accord. The Patent Office had broken the law.

The great door juddered and screeched, inching its way towards us.

"We can't hold it," yelled Lara.

"Tell them we'll give up!" I cried.

Lara threw herself towards the speaking grille and pressed the button. I gathered up the cards and ran towards the brass pipes on the wall.

"We give up!" she shouted. "We surrender!"

The scraping noise stopped. Chronis's voice was cold. "Remove your barricade. Then lie face down on the ground. Hands spread. Anyone who disobeys this simple instruction will be shot."

CHAPTER 32
October 13th

Applause is the reward of the bullet-catcher. But the con artist will be far away by the time his trick is seen.

THE BULLET-CATCHER'S HANDBOOK

On the third day after my arrest the cell door opened and Agent Chronis stepped inside. He waited until the jailer had relocked the door and walked away. I sat up from the narrow bed, clasped my hands on my lap and waited.

"Are you being treated well?" he asked.

"It's not the worst prison I've been in."

"The food?"

"Adequate."

"Good. Good."

He stepped to the window and went up on tiptoe to look outside. Then he turned, hands clasped behind him. I waited, sensing that the balance of our interaction had shifted in my favour.

"You did a remarkable thing," he said, breaking a silence that had become uncomfortable. "Getting so far, I mean. Though your capture was inevitable. What did you hope to gain? You must have known that you couldn't escape."

"How are the others?" I asked.

"As well as any who must hang. It's the boy I pity most. And then those young women."

"But not me?"

"It's hard to pity one who shows no remorse. You really are the worst of them. You and the dwarf. It's as if neither of you want to live."

"That may be true," I said. "I was surprised you didn't shoot us there and then."

He stood, as if waiting for me to say more, but I was happy to let time pass.

When he hadn't responded for over a minute, I said, "Thank you for your visit."

The dismissal seemed to irritate him more than anything I had yet said. His cheeks began to colour. "There is one more thing," he said. "A question of accounting."

"I'd be pleased to help."

"Well... We have been reviewing the inventory of the rooms through which you passed. The full task will take months. But our preliminary report suggests that some items are missing."

"Indeed?"

"We will find them one way or another. But there are so many places of possible concealment that the manpower needed for the search is considerable. If you could just tell us where these things were hidden, it would save us much trouble."

"Why would I want to save you trouble?"

"There could be rewards for cooperation. Some food of your own choice? Or perhaps a more comfortable cell?"

"Tempting," I said. "What exactly is missing?"

"Index cards."

"And what is on these cards?"

"I cannot say."

"Could they have been documents related to the rewriting of history? In contravention of the Great Accord, I should say. I did see such cards. What do you suppose would happen if the world were to learn about them? For example, do you think the rulers of the Kingdom of England and Southern Wales would be interested?"

"That cannot happen!"

"Can it not?"

"No one would believe you."

"Even if they saw the index cards themselves? I imagine some might very much want to believe the Patent Office guilty of a crime. What would they do with such evidence?"

Agent Chronis's face displayed a palette of emotions. Anger and frustration had caused it to redden. Now horror bleached it to a sickly pallor the colour of tallow.

"What did you do with the index cards?"

Ignoring his question, I stood and stepped to the window. But, even on tiptoe, I couldn't see out. "You mentioned a more comfortable cell. I should like that. And for my friends also."

"What did you do with the cards?" he asked again, his voice higher in pitch.

"I'm tired now," I said. "I should like to rest."

He took in a breath, as if to speak. I lay back on the bed and turned my face to the wall. I could hear him shifting behind me.

After a long moment he banged on the door and shouted for the guard. I could hear the tension in the rhythm of his footsteps as he marched away.

My cell was in an upper level of the International Patent Court. Whilst I waited, I imagined what must be happening in the offices below. Clerks would continue to search for the missing documents. Agent Chronis would write notes on our interview. They would be passed on up through ever more senior ranks as the index cards were not recovered.

One fear would be an accomplice within the Patent Office. Everyone who'd had access to the corridors would be questioned, John Farthing most of all. They would know we'd spoken down there. They would learn that he'd blocked up the hole in the door so that no one else could see what passed between us. Chronis had taken over command after that. Perhaps he was the more senior agent, or there were doubts about Farthing's loyalty, or Farthing had himself stepped aside, unwilling to authorise lethal force as he had threatened.

That last possibility held me.

Eventually, when everyone was questioned and all accounts were found to match, their minds must have turned to the pneumatic messenger pipes. As indeed my mind had turned whilst the door was being forced.

I'd stuffed the cards into a canister with a note of explanation – a plea and an apology for the danger I was sending. Then I'd addressed it to Richard da Silva and sent it off in the pipe to the Barristers' Mess. By the time the door had opened, I'd been lying face down next to my comrades.

If the Custodian of Marvels hadn't been running, I believe they might have shot us. But the hum of the engine and a scatter of cards had planted a seed of uncertainty. Through our captivity, the seed had begun to germinate.

Three days.

The missing cards could have found their way to the

Council of Aristocrats in that time. The Palace was only a mile distant. And they, the government with most hatred for the Gas-Lit Empire and its institutions – what would they do?

There were laws for the punishment of agents. But what would happen if there was even a hint that the entire agency had strayed so far from the Great Accord? There was no precedent for it.

I'd discovered that a battle and its technology had been wiped from history. I had not discovered why. But, as I lay in my cell, an idea had begun to form. Those terrible guns cannot have been long invented when Waterloo began. The generals sent their armies to attack, not understanding that a hundred men so armed might hold out against battalions. Ample time for reinforcements to arrive on both sides. Thus a single battle had been able to stretch for months, becoming an entire war.

After such a harvest of death, it was no wonder a revolution had followed in the old Great Britain. From that, the Great Accord had been signed and the Patent Office brought into being – its mission to freeze the development of unseemly science. But the science they most wanted to ban was already in existence. So they used their powers to wipe it from history. They took all the guns, all the history books, every reference to it. Operation Clean Start must have taken generations. Indeed, their pursuit of my book proved it was still going on.

The Patent Office had been set up to watch over the Great Accord. It was implicit that the governments of the nations must be watchers of the watchmen.

If those index cards reached the wrong people, might not the men-at-arms of the Kingdom be ordered in to take over the Patent Court? What would stop them seizing that great stockpile of weaponry? Against such power, the combined forces of the other nations would be impotent. Everything the agents had striven for in two centuries would be wiped clean in a single day. That is what they feared. Enough, I hoped, for them to agree to my bargain.

I'd once thrilled to the idea that the Patent Office might be overthrown. But that terrible arsenal had changed my thinking completely. The knowledge of such weapons had been erased. Laws had been broken. But I could find no fault in what they'd done.

So I waited, playing out permutations, hoping they didn't call my bluff. I thought of Yan, who had fallen, and of Tinker, worrying that he might not cope with captivity.

And of John Farthing. My thoughts always returned to him.

It was two hours after Chronis had left that the cell door opened and there he stood, breathing deeply, his forehead slick with sweat. I sat up on the bed as before, hands clasped in my lap, and was pleased with myself that I managed not to smile.

"Where are the cards?" he asked.

"No longer in this building," I said.

"Can you get them back?"

"Not from here. You'd have to let me go."

"It is done."

"And my friends. A pardon for all of us."

"It may take a day to arrange."

"In the meantime, please move us all somewhere more pleasant."

He nodded. "And will there be anything else?"

•••

Our new quarters were a set of connecting apartments on the fourteenth floor of the Patent Court. I was the last to arrive. The guard escorted me to a pleasant reception room where Lara, Ellie and Jeremiah sat drinking tea. He gave a curt bow before leaving, a politeness that was unfamiliar. But I heard the door being locked from outside after he left.

"What's happening?" asked Lara.

I'd just begun to explain when Tinker burst in from one of the side rooms. He seemed unnaturally clean, but wore a grin nonetheless. I staggered back under the impact as he launched himself to hug me, then he stepped back and looked me over as if to reassure himself that they had done me no harm.

"Are you well?" I asked.

"There was a tin of biscuits!" he said gleefully, then careened back into his room.

Ellie rolled her eyes. "Don't worry. We managed to hide a few."

I found Fabulo in one of the side rooms. He was sitting next to a bed, staring at the wall.

"They're going to let you go," I said.

"Then what will I do?"

"Whatever you want."

"I spent half my life looking after Harry. The only thing I wanted was for him to be happy. I don't know what else there is."

"Someone else to love?"

He looked me in the eye. "That's rich! It'll be a cold day in Hell before I take such advice from you, Eliza." This he said with a smile.

It took another week for the arrangements to be made and all the safeguards that I requested to be put in place. Then, when our pardons had been signed and witnessed, when they had been taken away and delivered into Julia's hand, a package arrived at the International Patent Court. When opened it was found to contain all the missing cards.

Having packed up our few possessions we were escorted back down flight after flight of stairs to the grand lobby. John Farthing stood waiting for us. I will confess that I felt my heart dilate on seeing him. He strode up to me, his face stern.

"Miss Barnabus."

"Agent Farthing."

"News of your release precedes you. There are people waiting outside."

"Thank you. I understand."

We were a strange procession crossing the lobby. A boy, a dwarf, two women and a man, all carrying bundles of clothes, an agent marching on either side and myself walking at the very front. People stopped to stare. Petitioners milling at the entrance parted to let us through.

The red coats of the Duke of Northampton's men-at-arms were conspicuous in the bright sunlight. As we marched down the low steps towards them I noticed a grand carriage waiting by the roadside.

I stopped just before the line of yellow bricks that marked out the boundary between the Kingdom and the Patent Court. The men-at-arms were standing to attention immediately on the other side. Then the carriage door opened and out climbed the duke himself, arrayed in furs. In his left hand he held a pair of iron manacles, in his right hand, a document.

"We meet again," I said.

He seemed older than before. His face was thinner. A muscle twitched below his eye. "You can't hide in there forever," he said.

"Nor shall I."

I stepped across the line of bricks. At first he recoiled, as if I might be about to attack him. When that didn't happen, he began to smile.

"Elizabeth Barnabus – by the power invested in this warrant, I, the Duke of Northampton, hereby take possession of…"

But, before he could finish, John Farthing stepped between us. "You are the Duke of Northampton?"

"I am, sir."

"Your grace, the Duke of Northampton, by the power invested in *this* warrant…" He produced a folded document from within his jacket, "…I, John Farthing, hereby arrest you for corrupting a public official in the course of his duties."

The duke's expression changed from surprise to confusion and then to a cold, dangerous anger. He moved closer to Farthing and lowered his voice. "I'll not forget or forgive you for this! Have you any idea what this girl has cost me?"

"You're still under arrest," said Farthing.

"No court in the land will hold me!"

"Forgive me if I didn't fully explain. No court in the land will be concerned with your case. It rests with the International Patent Office – since it was one of our officials that you bribed. He has already confessed."

So saying, he took the duke's arm and pulled him across the line. At first I thought the men-at-arms would try to pull him back. But they looked down to the yellow bricks and stood their ground.

I pulled the warrant from the duke's hand and passed it to Farthing. "This is evidence in the case."

"This is an outrage!" shouted the duke.

"It is indeed," said Farthing. "And did you know the penalty for your outrageous crime is death?"

CHAPTER 33
November 2009

Magic has ever lived in the gap between what we believe should be and what our senses tell us.

THE BULLET-CATCHER'S HANDBOOK

As my adventure had begun, so it came to end – with a waking in darkness and the knowledge that I was not alone. This time it was not a gun pressed to my cheek, but a hand rocking my shoulder. In my former life, I would have jolted awake with a cry. But, since returning to my boat, sleep had begun to bring me peace. And in that peace a kind of clarity had begun to grow.

I opened my eyes to find him bending over me. I could not see his face. The silver moonlight was behind him, making of his hair a halo. But he was close enough for me to know the delicate scent of him.

"John?"

"Elizabeth."

He knelt on the floor next to the cot, bringing his face closer still. "You know why I can't be here?" he whispered. His warm breath, touching my skin.

"I do not."

"I'm an agent of the–"

I put a finger against his lips to stop the words. "You are John Farthing. Beneath all the layers, that is what you are. And I am Elizabeth Barnabus. Right now it's all we need to be."

"But if someone discovered…"

"No one shall."

"I told myself I wouldn't come," he said. "But my feet carried me and I had no will to stop them."

There was a rustling on the other side of the cabin as Tinker sat up, shedding his blanket. "What's happening?" he asked, his words slurred by sleep.

"Nothing bad," I said. "But I need to talk to this gentleman alone."

The boy didn't ask further. Simple acceptance of the marvellous was one of his many gifts. He pulled on his coat, then sat on the step to lace his boots before climbing out through the hatch. The boat swayed as he jumped to the towpath. Listening to the crunch of his footsteps receding, I realised that John's hand still lay where it had been when I awoke. My nightshirt had slipped to the side and his touch rested on my unclothed shoulder. It seemed the most natural thing. I reached up and stroked his hair. His finger traced from the side of my neck to the soft skin of my ear.

"I'm driven by selfishness," he said. "You know I can never marry. There's nothing I can give you."

"You're giving more already than you know."

I brought my hand around behind his head and guided him closer. His lips brushed mine – a kiss as delicate, it seemed, as the touch of the moonlight. Then he pulled back.

"I'm a bad man."

"That which you think bad is the very part I most admire."

"You should send me far from here," he said, then pressed his lips again to mine.

The kiss was firmer than before and more succulent.

"Perhaps I should," I said, when next I breathed.

But, reader, I let him stay.

A GLOSSARY OF THE GAS-LIT EMPIRE

ACCESSION DAY

May 23rd 1828. The day when the Kingdom of England and Southern Wales finally signed the Great Accord. As the last major signatory, this event made it inevitable that the Gas-Lit Empire would grow to encompass the entire civilised world.

Negotiations leading to the signing had been long and fraught. The Kingdom, *de facto* leader of the unsigned nations, initially demanded a wide range of exemptions from the provisions of the Accord. But, as the number of unsigned nations dwindled, so did the Kingdom's influence. Risking a slide into insignificance, it finally capitulated, having secured exemption only from the provisions of the Twelfth Amendment, which had come into effect during the negotiation period.

The Kingdom presented this as a victory, since no other nation was exempt, ignoring the fact that none of the other signatories had wanted to be. However,

Accession Day was afterwards remembered by Kingdom nationalists as a shameful moment in their history. (See also: *London Time*.)

THE ANGLO-SCOTTISH REPUBLIC

The northernmost nation formed by the partition of Britain following the 1819 armistice. The city of Carlisle is its capital, the seat of its parliament and other agencies of government. It is a democracy, with universal suffrage for all men over twenty-one years of age.

The Anstey Amendment

An amendment to the armistice signed at the end of the British Revolutionary War. The border had initially been drawn as an east-west line from the Wash, passing just south of Derby. However, when news started to spread that Anstey was to be controlled by the Kingdom, new skirmishes broke out.

The Anstey Amendment was therefore drafted, redrawing the border to include a small southerly loop and thereby bring Ned Ludd's birthplace into the Republic.

The border had originally been drawn so that it would pass through sparsely populated countryside. An unforeseen consequence of the Anstey Amendment was the bisection of the city of Leicester between the two new nations and its subsequent flourishing as a centre of trade and communication.

ARMISTICE

The agreement which brought the British Revolutionary War to a close. Britain had been depleted of men and resources in the stalemate of the Napoleonic Wars. Three further years of civil conflict reduced it to economic collapse and the population to the point of starvation.

On January 30th 1819, the leaders of the opposing armies met in Melton Mowbray and signed the armistice document, which was later ratified by the two governments. (See also: The Anstey Amendment.)

THE BRITISH REVOLUTIONARY WAR

Also known as the Second English Civil War, it ran for exactly three years from January 30th 1815 to January 30th 1819 and resulted in the division of Britain into two nations: the Anglo-Scottish Republic and the Kingdom of England and Southern Wales. The untamed lands of northern Wales cannot be said to be a true nation as they are ruled by no government.

BULLET-CATCHER

One who performs a bullet catch illusion. The term is also used to describe stage magicians known for other large-scale or spectacular illusions.

THE BULLET-CATCHER'S HANDBOOK

The Bullet-Catcher's Handbook is a collection of sayings and aphorisms, accumulated by travelling conjurors. Some entries seem to be transcriptions from an early oral tradition, possibly medieval in origin. Others belong to the Golden Age of stage magic.

THE CIRCUS OF MYSTERIES

One of the many travelling magic shows to tour the

Kingdom of England and Southern Wales. Original home of Elizabeth Barnabus. After years of financial difficulty, it was finally closed in the early years of the twenty-first century after its owner, Gulliver Barnabus, was declared bankrupt.

THE COUNCIL OF ARISTOCRATS

The highest agency of government in the Kingdom of England and Southern Wales.

THE COUNCIL OF GUARDIANS

The highest agency of government of the Anglo-Scottish Republic. Sixty per cent of its membership is appointed. Forty per cent is elected by universal suffrage of all men over the age of twenty-one.

THE CROWN AND DOLPHIN

A public house in London on the crossroads of Cable Street and Cannon Street, outside which John Williams, accused of the Ratcliff Highway Murders, was buried, with a stake driven through his heart. The body was rediscovered during the digging of a new gas pipe. The skull was exhumed and subsequently displayed in the pub.

CULTURAL DRIFT

A phrase used to describe the origin of cultural differences between the Kingdom of England and Southern Wales and the Anglo-Scottish Republic.

The cultures of Kingdom and Republic were not dissimilar at partition. But years of priding themselves on their differences caused them to drift apart. In *A*

History of the Gas-Lit Empire, the process is described thus: "How often do we see an unhappy couple changing over time so that each more perfectly manifests the aspect of their character that annoys the other. So it was with the disunited kingdoms of Britain."

DAYLIGHT SAVING TIME

At 4am on the second Sunday in March, clocks were set forwards one hour throughout the Gas-Lit Empire. They were set back again at 4am on the second Sunday in October. This with the exception of the Kingdom of England and Southern Wales, which used the second Saturday in March to set clocks forward and the second Saturday in October to set them back again. (See also: *Twelfth Amendment.*)

DEPARTMENT OF CONSTITUTIONAL VERACITY

A department of the International Patent Office charged with monitoring the organisation's own compliance with the Great Accord and such amendments as comprised the treaties of its establishment.

It was brought into being under the provisions of the First Amendment, charged with detecting, prosecuting and documenting infringements. Its other duty was the delivery of a comprehensive triennial report to all nations signatory to the Accord.

Whilst its mandate included the imposition of capital punishment, few agents or officials were found guilty through its long history. It handed down death penalties on thirteen occasions, all of those cases falling during the chaos that characterised its final years.

ELIZABETH BARNABUS

A woman regarded by historians as having had a formative role in the fall of the Gas-Lit Empire. Born in a travelling circus, becoming a fugitive at the age of fourteen, with no inheritance but the secret of a stage illusion, she nevertheless came to stand at the very fulcrum of history.

No individual could be said to have caused the collapse of such a mighty edifice. Rather, it was brought low by the great, the inexorable tides of history. Yet, had it not been for this most unlikely of revolutionaries, the manner of its fall would have been entirely different.

THE EUROPEAN SPRING

The period of revolutions and utopian optimism in Europe that began with the overthrowing of the French monarchy in 1793 and ended with the execution of the King of Spain in 1825.

THE GAS-LIT EMPIRE

A popular, though inaccurate, description of the vast territories watched over by the International Patent Office. The term gained currency during the period of rapid economic and technical development that followed the signing of the Great Accord. It reflected the literal enlightenment that came with the extension of gas lighting around the civilised world. Though ubiquitous, the term Gas-lit Empire was misleading, as no single government ruled over its territories. From its establishment to its catastrophic demise, the Gas-Lit Empire lasted exactly two hundred years.

THE GREAT ACCORD

A declaration of intent, signed initially by France, America and the Anglo-Scottish Republic in 1821, which established the International Patent Office as arbiter of collective security. Following revolutions in Russia, Germany and Spain, the number of signatories rapidly increased until it encompassed the entire civilised world. The original text is reproduced below. Subsequent amendments extended it to twenty-three pages:

When men of high ideal and pure motive devote themselves to the establishment of an agency and of laws that will surpass the jurisdiction and sovereignty of the nations, it behoves them, out of respect to the opinions of others, to state the cause that impels them so to act.

Whereas some sciences and inventions have manifestly secured and improved the wellbeing of the common man, We hold it self-evident that others have wrought terrible suffering. Never has it been the way of science to separate the seemly from the unseemly. Therefore has the good of all been offered up for sacrifice on the altars of egotism and narrow self-interest. Since the nations have failed to rein in their scientists and inventors, it has fallen to Us to establish, through this Great Accord, a supra-national sovereignty, adequate to the task.

In adding our signatures to this declaration, We are not embarking on a campaign of military conquest; rather it is Our intention to subdue recalcitrant nations through the evident truth of Our cause. But, should any nation rise up against this Great Accord, We hereby pledge to combine

*all the strength at our disposal into one mighty army and
reduce the aggressor to abject submission.*

*We also pledge to offer up such funds as are necessary for
the establishment and maintenance of an International
Patent Office, whose task it shall be to secure the wellbeing
of the common man. This it shall achieve through the
separation of seemly science from that which is unseemly,
through the granting or withholding of licences to produce
and sell technology, through the arbitration of disputes and
through the execution of whatever punishments are deemed
fit. In creating an agency of such sweeping powers, We are
minded also to put in place the means for its dissolution.
Thus, should two thirds of the signatory nations agree, the
entire accord will be deemed null, the International Patent
Office rolled up and its assets divided equally between all.*

*With these high aims and clear safeguards established, We, the
representatives of the republics of France, America and Anglo-
Scotland, together with whatsoever nations may hereafter
voluntarily append their names and titles, freely enter into this
Great Accord on behalf of our peoples. In doing so, We hold
ourselves absolved from all previous alliances and treaties.*

GREENWICH MERIDIAN

The meridian bisecting the Greenwich Observatory was
maintained as the Prime Meridian for cartographers in
the Kingdom of England and Southern Wales, due to
the exemption of that nation from the provisions of the
Twelfth Amendment. Thus, charts produced in London
had longitudes offset by 2°20'14.03" westerly from those
produced in all other nations of the Gas-Lit Empire.

INTERNATIONAL CHRONOLOGICAL NETWORK

With the rise of fast air travel, diversity of local timekeeping systems started to became problematic. A passenger boarding an airship in Carlisle could not know when, according to local time, he would be landing in Amsterdam, since the clocks of the Netherlands had no fixed relationship to the ones in Anglo-Scotland.

Thus the International Chronological Network was established, based on the Prime Meridian (see also the Twelfth Amendment). The world's most accurate clock, designated ICN1, was constructed in the Paris Observatory as the global standard. This became the reference point for ICN clocks in each other signatory nation, which were set a certain number of hours ahead or behind Paris Mean Time. (See also: *International Patent Court*).

INTERNATIONAL PATENT COURT

A monolithic structure built on Fleet Street in London to house the Supreme Patent Court and other subsidiary courts. It was also the home of the clock designated ICN2. (See also: International Chronological Network.)

The land on which the court building rested was ceded by the Kingdom of England and Southern Wales as part of its treaty obligations. It was a self-governing enclave, referred to as the Jurisdiction of the International Patent Office. No commerce was permitted there.

No weapons were allowed within the court building itself, but the nations of the Gas-Lit Empire provided guards to patrol outside it. The task was seen by many as ceremonial, since an attack on the court building was thought impossible. However, the individual soldiers chosen for the honour were the elite of their respective armed forces and sworn to defend the building even unto death. Uniquely, the soldiers of the Kingdom of England and Southern Wales were not permitted to enter the enclave, though they kept guard beyond it.

INTERNATIONAL PATENT OFFICE

The agency established in 1821 and charged with overseeing the terms of the Great Accord. Its stated mission and highest goal was to "protect and ensure the wellbeing of the common man". This it did through enforcement of International Patent Law.

Agents of the Patent Office had wide powers to investigate, prosecute and punish patent crime by individuals and organisations. Were the Patent Office to have judged any nation guilty, it would have issued an edict calling on all other signatory nations to reduce the transgressor to dust.

THE KINGDOM OF ENGLAND AND SOUTHERN WALES

The southernmost nation formed by the partition of Britain following the 1819 armistice.

With its capital and agencies of government in London, it would be easy to mistake it as simply the rump of the older, larger Britain. However, with the rule of the country passing out of the hands of the king and the parliament and into the control of the Council of Aristocrats, it must be regarded as a revolutionary nation in its own right.

LONDON TIME

With its opt-out from the Twelfth Amendment, the Kingdom of England and Southern Wales held to the Greenwich Meridian as the basis for timekeeping. Thus it found itself out of step with the peoples of every other nation in the Gas-Lit Empire, who used the Paris Meridian. Kingdom clocks were set nine minutes and twenty-one seconds behind Paris Mean Time. Though inconvenient, the discrepancy was a matter of considerable national pride, symbolising its independence of spirit. (See also: Daylight Saving Time.)

Though an enclave within London, the Jurisdiction of the International Patent Office ran according to the international standard. Its clocks were set with reference to Paris Mean Time.

The Long Quiet

The cessation of open conflict and technological innovation that followed the formation of the Gas-Lit Empire. It was proclaimed by many political philosophers to be the end of history.

With the eye of the International Patent Office watching over them, no nation could attempt to out-develop the others in the technology of killing. The armaments industry had previously been an advocate of war. Now it atrophied. Bound by international treaty, governments could no longer use their armies as a means of enforcing foreign policy. On the social front, technological innovation had previously been a driver of social change. During the Long Quiet, that too was reduced to almost nothing. The Anglo-Scottish Republic embraced this aspect of the Great Accord more vigorously than others. But even in the Kingdom of England and Southern Wales, the least enthusiastic signatory, innovation came to mean the application of mere cosmetic changes. Between 1900 and the year

2000 there were fewer patents filed in London relating to engines than there were to differing designs of clock face.

NED LUDD

Inspirational figurehead of the Luddite movement which precipitated the British Revolutionary War of 1816-1819. Ned Ludd was posthumously named "Father of the Anglo-Scottish Republic".

NED LUDD DAY

The annual celebration of Ned Ludd's life. It takes place on March 21st, though there is no reason to believe this was his actual birthday. It is traditionally marked by the presentation of gifts and the symbolic destruction of models of "unseemly machines" by the head of each household. Bank Holiday in the Anglo-Scottish Republic.

OLD CALENDAR

The Old Calendar (OC) was largely superseded by the New Calendar (NC) on the signing of the Great Accord. Thus, 1821 OC is equivalent to the year 1 NC. Uniquely, the Kingdom of England and Southern Wales continued to use the Old Calendar.

PARIS MERIDIAN

The Prime Meridian used to define longitude on maps and charts produced in the Gas-Lit Empire.

Prior to 1824, several different meridians were in common use. The International Meridian Conference was convened in 1823, following the USS *Thomas Paine* disaster. The Twelfth Amendment was drafted at the conference and brought into law the following year.

Patent Crime

The development or use of any technology deemed "unseemly" by the International Patent Office.

Revolutionary Nations

Those nations established during the European Spring.

The Second Enlightenment

The long period of relative peace that followed the establishment of the Great Accord. Though nations have engaged in border squabbles, imposed trade embargoes on each other and used the economy as a weapon, there has been no pan-European conflict since stalemate and exhaustion ended the Napoleonic Wars in 1815.

The Twelfth Amendment

The 1824 amendment to the Great Accord which standardised the Prime Meridian for signatory nations. From the signing of the amendment, longitude on all charts and maps was recorded as the angular distance east or west from the Paris Observatory. It also established the metric system of weights and measures and the standardisation of timekeeping. (See also: International Chronological Network.)

Unseemly Science

All those sciences and technologies judged by the Patent Office to be deleterious to the wellbeing of the common man. Such judgements are difficult, inasmuch as it is impossible to be certain of the future implications of any invention. Mistakes are minimised through a combination of three factors: a century and a half of case law, the combined wisdom of the patent judges, and the application of the precautionary principle. It is axiomatic that the science of medicine is always for the benefit of the common man. Thus its research can never be regarded as unseemly.

ACKNOWLEDGMENTS

I would like to thank Ed Wilson, Marc Gascoigne, Phil Jourdan, Penny Reeve and Will Staehle, whose input in various forms has been of immense help during the writing and publication of this book. I would also like to thank Terri Bradshaw, Dave Martin, Jacob Ross and all the other members of LWC who gave feedback and encouragement. But my greatest debt of gratitude is to Stephanie, Joseph and Anya, who saw the whole process through from the start and without whose support and patience this book could not have been written.

"Take off the disguise
    and another is revealed beneath..."
      — THE BULLET-CATCHER'S HANDBOOK

CATCHER'S

THE • BULLET-

DAUGHTER

"Compulsive reading... a magic box
pulsating with energy." – GRAHAM JOYCE

ROD DUNCAN